MORYAK

A NOVEL OF THE RUSSIAN REVOLUTION

Lee Mandel

Copyright © 2012 by Lee Mandel
All rights reserved.

ISBN-10: 1475286090
EAN-13: 9781475286090

"He loved his country as no other man has loved her; but no man deserved less at her hands"
The Man Without a Country
Edward Everett Hale

"There is nothing new in the world except the history you do not know."
Harry S. Truman

BOOK ONE

PROLOGUE

Prime Minister's residence
St. Petersburg, Russia
October 16, 1905

As the carriage pulled up to his home, Sergei Witte already knew what he needed to do. A master of intrigue himself, he had considered the possibility of having to abort the mission, as unlikely as it seemed at the time. He stepped through the door and asked his valet to come into the library with him. After hanging up the count's coat, the valet dutifully followed Witte into the library and closed the door behind him.

The valet, a loyal and dedicated servant named Boris, came from a large family that had been St. Petersburg residents for generations. Boris had served in the Imperial Army and had been highly recommended to the Wittes when he had applied for the job as valet. It amused Witte to know that while he had no doubts about Boris' loyalty to the Tsar, he had cousins who had revolutionary leanings. Despite their vast political differences, Boris still had cordial relations with them all. Witte had the instinctive feeling that this good will might come in handy over the years, and he was right. During the original planning phase of the mission, Witte knew that whomever the British selected for the job, he would need a team of local people to assist in executing the mission. For assistance, he had turned to Boris for help.

Through his first cousin, Boris had arranged to meet with a local Bolshevik. He offered the man a large sum of money to assemble a team to assist the foreign agent with the mission. The Bolshevik seemed all too pleased to accept. Boris had gone to the meeting under an assumed identity and dressed like a laborer, ensuring that he could never be traced back to Witte. He was simply the broker between the recruited team and the foreign agent. He had been successful in his role.

That night, Witte told Boris about the abrupt change in plans. He informed the valet that the mission was to be aborted, effective immediately. Witte ordered him to make contact with the Bolshevik immediately. Boris nodded in assent and then thought for a few seconds. "Count Witte, what about that British agent and his partner?"

Witte sighed and admitted, "They have become expendable. In fact, looking at the whole picture realistically, they must never leave Russia. They know too much." Scratching the back of his head, he continued. "In fact, dear Boris, it may be best to have the secret police work for us in this matter, if you know what I mean. They have ways of dealing with threats such as this."

I

Sagamore Hill
Oyster Bay, New York
August 1905

The sun infused the chauffeured car with a relentless heat. Sergei Witte, the prime minister of Russia, took out a silk cloth and wiped his brow. He felt relief when he spied the main gate at Sagamore Hill. The car coasted to a stop in front of a uniformed guard.

The guard ran a quick check and waved the car past. A few moments later, the car approached the mansion. Several darkly clad individuals waited for Witte on the front porch. No doubt, they represented the famous U.S. Secret Service.

The car stopped. An agent opened the door and let Witte out. At six-feet-six-inches tall, he towered over the agent, noting with pleasure that the man had to look up when he said, "Welcome to Sagamore Hill, Mr. Straub."

The Straub subterfuge had been a necessary contrivance to conceal his true identity. The plan he was about to propose could be thwarted if the Tsar became aware of this visit.

The agent invited Witte to proceed up the porch stairs. "President Roosevelt is expecting you and will join you shortly. He asked that you be escorted to the study." The Secret Service agent dutifully logged the guest's assumed name into his register at the door and then escorted Witte to the president's study. "Please have a seat. I'll inform President Roosevelt that you're here."

As the agent departed, Witte strolled over to the window and gazed out over Long Island Sound. The sunlight shimmered on the blue water, creating the picture of a beautifully peaceful summer day with many sailboats on the sound. What a pity that his business, his reason for visiting Sagamore Hill, would potentially ruin the president's day. This possibility was clear from the moment Witte had requested the clandestine meeting with the young American leader.

As he waited, Witte wondered how all of these events of the past year could have happened. How could the situation have gotten so out of hand? How did he, the prime minister of Russia, end up sitting here in the summer home of the president of the United States, waiting to discuss a topic so sensitive it could never be recorded for history's sake? History might call the topic treason, but Sergei Witte knew it was the only way to preserve Russia. With much sadness, he reflected on the events of the past year. It had been a nightmare. Mother Russia was being ripped apart by revolution, a senseless war, and the utterly ineffective leadership of the supreme autocrat of Russia, Tsar Nicholas II.

As Witte stood, perusing the many books lining the mahogany shelves of the president's study, the door opened and in bounded President Theodore Roosevelt. His very presence radiated energy and confidence. Witte towered over Roosevelt, but the president shook Witte's hand so vigorously that the prime minister winced.

"Welcome to Sagamore Hill, Mr. Witte," Roosevelt exclaimed. "I am honored by your visit, but I am equally confused. Please be seated, and we'll chat." They sat in the two facing leather chairs, and the president began the conversation almost immediately in his animated style.

"Mr. Witte, I truly appreciate His Excellency the Tsar's willingness to send you as his representative. I must say, however, I'm a little surprised and confused by your request for this visit. We'll both be in New Hampshire tomorrow for the beginning of the peace negotiations. So, this matter must be very urgent. As requested, you are listed on the official guest roster today under an assumed name. No one other than the two of us will ever know that this meeting has taken place. Now, having said all of this, you must tell me, what urgent matter do you wish to discuss?"

"Mr. President, I'll get right to the point," replied the Russian. "These negotiations will not succeed. Tsar Nicholas will never enter into any agreement." He paused for a moment to gauge the young president's reaction. Roosevelt sat stone-faced as Witte continued. "I felt that you needed to know this reality before the whole process began."

Roosevelt stared past the older man for a few seconds. He then looked at him directly as he responded, the muted anger in his voice very apparent.

"Then why are you here, Mr. Witte? Why did Nicholas send you? If an agreement is not possible, why waste everyone's time? You are well aware that the eyes of the world are upon us! Japan is here in good faith and ready to negotiate. Your message is both unsettling and infuriating!"

The president stood up and with his hands folded behind his back, walked over to the large picture window overlooking Oyster Bay. After what seemed an eternity to Witte, the president returned to his chair, sat down, and stared hard at Witte.

"Be frank with me, Mr. Witte. I have the feeling that something else is going on here. What is it? Why did you want this meeting?"

"Mr. President, you must believe me when I tell you that I believe in peace, and I believe that this senseless war must end." After recounting the events of the past year for the younger man, Witte paused and then sighed. "Mr. President, Russia is on the verge of collapse. The people are on the verge of rebellion. We will lose the support of the people entirely if we don't end this senseless war and, more importantly, surrender to their demand for a form of representation in our government. Even a limited form of a Duma, comparable to your House of Representatives, would be acceptable, but Nicholas has refused this solution. I have begged him to accede to the demand but he absolutely refuses. Every day more demonstrations and more strikes occur. The country's industries are paralyzed. If we could reach a peace agreement in Portsmouth, it would be helpful, but it would only delay the rebellion. Without a Duma, Russia is doomed to anarchy."

"Again, Mr. Witte," began Roosevelt, "why are you telling me this? Russia's internal affairs are its own, and—"

"Mr. President," interrupted Witte, "a group of us in the highest levels of the government believe in the future of Russia and believe that our country can be spared from the horror of the upcoming rebellion. We have a plan, and we have the will to act. We believe it is our only hope. That is why I'm here in total secrecy.

"The Tsar's uncle, Grand Duke Nicholas Nikolaevich, is totally sympathetic and is willing to do whatever is necessary.

He is the commander of the Petersburg Garrison, and the military is completely loyal to him. This man will become the new leader of Russia. He will grant the Duma. Our new government will solidify its power while actually listening to the people, *all* of the people." He put an emphasis on the word 'all', knowing that it would appeal to the idealistic Roosevelt. "This plan has been discussed and approved at the highest levels of the Russian government. The Imperial family, of course, knows nothing about it. This approach is our only hope, Mr. President, and we need your help. Of all the world's leaders, you are the one we appeal to in secrecy."

As Roosevelt absorbed all of this information, he studied the older man's eyes. They were tired eyes, eyes that had seen much, eyes that harbored much sorrow and pain. The president prided himself on being a good judge of character. He sensed a goodness and a decency in this man, in spite of his statements that were tantamount to treason.

"Would you like a drink before we continue, sir?" the president asked, sensing that Witte needed to steel up his courage for what was to follow.

"Yes, I would," he replied. The president went over to the bar near the desk and poured a couple of glasses of wine. He handed Witte a glass, held up his own, and proposed, "To peace and democracy!" The older man smiled, touched his glass to the president's, and sipped his wine. Roosevelt stared at his glass for a second and then asked, "What are you planning? What do you need from me?"

"Mr. President, the Japanese have defeated us. They have no need to make any concessions to us. However, we need you to coerce them into acquiescing to some of Nicholas' demands, enough to allow him to save face and encourage him to agree to a peace treaty. This tactic will buy us time, but as I told you,

Nicholas will never agree to a Duma. His refusal will be the last straw." Witte stared down at his glass before continuing, almost afraid to look the president in the eye.

"Sir," he continued, "Nicholas must be removed from Russia by any means necessary so that Grand Duke Nicholas Nikolaevich can take over the government." Witte looked up at the president and repeated, "By any means necessary."

Witte shifted uncomfortably in his chair. "Our contacts with the British tell us that King Edward will not allow the Tsar into the country, even if he were to voluntarily request residence there. Yes, the king is quite angry with his cousin. He certainly doesn't want a working-class rebellion spreading to Great Britain. The British intelligence service is willing to help us covertly, but they will only do so with American assistance. They want you to send an agent to help their agent take the Tsar out of Russia. They asked me to tell you that if you decide against this request, the British will not undertake the mission alone. In fact, they will deny any knowledge of the plan or of our conversation pertaining to it. Yes, Mr. President, there is definitely a serious plan in the works."

"You expect me to believe this on your word alone? You want me to believe that England is willing to arrange what is tantamount to a kidnapping of the Tsar by the British and the Americans? Really, Mr. Witte, you expect too much from me!"

Witte cleared his throat and began again. "Of course not, Mr. President. I wouldn't expect you to take my word alone on something as crucial as this matter." He placed his wine glass on the table next to him, reached into his breast pocket, and produced an envelope. Roosevelt noted the embossed seal of the British royal family in the upper corner. The envelope contained a handwritten letter, personally addressed to Roosevelt from King Edward VII. It served to confirm what Witte had related to him.

The letter stated that Edward, too, had been briefed by Witte before his departure for the United States and was told about the action that the Russian prime minister proposed. Edward informed Roosevelt that only with the assistance of an American agent would he authorize a British agent to carry out the mission. Both governments would assert plausible deniability. Should either agent or both agents be captured, the king insisted that both governments feign ignorance of the agents' actions and deny any responsibility for these rogue agents. Edward stated that the only other person in England who knew of the proposed mission was William Melville, who had served as England's director of foreign intelligence operations. Melville had been designated the head of the operation and, from that point on, Edward declared he would step back and allow Melville to have total control of the operation. Edward would no longer be involved. He concluded the letter by inviting Roosevelt to assign an agent to work with Melville's man, again noting that England would not attempt this mission without American participation. Edward asked Roosevelt to burn the letter when he finished reading it.

Roosevelt walked over to his desk and produced a match from one of the drawers. As requested, after lighting the match, he placed the flame up to the letter and watched it char into ashes. When it was consumed, he turned to Witte and stared at him for a moment before beginning. "If you want the Tsar out of the country, why not do it yourself? If there is support for this action at your level, you must have people who can handle it for you. Why must this be a foreign operation, and why must an American be involved?"

"Because, sir, we are a police state that is riddled with informers and double agents. You may not know this, but the Tsar is protected by his secret police, the Okhrana. They have arrested two agents in the past three months that we had hired from within to do the job. Both were exposed by informants to the Okhrana and were summarily executed. Fortunately, these agents had no idea for whom they were actually working. But the sword cuts both ways, Mr. Roosevelt. Most of the revolutionary factions in Russia have informants that are actually on the Okhrana's payroll. At the same time, we have learned that many Okhrana officials have been bribed by revolutionary factions and anarchists. We have concluded that it would be impossible for a Russian to achieve success with the mission. Anyone with the necessary talents for the job would be known to one side or the other and would be exposed before even getting near the Tsar. That is why we approached the British in the first place. As it turns out, they have an excellent agent who speaks Russian like a native and has espionage experience. He needs a partner. This partner must be fearless, fluent in Russian, and, if necessary, willing to sacrifice his life. Hopefully, that outcome can be avoided.

"The British fear that rebellion of the working class may spread to the British Isles. That is why they will help us. They believe that this mission will provide stability to all of Europe. The removal of Nicholas will be a small price to pay for this stability. Incidentally, if the death of Nicholas becomes necessary, it will be announced that he died of heart disease or something else along those lines. The rest of the Imperial family will not be harmed."

Roosevelt sighed. "The British have requested an American agent, or they won't participate, so the whole plan now falls onto my shoulders."

"Yes, Mr. President. The British have insisted they will not be the only foreign power involved, and they only trust America. As King Edward indicated, they are insisting on a policy of total deniability. If these agents are apprehended or killed, both governments will disavow both men. That must be understood from the beginning. The British agent who has volunteered understands this risk completely."

Roosevelt got up and began pacing, his arms clasped behind his back. Again, he walked to the large picture window and stared out to the bay. Witte couldn't help but notice that the president was a powerfully built man with very broad shoulders. He had read that this young American was an avid outdoorsman, and the president certainly appeared to be a vigorous, athletic individual. Roosevelt turned around and walked up to the Russian, who stood as the president approached him.

"I don't think it will surprise you when I tell you that I'll need to think about this proposal," Roosevelt stated. "This information is a lot to digest, especially so unexpectedly. I've done my homework on Russia, and I know all about you, Mr. Witte. You are considered one of the backbones of Russia; at least, that is what my own experts tell me. I'm told that the increasing disarray that is occurring in your country would be even worse were it not for your guidance and steadying influence on the Tsar. You are a man of respect and honor, which is, quite frankly, the only reason I did not ask you to leave here immediately."

"Mr. President," replied the Russian, "we are short on time, and I do appreciate your even listening to me. I have dedicated my life to the service of Mother Russia, so this whole circumstance is tearing at my soul. Russia is at risk of total dissolution into anarchy and rebellion. If you can convince the Japanese to make some concessions, I believe I can convince Nicholas to end this insane war. This tactic will buy us precious time. However, he will never, and I repeat, never agree to allow a representative Duma, even a token one. This disappointment will break Russia. We must have him removed and let the Grand Duke take over. He will be able to steady the nation. I am ... *we are* ... begging you, Mr. Roosevelt. We are truly begging you."

The men stared at each other, and Roosevelt announced that the meeting was concluded. It was time for the Russian to leave if he planned to make it back to New York City. There he would board the official train that would be carrying both the Russian and Japanese delegations to the Portsmouth, New Hampshire, peace talks. Roosevelt would be arriving shortly thereafter. As the men shook hands at the door, Witte once again thanked the young American leader for receiving him. Before letting go of Roosevelt's hand, Witte said, "Please, Mr. President, send us a man, a brave man, fluent in Russian, and willing to work to make this insane world safe. The contact point in Great Britain is William Melville, head of the war office intelligence division. He's the only one who knows of the plan."

As Roosevelt watched the huge Russian leave down the hallway, he reflected on the just-ended clandestine meeting. Here, a senior official of the Russian government had just asked him to become part of a conspiracy against a foreign head of state. Unthinkable! Yet he was being told that if he didn't assist the Russians, the peace conference was surely doomed, and Russia would disintegrate into chaos. Roosevelt wholeheartedly agreed with Witte in that regard—Europe would then be completely destabilized.

As he walked back into his study, Roosevelt felt the urge for another glass of wine. After pouring it, he walked over to the picture window and stared out at the water. God, how he loved the sea! It had a soothing quality. He always felt that he could relax and think better around the water. He downed the wine and realized that he was running a little late. He needed to pack because he was also going into the city to take the presidential train to New Hampshire that evening.

The thought of the upcoming peace conference being sabotaged before it even began made him angry. All of the work that he had poured into the conference was potentially for nothing. He had had no real opinion about Tsar Nicholas in the first place, but now he had a growing contempt for him. The prime minister's last request served as the final surreal aspect of the just-concluded encounter. Roosevelt smiled to himself as he recalled it. "Send us a man," Witte had said, "one who is fearless, fluent in Russian, and if necessary, willing to sacrifice his life." As if this sort of man could be easily found!

Ironically, it seemed to the young president that he believed he had just met such a man only a few short weeks ago.

***

Sergei Witte watched the Connecticut countryside pass by and reflected on his secret meeting with the American president. Considering his request, the meeting had gone about as well as he could have hoped. He was unsure if Roosevelt would act. He would have to wait for a sign. If the president didn't act, Russia would have no future.

He had been impressed with the president's energy and presence. Most of all, he admired the president's integrity, his sense of compassion for the common man. Witte had tried to exploit this very trait when he told the president only part of the truth about the plan.

It was true that Grand Duke Nicholas would ascend to the throne, and he would indeed grant a Duma. It would be a representative body with no power, a token morsel thrown to the people. The Grand Duke would serve as a military dictator.

The right-leaning aristocrats had no real intention of ceding much power to the people; only the illusion of sharing would be needed. The Tsar never could understand that basic principle. Witte was considered among the most liberal of the ruling class. He believed in a constitutional form of government with limited representation of the people, but he was in the minority. He felt awkward being in the unenviable position of having to support an option that was not entirely palatable to him. It boiled down to the lesser of two evils: a military dictatorship with the preservation of Russia, or continued rule by the Tsar with chaos and a downward spiral.

Witte felt mildly conflicted not being completely honest with the president about the true intentions of the cabal to appoint a military dictator, but he felt the means would justify the end if Russia were to be preserved. In the final analysis, preservation was all that mattered.

2

As the presidential train proceeded through upstate New York, Roosevelt finished a short meeting with his foreign policy advisors. He felt prepared for the conference. He knew the issues, and he felt that his role would be more as a facilitator and moderator. Both sides wanted peace. Japan would be negotiating from a position of strength. The Japanese had clearly prevailed in the war. On the other hand, Russia had nothing. The dire position that Russia was in was the reason that the meeting with Witte had surprised him so much. He had been under the impression that the Russians would want to end the conflict and would be negotiating in good faith. While he hadn't heard much about the personality and style of the Tsar, he was upset and disappointed by Witte's characterization of him. He, the president, the organizer of the peace conference, had knowledge that no one else on the train had: the conference had no chance of succeeding.

Just as the last member of his policy team started to leave the conference room, Roosevelt grabbed him by the sleeve.

"Charles, please stay. There is a matter I need to discuss with you."

"Yes, Mr. President," replied Charles J. Bonaparte. He sat down as Roosevelt closed the door and joined him at the table. He had appointed Bonaparte as secretary of the navy earlier that year, and Roosevelt had been extremely happy with his choice. In addition to his background as a highly competent lawyer, Bonaparte had also proved to be a superb administrator. Roosevelt was doubly amused that a distant relative of Napoleon Bonaparte was a cabinet member. Bonaparte looked the part of a New York lawyer, always clad in high-starched collars and pinstriped suits. One of Bonaparte's aides had provided Roosevelt with a highly detailed briefing on the situation in Russia. This young man had greatly impressed the president.

"Charles, remember that briefing on the situation in Russia that you had your aide give me about two, three weeks ago?"

"Yes, sir, I do. Quite impressive, wasn't it?"

"Indeed it was. Who was the young man who gave that presentation?"

"That was Lieutenant Junior Grade Stephen Morrison of the United States Navy."

"That's right. He's Oscar Leavitt's son-in-law, correct? Isn't he related somehow to the late Congressman Morrison? I seem to remember that about him. The young man speaks Russian, doesn't he?" Before allowing Bonaparte to answer, he added, "He's got those eyes that look right through you. There's a lot of anger in those eyes," said Roosevelt, almost to himself. After reflecting to himself for a few seconds, he asked, "What can you tell me about him?"

"Well, sir, he is the late Congressman Morrison's adopted son. He is a graduate of the Naval Academy, Class of '93. His real father was a Jew, an influential rabbi in New York City , who disowned him years ago. He emigrated from Russia. You see, Morrison has Russian blood. He has always maintained an avid interest in Russia, and I believe he still has contacts in that country. I would venture to say that he is probably one of our country's experts on Russian internal affairs."

"Congressman Morrison was an Irishman, a Catholic. Is young Morrison a convert?"

"That's somewhat interesting, Mr. President. Lieutenant Morrison is a Jew, a nonpracticing one to be sure. I talked with some of the late congressman's staff about him before he joined my own staff. Congressman Caleb Morrison was legally Lieutenant Morrison's stepfather. The lieutenant, however, remains a Jew. I presume it is a long and interesting story as to how the religious situation all came about, but I really don't know many of the details. Lieutenant Morrison is tight-lipped on the subject."

"He certainly looks rugged enough. I'm a little surprised to learn he's a Jew. What can you tell me about his naval career? Has he shown courage and initiative? For goodness' sake Charles, why would the son of an immigrant rabbi want to be a United States naval officer?"

Bonaparte thought for a few seconds before speaking. "Mr. President, I really can't answer your last question. I did investigate his background before taking him on as my aide, of course. The congressman had never used any influence on his son's behalf. I learned that Morrison was nearly expelled from the Naval Academy for a severe hazing incident. Apparently, the word got out about his Jewish background shortly after he arrived at Annapolis, and he was pretty much ostracized during his four years there. The incident I'm referring to, interestingly enough, was a serious beating that *he* received at the hands of some other naval cadets. Of course, the hazing was because of his religion even though he was a nonpracticing Jew."

"And he was the one nearly suspended?" asked the amused Roosevelt.

"Well, Morrison refused to cooperate with the investigating officials at the academy. He wouldn't name the cadets who attacked him, although everyone, including Morrison, knew who had done it. It put the defenders of the honor code in quite a dilemma. He refused to betray fellow classmates, even when he was threatened with expulsion. Ultimately, they dropped the threat because he refused to name names. He went on to graduate second in his class.

"There have been other incidents since he received his commission. All apparently have involved ethnic slurs, and he has proven to be very quick to respond with his fists. Before becoming my aide, he served aboard the battleship *Indiana* where he worked with William Sims on that famous gunnery exercise a few years ago. After the *Indiana* won that gunnery competition, several crews were at the officer's club at the Philadelphia Navy Yard. Morrison's counterpart from the *Massachusetts*, which just happened to finish second in the competition, was near him at the bar and quite intoxicated. Apparently, he made a comment that they lost unfairly because the *Indiana* had a 'cheating Jew bastard,' or something to that effect. It was very unsubtle. Morrison immediately pounced on him and beat him to a pulp."

"What's your personal assessment of this man, Charles? Would you trust him with your life?"

Bonaparte put his hand to his chin and stroked it, deep in thought. He appeared to be choosing his words very carefully. "What do I think?" he asked himself aloud. After nearly a minute of contemplation, the secretary of the navy looked up at the president and began to speak. "Mr. President, even though we haven't worked together very long, I can tell you that Lieutenant Morrison is a highly intelligent, dedicated naval officer. He is a fearless individual who is not in the least bit timid about fighting if provoked. His loyalty to the United States and the United States Navy is unconditional. Yes, I would trust him with my life.

"There is another facet to him, sir. I, too, sense a deep anger within him. You mentioned his eyes. I've seen that anger, too. It's almost as if he is a controlled volcano waiting to erupt. Mind you, he is a polite, controlled individual. I've never seen lose his temper. I just have this feeling about him. I can almost imagine an explosive response to a provocation. I suppose I just don't understand."

"You don't understand what, Charles?" asked Roosevelt.

Hesitatingly, Bonaparte replied, "He doesn't look like a Jew, Mr. President. I never would have known. It seems to me that his life could have been so much simpler if he had converted when he was adopted. It's almost as if he wears the issue on his sleeve, just daring people to engage him on the subject. I know my interpretation of his motives sounds terrible, but it seems that he wants it both ways: he wants to fit in, yet he doesn't want to fit in. That's what I don't understand."

"What do you know about his family life?"

"He was married less than a year ago. His wife is the daughter of Oscar Leavitt, whom you know. He, of course, was formerly the United States Minister to the Ottoman Empire. She is a very wealthy woman in her own right. They have no children. I don't know a lot of other details because he is a very private person."

A wife- that may complicate things, thought Roosevelt. He sat silently for a moment, taking in all that Bonaparte had just told him. He paused and then asked, "Would you trust this man to act unhesitatingly on behalf of his country, to carry out any mission for his government as an exemplary representative of the United States?"

"Absolutely," replied Bonaparte without hesitation.

"Well, then," said the president, "after dinner tonight, we need to have a private meeting. On my schedule, I will have the meeting listed as a briefing on the new battleships we are building." Roosevelt stood up and looked at Bonaparte. "I have been advised to send an exceptional naval officer to England to work with Admiral Fisher on that new battleship they are building. In fact, the keel is scheduled to be laid for the new ship on October 2, and we need to send a representative for the ceremony. Why don't we make the trip more than just a ceremonial visit? I believe that this Lieutenant Morrison is just the man for the job."

3

State, War, and Navy Building
Next to the White House
One Month Earlier

Theodore Roosevelt had been both flattered and delighted when the Japanese ambassador secretly requested that the young president both initiate and facilitate a peace conference to end the war. This opportunity would be the first real chance for an American president to have an active role in international affairs. Determined to end the conflict, Roosevelt already knew how the Japanese stood on the issue, but the Russians were largely a mystery to him.

The following day at a cabinet meeting, Roosevelt requested a comprehensive briefing on Russia. He wanted to hear from a subject-matter expert. He wanted to be totally prepared to deal with the Russians. To Roosevelt's delight, the secretary of the navy announced that he could arrange a detailed briefing for the president and the cabinet in forty-eight hours.

The members of the cabinet had already assembled in the main conference room when Secretary of the Navy Bonaparte arrived with his aide to begin preparations for the briefing on Russia. The naval aide distributed a booklet of papers in front of each seat at the table and then set up an easel at the head of the table. Just as he finished his preparations, President Roosevelt entered the room, and all of the cabinet members stood in place. "Please, gentlemen," said Roosevelt as he approached the seat at the head of the table, "be seated." After everyone sat down, Bonaparte stood and announced, "Mr. President, our briefer today will be my aide, Lieutenant Junior Grade Stephen Morrison."

"Excellent!" barked the president. "Please begin, Lieutenant."

The young officer had been standing at parade rest after the president was seated. He walked to the front of the room and took his place at a mahogany lectern. Standing ramrod straight in his choker-white uniform, he picked up a pointer and began. To Roosevelt, the officer appeared every inch an all-American boy, the type he himself had led up San Juan Hill during the Spanish American War. The lieutenant stood about six-feet tall and had dark brown hair. He obviously was accustomed to public speaking. The lieutenant had several charts affixed to the wall, in addition to the easel in the front of the room that contained a flip chart. The first page contained a large wiring diagram with several photographs attached. He immediately called attention to the briefing binders on the table in front of each member of the high-level audience.

"Mr. President, distinguished members of the cabinet, I am Lieutenant Junior Grade Stephen L. Morrison, United States Navy, naval aide to the secretary of the navy. Our topic today is

Russia. My goal is to impart to you a working knowledge of the social and political climate in that country today."

The lieutenant began his presentation and proved to be an impressive speaker. He spoke fluidly and never referred to his notes. He covered various topics, starting with the governing structure of Russia. Roosevelt was fascinated to learn the history of the Romanov dynasty, starting with Tsar Michael in 1613 through the current Romanov ruler, Tsar Nicholas II. Other subjects covered included the Russian economy and a detailed discussion of the Russo-Japanese War. The young officer then turned to the social structure of the Russian people.

"The Russian people are in a state of turmoil," he began. "Russia is an overwhelmingly poor country. Their industrial revolution occurred later than in most western countries. Even after Tsar Alexander II freed the serfs in 1861, the peasant class remained without basic civil rights, tied to the land, and in an endless cycle of debt. There was a glimmer of hope; one of Alexander II's reforms was to grant some basic governing authority to the local provinces. That was short-lived. The country has been run as a strict autocracy since 1881 when Alexander II was assassinated. His son, Alexander III, revoked many of the moderately enlightened social changes his father had enacted. Nicholas II, the son of Alexander III, continues this strict autocratic rule. A rigid bureaucracy rules the many Russian provinces. Nicholas appoints the local governors, who then serve as his personal emissaries.

"The peasants are so far removed from the government that in their little villages their everyday, miserable lives are ruled by town elders. Unfortunately, the appointed governors and other assigned nobility have nothing to do with the population. The nobility doesn't have a clue what the actual living conditions are because they never leave their social strata. For years, the local governors were viewed with reverence by the peasantry, most of whom remained illiterate and content to work the lands. Remember also that, in both the cities and the countryside, strict censorship of the press exists, and no criticism is allowed of the Imperial family or its policies."

Lieutenant Morrison paused to take a sip of water from the crystal goblet that sat on his lectern. He cleared his throat and continued his lecture. "A demographic change in the peasant population has occurred over the last thirty years. While it's still basically an agricultural nation, the burgeoning industrial revolution has transformed the country. A large-scale migration of the peasants has occurred to the cities to work in the factories. Their working conditions and their living conditions are abhorrent. Unlike in the western countries, no labor unions or trade unions protect them. Interestingly, the literacy rate has likely doubled over this time. Hence, the new Russian peasant is an urban dweller, is overworked and underpaid, lives in squalor, and wants a better life. Several labor strikes have erupted over the years, beginning in the 1880s. The intelligentsia and the student classes have become increasingly active socially and much more vocal. These now-literate Russian masses have been reading tracts calling for social change or even more drastic, social revolution and the overthrow of the status quo. This increasing unrest and radicalization of the population has greatly increased over the past decade. Nicholas seems unwilling or unable to acknowledge this change, largely accounting for the current chaos in Russia."

The lieutenant paused, then walked over to his flip chart, and turned over a page to a new one that had several individual photographs. He returned to the lectern and began again. "The last subject I am going to cover concerns the political climate that currently exists within Russia. I have given you a brief overview of the social structure of Russia, and I want to finish with today's political realities, which are the crux of the problem. The following internal political movements represent the biggest threat to the stability of the Imperial government. While they differ in style, temperament, and philosophies, they have this one uniting factor in common: they are totally opposed to the war and use their opposition as a rallying point. They all preach the ceding of governing power to the common people, or proletariat, as they call them. My study of these groups indicates that this last feature is pure smokescreen. While they preach a concept of a 'worker's paradise', their ruthlessness leads me to believe that their motives are less pure.

"The largest group is called the Socialist Revolutionaries. These are the anarchists, the violent revolutionaries. If you can conjure up an image of a wild-eyed bomb thrower, you have just pictured a typical member of this group. Their method of achieving their goals is by terror and assassination. This group is highly influenced by the terrorist group Narodynaya Volya, or People's Will. They were responsible for the assassination of Tsar Alexander II in 1881. They are led by a thug named Viktor Chernov," Morrison said, using his pointer to indicate a grainy photograph on his easel chart. "I obtained this police photograph through a contact of mine from Great Britain," he said with a slight smile.

"The other major group is called the Social Democratic Workers Party. This party was formed in 1898 in Minsk to combine all the various revolutionary factions. In recent times, this group has suffered an internal power struggle and, in fact, has fragmented into two rival factions. Both factions derive their dogma from the work of the German writer and social theorist, Karl Marx; hence, they are known as Marxists. The more democratic faction that adheres to a more pure form of egalitarian

Marxism is lead by Julius Martov," he said, indicating Martov's photograph with his pointer. "This faction has come to be called the Mensheviks, which is Russian for Minority Men.

"The smaller faction is lead by one Vladimir Ulyanov, known by a revolutionary pseudonym of Lenin. These Russian dissidents are enamored with revolutionary pen names. I apologize, but I was unable to obtain a photograph of him on such short notice," Morrison said, pausing for a second. "This faction is basically a dictatorship under Lenin. All must toe the line, and no dissent from within is tolerated. They have a long-range plan for winning the minds of the Russian peasantry. Their form of Marxism is less pure, more severe, and more subjective. They believe in conspiracy and infiltration. While they are not the avid bomb throwers that the Social Revolutionaries are, they do not hesitate to kill if killing will further their aims. They have come to be called the Bolsheviks, or Majority Men.

"The basic underlying philosophy of the revolutionaries has evolved over the years. At first, many of them felt that an enlightened peasantry would be the key to revolution. Earlier efforts were geared toward educating these masses. Some even envisioned a period of capitalism before the country would be able to evolve into a socialist state. In recent years, this populism, as they called it, has fallen out of favor. Now the efforts seem to be geared toward the workers in the cities. They will be the ones to lead the revolution and overthrow the Tsar. It has become more of an issue of style and technique among the various factions."

The lieutenant turned to his small audience and put his pointer down on the table. "If there are any questions at this time, I will be glad to answer if I can," he said with a smile.

"I have a few questions," said the president. "First off, I want to thank you and compliment you on a most excellent brief. It was surely finer than any talk I ever heard in my four years at Harvard!" A ripple of laughter spread among the cabinet members. "Do you speak Russian? Your pronunciation of the names and the cities you spoke of leads me to believe that you do."

"Yes, sir, I am fluent in Russian."

"Where did you learn to speak it so well? How do you account for your interest and knowledge of this country?"

"Mr. President, my parents were Russian. I was born there in the city of Perm, and we came to the United States when I was eleven years old. The year before I started at the Naval Academy, I traveled throughout Russia. I still have contacts in the country as a result of that trip. In all likelihood, I may still have relatives who live in Russia, although I've never met them."

"Very interesting, Lieutenant. Let me get to my most important question. As you know, in less than a month, we will have representatives from both the Japanese and Russian governments here, meeting at Portsmouth, New Hampshire. I know that both countries want to end this senseless war. As your lecture has pointed out, Russia is on the verge of anarchy, and if the Tsar's government falls, all of Europe is in danger of being destabilized. Tell me, which internal group do you see as the biggest domestic threat to the Tsar? It seems to me, based on what you presented, it would be the Social Revolutionaries. Would you agree that these violent killers are the Tsar's greatest threat?"

"With all due respect, Mr. President, I disagree with that assessment. To me, the real threat lies with the Bolsheviks."

"And why do you say this, Lieutenant?"

"This is all conjecture and analysis on my part, sir, but I worry about the Bolsheviks and their power to influence people, especially this Lenin character. He is a ruthless, but charismatic, leader. He is unbending and rigid in his doctrine. For him and his followers, his doctrine is almost like a religion. He knows what to say, and he knows what the proletariat wants to hear. He has completely neutralized the Menshevik faction with his persuasive and corrupting influence. Take, for example the names Bolshevik and Menshevik. They derive from the breakup of the Socialist Democratic Workers Party two years ago. They had their second international meeting in Belgium. Although Martov was striving for unity, Lenin saw Martov's position as his weakness.

"Lenin and his people blocked every resolution that Martov and his people tried to advance. Not once did he compromise. On one vote when his faction outvoted the Martov faction, Lenin derisively called them Mensheviks and began to call his own faction the Bolsheviks, or Majority Men, on every issue since. These names have persisted, and Lenin has effectively taken over the movement by capturing the minds and spirits of the party members while humiliating Martov and his followers. It is a powerful man who can win battles against alleged allies without firing a shot or throwing a bomb."

"How can you know all of this?" asked the amazed Roosevelt. "I mean, how can you know what has transpired in Russia to give this man power?"

"Sir, as I mentioned, I have contacts in Russia, and I have traveled around that country. But one only needs to read what Lenin is currently writing to know his mind and his motives. He publishes a revolutionary newsletter that he calls *Iskra*, which in Russian means, 'The Spark.' I have read every issue he has managed to publish. If one reads these publications and also reads between the lines, I believe it is quite clear where Lenin is heading and what his plans for power are. Mr. President, you asked me what the biggest threat is to Russia. Maybe in the short term it is the Social Revolutionaries, but if the evolution of rebellion in Russia becomes drawn out over many years, it is Lenin and his Bolsheviks whom I fear most."

Roosevelt then asked, "What about Tsar Nicholas II? What sort of man is he?"

"Actually, sir, I met him over a decade ago. He was a bit of a surprise for me. His father, Tsar Alexander III, was a huge man, very outgoing and boisterous, but Nicholas is a physically unimpressive man. He didn't strike me as much of an intellectual, but I suppose looks can be deceiving. He is quiet and very shy. He came across to me as a man who prefers to avoid confrontations, at least directly. He has a very aristocratic, condescending air about him."

"Tell me, Lieutenant, do you know anything about the Russian prime minister, one Sergei Witte? Can he be trusted to deal in good faith?" Roosevelt stood up and walked over to a picture of the Tsar and his advisors that Morrison had affixed to the wall. The prime minister certainly had an aristocratic appearance, highlighted by a neatly trimmed Vandyke beard.

"Witte has been in the service of Russia for many years. He was a trusted advisor for Nicholas' father, Tsar Alexander III. Alexander was a brutal man who ruled with an iron fist. Although Witte was greatly respected by him, he was also considered a little too cerebral and liberal leaning for Alexander's taste. Nonetheless, he became regarded as the conscience of the Imperial family—if there is such a thing," noted Morrison, his voice trailing off with a touch of sarcasm.

"Under Nicholas," continued the lieutenant, "Witte has become also something of a father figure. Unlike Tsar Alexander, Nicholas is a much more timid individual. Physically, he is not imposing like Alexander was, and as I mentioned before, I am told that he detests confrontation. Whereas Alexander was a large, outgoing man with a bit of a violent streak, his son Nicholas is a small, passive individual. Complete opposites. I am told that Tsar Alexander III called his son a dunce. My own impression is that Nicholas is the wrong ruler at the wrong time in Russia's history. He needs someone like Witte."

"And so," interjected Roosevelt, "you feel that Sergei Witte is a man who can be trusted to do what needs to be done, not only for Russia, but now for the sake of Europe?"

"Yes, Mr. President, I would trust this man," said the lieutenant earnestly.

As the meeting ended and people started leaving the briefing room, the president watched the young lieutenant as he took down his briefing charts and gathered his materials. *He's a smart one*, thought Roosevelt to himself. *Very knowledgeable, confident, and most of all, honest and straightforward.* He cut an impressive figure in his starched white uniform, trim with broad shoulders. Roosevelt guessed him to be in his early thirties. His eyes struck Roosevelt the most. To him, they were very cold brown eyes. *A lot of anger in those eyes*, he thought.

A lot of anger.

Russo-Japanese Peace Conference
Portsmouth, New Hampshire
August 1905

President Roosevelt was pleased with the progress that had been achieved thus far. The conference had gone on for nearly three weeks, and Roosevelt felt very encouraged. The Japanese delegation, lead by Baron Komura, appeared to be earnest and accommodating for the entire peace process. Even the Russians seemed to be flexible on the issues, leading Roosevelt to wonder if Witte had given him an accurate picture of the Tsar's intentions.

The Russians agreed to abandon the Liaotung Peninsula and to withdraw from Manchuria completely. Despite these encouraging developments, the negotiations came to a standstill over the issue of reparations. The Japanese insisted that the Russians be punished financially and demanded a huge financial sum, as well as possession of the island of Sakhalin. The Russian negotiators, lead by Witte, remained steadfast in their opposition to these demands. To all observers, the conference appeared to have reached a stalemate. Although not an active participant in the actual negotiations, Roosevelt felt compelled to become active behind the scenes.

On August 23, he sent a confidential letter to Baron Komura, requesting a private meeting between the two men. It would be held at the president's hotel suite. In addition, Roosevelt took a special precaution— there would be no documented record of the meeting.

***

The final session of the conference was scheduled for August 29, and the meeting still remained deadlocked. The world had already assumed that the conference would end in failure. That afternoon, Roosevelt heard a pounding sound on the door of his hotel room. Irritated that he had to interrupt his correspondence, Roosevelt opened the door to find his personal secretary all but convulsed with delight. "Mr. President," he said, breathing hard with excitement. "Have you heard the wonderful news?"

"What wonderful news?" he replied, irritated at the intrusion.

"It's a success! The Japanese have dropped their demands for reparations. Both sides are now totally in agreement. The newspapers are currently breaking the story."

At first, Roosevelt could not find the words to express his joy and amazement. A broad smile broke upon his face as he embraced his assistant. "This is wonderful! Absolutely delightful! I must get down to the Navy Yard immediately. Please notify my cabinet members," he said as he dashed over to the chair to grab his jacket.

"And just think, sir, it's all of your doing. The meeting was your idea. You know that the world will laud you as a great peacemaker. Your place in history will certainly be even further embellished with this great accomplishment. You deserve the lion's share of the credit!"

More than you will ever know, Roosevelt thought to himself as he headed out the door. *More than you will ever know.*

***

The signing of the peace treaty concluded the Russo-Japanese War. Baron Komura signed on behalf of the Japanese emperor, and Sergei Witte signed on behalf of the Tsar. That night, a large reception was held at the Portsmouth Navy Yard's Officers Club. Everyone shared a definite sense of history being made. Many had doubted that the conference would succeed. Both sides had surprised everyone, especially Sergei Witte.

As Witte lifted the wine glass to his lips, his attention drifted from the speaker, President Roosevelt. All the other members of the Russian delegation sat in rapt attention as the young president spoke in his usual animated style. Going through a translator did nothing to diminish the impact of his words on the non-English-speaking members of the delegation. *How did it happen?* Witte wondered to himself. *Had Roosevelt gotten to them?* Witte was astonished when the Japanese suddenly dropped their reparations demand. In addition, they agreed to divide Sakhalin Island with Russia. He knew the Tsar would approve of these latest offers by Japan because it allowed him to save face. It looked as if the Japanese had backed down. *The fool,* thought Witte. *Russia is on its knees and on the verge of destruction, and he worries about saving face!*

President Roosevelt met briefly with each delegation leader before the celebration ended. Baron Komura would be delighted to bring back a secret aid pledge from the United States to deliver to the emperor. No one in the American government would know it, but some presidential discretionary funds intended for the construction of the Panama Canal would soon be diverted to Japan.

When the president went to bid farewell to Witte, the Russian stood at attention and firmly grasped the president's offered hand. "Congratulations on a job well done," said the president while pumping the Russian's hand.

"Mr. President, I don't know if the world can thank you enough for your efforts. On behalf of my government, we are indebted that you arranged this peace effort."

At that point, Roosevelt stopped pumping Witte's hand. He gently began squeezing it with ever-increasing pressure. He just stared into the Russian's eyes, not saying a word. The eyes spoke for the both of them. Although in pain, the Russian said nothing.

Witte knew. The president had thought about Witte's proposal to remove the Tsar, and he now signaled his assent.

Aboard the RMS Oceanic
Mid-Atlantic Ocean
September 1905

Lieutenant Junior Grade Stephen Morrison felt odd to be dining aboard ship with civilians. The luxurious first class dining room of the *Oceanic* was a far cry from the spartan wardrooms of the United States Navy vessels on which he had served. However, on this night, he dined in civilian formal attire, sitting with seven other complete strangers. He had boarded the ship in New York City for the trans-Atlantic crossing to England. His ultimate destination would be the Royal Naval Dockyard in Portsmouth, England. His orders had him reporting directly to the office of the First Sea Lord, Admiral Sir John "Jacky" Fisher. Although his official orders called for him to be in England for four weeks, the British naval authorities had been notified that they would be hosting the representative from the United States Navy for a week. His assignment would end after the keel-laying ceremony for the new battleship, HMS *Dreadnought*.

Shortly after the Portsmouth Peace Conference, President Roosevelt notified Bonaparte that he wanted to meet Lieutenant Morrison, the young officer who had so impressed him at the briefing on Russia. "I'm sending him to meet with the British to study the new battleship they are constructing. He was personally recommended to me by my aide, Commander Sims, you know." In their private meeting, Roosevelt tasked Stephen Morrison with the assignment of liaison officer to the Royal Navy for a week. Only after swearing him to secrecy did Roosevelt inform him of the mission to Russia.

"You are certainly free to turn down this assignment, Lieutenant. Nothing unfavorable will reflect on you if you decline. After all, you and I are the only two people in America who know about this mission. However, I do believe you are uniquely qualified for this assignment. In fact, given your background, your knowledge of Russia, and your fluency in the language, I do not believe there is a better qualified man in the entire country than you." He gave Morrison until the next morning for his answer.

That night, Morrison stayed late at his office, weighing the pros and cons of accepting President Roosevelt's assignment. *Why do this?* he thought to himself. *My life is so good now. I have a wonderful wife and a great job. My career seems to be on track.* Just when he seemed to have talked himself out of the job, he felt a sobering sense of responsibility start to gnaw at him. *The president is right; I am probably the most qualified person in the country for this assignment. If not me, than who? How does one turn down a request from the president of the United States? Didn't I take an oath when I was commissioned?* He barely slept at all that night. The following morning, he notified the president that he would volunteer for the mission.

Breaking him out of his reverie, the bejeweled elderly lady to his left asked, "And what line of business are you in, Mr. Morrison?" All of the other diners at the table appeared to be members of the moneyed class of either England or the United States. The elderly woman eyed the young man, noticing that he was very clean cut with short hair, and that he had ramrod straight posture.

"I'm an officer in the United States Navy, ma'am. I'm stationed in Washington, and I'm currently headed to England on official business." he replied as he sliced his filet mignon. She nodded approvingly in reply and said, "Well, well, that sounds important!"

"Not really," he replied after sipping his red wine. "I'm going to be looking at a new battleship the British are building." Morrison hoped she would not continue to question him throughout the dinner, but the other diners at the table began peppering him with questions. In a way, he felt as if he was back in Washington in his job with Secretary Bonaparte, having frequent opulent dinners with wealthy, important people.

After the main course, the questions stopped, much to his relief, and the conversation drifted to other topics. As the waiter placed their desserts on the table, his mind wandered back to two nights prior when he and Helen had dined with her father at his Georgetown home. It was during dessert that he informed them of his urgent assignment.

"England!" exclaimed Helen Morrison, "Why England? And why tomorrow? I don't understand. What is so urgent that only you can be assigned to this mission? I thought you'd be safely tucked away here working for Secretary Bonaparte.

That's what we both thought! And how can he spare you for all that time away? For an entire month!"

Both she and her father stared at him with a mixture of confusion and disappointment in their eyes. "She's right, Stephen. This is sort of sudden, isn't it?" asked his father-in-law. "What is this urgent assignment that you are being given?"

He placed his knife and fork down and smiled back at them. "Well, you both must understand. Because of my background in naval gunnery, I apparently have the unique skill sets that Secretary Bonaparte wants for this assignment. I don't know if you've been following it in the news, but the British are about to build this new class of battleship that is revolutionary. We've truly never seen anything like it. They are calling it the *Dreadnought*. It is the brainchild of their First Sea Lord, Admiral Sir John Fisher. You remember meeting him earlier this year, darling? He was quite the dancer at the embassy reception." Helen nodded in acknowledgement as Morrison continued. "It's going to be an all big-gun ship, featuring only twelve-inch guns in rotating turrets, and it will be powered by the new turbine engines that will allow it to achieve speeds that have been unheard of before now."

"That's all very good, Stephen," interrupted Helen, "but you still haven't answered our question. Why you? Why does it have to be you?"

"Actually, it's quite a personal honor," he answered. "Admiral Sir Fisher has personally requested me as his gunnery expert, among other things. On his staff is Captain Percy Scott, the British officer who taught Commander William Sims the technique of continuous-aim firing. Sims has strongly recommended to President Roosevelt that I be assigned this task. They are concerned with the placement of the gun turrets. On the ships we are planning, Commander Sims would like them to be superimposed forward and aft, with one turret above and slightly behind the other in each position. Some of the British experts believe that the lower turrets in this arrangement cannot be manned when the upper one is firing. We, in fact, are committed to try this technique on two battleships that we're building. Lord Fisher may need me to personally testify before his committee on designs."

After a few moments of silence, his wife asked, "How long will you be away, really?"

"Oh, it should only be five weeks, six weeks tops. You know how these political processes can play out."

This cover story, of course, contained a kernel of truth. Designed by President Roosevelt, it provided a credible rationale for Morrison's trip to England. The mission planning had been unknowingly assisted by Secretary Bonaparte and his own naval aide, Commander William Sims. Passage was booked on the *Oceanic* for England, and arrangements had been made with the British admiralty. As he now sat dining with seven other wealthy strangers, he really had no desire for their idle chatter. In his mind, he repeatedly reviewed the broad outlines of the assignment for which he had volunteered. He recalled his final conversation with the president.

Roosevelt had made it crystal clear that if something went wrong, if Morrison was caught in the act of carrying out this mission, or if he was killed, he would have nothing identifying him as an agent of the United States government, or as an officer in the United States Navy. If he were identified as an American, the United States government would disavow any knowledge of him or his actions. Morrison would simply disappear. Roosevelt stressed this point repeatedly, almost as if he couldn't believe that anyone who truly understood the consequences would volunteer for this mission.

Morrison knew that Roosevelt would never truly understand his reasons. In addition to his sense of duty, Morrison couldn't deny to himself that there were personal reasons for accepting the mission. The thought of returning to his native Russia provoked ambivalent feelings. He harbored both a desire to destroy the country that had persecuted and driven his family out, yet he also felt that this was a chance to effect positive changes in Russia. In addition, there was always his ever-present desire to be the consummate American naval officer. *If I am honest with myself,* he had reasoned, *if I can pull this assignment off, I'll no longer just be the rabbi's boy, the outsider. With success will come acceptance...*

"And so," exclaimed the distinguished gentleman in the white Vandyke beard, sitting opposite Morrison. "Let us lift up our glasses and let me propose a toast!" Numerous cries of "Here! Here!" erupted around the table. The wine steward proceeded to fill all of the glasses, and as all the diners raised their glasses, the gentleman continued. "To much health and happiness, to peace and prosperity. And a special toast to President Theodore Roosevelt. I have it on good authority that he may well win the Nobel Peace Prize." Immediately after all the diners clinked glasses with one another, they all downed their expensive wine.

Yes, thought Morrison to himself as he savored the wine, *to President Roosevelt, who is doing more for world peace than any of you will ever know.*

Royal Naval Dockyard
Portsmouth, England
September 1905

Shortly after the *Oceanic* docked, Stephen Morrison disembarked the ship. Waiting for him at the pier stood an earnest-appearing ensign who worked directly for Captain Reginald Bacon, naval assistant to the First Sea Lord. "Welcome to England, Mr. Morrison!" beamed the youthful ensign as he saluted. "I'm here to take you to Captain Bacon's office. He's expecting you for lunch, sir."

Morrison returned the salute and offered, "That's very kind of him."

Both men got into the car and sped away to the Royal Naval Dockyard. As they drove, the young ensign proved to be a chatty host. "Will you be working with us on the *Dreadnought,* sir?"

"I'll be with you for a week. I'm scheduled to shove off after the keel-laying ceremony."

"That will be quite the celebration. You know, that's the official start of the Battle of Trafalgar celebrations. The month of October is the one-hundredth anniversary of Lord Nelson's victory at Trafalgar. His Majesty King Edward will be here for that celebration. You know, he and Admiral Fisher are good friends."

"So I've heard," replied Morrison as the car pulled up to a two-story, red brick building at the head of a drydock. As he got out of the car, the ensign pointed to the large piles of metal plates and other materials stacked on either side of the drydock. Hundreds of shipyard workers scurried busily all over the drydock area. The whole area seemed to be alive with energy and purpose. "As you can see, sir, we're ready to go." He led Morrison through the front door where a young yeoman issued him a special identification badge and stamped his orders. He followed the energetic ensign up a flight of stairs to a door that had "Captain Bacon" neatly painted on the frosted glass pane. "I'll leave you here, sir," the ensign said as he opened the door for Morrison. To the young lady at the desk, he barked, "Let Captain Bacon know that Lieutenant Morrison of the United States Navy is here." The young lady jumped to her feet and disappeared behind a door in the rear of the small office.

Several minutes later, a tall, distinguished-looking officer emerged from the back room. "You must be Lieutenant Morrison," he said, extending his hand. "I'm Captain Bacon. Welcome to Portsmouth."

As they firmly shook hands, Morrison replied, "I'm delighted and honored to be here, sir."

"Excellent! I hope you're hungry. We're headed for the officers' club for lunch. Captain Scott will be joining us. He knows you by reputation and is looking forward to meeting you."

The lunch at the officers' club evolved into an excellent social engagement for Morrison. He found Captain Percy Scott to be a very interesting individual. Acknowledged as the Royal Navy's foremost expert on gunnery, Scott had revolutionized naval gunnery into a true science. These techniques had been brought to the American navy by one of Scott's protégés, then-Lieutenant William Sims, who had become one of Stephen Morrison's most influential mentors. Scott was a short, hyperactive individual, the type of man who dominated every conversation. Most people found it hard to get a word in when conversing with him. Scott seemed excited to meet Morrison, considering him another one of his gunnery disciples. "I've heard about the exploits of you and Commander Sims aboard the *Indiana*. Well done indeed! I also read the after-action report once it was forwarded to the Royal Navy. You two have changed gunnery techniques forever back in the states. God, it wasn't very long ago in the British navy that if a projectile fired by a naval vessel actually hit a target, it was a cause for celebration. Now, you Americans have learned the art and the science. Again, well done, Mr. Morrison!"

"Well, sir, we had a pretty good teacher, if I must say so."

"Oh, you must!" blurted out Scott. "You certainly must!" Both Bacon and Morrison erupted into laughter. Morrison could sense he would enjoy his week with the British.

After lunch, they returned to Bacon's office for a briefing. Bacon had prepared a briefing folder for him, and they sat down in the conference room next to his office. "Lieutenant, I'm going to give you an overview now on *Dreadnought*; how it was conceived, what exactly is going into the design, and what the timeline is for the project. Are you familiar at all with *Dreadnought*?"

"I know that it's going to be an all-big-gun ship, only twelve-inchers. In addition, I know it will be fast. It appears to be based on that concept presented by the Italian naval architect, Cuniberti, a couple of years ago in an issue of *Jane's Fighting Ships*, correct?"

"No doubt that concept helped influence Lord Fisher's thinking, but the ideas are all from his brain. He has been envisioning this type of ship for years. Now that he has attained the position of First Sea Lord, his intention is to make his vision a reality. We're totally committed to it. We'll begin with a little background. Admiral Fisher assumed office in October of last year. One of the five main reforms he proposed for the naval service was to design and build a new class of battleship equipped only with twelve-inch guns and capable of twenty-one-knot speeds, two unheard of concepts up to this time.

"Beginning the end of last December, Admiral Fisher formed the Committee on Design to conceptualize the project. I was a member of the committee, along with six other naval officers and nine civilians. Admiral Fisher was not actually a member of the group, although his heart and soul were present in the room at all times. In fact, he oversaw the entire process. The committee met for seven weeks and based our work around the two governing principles as elucidated by Admiral Fisher, guns and speed. We decided on ten twelve-inch guns mounted in five turrets: one turret forward, one wing turret on either side of the superstructure, and two aft turrets."

"I don't mean to interrupt, sir, but why didn't you superimpose two turrets forward, with the upper one higher and slightly behind the lower turret? We're putting that type of arrangement in the new battleships we're designing, and we feel it will be more effective."

"We actually considered that arrangement, but the committee was split on this issue. Some felt strongly that in this arrangement, the firing of the upper turret would cause too much of a blast effect and render the lower turret unusable. I have mixed feelings myself. In the end, Admiral Fisher decided on the chosen arrangement of the turrets."

"What about the propulsion plant? I read that you are going to change from reciprocating piston steam engines to turbine engines. I'm not familiar with this concept. Can it work on a battleship?"

Bacon smiled before continuing. "It can, and it will! You've been in the engine rooms on modern ships, Lieutenant. Can you carry on a conversation or use the phone? In fact, can you even hear yourself think?" Seeing the smile develop on Morrison's face, Bacon continued. "I thought not. Our engineers have devised a steam turbine technology they guarantee us will be much quieter and much more durable than piston engines. Instead of pistons slamming up and down in cylinders, causing metal fatigue and ultimately cracked metal, we'll have rotating metal discs mounted on the shaft that will spin continuously. We'll reduce metal fatigue and run a hell of a lot cleaner, too. Can you ever remember going down into the engine room and not sliding all over the place because of all the fuel oil over the deck? This new technology will be much cleaner, and engine room duty will be much more palatable. Our engineers have a design that will generate twenty-three thousand horsepower from this turbine engine."

"What is the anticipated weight of *Dreadnought*? That's a lot of horsepower," Morrison commented.

"The weight will be seventeen thousand tons." When Bacon finished the sentence, Morrison whistled when he heard the number. "Those are quite impressive numbers! Almost a little mind-boggling, if you don't mind my saying so, Captain." He ran some figures in his head for a few seconds. While deep in thought, Morrison said, almost as if talking to himself, "You know, given the horsepower generated, twenty-one knots would be feasible for a seventeen-thousand ton ship. Yes, yes it would!" exclaimed Morrison, feeling intellectually stimulated by the thought of this new ship design.

Bacon smiled at the young American. "I see the lights going on in your head, Lieutenant. It is intriguing, isn't it? I can see your enthusiasm growing as we talk. Actually, one has only to spend ten minutes hearing Admiral Fisher wax eloquently about *Dreadnought* to become a true, devoted believer." Pouring a glass of water for himself and Morrison, Bacon instructed, "Turn to page ten of the briefing book. You're in for a surprise."

Morrison did as instructed and gasped. After reading the proposed timeline for the ship's construction, he blurted out "Sir, you can't be serious. From keel laying to completion in twelve months? That's impossible!"

"It would seem that way, if one were wed to tradition. You know, the keel laying is next week. Did you see what was going on in this yard when you approached the drydock? All of the materials are stacked and ready. All of the metal plates for the hull and armor belt are pre-cut and positioned for installation. The work force is motivated and committed to the project. They have been literally counting the days until the work begins. Lastly, don't forget the driving influence of the First Sea Lord, Admiral Sir John Fisher himself. Never underestimate that last factor, ever."

"May I ask a question, sir, and I mean no disrespect?"

"Fire away."

"What is the quickest time that a battleship has ever been constructed in your drydock?"

Bacon paused and reflected. Finally, he replied, "About two-and-a-half years. Yes, that's about right."

Morrison just sat there with a skeptical look on his face. Bacon smiled at him and said, "Just remember all of the facts that I have just outlined for you concerning the construction of *Dreadnought*. All of them will guarantee the success of the venture. Most of all, Lieutenant—and this is important—never, I repeat never, underestimate the power of the last factor I described to you. The influence of Admiral Fisher is what will ensure that we complete the construction exactly on time."

***

Over the next several days, Stephen Morrison met with many of the individual project managers who would be overseeing the various aspects of *Dreadnought*'s construction. He had been allowed to sit in on all aspects of the pre-construction phase that had been concluded by the week's end. Back in his room at the bachelor officers' quarters each night, he transcribed copious notes into a log that he would use to assemble his final report to Secretary Bonaparte. He planned to have at least a rough draft ready to submit before he left for Russia.

The thought of Russia continually weighed on his nerves. He had no idea how he would be contacted by the British agent with whom he would be working. He had been told by the president that the agent would contact him upon arrival in London, but other than that, he had nothing. No name, no address, nothing. He had been informed that the project was to be run by the head of British Intelligence, but nothing else had been revealed. Roosevelt had told him that in England, only the king, the prime minister, and this intelligence director knew of the mission. They would be given the name of an American, Lieutenant Stephen Morrison. With so many

Lee Mandel

unknowns, Morrison even began to wonder if the mission had been aborted.

That morning, he had been awakened by a nightmare. It was an odd premonition. He had had varying versions of the same nightmare since he was a teenager, but he hadn't had any episodes in over a year. As he lay in his bed, drenched in sweat, he realized that the uncertainty was starting to get to him. Why else would the nightmare have returned at this particular time? The keel laying would be in two days and still no contact or instructions from the British. He got out of his bed and walked over to the mirror hanging over his chest of drawers. Staring deeply into the face looking back at him, he began thinking. What was he trying to prove to himself by volunteering for this mission, returning to Russia after all these years? How long had it been, he wondered? Sixteen years? How many different lives had he led that brought him to this point? He was an American in England, awaiting orders to go into Russia and take part in a kidnapping and possible assassination of a foreign monarch. He smiled and thought, *No wonder the damn nightmare returned!* Splashing water on his face, he forced his thoughts back to his work and his wife. He would get through this challenge. Once the mission began, he would be all right. *Focus on the mission,* he thought. *That's the key.*

Later that day, Captain Bacon's secretary stopped Morrison as he entered the main office and said, "Oh, Lieutenant, these are for you." She handed him two envelopes. He thanked her as he tore open the first envelope. Continuing down the corridor, he began to read its contents. The memo from Captain Bacon contained a general reminder to all hands that everyone must be seated by 0945 on Monday, October 2, for the arrival of the official party, which would include Admiral Fisher and King Edward. On the bottom of the note, Bacon had scrawled,

"Good news, Lieutenant. You'll be riding back to London on the afternoon train with Admiral Fisher. The First Sea Lord wants to meet you." The prospect of meeting this naval legend both surprised and delighted Morrison. He knew that an official function, a ball to commemorate the Battle of Trafalgar, had been scheduled for that night at Buckingham Palace and that Fisher would be returning to London to attend it. The train ride back to London would take about an hour-and-a-half. He would have plenty of time to have a great conversation with the head of the Royal Navy.

As he started to toss the message into a wastebasket, he remembered that he had a second larger envelope. Opening it, he pulled out an official invitation that featured the crest of His Highness King Edward VII. It was an invitation to the reception at Buckingham Palace the night of the keel laying. This unexpected honor brought a big grin to his face. Meeting "Jacky" Fisher and going to a reception at Buckingham Palace, all in the same day! His day had certainly improved since he had awakened drenched in sweat from his haunting nightmare. It was turning into a fine day, in fact. As he started to put the invitation back in the envelope, he saw that the word "over" was handwritten in blue ink in the bottom corner.

He turned the invitation over and saw, written on the back: "The Music Room 9:30 P.M."

It was signed with the initials HRH.

***

Monday, October 2, turned out to be a clear, cold day. Amidst strict security, the entire dockyard workforce had assembled in place by 9:30 that morning. Like clockwork, the king's train arrived at Portsmouth exactly on time. As the crowd watched, the official party led by His Majesty King Edward VII took its place on the podium. The First Sea Lord, Admiral Sir John Fisher, sat next to the king.

The entire ceremony lasted less than half an hour. When the master of ceremonies introduced Admiral Fisher, the crowd erupted into wild applause. Waving like a celebrity, Fisher then began his speech, which lasted about fifteen minutes. *He is quite an energizing and charismatic speaker,* thought Morrison. Extremely buoyant and frequently gesturing with his arms, he seemed almost like an actor on a stage.

When Fisher finished, he introduced King Edward. Immediately, the crowd was on its feet, applauding wildly, and then it burst into a chorus of "God Save the King." When the tumult finally died down, the king spoke to the crowd. He delivered a short, inspiring pep talk stressing the importance of the work about to commence. The motivated work force loved it, and when the king had finished, they broke into another standing ovation.

After the king returned to his seat, the workman brought out the pre-cut metal plates of the keel of the battleship and positioned them while other workers stood by, ready to begin welding. They had rehearsed this moment for over a week, and with the teamwork of a choreographed ballet, the job was completed in minutes. Fisher returned to the lectern and announced, "Gentlemen, you may commence construction of the HMS *Dreadnought* upon the departure of the official party!" The crowd stood at attention as the official party departed. The king would be leaving for London immediately. Fisher would be staying until mid-afternoon, when he would be departing on the king's train, which was being sent back to Portsmouth to transport him and his staff to London.

As soon as the official party departed the dockyard perimeter, a shrill whistle blasted from the top of the nearby water tower, a signal to commence the construction of the new battleship. Morrison watched with amazement and admiration as the hundreds of workers actually began running to their workstations. Cranes started to move, welding torches were lit, trucks hauling parts began moving and the dockyard came alive in a continuous buzz of perpetual activity. Admiral Fisher had decreed that *Dreadnought* would be constructed in one year. They had their marching orders. "Watch us now, Lieutenant!" shouted one of the young British officers with whom he had been working that week. "Tell Mr. Roosevelt that you saw history being made this month!"

"I certainly intend to," shot back Morrison to the young ensign. With a smile, he waved and headed back to his quarters to pack his bags. He had just enough time to finish the first draft of his report and then make the train headed for London.

***

As Morrison read the draft of his report, the rhythmic slight swaying of the train's motion nearly rocked him to sleep. A hand on his shoulder, gently shaking him, suddenly startled him. "Excuse me. You're Lieutenant Morrison, correct?" asked a young British yeoman.

Sitting upright, he replied, "Yes, that's me."

"Sir, Admiral Fisher will see you now. Please follow me." Morrison stood and followed the young man as they headed for the rear of the train. Fisher was in the last car. As Morrison approached, he stood and extended his hand, bellowing out, "Hello, Lieutenant! I'm sorry we haven't been able to meet before now." Fisher was a stocky man with short gray hair and a twinkle in his distinctive green, almost oriental eyes. He had a crushingly strong handshake, which Morrison reciprocated, saying, "Admiral, I can't tell you what an honor it is for me to meet you."

"Please, Lieutenant, sit down, and we'll talk. Would you like a drink?"

"Water would be fine, sir." Fisher nodded at the enlisted man who stood nearby. "Please make that two waters, young man." Morrison noted that the admiral had a sallow, almost yellow, complexion. He had heard the rumors that his coloring was the result of several previous bouts of malaria. It became apparent immediately that Fisher loved to talk, and he seemed especially pleased that the United States has sent a representative to study the *Dreadnought*. "Tell me," he began, "what do you think of our project?"

"Very impressive, sir. It is a fantastic concept. You have quite a team putting it all into place. Captain Bacon is a most capable man. He and his staff have been quite kind to me this week, and I truly appreciate their efforts."

"Captain Bacon is impressive, isn't he? To be candid, no one could work as my naval aide and not be impressive, not the way I drive them! I'll let you in on a little secret, one that is probably the worst-kept secret in the Royal Navy," he said as he winked at Morrison. "Captain Reginald Bacon will be the first commanding officer of HMS *Dreadnought* when she is commissioned next year."

"I can't say that I'm surprised, sir. I'd love to serve under such a capable CO as him."

"Well said, Mr. Morrison! Reviewing your record, it looks as if you've had a few impressive commanding officers in your career thus far. Tell me, what do you think of the timeline that we've laid out for the ship's construction? Do you believe we can do it?"

"Well, sir, if you say it can be done, I wouldn't doubt you."

"I can tell you're stationed in Washington and have been around diplomats with that answer. Obviously, you really don't think it can be done. But make no mistake, the *Dreadnought* will be commissioned and ready for sea trials in one year. To show you how confident I am of this goal, I'm extending you an invitation to return next year for the commissioning. If you like, we'll arrange for Captain Bacon to take you out to sea!"

Morrison tried his best not to appear startled and thanked the admiral profusely. "I can think of nothing I'd like better. Thank you so much, Admiral."

"Tell me, Mr. Morrison, I hear you disagree with the placement of our forward turret and instead would have recommended two forward turrets, one on top of the other. Do you realize that I personally overruled that idea? Why would you have recommended otherwise? You must realize that careers are ruined by such disagreements with superior officers."

Morrison suddenly felt as if he was being set up for a fall. Why else would Fisher have brought up the whole matter? He decided to answer candidly. "With no disrespect meant, sir, our engineering studies show that the superimposed turrets, when placed correctly, pose no difficulty either with the firepower of the lower turret when the upper one fires, or with the habitability of the lower turret under those circumstances. With correct venting of the spaces, as well as required hearing protection, this is a better arrangement. It also puts more of our firepower directly forward as we pursue and attack the enemy.

"Pursuit and attack. This is where the placement of the forward turrets really comes into play in our overall strategy and battle doctrine. You see, Admiral, we have been heavily influenced by a brilliant naval strategist who once said something to the effect that, 'I am an apostle of End-on Fire, for to my mind, broadside fire is peculiarly stupid.' I believe I'm capturing the essence of his words correctly."

Fisher stared directly into Morrison's eyes upon hearing his own words being recited back to him. Morrison feared he had crossed the line; Fisher appeared about to explode with anger. For about fifteen seconds, that impassive look of welling anger continued to be written all over the admiral's face. Then, suddenly, he threw his head back and began roaring with laughter. "Oh, my God, Mr. Morrison! Well done! Well done!" He continued to shake with laughter, finding it hard to speak at first. "You have knowledge and audacity—a very valuable combination in this day and age. A combination that, unfortunately, I see very rarely in the Royal Navy." He continued laughing and finally settled down to say, "The look on your face was priceless! You looked like a sailor from the age of sail who was about to be keel-hauled."

"To be perfectly honest, sir, you looked like a captain from the age of sail who was about to order me to be keel-hauled!" Smiling as he spoke, Morrison was glad to see the admiral again burst into laughter with his response. Their meeting seemed to be going well.

The admiral meandered on about his youth and how he had entered the Royal Navy as a penniless thirteen-year-old. He seemed especially proud as he recalled his accomplishments as he struggled to claw his way to the top of the British Navy. "You see, Mr. Morrison, I'm not sure you can relate to these types of struggles. You are a graduate of the United States Naval Academy and the son of a United States congressman. Don't look surprised. I had my staff do some homework on your background."

Morrison cleared his throat and replied, "Actually, Admiral, I can relate to these types of struggles. Congressman Morrison was my stepfather. I was born in Russia, the son of a rabbi who immigrated to the United States when I was eleven years old. I know exactly what you mean about starting out in life with absolutely nothing."

Fisher's jaw dropped as he said, "What? You mean you're a Jew? But you don't look … I mean how …?" He seemed unable to express the questions that shot through his mind.

"I know. I don't look like a Jew, whatever exactly that means. I've heard that all my life. It's a long story how I ended up as a naval officer and currently aide to the secretary of the navy, and it's probably a story for another time, sir."

"Hmmm," mused Fisher, as he looked at the young American and smiled. "Another Disraeli!" he said, referring to England's Jewish prime minister of the late nineteenth-century. He stood up, and Morrison immediately followed suit. Fisher extended his hand and said, "Shake hands, Lieutenant Stephen Morrison." As they pumped each other's hands with firm, powerful grips, Fisher smiled and continued, "From one penniless wretch who made it into the service of his country's navy to another."

Morrison smiled broadly and replied, "Amen to that, Admiral."

7

Buckingham Palace
London, England
October 2, 1905

The ballroom at Buckingham Palace had been decorated in nautical tones, in keeping with the Battle of Trafalgar theme. As the orchestra played, Stephen Morrison circulated around the room. It was a pleasant ending for a very exciting day, all things considered. After arriving in London, he learned that Admiral Fisher had arranged lodging for him at the Navy Club downtown and for an admiralty car to pick him up and take him to Buckingham Palace. He had his first encounter with the king when he went through the receiving line. When he reached the monarch, his aide announced, "Lieutenant Junior Grade Stephen Morrison, United States Navy." They shook hands, and the Edward simply welcomed him to the reception.

After about a half-hour of mingling, Morrison spotted Admiral Fisher regaling a small crowd of fellow guests, and he walked over to join them. As he approached the group, Fisher spotted him and announced to the others, "Ah, there he is, our representative from the United States Navy! Everyone, this is Lieutenant Morrison. Lieutenant, these good people were just telling me that they don't believe that *Dreadnought* can possibly be constructed in a year. What is your opinion? Mind you all, he's a disciple of Percy Scott, so we don't know if we can really believe him!" Everyone laughed, turning to the earnest young American who had just joined them.

"What is my opinion?" he repeated for the theatrical effect. "Hmmm. It is my humble opinion that the ship will be finished in exactly one year, and I say that for two reasons," he smiled.

"And just what might those reasons be, young man?" inquired a bejeweled, stately looking woman, speaking for almost everyone assembled around Admiral Fisher.

"Well, ma'am, first, tonight we honor England's great naval hero, Lord Nelson, for his incredible victory at Trafalgar. But are we not also honoring his heir apparent, England's greatest living admiral, Admiral Fisher, and his pledge to construct the greatest battleship in history? Just as we would never doubt the greatness of Nelson, would we dare dishonor his memory by doubting the ability of his heir, who is the living embodiment of Lord Nelson? Ladies and gentlemen, I think not!"

As he looked around, the small spellbound crowd was impressed, one woman even saying, "My, you've trained this American well, Jacky!"

"More importantly, the *Dreadnought* will be finished in exactly a year because I'm coming back to England in exactly a year to go to sea with her, as Admiral Fisher promised me. And I have warned the admiral that the ship must be ready because there is no more pathetic sight than an American naval officer crying in his beer, which is exactly what will happen if it isn't ready!" With that, the small crowd burst into laughter, and several began applauding and shouting, "Bravo!"

After the small crowd dispersed, Fisher took Morrison by the arm and announced, "I have a very important question for you, Mr. Morrison!"

"Yes, sir, what might that be?"

"If you're an aide to the Secretary of the Navy, you must attend a good number of these damn state functions. So my question is, are you a decent dancer?"

Morrison smiled at the seemingly earnest look on Fisher's face and replied, "I have never broken any woman's foot, and I've had no major complaints thus far."

"Good!" beamed the admiral. "They are about to play a waltz, and I promised my niece that I'd waltz with her. Please, come with me, Lieutenant. I'm going to introduce you to my wife, Kitty, and I'll have you waltz with her." He stopped, gave the younger man a stern look, and announced, "That is a direct order." Arriving at the side of his elegant wife, Fisher introduced Morrison to her and said, "Darling, let's see if an American naval officer half my age can match my dancing skills."

Morrison smiled at her and said, "Ma'am, it would be an honor to escort you to the dance floor."

As the orchestra began to play a Strauss waltz, they began to dance and Mrs. Fisher complimented her young partner. "You are a good dancer, Lieutenant. I really shouldn't be surprised. You've made a good impression on Jacky." Seeing the young man blush, she continued, "You needn't be so modest. Feel honored. It's rare that he meets someone and gets to like him so quickly."

Not certain what to say, Morrison simply said, "Thank you, ma'am. You flatter me. I don't know what to say."

"Well then, young man, say that you are a lucky man with a great future ahead of you. Say that you are a man who has greatly impressed the most important man in the British Navy. Most of all, say that your wife is a lucky woman to have a husband as dashing, as intelligent, and as promising as you, and you are a lucky man to have a wife as devoted and understanding as she must be." She smiled as the waltz came to a finish. "You didn't hear this from me, Lieutenant, but Jacky—I'm sorry—Admiral Fisher, intends to request that the United States Navy send you here as an exchange officer in the near future."

All of the dancers politely applauded the orchestra when the music ended. Morrison took her hand in his and said, "Thank you very much. It was a treasured moment to share this dance with you." He bowed and gently kissed her gloved hand. As he stood back up, he noticed the large clock on the far wall read 9:20 P.M.

***

It didn't take him long to reach the music room. As he walked down the hall toward his destination, he noted a military guard stationed outside of the door. As he approached it, the guard, noticing his American naval uniform asked, "Are you Lieutenant Morrison?" When he answered in the affirmative, the guard turned, grabbed the doorknob, and said, "They're expecting you. Please enter."

Entering the beautifully paneled room, Morrison saw King Edward and Prime Minister Arthur Balfour sitting in two leather chairs that had been pulled together with a third one, obviously intended for him. "Ah, Lieutenant," said King Edward, "come on in and join us. This is Prime Minister Arthur Balfour." The prime minister extended his hand and nodded to the chair as Morrison shook his hand. When he sat down, the king thanked him for coming.

"My purpose in asking you here is twofold," said the king, reaching into his vest pocket and removing a gold cigar case. "First, I wanted to meet the man who would volunteer for such a potentially perilous mission. I wanted to thank him personally." He stood, walked over to Morrison, and placed a hand on his shoulder. "Young man," he continued, "you are a hero. You are a patriot, and the world will owe you a debt it will never be able to repay. I wanted to tell you that personally and to thank you. Lastly, I wanted to shake your hand."

Morrison stood up, the monarch extended his hand, and they shook hands firmly. "God bless you, Lieutenant Morrison," he said with all sincerity. "I'll be leaving you now with the prime minister." Balfour stood as the king exited the room. The prime minister invited Morrison to sit down again.

"I asked His Majesty to let us meet privately from this point on. Actually, I had advised him not to meet you. The less he knows about all of this, the better. However, he insisted on meeting you and personally thanking you. In fact, before I say another word, I, too, want to thank you for volunteering."

Balfour leaned toward Morrison and said, "Tomorrow morning you are to go to an address on Victoria Street, 64 Victoria Street. It's located on the Victoria Embankment. Be there at 9:00 A.M. sharp. The address houses a nondescript-looking office, and the signage on the door reads W. Morgan, General Agent. There you'll meet William Melville, who runs all of our foreign service espionage operations."

"Is it Mr. Melville with whom I'll be going into Russia?"

"No, he has an agent already picked out and ready with a plan for the mission. Like you, this agent is fluent in Russian and can pass for a native. This agent will be there tomorrow."

"Do you know when we'll be leaving?"

"No. You'll get all the details tomorrow. I suspect you'll be leaving almost immediately. We all want this mission completed as soon as possible before Russia crumbles into anarchy." The prime minister stood, walked to the small bar, and poured himself a brandy. "Can I interest you in a brandy, Lieutenant?"

"No, thank you, sir. If it's all right with you, sir, I'd just as soon go back to the Navy Club and get some rest. I have a feeling I won't be getting much rest over the next few weeks."

"Yes, of course. Please, feel free to leave. I wish you the best of luck." After shaking hands with the prime minister, Morrison turned and began walking toward the door. When he reached the door, Balfour called out to him, and he turned. "Thank you, Lieutenant Morrison," Balfour said, "Thank you, and God speed!"

As Stephen Morrison walked through the vast halls of Buckingham Palace, the words of Kitty Fisher kept ringing in his ears, "You are a lucky man to have a wife as devoted and understanding as she is." Mrs. Fisher was right. He had to let Helen know. Tonight.

***

The uneasy feeling in his gut began as soon as Morrison returned to the Navy Club. He was embarking on an assignment with potentially dangerous consequences. His life might be forever altered. The reality of this mission suddenly weighed heavily on his soul. After sitting in a corner chair and contemplating what might lay ahead for him, he got up and began to prepare for the next day. As instructed, he would be dressing in plain civilian clothes. He laid out the outfit on his bed. Next, he sat down and withdrew a large envelope from the desk drawer and began to erase the identity of Stephen Morrison.

Into the envelope, he placed his identification card and wallet. He removed his Naval Academy ring and then, with a sad feeling, he removed his wedding band, and placed them both into the envelope. From that point on Stephen Morrison would cease to exist. Walking over to the closet, he removed his suitcase and began to pack the rest of his clothing. Completing the task in a few minutes, he lay down on his bed and put his hands behind his head. His thoughts turned to Helen. Kitty Fisher was absolutely correct. He wanted to reach out to Helen one last time before he started the mission.

Returning to the small desk, he removed paper, took his Waterman fountain pen in hand, and sat down to write.

2 October 1905

My Dearest Helen,

I wish you could know how much I prayed to God that you could be here with me in London tonight. I am dog-tired after this exciting day. It began with the keel-laying ceremony at Portsmouth, and I have just returned from a reception at Buckingham Palace to kick off a month-long commemoration of the 100-year anniversary of the Battle of Trafalgar. I'm meeting some fascinating people, especially Admiral Fisher! He is everything that we heard - brilliant, dynamic, forceful, and possibly the most charismatic person I have ever met. The battleship will be a huge technological leap forward. I'm honored to be able to spend a few more weeks here observing the construction.

Do you realize that we're coming up on a very important anniversary? That's right. In a little over two weeks, we'll have been married for seven months! Seven months, and you still haven't gotten tired of me. And you better not, Mrs. Morrison! I intend for us to grow old and senile together. All silliness aside, I just wanted to tell you how much

I love you and miss you. I thank God that you came into my life, and I'm living for the day when we can be together again. God willing, I'll be home to you in four or five weeks.

Based on our projected workload, I may not have much of a chance to write again before I return. Never forget that you are always in my heart. I live for the day when you are in my arms again.

Just thought you'd like to know.
All my love, forever
Stephen

*Victoria Street
London, England
September 1905*

The middle-aged gentleman fumbled with his keys as he stood in front of his office on the Victoria Embankment. Finally unlocking the door, he entered his office on the first floor. The directory listed the occupant of the nondescript office as W. Morgan, General Agent, but that wasn't his real name. His real name was William Melville, and for over ten years he had served Scotland Yard as the head of the Special Branch, known among inner circles as the British Secret Service.

As he entered his office, Melville thought back to the evening several weeks ago when he was summoned to 10 Downing Street by Prime Minister Arthur Balfour. On many occasions, he had briefed virtually every senior member of His Majesty's government; he didn't suspect that meeting would be anything but routine. The presence of Sergei Witte, Prime Minister of Russia, in Balfour's study quickly confirmed that this meeting would be different.

Balfour introduced Melville to Witte, whom Melville recognized from his photographs in the newspapers. Balfour began the meeting by giving Melville a stern disclaimer. The meeting would be top secret, and everything they discussed would be strictly for Melville's ears and very much off the record. Melville acknowledged his agreement. Only then did Sergei Witte reveal the reason for his secret visit to the prime minister's residence. He described the plan within the top circles of the Russian government to remove Tsar Nicholas II from Russia and to replace him with a military leader, the Tsar's uncle, Grand Duke Nicholas. He implored the prime minister and Melville to send a British agent to perform the mission of actually removing the Tsar from Russia.

Witte assured them that the Okhrana was too riddled with double agents and informers to successfully get the job done. It had to be an agent from a foreign power. Melville was very familiar with the Okhrana and knew that what Witte said was true. Witte went on to speak for over an hour, relaying the grave state of affairs in Russia. He closed by saying, "Gentlemen, the fate of Russia is at stake. Nicholas will bring our country to ruin. Anarchy is breaking out all over the country. This mission is important to England as well. There is much social unrest here, too. The collapse of Russia will destabilize all of Europe. I implore you to help us. Send an agent to remove the Tsar and preserve a stable Russia!"

After Witte departed, the prime minister poured a brandy for Melville and himself. They sat down in the study, and Balfour asked Melville what he thought. "Is what Witte asks even feasible, William? Who in God's name could ever pull off such a mission?"

Scratching his cheek, Melville slowly and methodically responded. "Well, sir, it is one hell of a request." He studied the fine-cut crystal glass that contained his drink for a few seconds and then continued. "He is absolutely right, you know. The Okhrana is like a sieve when it comes to secrets: too many agents on too many payrolls. I seriously doubt that this sort of mission can be accomplished from the inside, so to speak." He appeared pensive, lost in thought, as if formulating a plan in his head. "The mission itself, should we attempt it, would be very risky and very difficult, but not impossible. With all due respect, Prime Minister, shouldn't we inform King Edward of this request, given the potential international repercussions?"

"We actually met with His Majesty last night," replied Balfour. "Witte made his request in my presence, explaining the possible effect on England should a revolution occur in Russia. This situation concerns the king very much. His Majesty authorized me to proceed under the condition that there be total deniability of his knowledge. He also declined knowledge of any details should we accede to Witte's request. I gave him my word on both counts before I contacted you yesterday. Now, William, as you heard, time is short. The mission would have to be completed by the end of the year, lest those riots that he described break out in January."

"My sources have confirmed that, indeed, a series of strikes and demonstrations—no, you're right, riots—are scheduled to begin on January 5, the anniversary of 'Bloody Sunday.'"

"William, could anyone go to Russia and accomplish this mission? It seems virtually impossible to me."

"Actually, sir," Melville replied, "there is a man whom I believe is clever enough to do it. He's done other jobs for us.

In fact, he was born in Russia. He currently goes by the name of Sidney Reilly. He was instrumental in protecting our government's oil interests in Persia earlier this year."

"Wasn't he the one who made sure that the Rothschilds didn't get those oil concessions?" the prime minister recalled. "I've heard a little about him. Sounds like a bit of a scoundrel. Can this man be trusted?"

"I believe he can be trusted with a mission as long as there's excitement in it, and of ultimate benefit to him. He's a strange one. Lives the life of an English gentleman, but he's a Jew from Russia whose name was originally Salomon Rosenblum. He came here nine years ago under mysterious circumstances. Quite the ladies man, also. Oh, yes," he reminded himself, "he's also a versatile linguist. Speaks French, German, Italian, and of course, Russian. He also has established business interests and contacts in St. Petersburg."

"Wouldn't he be recognized?"

"That's another interesting facet about him. He's good with disguises and identity changes. I believe he has six different passports. He can pass for Russian, Greek, Italian—you name it." Pausing to reflect a minute, Melville continued, "Yes, I believe that this mission would be tailor-made for Reilly."

"Would he accept such a mission?"

"Yes, I believe he would. He's too ambitious and vain to decline it."

The prime minister stood up and began pacing the room, his arms behind his back. Melville sensed something else was bothering Balfour, something he hadn't mentioned yet. Finally, Balfour stopped pacing and looked at Melville. "There's a complication, William. I don't like the idea that this mission should solely be a British mission. We're not the only ones who would feel the repercussions should the revolutionaries overthrow the Tsar and plunge Russia into anarchy. The entire western world would feel the effects. If the mission were to fail and be uncovered, I wouldn't want all the condemnation falling on England's shoulders. This whole thing is too risky."

"What do you suggest, sir?"

Balfour kept pacing, much to Melville's annoyance. Finally Balfour stopped and said, almost as if with a revelation, "We need to get the Americans involved with this mission, to make this a joint Anglo-American mission. This partnership would be an insurance policy that England wasn't acting alone in the event that the plan goes sour. Because President Roosevelt is making public pronouncements about mediating the end of the war, we need to involve him, especially after Witte tells him that the Tsar will never agree to a peace agreement, as he informed us last night."

"He actually told you that? Will Witte tell Roosevelt the same thing?"

"Witte leaves for the United States the day after tomorrow. He has a secret meeting scheduled with Roosevelt at his New York home next week where he will deliver the bad news of the Tsar's real intentions." He paused for a minute and continued. "That's it, William. I'll inform Witte in the morning that we will only act on his request if he can convince the Americans to join us on this mission. If they do, then I will leave all facets of the planning in your hands. You understand what I'm telling you. Like His Majesty, I require total deniability. If the plan goes wrong, your agents—this Reilly fellow and anyone working with him, including any Americans—are on their own. The British government will deny any awareness of their actions, and we can assume the Americans will respond the same way. Total deniability. It has to be this way."

**

On the current, cool October morning, as Melville sat at his desk, he heard knocking on the door. He walked over and opened it. Smiling, he announced, "Hello, Sidney, come in," as he shook Reilly's hand. "The American will be arriving momentarily." Reilly followed Melville to his office and took a seat. "Is everything satisfactory with your new flat?"

"Yes, sir, it is. Thank you for asking," replied the young agent. "Tell me, sir, do you know anything about this American?"

"Only that he's a naval officer and that he's fluent in Russian. They told me that he is very knowledgeable in Russian affairs. Sounds as if he is the right man, if the right man truly exists!"

"We shall see, sir. I hope you'll allow me to have final approval of this American, given that I will be going into the abyss with him."

"Of course," replied Melville. As he spoke, there was a knock on the door. "That must be him now. Let me fetch him."

Melville opened the door to see a rugged-appearing man in his mid-thirties. "I'm looking for William Melville," spoke the young man.

"That's me," replied Melville and extended his hand. "Come on in." He motioned toward his back office. As Morrison entered, he saw a dapper gentleman sitting in one of the chairs at the head of the desk. Extending his hand toward him, he announced, "I'm Lieutenant Stephen Morrison, United States Navy. I'm reporting as ordered."

"Please, be seated," invited Melville. "This is Sidney Reilly. He is in charge of your mission. Thank you so much for volunteering, Lieutenant." Morrison looked at Reilly as they all were getting seated. *A little too smooth looking*, he thought to himself. *I'll have to keep an eye on this one.*

"Lieutenant, you understand the goal of this mission. Total secrecy is imperative. You two will also be working under the concept of total deniability. If either or both of you are caught or killed, both His Majesty's government as well as the Roosevelt administration will deny any knowledge of your actions. That fact needs to be very clear up front."

"Sir, I was briefed by President Roosevelt himself," responded Morrison. "He is the only person in the United States, other than me, who knows about this mission. I assure you of that. He also stressed the stipulation of deniability. I understand and accept this risk."

Reilly was watching the American as he spoke. He appeared very intelligent and articulate, but Reilly needed to satisfy his curiosity. If they were going into danger together, he had to be sure about this American. "Tell me, Lieutenant," he asked in Russian, "how well do you speak Russian? I've heard you are very knowledgeable in Russian affairs. Have you ever even been in Russia?" he asked, appearing skeptical.

Morrison noted the smug look on Reilly's face before he answered. "I have been told that I speak Russian like a native," replied Morrison in flawless Russian. "Yes, I have been to Russia. For your information, I was born in Russia, and I have lived in Perm and Odessa. Before I began my studies at the United States Naval Academy, I spent a year touring the Russian countryside. I still have contacts inside Russia that keep me informed about Russian politics. Any other questions? Shall we continue this conversation in Russian, or can we speak English?"

Reilly looked at Melville and smiled. "Well, I suppose that Lieutenant Morrison has the right qualifications. Sorry, Morrison, I had to know now if you could pass as Russian. I didn't know your background."

"Excellent!" responded Melville. "Lieutenant, I understand that as far as anyone knows, you're still studying our *Dreadnought*. We will continue with that cover story until you return from this mission. Mind you, when you walk out of this office today, Lieutenant Stephen Morrison will cease to exist, at least until the mission is completed. Did you bring me the things I requested?"

"Yes, sir," he replied as he reached into his coat pocket and removed the envelope. Handing it to Melville, he said, "It's all here, including my wedding band. Please be careful with it."

"I will indeed," reassured Melville. "Your code name, as well as the mission's code name, will be Double Eagle. As you know, the double-headed eagle is on the official crest of the Romanov family. Reilly has developed a plan that I've approved. I'll let him brief you on this plan after you both leave here."

Melville then stood and walked over to the corner of his office where a small chest sat on the floor. Opening the lid, he reached into the ice that filled the chest, pulled out three bottles of Guinness beer and brought them to his desk. After opening the bottles, he handed one to each of his guests and lifted his own. "Gentleman, a toast! To the success of Double Eagle!" All three raised their bottles and lifted them to their lips. They stayed for about fifteen minutes making small talk. Finally, Reilly put down his bottle and said, "Come on, Double Eagle. Let's get going. We've got work to do."

***

Reilly had booked a room for Morrison at the Hotel Europa on Grosvenor Square. After leaving him there, Reilly returned to his own flat in Paddington to change for dinner. As he laid out his dinner attire, he stopped and began to think. *This American seemed impressive enough, and he certainly could speak Russian like a native. One less thing to worry about.* However, Reilly knew virtually nothing about this new partner, other than the fact he was an officer in the United States Navy. The story he told them was impressive. *Born in Russia, he's an American who graduates their naval academy, and now he's a volunteer for a mission that may well be suicidal. This Stephen Morrison has a surreal, almost unbelievable, quality. There must be more to him than meets the eye. He definitely is not what he appears to be and I sure as hell intend to find out more about this new partner of mine at dinner tonight,* Reilly thought to himself as he dressed.

As Melville had quickly learned, there was also more to Reilly. Appearing to be an aristocratic Englishman, he was, in fact, a native of Russia, from Odessa before he had immigrated to England a decade earlier. To cover his trail, he had created an elaborate background story that was both unbelievable and impossible to disprove. He appeared to be an English gentleman of leisure, and he had adopted the lifestyle, along with a new name. Although born Salomon Rosenblum, he had adopted an Irish-sounding name, Sidney Reilly.

Reilly had immersed himself in a myriad of business schemes throughout the continent and, given his natural flair for languages, he became an international businessman. This role provided the cover for the intelligence operations he performed on behalf of His Majesty's government. Having caught Melville's eye, he had impressed the head of the British Secret Service with his resourcefulness and ingenuity. He had a natural flair for spying and espionage in general. He also proved to be a master of disguise.

What worried Melville most about Reilly was his womanizing. Although married, he had a way of ending up in the beds of many upper-class society women, who seemed to find him irresistible. He often counseled the young agent about discretion and avoiding compromising positions. Reilly would smile and agree, and then head to his next sexual conquest.

Miraculously, and to the relief of William Melville, he never seemed to get into trouble over his bedroom antics. Melville had to write off the anxiety he felt over Reilly's sexual habits as the cost of doing business with him. This agent got results, and, ultimately, that was all that mattered.

Melville also believed that Reilly was the one agent audacious enough, and crazy enough, to take on the mission to Russia.

***

Reilly had made reservations for them to dine at Claridge's. Arranging to meet in front of the hotel on the corner of Brook and Davies Street, Reilly saw the American walking toward him and waved. They shook hands and Reilly took Morrison by the arm, escorting him into the lobby. "There is no reason not to enjoy some of England's finest cuisine tonight, considering where we're going. We'll go over everything while we dine."

The maître d' recognized Reilly as the two entered the dining room. "Mr. Reilly! So good of you to dine with us again tonight. We have your usual table ready for you and your guest." The two followed their host to the table and sat down. Immediately, Reilly ordered champagne for them.

Reilly started the conversation. "I assume you know the details of Russia's current status? After all, I'm told you are an expert. How good are your inside sources?"

"My sources tell me that Russia is on the verge of a revolution," replied Morrison. "Things have been spiraling downhill, and this senseless war with Japan has really been the final straw. The Tsar has fooled no one with his usual stupid antics, such as the pogroms against the Jews. The Russian people can see what the real issues are. Nicholas is a weak, sad excuse for a leader. He has capable men like Witte to advise him, and instead, he relies on his wife and, worst of all, this crazy so-called holy man named Rasputin, a real degenerate, who seems to have some sort of major influence over the Tsar.

Morrison paused for a moment. "Japan has defeated Russia in this war. The Tsar is either too vain or too stupid to grasp this fact," he said, shaking his head in disgust. "You know, Reilly, the revolutionaries are planning massive riots in January on the anniversary of the Winter Palace massacre. The nation is really on the verge of implosion."

Reilly listened to his new partner and then raised his champagne glass. They toasted with the excellent French champagne to the success of the venture. Reilly looked at Morrison and said, "You know, I like to know a little something about the people that I work with. I mean, we do have to trust each other and all that sort of stuff."

"What is it you want to know?" asked Morrison as he savored the drink.

"Well, for one, why would an officer in the United States Navy volunteer for a mission like this one? You're not an intelligence agent, are you?"

"No, I'm not an intelligence officer. I'm just a regular line officer. Let's just say that I have my reasons for volunteering and leave it at that."

"How does a boy born in Russia end up as an American naval officer? I'm sure there's quite a story behind this!"

Morrison smiled and admitted, "Yes, it's quite a story. The short version is that I was born in Perm, my father was a rabbi, and we immigrated to New York in 1881. As far—"

"You're Jewish?" asked Reilly incredulously. "Christ Almighty, you sure don't look it! I never would have guessed."

"As I was saying, as far as my naval career, I've always been fascinated by the sea. I've wanted to be a naval officer since I was a little boy in New York City" As he finished, the waiter brought their entrees. "That's the short version, partner. Why are you grinning?" he asked when he saw Reilly smile and shake his head.

"This is almost too much. Simply too much!" laughed Reilly as he began to cut into his steak. "Talk about irony and coincidence." Sensing that Morrison had no idea what he was talking about, he explained. "As a matter of fact, I was also born in Russia, in Odessa. My birth name was Salomon Rosenblum. Can you taste the irony, Double Eagle? Two Russian-Jewish expatriates, going back into Russia to kidnap the Tsar? It's almost too good to be true."

As Morrison washed down a morsel of lobster with the fine champagne, he looked at his partner and quipped, "Well, you could have fooled me, too. I had you pegged as a proper English gentleman." Reilly began to chuckle as he thought over the situation, when Morrison finally said, "You know, we've done enough socializing and fine dining. What exactly is your plan? Let's cut the social stuff and get down to business. When are we leaving for Russia?"

Reilly wiped his lips with his napkin and suddenly became very business-like. "We leave in the morning." He raised his glass and took a sip before continuing. "The plan is not very complicated," he continued. "I have an import-export business in St. Petersburg on Nevsky Prospekt. It's a legitimate, functioning business. In the past, I've brought in associates from our fictitious foreign offices; hence, bringing you into the country will cause no particular notice. Our main import is precious gems. As a result of considerable bribery, we gained access to the purchasing agents of Faberge. Are you familiar with that company?"

"I've heard of it," replied Morrison. "Isn't Faberge the 'jeweler to the Tsar'?"

"Exactly. They are the exclusive suppliers of all jewelry to the imperial Russian family. Every year, they produce for the Tsar these exquisite eggs, which the Tsar collects and gives as gifts to the Tsarina and his mother. I tell you, Double Eagle, these eggs are magnificent; they are priceless. The craftsmanship is beyond words. They are pure gold, and they are all gem-encrusted as well. Magnificent works of art!

"It is at Faberge where our plan begins. Through an arrangement brokered by Melville himself, we will be bringing in diamonds from the British royal family's collection. I was with Melville in the Tower of London when we picked them up. In an arrangement set up by Grand Duke Nicholas with Peter Carl Faberge himself, we will be arranging a private showing of these British jewels to the Tsar personally at Faberge's workshop in his building. Already we know that the Tsar is fascinated with the prospect of owning these gems, as is Faberge in using these gems for his newest creations."

"I'm a little confused," said Morrison as he cut another piece of lobster and dipped it into the drawn butter. "Are these supposed to be stolen gems that will be presented to the Tsar? Doesn't this scenario seem somewhat suspicious?"

"Of course not!" shot back Reilly, somewhat miffed at his American colleague. "Through official channels, His Majesty has contacted his cousin the Tsar and offered to sell the gems in a very quiet manner to raise revenue for his new battleship, the one you are supposedly working on at the moment, instead of raising taxes. I suppose Russia isn't the only country concerned with oppressed workers," laughed Reilly sarcastically. "Since Grand Duke Nicholas has brokered the arrangement, he will personally bring the Tsar to the Faberge Building. This is where the abduction will take place."

"I certainly hope that the Tsar hasn't read the British newspapers too closely. He'd know that the *Dreadnought* is being financed by the money that Admiral Fisher is saving by retiring over one-hundred-fifty ships from the Royal Navy," countered Morrison.

"I assure you that Nicholas is not the type of leader that gets into fine detail. In fact, I hear he's not much of an intellect at all." Reilly paused for some more champagne and continued. "The Tsar will be drugged into unconsciousness, and we'll shave off his beard and mustache so he won't be readily recognizable. Unbeknownst to Mr. Faberge, we will then detonate a small bomb in the back of his workshop, setting off enough of an explosion to destroy a small part of the factory. Unfortunately, casualties are necessary for the plan to succeed. One must crack eggs to make an omelette, you know.

"At that point, you and I will change into outfits of St. Petersburg rescue workers from the nearest hospital. We will then adopt completely different identities, supported by papers identifying us as working-class St. Petersburg hospital laborers. The Tsar will be changed into the outfit of a worker. When the rescue squads arrive, you and I will transport the unconscious Tsar by stretcher into a waiting ambulance. This particular ambulance will not go to the hospital. We will change the Tsar into clothing of a gentleman, and we will do the same. A block away from Petrovskaya Embankment, we have secured a garage. We'll exit the ambulance there and walk our 'drunken' associate to a waiting pleasure craft at the waterfront. We'll cause no notice; we will just be three well-to-do Russian businessmen out for an early evening boat ride. About five miles out, we'll transfer to a ship heading to Helsinki.

t, we'll be British physicians accompanying a ...ient back to England for treatment." Once ...y stopped and took a deep swallow of his drink. He ...ed with pride at the American lieutenant whom he would refer to from this point on only as Double Eagle. He could tell from his unimpressed look and his angry eyes that the American had many questions. "You obviously have questions, Double Eagle. Fire away!"

"Obviously, the two of us alone cannot pull this off. I assume you have inside people," said Morrison as Reilly nodded affirmatively. "How many are we talking about, and how reliable are they? I'm told that both the Okhrana and all the revolutionary groups are riddled with double agents. And what about the Tsar? What happens after the explosion? Won't someone be bound to notice that the Tsar of Russia is missing?"

"That is the beautiful part," replied Reilly. "As I told you, some people will die during the explosion. It's an operational necessity. In fact, the unwitting bomber will be bringing in the explosive in his lunch bucket. This worker has been studied for weeks, and he is a creature of habit. When he opens the lunch bucket that night, he will detonate the bomb, and he will be blown up beyond recognition. His body, or what's left of it, will be passed off as the Tsar's body. Hence, the Tsar is killed by an anarchist bomb, and Grand Duke Nicholas will assume the throne. Incidentally, several other bombs will be set off simultaneously all over St. Petersburg, just to keep the police busy and divert attention away from our mission."

"And who are your inside workers, and how reliable are they?"

"They're pretty good men. They absolutely hate the Tsar, so they are committed to seeing this plan succeed. Almost all of them are from this Bolshevik faction, so they're a little crazy and very ruthless. They are also starved for money. I pay them very well, so I've bought their loyalty. They will also be completely loyal to you. They know this mission has another team leader. Although they know nothing about you, they know that they take orders from both of us. If something should happen to me, they are to obey you completely. Believe me, Double Eagle, they are loyal to whoever pays them the most money. No one can come close to what I'm paying these men. Couple that with their intense hatred of the Tsar, and we have very able and capable assistants for this mission."

"From what I know of the Bolsheviks, they're fanatical," said Morrison. "Reilly, I don't mind telling you that this makes me feel very uneasy. To have our plan hinge on the trustworthiness of these people doesn't exactly give me a warm feeling."

"It is your knowledge of Russia that makes you absolutely perfect as my partner in this job," Reilly relpied. "I'm told you are an expert in Russian affairs so you know the type of people we are dealing with. You are of Russian blood, you speak Russian, and you understand the Russian mindset. We'll need all of those talents to pull this off. I tell you, Double Eagle, I believe we can trust these people. The truth of the matter is that we must trust them, as we have no other option given the short time frame. I need a leader, a leader who, just coincidentally, has all of your traits, for us to succeed. So please don't break my balls! If you're not up for the mission, say so. If you can devise a better plan in the next fifteen minutes, for God's sake, let's hear it."

Morrison could see that he had rattled the normally confident and tranquil-appearing Reilly. The man was right; what other options did they have at this time? They were beyond the point of no return. "I'm sorry. I didn't mean to be so skeptical. I did volunteer, and we'll implement your plan. However,

I will tell you this, Reilly. If I even suspect that any of your men is selling us out, I won't hesitate to kill him. I expect you to be prepared to do the same."

Reilly stared for a moment at the American. Morrison was indeed the man for this job. His eyes seemed to burn with hatred when he was angry. The situation still struck Reilly as funny, for he would have never suspected that this tough-looking individual with the killer eyes was a Jew. What a quirk of fate it was to bring together two men with such similar origins.

"Of course, I am prepared!" snapped Reilly. "Never forget that you and I are basically cut from the same bolt of cloth. You wear the uniform of an officer in the United States Navy, and I wear the uniform of an English gentleman. Beneath those surface trappings, we're the same kind of animal, Double Eagle. We were both born not belonging, and we both want to belong, albeit in different ways. No doubt, volunteering for this mission is your way of trying to belong. Well, take it from me, my friend. Even if we pull this mission off, you will never belong. We're not that different at all, my friend. The only difference is that you still believe in acceptance, but I already know that it's not possible. You will just have to learn that fact for yourself."

Leaning forward on his elbows, Reilly paused for effect and then continued with a touch of anger in his voice. "Please spare me the theatrics of wrapping yourself in an American flag and thinking that you fool me. Believe me, I see through you like I'm looking through plate glass."

Reaching into his jacket pocket, he pulled out a passport and handed it to his American partner, whose eyes smoldered with anger. "Here's your first gift. You'll need it tomorrow." Morrison opened the British passport and saw that the photographs that he had made before he left the states were affixed.

It listed his name as Brian Anderson, a resident of the Mayfair section of London.

"This will be your first identity while we travel to Russia. You, of course, are one of my business associates," said Reilly. "I'll keep our other passports. Incidentally, in St. Petersburg, my name is Sidnei Raille. Might as well start using that name now." Looking at his pocket watch, Reilly smiled and said, "You know, Double Eagle, the hour is growing late. I recommend we both get some rest. I will be sending a car for you at 7:00 A.M."

"Good idea. I am a little tired." With a stony expression on his face, Morrison continued. "I think we understand each other. Thank you for dinner."

"Sort of a Last Supper, hmmm?" quipped Reilly.

"Yes, I suppose it is."

Passazh Arcade
Nevsky Prospekt
St. Petersburg, Russia

The following morning they departed London by train for Dover, where they boarded a ship for Copenhagen, Denmark. There they boarded a ship headed east across the Baltic Sea, destined for St. Petersburg. It had all gone according to plan. Morrison had to give Reilly credit for the operation thus far. To other passengers on the ships, they appeared to be two business associates, one Russian and one British, headed for Russia on routine business matters. On the voyage to Russia, Morrison was careful not to speak any Russian since his cover required him to be minimally capable of speaking the language. Upon arrival in St. Petersburg, Reilly did all the speaking for the two of them, explaining to the customs agent that they were both visiting on business. Had the customs agent known their true intentions, he would have had them arrested on the spot. The purpose of their trip was not to conduct commerce in any sense of the word. They were in the country on a mission. A mission to topple the Russian government.

Reilly arranged for a hansom cab to take them to his small apartment, located near his business office. Reilly invited Morrison to unpack and offered him the second bedroom. As Morrison placed his shirts in a drawer, he heard his partner call out, "I hope you're hungry, Double Eagle! I myself am famished. I'll take you to a fine restaurant as soon as we freshen up a bit. By the way, how long has it been since you last set foot in Russia?"

Morrison thought for a second and replied, "About seventeen years. I left from the Pacific port of Vladivostok. It's closer to eighteen years since I was last in St. Petersburg."

"You'll see that the beauty of the city is still the same. The political atmosphere, however, is quite explosive. You'll sense it everywhere. Rebellion is in the air, anarchy is looming, and yet that fool Nicholas lives in his fantasy world." Sticking his head into the bedroom, Reilly implored, "Come on, Double Eagle, I'm starving to death. I want to take you to Davidov's. It's one of my favorite restaurants."

As usual, Reilly had impeccable taste in restaurants. Morrison certainly couldn't complain. In fact, it surprised him how much he was enjoying being with Reilly, who was a gourmet, a wine expert, and came across to all as an Englishman of means. Able to talk authoritatively on virtually any subject, he and Morrison were well paired. Reilly's incessant talk of all of his female conquests seemed to be the only thing that Morrison disliked about him. His tales of womanizing began to grate on Morrison's nerves. Fortunately, that evening Reilly had chosen not to share any such stories with his partner. As their dessert was served, Reilly informed his American partner that they would be meeting his Bolshevik contact that night, immediately after dinner.

The walk over to the Nevsky Prospekt in the cold October evening took only minutes. They entered the indoor mall-like structure known as Passazh Arcade. Shoppers, browsers, and tourists still walked throughout the arcade as Morrison and Reilly approached a small office near the far side of the arcade. The sign on the door read 'Continental Exports' and underneath that was the name of the proprietor, 'S. Raille.'

As Reilly opened the door, he remarked, "Most likely, he's already waiting for us in the back. I gave him a key for the office while we're working on this project." Seeing a slip of light from under the door to the back room of the office, Reilly smiled and said, "Yes, he's waiting for us. If nothing else, he's extremely punctual." The two walked to the back door and opened it.

The room appeared to Morrison to be configured as a small conference room. The man sitting on the side of the table slowly rose to his feet as he and Reilly entered. The short, stocky man with a dark complexion had a thick handlebar moustache. With his thick black hair combed back and parted in the middle, he looked to Morrison like a typical Russian laborer. Reilly turned to his partner and began the introductions. "Double Eagle, this is Olovyanniy, the leader of our team." Staring straight into Morrison's eyes, the gruff-looking man reached across the table and took Morrison's hand.

Olovyanniy, the Tinman. These Bolsheviks sure love these revolutionary names, thought Morrison. Reilly continued, giving a little of the man's background. "He works at the Putilov Metal Works, and he is active in attempting to organize the metal workers. Olovyanniy is a committed Bolshevik and is dedicated to the overthrow of the Tsar. His entire team is as dedicated to the project as he is." Turning to address the Bolshevik, Reilly looked at him and said, "Double Eagle is the man I've been telling you about. You will give him the same loyalty and respect, as will all of your people, that you give to me. Is that understood, Olovyanniy?"

The Russian continued to shake Morrison's hand, applying more pressure and never breaking direct eye contact with him. "Of course," replied the Russian. "Why am I not surprised to see another well-dressed British dandy? Is this man you have been telling me about up for this mission, or will it wrinkle his nice outfit?" The Russian then bellowed with laughter.

Just as the Russian's head reared back, Morrison yanked his hand, reached across the table, and grabbed his jacket lapel. In one motion, he lifted him in the air and flung him down on his back onto the table. Morrison immediately shoved his right forearm tightly against the gasping Russian's neck.

"Let's get this straight, you ugly bastard," growled Morrison, his face inches from Olovyanniy's face. The Russian began to turn blue from asphyxia. "The only question in my mind is if *you* are up for the job. If you ever speak to me like that again, I will kill you on the spot. Do you understand? You, or anyone on your team, understood?" The Russian only gasped for air, and Morrison repeated, "Do you understand?" Unable to speak, the Russian nodded in assent. Morrison removed his forearm, and the Russian, choking and gasping, rolled off the table and collapsed to the floor.

"Christ Almighty, we don't have time for this bullshit!" shouted Reilly. "What the hell did I just finish telling you, Olovyanniy? Now can we please conduct a little business?" He went over to the Russian and helped him up into one of the chairs. *Double Eagle is a violent man,* Reilly thought to himself. *He has a very civilized, cultivated veneer and is obviously a very highly educated man, but underneath lurks the soul of a very dangerous man, filled with anger, hatred, and self-hatred.* Morrison sat down opposite Olovyanniy, who was just beginning to catch his breath and regain his color. He stared directly into the Russian's eyes, and he could see that he had intimidated him.

Reilly began with the latest update of the project known as Double Eagle. "One week from tomorrow, October 18, it is set for about 9:00 P.M. Olovyanniy and his men have been arranging all the details, as I explained to you earlier. I have greased the entire trail with ample amounts of money. How is the plan progressing at this point?" he asked the Bolshevik.

"Quite well, Comrade Raille," replied the Russian, as his breathing pattern returned to normal. "The team is ready, and we have already bribed an ambulance crew from the hospital. That aspect is all fine. The workers at the Faberge plant are all okay. They took the money and asked no questions."

"Is the bomb ready, and is the plan to get it into the pigeon's lunch bucket satisfactory?"

Yes, comrade, all is in place."

"I have a question," interrupted Morrison. "The plan calls for the Tsar to be drugged or sedated. How will we accomplish that task?"

Reilly stood and walked over to a filing cabinet in the corner. He reached into a drawer, picked up a small box, and placed it on the table. He removed the cover to reveal four syringes filled with a tan-colored liquid. Smiling, he quipped, "Courtesy of my personal physician. He was only too glad to help me with the medication when he saw the money in the envelope I had left for him. Any other questions?"

"Just one. The body that will be offered up as the Tsar's body. I doubt that this ruse will hold for very long, even if we control the explosion scene. Have you thought about that?"

"Actually, I have. You're right, that is the thinnest part of our plan. We're counting on the speed of execution- get in and get out. By the time the authorities realize that they may not have the Tsar's body, Grand Duke Nicholas will already be in power and will control the situation. It will be a moot point by then." Looking back and forth at both men, he summed up the mission. "If we are careful, do not panic, and stick to the plan, everything should work well. This I truly believe, so let us proceed. Gentlemen, we are about to change the history of mighty Russia!"

Morrison glanced over to Reilly and then back to the Bolshevik. He noted the hatred simmering in the Russian's eyes. "We'll meet in two days for updates," said Reilly. "Let's call it a night, shall we, gentlemen? Olovyanniy, let yourself out about fifteen, twenty minutes after we leave." They all stood and Morrison and Reilly began to leave the room. Before he exited, Morrison paused and stared back at Olovyanniy. He then turned and walked out of the room with Reilly trailing behind him. After Reilly shut the door, the short Russian sat down, pulled out a flask of vodka, and took a deep swig. *Double Eagle,* he thought to himself. *I don't know who you are Mister Double Eagle, but I don't like you at all.* He then started laughing to himself hysterically. *Yes, Mister Double Eagle, I don't like you one bit, you lousy British snob.*

10

The Winter Palace
St. Petersburg, Russia
October 16, 1905

Serge Witte thumbed through the various official documents he had prepared for the Tsar's signature. As October progressed, he sensed he had become a bundle of nerves, and he hoped his stress didn't show. As he sat in the Tsar's outer study, he wondered what urgent business had caused the Tsar to summon him to the palace on such short notice. The Tsar had hastily returned from his main residence at Tsarskoe Selo earlier in the day, traveling the fifteen-mile journey on his personal train. Witte had been summoned from his dinner table where his family was celebrating the joyous news that had just been announced the previous day. The Tsar was so pleased with the outcome of the Portsmouth Peace Conference that he had created a title for Witte, who was now Count Witte.

Only four days before, Witte had made his final attempt to convince the Tsar to grant a Duma, but he knew his gesture was futile. In the lengthy memorandum he had prepared, Witte recounted the disastrous policies that had brought the country to the brink of rebellion. He stressed how the public dissatisfaction had now grown into a true hatred of the government, and how the government was now neither respected nor trusted. Witte knew the truth in his words. He also knew that the foolish Tsar, the Tsar obsessed with the concept of autocracy, would never succumb to the logic of the memorandum. Still, Witte felt he needed to make the last effort to convince him, no matter how futile the effort might be. It appeared obvious to Witte that the Tsar would not act.

The Tsar suddenly bounded into the room with unusual energy. He appeared both excited and confident, two qualities he rarely exhibited. "Please do come in and sit down, my good Count," he began as he walked over and sat behind his own massive desk. Witte lowered himself into the leather chair next to the desk as the Tsar continued to speak. "I've come to a momentous decision that I want to discuss with you. In fact, you are the main inspiration for the decision. I have read your memorandum with great interest, and I believe you are correct.

"I have come to the determination that I must indeed grant to the people a Duma. I intend for it to be more of a token, a morsel for them to chew on. Oh, come now, Count, please don't look so shocked," he exclaimed, watching the astonished Witte's jaw drop.

"Your Majesty, I ... I simply don't know what to say. You were so opposed to the whole concept for, well, for over a year now." Thoroughly dumbfounded, Witte tried not to express the total shock he felt. "What changed your mind?"

"It was a number of things, my good man. You may not think I appreciate the great people such as yourself that I have advising me, but I do. What you accomplished in America at the peace conference is nothing short of miraculous. Also, the input from my mother contributed a great deal to my decision. However, it is the advice of the Tsarina and the holy father that really allowed me to make the most rational decision. It is as if God himself is whispering in my ear."

My God, thought Witte, *it is the devil himself, the self-anointed holy man, that peasant Rasputin, who is behind this change!* Ever since the heir to the throne, Alexei, was born the summer before, the downhill spiral had accelerated. No one outside the royal family and the immediate cadre of advisors knew the truth about Alexei- he had been born with hemophilia and had uncontrollable bleeding from even the most minor cuts or trauma. The Tsarina Alexandra believed that only Rasputin had the ability to stop the bleeding episodes, and she had fallen more and more under his influence. Now he appeared to be giving the royal family advice in affairs of state. *This decadent holy man actually has more influence with the Tsar than I do,* thought the stunned Witte to himself.

"The holy father knows that we must keep the empire safe and intact for Alexei when his time comes," continued Nicholas. "I'm not blind, you know. I can sense the anarchy and feel the rebellion in the wind. The holy father recommended I follow your advice and grant a Duma, and the Tsarina now agrees. Oh, it will be more show than substance, just enough to allow things to settle down. However, we will have the press ring out the praises of a just and caring Tsar," outlined the excited Nicholas, his eyes staring off in the distance as he continued. "A Tsar who grants a voice to the people. A Tsar who will promulgate an October Manifesto outlining his just plans for his people. I tell you, dear Witte, this plan of mine will definitely produce the desired effect. This can keep Russia together. It will give us time."

"It certainly would keep the kingdom together, Your Majesty. I believe that just the announcement of the formation of a Duma will usher in a new era of stability," agreed the count. "When do you intend to make the announcement?"

"It will be released by the newspapers tomorrow night. In fact, the announcement is already at the publishers, and they are sworn to secrecy until tomorrow night. Yes, my good Count Witte, it will be a night for celebration. Come with me on the eighteenth to Faberge. I'm viewing some exquisite gems from the private collection of my cousin King Edward of England. I want to buy something for you and your family. You have been right all along, and you have served your Tsar well."

"Your Majesty, I don't know what to say"

"Then say you will accompany me on the eighteenth. It's a private, unannounced showing, and there will be absolutely no publicity. Not even the Tsarina knows about it. Yes, this is a new beginning, my good Count, one that buys me time." The Tsar's demeanor suddenly turned frosty, and he stared for a moment at the count. "Time I need to consolidate my power, and time to track down the scum, the anarchists, that brought me to this loathsome decision."

Witte couldn't help but notice the irony. It was almost as if he was hearing both Tsar Alexander III and Grand Duke Nicholas themselves speaking. Perhaps, deep inside of the veneer of this simpleton born to royalty dwelled a cunning, clever autocrat, one who would rarely expose his true feelings. "Of course, your Majesty, I would be honored to accompany you to Faberge," replied the count, mustering up all the feigned enthusiasm he could manage. Satisfied with Witte's response, the Tsar dismissed him and Count Witte made his way out of the palace onto the chilly St. Petersburg street where his carriage waited for him.

As the carriage maintained a steady pace, the events of the meeting reeled in Witte's head. A disaster loomed, just as the plan would be unfolding. *Now, of all times, the Tsar develops a sense of political realism. The timing couldn't be worse. The press already has the story about the Tsar's decision to grant a Duma. If the plan proceeds now, it could produce an even worse outcome than the one certain to occur if Nicholas remains unyielding in his autocratic ways. The people will think the Tsar was unjustly killed for becoming an enlightened man of the people. A martyr! In addition, the Americans and the British will feel betrayed; sent on a mission for no purpose. After all, they agreed to become involved only because they were told that the Tsar would never grant the Duma! No,* thought Witte, *things had changed abruptly. It had to be called off for now. The timing wasn't right. They had to change strategy.* However, the abduction was scheduled to take place within forty-eight hours at the Faberge building. He would have to act fast.

As Witte entered the front door of his residence, he called for his valet Boris. He informed him that the mission was to be aborted. Boris needed to act with haste. Unfortunately, the foreign agents that he requested to be sent to Russia to execute the mission were now expendable. He made certain that Boris understood that they must never be allowed to leave Russia alive. Both men agreed that this matter would best be handled by the Okhrana.

***

Later that night, the valet sat quietly at a back table in the dark pub where the air, thick with cigarette and cigar smoke, started to sting his eyes. The valet, only a short while ago garbed in formal wear, now was dressed in dingy peasant clothing, nursing his vodka while he waited for his contact. He didn't know the contact's name, but he regarded him as a most disreputable character. They had only met twice before, and Boris had hoped he would never have to deal with this arrogant rabble again. The valet spotted the contact and signaled to him. The contact walked over to the table and sat down, signaling the waiter to bring a drink.

After downing his drink, the contact looked straight at the valet and spoke. "So comrade, what is so goddamn important that you needed to see me tonight? We are quite busy, as you know."

"It's off," blurted the valet. "The mission has been terminated."

The contact looked up from his drink, startled, but with fury in his eyes. "What? Why? Look, you son of a bitch, you owe my men and me a lot of money. We have worked our asses off, and we're the ones taking the risk, and—"

"Shut up! Just shut your mouth and listen!" demanded the valet. "You will all be paid exactly as promised. The mission is cancelled. Don't ask why. It's none of your concern. Suffice it to say that the mission is officially aborted as of this moment. One other thing must be done. You'll need to complete this task if you want to receive full payment. Are you listening, my friend?"

"Yes, yes, I'm listening. Of course, I'm listening!" exclaimed the coarse Russian as he downed another vodka. "What else do you want us to do?"

The valet leaned forward. "The two Englishman must never make it out of Russia. After all, they are here to overthrow a monarch. They know too much to allow them to ever leave

Russia. Whether they die or not is up to you. Whether you want to do the job or let your contacts in the Okhrana deal with two foreign criminals is entirely up to you. You will receive full payment once these two have been neutralized. There is no negotiating this point. Lastly, this meeting, like our prior meetings, never took place, understand?"

"Yes, I understand," replied the sneering Bolshevik. "Tell your people, whoever the hell they are, not to worry. We'll take care of it." He grinned as he thought of the possibilities. He had many contacts in the Okhrana who took bribes and played both ends against the middle. Maybe a well-placed informant's tip would do the job nicely.

"Very well then. Our business is concluded. Your payment will be left at the usual drop point. We will never meet again." At that point, the Russian stood up, gave the valet a mock salute, did an exaggerated about-face, and walked to the door of the pub. The valet let out a sigh and poured himself another drink. He never felt comfortable acting as an intermediary for this type of intrigue, and he especially took comfort in the fact that he would never have to deal with that arrogant, unseemly Russian peasant with the handlebar moustache again.

***

Morrison was extremely annoyed with Reilly the next day. They had an appointment that afternoon to meet with the owner of the watercraft they would be using to transport the Tsar to the Helsinki-bound ship. That morning, Reilly announced that he had some 'romantic' business he had to attend to first. He smiled as he said, "You know, Double Eagle, I can arrange some company for you, too, if you'd like." When Morrison shook his head and reminded him that he was a married man, Reilly erupted with laughter and exclaimed, "That has never been an issue with me, my good friend." He promised to be back at the apartment by 2:00 P.M.

Glancing at the clock, Morrison saw it was now close to 4:00 P.M. *Here it's late afternoon, and the sun is beginning to set. In less than forty-eight hours, we are going to undertake a critical mission for our respective countries, and my partner is out whoring,* he thought to himself with disgust. *Fine with me if he wants to do that sort of thing, but not if he makes us late for an appointment that is critical to the mission.*

Morrison lay back on his bed with a copy of the daily newspaper and began to read. His thoughts turned to his father, his real father. He wondered what his father would think if he knew his son had returned to Russia, the country from which he had emigrated so many years before. *Emigrated,* he thought ruefully. *Hell, fled is more apropos! Well, Rabbi Zvi Kambotchnik, your son has returned to Russia on a mission for the United States government. Not that this would have made you proud of me or even impressed you. Enough of these thoughts!* "Damn!" he said out loud, "Where the hell are you, Reilly?"

The loud slam of the front door being closed broke Morrison's chain of thought. "It's about time you got back here!" he yelled. "We're late already, you know!" As he sat up on the bed, he could hear more than one person in the outer room of the apartment. "Don't tell me you brought some company back here with you. Christ, are you ever satisfied?" He looked up and saw four strangers standing in his doorway, rushing toward him.

Their leader, with his pistol drawn, shouted, "Get him! Hold him down!" Morrison leaped up and attempted to run over to the bedside table where Reilly kept a loaded pistol. He had barely arisen when they were all over him. It took three of the assailants to hold him down, and he realized that further struggling would be futile. The leader of the four wore a furry traditional Russian hat and bent over the supine Morrison. He produced what looked like a badge.

"Mr. Brian Anderson, by my authority as an officer of the Okhrana, I am placing you under arrest." Morrison understood him perfectly, but pretended not understand Russian.

"I don't speak Russian. I'm a British citizen, and I've done nothing wrong! What am I charged with? What right do you have to break into this apartment?" shouted Morrison. He found it difficult to breathe as one of the Okhrana agents now had his knee on his chest.

"Look, Mr. Anderson, I know that you are fluent in Russian, so let's stop the games. What are the charges? Well, let us start with plotting to kill the Tsar. You know—"

"That's a damnable lie!" blurted out Morrison, unwittingly revealing that he did speak Russian. "I'm a businessman here on a business trip. Just ask my associate, Mr. Raille!"

"Ah yes, Mr. Raille! We were expecting him to be here with you. Where is he at the moment, Mr. Anderson?"

"I don't know," replied Morrison truthfully.

"Well, maybe your memory will improve after you spend a little time with us in jail." To the other three men he barked, "Shackle him and bring him out to the car. But first, search this room for evidence. Make sure there are no weapons here. When you're done, get him out of here."

***

He had spent a day in a jail cell, along with several other common criminals who looked at him menacingly, but kept their distance. At last, his appointed lawyer, a Mr. Birkinov, arrived and escorted him to a holding area where he reviewed the charges against him. Birkinov seemed confident that an arrangement could be made where 'Anderson' would be deported from Russia. The only catch seemed to be his partner. The Okhrana very much wanted to know the location of the elusive Mr. Raille. Morrison kept insisting he had no idea. "I believe you, Mr. Anderson. Let's hope that, tomorrow, the magistrate also believes you," Birkinov said in a tired voice.

At that moment in a small alleyway on Petrovka Street, a scruffy young man kept pounding on a doorway until Sidney Reilly finally opened the door. The young man could see that he was interrupting a sexual tryst, but he conveyed his message: Double Eagle had just been arrested. After thanking the young man, Reilly returned to the bedroom and sat at the small desk, while his paramour lay asleep and snoring loudly. Looking at his pocket watch, Reilly realized that he was nearly three hours late for his meeting with Morrison. It occurred to him that his tardiness had actually saved him from being captured along with Morrison. What the hell had gone wrong? They were so close! But he had no time to figure out what went wrong; he had to act immediately. Clearly, the mission had failed. Survival, to fight another day, must become his only objective. His mind wandered to the multiple passports he had hidden at another safe house; he had never told Morrison about them. He must get out now. He quickly decided that he would be leaving Russia as a Turkish engineer. With a rueful sigh, he spoke softly to himself. "Goodbye, Double Eagle, have a nice death."

***

The magistrate, a humorless appearing man, seemed bored with all of the proceedings in front of him. Birkinov sat next to his impassive client, staring straight ahead. His client had no idea that the attorney had actually been called in front of the magistrate at his home the previous night. Under the threat of death from the Okhrana, he would not raise any objection to the harsh sentence that would be given to this enigmatic British agent who refused to talk. Birkinov's family remained foremost in his mind as he stared forward at the magistrate.

He had argued convincingly that there appeared to be no evidence that Mr. Anderson was a spy, but he, unlike his client, knew it was all a show. The magistrate, after seeming to review papers in front of him, then ordered the accused to stand in front of him. In a booming voice, he spoke out. "Mr. Brian Anderson, the Court of the Imperial Tsarist Authority hereby finds you guilty of espionage and guilty of attempting to assassinate his Majesty, Tsar Nicholas II. This is a capital crime, and you are hereby sentenced to death. You will be imprisoned in the Peter and Paul Fortress until such time that your sentence will be carried out. The sentence is death by hanging. Guards, handcuff this criminal and take him out of my sight!"

As he was being roughly escorted by the guards to the doorway, Morrison looked back toward Birkinov who stared straight ahead. As the doorway slammed shut behind them, Birkinov could only speak softly to himself. "God have mercy on you, Mr. Anderson, or whoever you really are. I assure you that the Russian government will not."

11

Peter and Paul Fortress
St. Petersburg, Russia
October 1905

As he was brought through the main entrance, Morrison recalled that the fortress, built by Peter the Great, was the first building constructed in St. Petersburg. In more recent times, it served as a prison for political dissidents and often served as a way station for the transport of these prisoners to internal exile in Siberia. It also housed hardened criminals charged with capital crimes against the state.

Bored, indifferent bureaucrats processed Morrison quickly into the prison, first by confiscating and then destroying all of his personal identification. They arbitrarily assigned a number as his only source of identification: Number Ten. After his in-processing, a scruffy but pleasant young man arrived to escort him to the warden's office in the administrative section of the fortress. With his hands cuffed in front of him, Morrison was led by the arm into the office where the warden sat working on some paperwork. He didn't look up at the new prisoner and ordered the escort to wait outside the office.

"Welcome to Peter and Paul Fortress, Number Ten. I see you are charged with espionage and attempting to assassinate the Tsar. Very impressive indeed." He looked up at his new prisoner and informed him, "You are scheduled to be hanged by the end of the month. I believe that you will find the accommodations here to be suitable for a criminal such as yourself. In actuality, I am short-staffed here so you capital criminals are often grouped together with the political prisoners. So much of the government's time is taken up keeping the political factions under control, you know. Do you have any questions, Number Ten?"

"No, sir, I do not," replied Morrison crisply.

"I also should warn you. The guard of your cellblock is a fat, sadistic bastard. He takes a special delight in tormenting prisoners and, frankly, I find him a distasteful individual. I wish I could get rid of him. However, he has friends in high places in the Okhrana and spies on the prisoners for them. I've tried to remove him, but my efforts are blocked every time, so be forewarned. As I said, we're short-staffed and have to make do.

"Now, Number Ten, do not make trouble for me. I don't know anything about you, other than they think you are a foreign agent and, frankly, I do not care. Obey the rules here. You won't lack for company. Last night, the Okhrana arrested the entire St. Petersburg Soviet—you know, the worker's council—and they are here as prisoners awaiting trial. I think you'll find them interesting. The remaining few weeks you have left on Earth should be interesting, if not comfortable." The warden stood up, walked to the door, and called for the escort to remove Morrison from his office.

The chatty escort accompanied Morrison from the warden's office to his cell. The seemingly pleasant young man confirmed the fact that they were short-staffed in the prison. As a result, he revealed that the prison allowed the inmates many individual freedoms, such as visitors, reading materials, and the right to associate with other prisoners during mealtimes. "The political prisoners, virtually all of whom will be going into exile either in Siberia or abroad, are allowed to wear their own clothing," he explained. "The convicted criminals, such as yourself, are given numbers for identification and are required to wear orange one-piece coveralls to be easily differentiated. At night, all convicted criminals are chained to their cots by ankle irons when the lights are extinguished. The cots are bolted to the floor. Any questions, Number Ten?"

Morrison remained silent.

As they walked down the long passageway of the cellblock, Morrison noted the foul smell of waste and sweat. The entire wing seemed dank with moisture. Arriving at his assigned cell, the escort removed a large loop of keys from his pocket, opened the cell door, and proceeded to lead his prisoner inside. The cell was approximately ten feet by six feet in size. A bucket in the corner contained human excrement from the prior occupant. On the floor lay a flat mattress on a small cot frame that had straw protruding from the ends. An orange set of coveralls sat neatly folded on the edge of the mattress. The escort ordered Morrison to remove his clothing and put on the coveralls. Before leaving him, the escort opened the ankle iron on the floor, placed it around Morrison's ankle, and locked the end of the chain to his cot frame.

Morrison was paralyzed with disbelief. As he lay on the cot in total darkness, his mind raced. *How had the mission gone so badly? And where the hell was Reilly? Did Reilly set me up? Did he betray me, and if so, why? Perhaps that disgusting Olovyanniy is to blame.* These thoughts raced though his head repeatedly, and he realized that he couldn't stop them. It actually distracted him from facing the reality that he would not be rescued by the Americans or the British. That much seemed clear to him. But the thought of spending the last few days of his life here, to be executed shortly, still didn't seem real. His thoughts turned to his wife, his beloved Helen. They would never see each other again. She would never know how or where he actually died. Tears formed in his eyes and rolled down his face as he thought of her.

Lieutenant Stephen Morrison had returned to his native Russia and now would die there after accomplishing nothing. *I've done this to myself,* he thought. *Accepting this insane mission, and for what? So I could finally feel redemption for being born a foreigner, a Jew? Reilly had said that I was looking for acceptance that would never come. Perhaps Reilly was right,* he thought, as self-pity and self-disgust washed over him. Several rats scurried by his feet as he continued to lie on his cot, his hands over his eyes. *I have to take one day at a time,* he said to himself, *one day at a time.*

The following morning, his guard arrived to unshackle him from his cot. The obese man appeared to be hung over. He reeked of alcohol and smelled as if he hadn't bathed in weeks. "Off we go, Number Ten! Time to meet the other human garbage at breakfast. Enjoy it because you won't eat again until tonight." His head reared back as he roared with laughter. "I'll escort you to the room this time because you're new here, but from now on, you make your own way, you understand me?" Morrison nodded and followed behind the guard. As they walked, the guard turned to him and said, "I forgot to tell you, but from now on, you call me Khozyain—the Master—understand?" Morrison nodded again. *This is the time to listen and keep my mouth shut,* he thought. *The warden was right; this is a very disgusting individual.*

The room where the meal was being served did not appear to be very large, and Morrison counted about forty people in the room. The austere room featured bare brick walls and a stained concrete floor. At the end of the room stood a large kettle where a man ladled out some sort of gruel into the prisoners' bowls as they passed by in line.

Morrison noted four long tables where the prisoners sat. About half the prisoners were dressed in civilian clothing. Some appeared rather well dressed, which surprised him, considering the environment. "Most of these well-dressed dandies were brought in here the night before last," said the guard to Morrison. "We arrested this bunch of revolutionary bastards who think they can run the government instead of the Tsar! Ha! They have the fancy clothes, but they are scum just like you, Number Ten! Now, enjoy your breakfast!"

Near the end of one of the tables sat a well-dressed young man wearing pince-nez eyeglasses on his nose and sporting a shock of unruly brown hair. He looked vaguely familiar to Morrison, so Morrison sat down next to him. The well-dressed man chatted enthusiastically with his other colleagues; he seemed very eloquent and well-spoken. When he finished talking, he turned to the new prisoner sitting next to him.

"Hello, comrade! Who might you be, and why are you here?" asked the young man cordially.

"My name is Number Ten. Let's leave it at that. I'm here because they had no room at the Hotel Astoria," he replied with a straight face.

The young man and his friends roared with laughter at his witticism. "My name is Leon Trotsky," said the young man, offering his hand, "leader of the St. Petersburg Soviet. We are here because we believe in something that the Tsarist government of Russia does not believe in: human freedom and dignity. We believe in the people, which the Tsar does not. We believe the Tsar's days are numbered and that Russia will be returned to the people." He paused to ingest a spoonful of the gruel and continued. "Number Ten, these walls won't hold us. We must continue the revolution that began last January at the Winter Palace. There you have it, me, my philosophy, and my life's work—all in a nutshell." The eloquent Trotsky smiled at Morrison and continued to eat his breakfast.

Morrison suddenly recognized him. It was indeed Trotsky! He had shown a picture of the revolutionary to President Roosevelt. His contact in Russia had written to him about Trotsky. He was a leading figure among the Mensheviks. He was aligned with Martov against the renegade, Lenin. Trotsky, the brilliant fiery orator, was sitting next to him that morning. Morrison thought of the irony of fate that had allowed this meeting to happen shortly after his mission had failed. His mission would have removed the Tsar so that men like the verbose young man sitting next to him would not have the opportunity to take over Russia and plunge it further into chaos. Looking down at his bowl of gruel, Morrison said, "Spoken like a true Menshevik."

The stunned Trotsky looked over at the man who would only identify himself as Number Ten. "Good sir," be began. "What part of Russia are you from? You have no distinctive accent of any sort. I am delighted you know something of the workers' movement."

"I've read *What Is To Be Done*, both Chernyshevsky's book and Lenin's pamphlet, as well as *Revolutionary Catechism*, if that sort of thing impresses you. I'm also familiar with the works of

Karl Marx." When he finished, Morrison saw the look of both surprise and delight in Trotsky's face.

"You, sir, are a most unusual and mysterious acquaintance. I see our breakfast time is nearly over," he said as he motioned toward the guards who entered the room. "We must talk more at meals. Listen, we are going to be tried for whatever charges they dream up against us. I'm not worried because I will be representing us in court. Let me see if I can help you, too, Number Ten." Looking at the approaching Khozyain, Trotsky whispered to Morrison, "Watch out for that one. He's a killer, a crazy killer. But I suspect that you already know that about him."

"And how is that?" asked Morrison.

Smiling, Trotsky replied, "Because you, too, have the eyes of killer. The angry eyes of a killer."

***

Over the next several days, Morrison fell into a routine. After breakfast, he would read books that circulated around the prison and then start his calisthenics. His routine consisted of push-ups and sit-ups, followed by jumping jacks. With his hanging scheduled in only a couple of weeks, he couldn't really explain to himself why he had the compulsion to exercise, other than it helped to take his mind off his circumstances.

Khozyain continued to harass him and, on occasion, would strike him with the large swagger stick that he carried. One of Khozyain's favorite harrassments quickly became apparent: He obviously enjoyed singling out one prisoner in particular for additional brutal treatment. That prisoner was Leon Trotsky. Something about his dapper style of dress and his eloquent manner seemed to infuriate Khozyain.

Morrison always dined with Trotsky. One evening, Morrison saw that Trotsky had a black eye and a new laceration on his forehead.

"My God, what happened to you?" he asked of his fellow Russian prisoner.

"Oh, you mean this? It's a gift from that fat prick, Khozyain. He really seems to have it in for me. I don't know why."

"Have you complained to the warden?"

"In fact, I have. The warden says he's powerless to do anything about it. The fat animal is well connected, and any attempt to remove him would bring the Okhrana down on the warden's head. You see, Number Ten, I have no fear of fighting the Tsarist government, but this bastard may well kill me before I can get out of this place."

"Maybe I can help you, Comrade Trotsky," offered Morrison. "I'm a condemned man and will be executed shortly anyway. The shit deserves to die. I'm getting a little sick of the way he treats me anyway."

"Please, Number Ten, don't do anything impulsive. It will only bring the system down on us even more. I have my life's work to do, and I'll take the abuse by one sadistic pig until I'm free, rather than risk losing the opportunities. Please, I'm begging you not to do anything rash."

Morrison nodded his head in agreement. He thought to himself, *I, too, have my life's work to do. Ironically, it once included putting revolutionaries like you out of business.*

***

At the end of his second week of imprisonment, Khozyain ordered Morrison to the warden's office where the warden informed him of his status. He would be hanged one week from that day in the courtyard of Peter and Paul Fortress. Upon returning to his cell, he began his daily regimen of calisthenics. *If I am going to be hanged, I'll die in perfect physical shape,* he rationalized. He had also decided that he would refuse a blindfold. He would look his executioners in the eyes as he died. As always, his thoughts turned to Helen. *What she was doing at that moment? Has the United States government told her that I am dead?* With his longing for his wife came the additional self-torment over his deception toward her concerning his mission. Invariably, his thoughts returned to the failure of his mission. Between his anger over Reilly's betrayal and his disgust over his own questionable motives for accepting the mission, a cynical depression settled into his mind. *With all that I've accomplished,* he thought, *now I'm going to die in a stinking Russian prison.*

Earlier that day, Khozyain had received a report that he had requested from the Okhrana concerning his most detested prisoner, Leon Trotsky. In the report, he gleaned a new piece of information that he suspected all along, and it served to further infuriate him. He learned that Trotsky was a Jew born in the Ukraine and that his real name was Lev Davidovich Bronstein. Khozyain needed no further reasons to fan his fury. Proceeding immediately to Trotsky's cell, the revolutionary looked up from his book at the approaching guard who began to strike him again and again with his swagger stick. He punched him in the ribs, and Trotsky felt a sharp pain in his chest wall as he collapsed to the floor. As Khozyain walked out of the room, he turned back and said, "There's more of this in store for you, you yid bastard!"

When Morrison arrived for dinner, he found Trotsky leaning forward on the dining table, breathing rapidly and shallowly with obvious difficulty. He smiled weakly at his mysterious friend.

"What the hell happened to you? Was it Khozyain?"

"I'm afraid so, good sir. I think he broke some of my ribs. It's a little difficult for me to speak." After trying to catch his breath, he continued. "He apparently found out that I am a Jew, like that was some great secret. Number Ten, I think he will kill me. For the first time, I am afraid. You see, my friend, you have no idea what it is like to be a Jew in Russia; you just have no idea. You appear to be educated and refined, in spite of the veneer you want me to see. I can't believe that you personally would be drawn to anti-Semitism as much of Tsarist Russia is."

"Comrade, I don't have many thoughts about the Jews," began Morrison with a lie. "I've read *The Protocols of the Elders of Zion*, and I know it is a bunch of horseshit. One thing I do know is that you will never have a problem with Khozyain again. That I guarantee you."

"Please, Number Ten, be careful," Trotsky implored as he gasped for breath.

That night, as Khozyain escorted Morrison back to his cell, he appeared to be in a buoyant mood. He hit Morrison a few times with the swagger stick, which wasn't unusual. Humming folksongs as he led Morrison to his cell, he ordered him to sit on his cot so he could apply the ankle iron to his right ankle. As Morrison sat, the guard lifted the heavy anklet and was about to wrap it around his prisoner's leg when Morrison violently smashed his knee up against the underside of the guard's jaw, sending him reeling backward to the floor. Leaping off the cot, he grabbed the guard by the shirt, and punched him in the jaw with a crushing blow from his right fist. "You disgusting fat fuck," said Morrison in a low voice, "tonight, you die!"

Khozyain slowly rose to his feet on wobbly legs, his eyes filled with rage. He turned his head to the left and spit out several teeth, as well as a large amount of blood. He reached for the whistle dangling on a lanyard around his neck, but the younger man proved too fast for him. Morrison ripped the whistle off his neck and threw it out of the cell. The guard attempted to rush into his prisoner head first and only managed to pin Morrison against the wall for a moment. Morrison grabbed the guard's hair, raised his head, and violently slapped both of his ears with his open palms, shattering the man's eardrums. As Khozyain cried out in pain, Morrison kicked him in the groin, bringing the obese guard down to his knees. The guard remained on all fours, barely able to breathe and unable to get to his feet.

Morrison walked around the guard until he stood directly behind him. He leaned over and placed his mouth directly behind the guard's left ear. "Listen to me, if you can still hear. Can you hear me at all?" He kicked the man in the butt and yelled, "Answer me! Nod if you can hear me!" The guarded slowly nodded his head. "Good," said Morrison, "because I want you to hear this. I want you to know that the last thing you will ever know in your miserable life is that you are about to be killed by a Jew who easily kicked your fat, worthless ass!" He then put his right hand on the guard's jaw and his left hand on the back of his head and in a violent wrenching motion, broke the man's neck.

Morrison looked around and saw that the cell door was still open. He reached under the guard's arms and pulled the obese man into the corridor. He sat the dead body up against the wall and stood back to take a good look at it. The guard's eyes bulged wide open with a look of disbelief on them. His thick, blue tongue protruded out above his gaping jaw. *Something is missing,* Morrison thought. *Ah, yes, the final touch.* He walked back into the cell and retrieved the guard's swagger stick. He walked over to the corpse and inserted the tip of the swagger stick in its mouth. *This is for you, Rabbi Zvi Kambotchnik,* he thought to himself as he rammed the stick down the dead guard's throat.

***

He lay back on his cot, strangely at peace with himself. He had just killed a human being. Granted, the guard was a wretched excuse for a human being, but a human being nevertheless. It was incredible. He had just murdered someone, and he felt absolutely no remorse. In fact, he marveled at how easy it seemed, and how relaxed he felt. The act of murder was, for him, an emotional catharsis. The seething anger living inside him all these years had been released. Morrison was being honest with himself when he realized that he actually enjoyed the killing.

He slept soundly the remainder of the night, at peace with himself for the first time since his arrest, possibly for the first time in his life.

The next morning, one of the other guards discovered Khozyain's body and summoned the warden, who dispatched three armed guards to the cell of prisoner Number Ten. The killer of the obese guard was no mystery; the dead body was sitting right outside of Number Ten's cell. The armed guards escorted Morrison to the warden's office with his hands in handcuffs and wearing leg irons. The warden ordered Morrison to sit and then excused the guards. The warden looked directly at the prisoner and asked, "Do you deny that you killed this guard?"

"Of course not," replied the prisoner. "Look, if you recall, I am scheduled to hang in less than a week. So I'm afraid there isn't much more you can do to me now, is there?" He had a stony, smug look on his face as he replied.

"Actually, Number Ten, you have done me a great favor. I've been wanting to get rid of that pig for months, and now you have done the deed for me. For this act, I am indebted. It's funny how fate works, isn't it?" He reached for a small stack of papers on his desk and held them in his hand. "Yes, fate is a funny thing. You know, I have a prisoner who is to be taken to the train station tonight. He is the leader of that naval mutiny that caused all that notoriety this past summer. His destination is the Imperial Labor Camp on Solovetsky Island. He has been given a lengthy sentence of hard labor. I think I have a way out of our dilemma."

"What dilemma?"

"Well, the guard you killed is well connected, and his death must be punished. And you must be repaid for helping me out, however unintentional your actions were in that regard. Number Ten, I'm going to hang that other prisoner. I plan to blame him for that obese piece of shit's murder. My gift to you is your life. You are the prisoner I will be sending to Solovetsky Island. All they care about there is that a prisoner arrives, and they'll assume it is the correct one. That is my gift to you." He paused and leaned forward on his elbows, staring directly into Morrison's eyes. "You are a proficient killer, Number Ten, and that skill should serve you well where you are going."

The sudden change of events stunned Morrison. Less than a minute ago, he believed he had only a week left to live. Now he was getting a reprieve, a gift of appreciation for killing another man. Again, he thought, *one day at a time. Perhaps it is not all over.* He looked at the warden and quietly said, "Thank you, sir."

"Thank me? You want to thank me?" he replied with his head thrown back in laughter. "You said to me a minute ago, 'There isn't much more they can do to me, is there?' Oh yes,

Number Ten, believe me, there is much more that we can do to you. Every day you are at that hellhole of a labor camp, you'll know just how much more we can do to you! You will likely wish that we had hanged you. I really do want to spare your life, but this is the only way I can do it. I'm sure, in the long run, you'll wish you hadn't thanked me. Now get out. You've got to be on a train in a few hours. Good-bye, Number Ten."

Two guards escorted Morrison back to his cell in shackles. Upon entering the cell, they ordered him to sit, and they chained his ankle to the leg of the cot. The guards quickly departed, slamming the door shut behind them. They stood outside the door as ordered. Until the prisoner was transferred to the train station later that day, the guards were ordered to be stationed outside his door.

Morrison sat there, staring at the tiny window intersected by small bars in the upper half of the door. He could see the back of a guard's head blocking most of the window. Sitting quietly, he tried to comprehend the sudden change of fate that had been thrust upon him only minutes before. He believed that he was to be executed later that week, and now it appeared that the sentence had been commuted by chance to a lengthy stay in a prison camp. *This must be a sign from God,* he thought to himself. *It's not over.*

Minutes later, the guards could hear some soft singing from inside the cell. They didn't understand the language that the prisoner sang, so they had no idea what the words meant. It seemed like a pleasant foreign folk song and, as they listened, they heard the prisoner softly singing, "I'm a Yankee Doodle Dandy, a Yankee Doodle do or die…."

BOOK TWO

1

Lower East Side, Manhattan
New York City
May 1883

The spring morning sunlight pierced the darkness of the musty room of the Manhattan tenement on Ludlow Street in the Lower East Side of Manhattan. Twelve-year-old Lev Kambotchnik shifted uncomfortably in his chair. Once again, he braced for another conflict with his father, Rabbi Zvi Kambotchnik. Over the past year, these conflicts were occuring more frequently. They centered mainly around the rabbi's frustration over the young boy's behavior. "Be a scholar," he always exhorted his son. A boy destined to become a rabbi shouldn't behave the way he did. Young Lev gave his father the impression that he merely tolerated his studies. His mind always seemed to be elsewhere.

Rabbi Kambotchnik also had other concerns. His son would frequently wander all over lower Manhattan. Lev seemed fascinated with the waterfront, fascinated with that new bridge being built. The boy could sit at the water's edge for hours, transfixed by the bridge construction. He seemed mesmerized by the passing boats and ships. He missed many lessons and was late for many others because of his fascination with the waterfront. What concerned the rabbi most was his son's inevitable interactions with the goyim, the non-Jews, with whom he often fought. "This is not the proper behavior for a yeshiva student," the rabbi frequently scolded Lev.

The police had brought the boy home an hour before. Lev had been in a fight on the way home from the waterfront. As he sat in the musty study, his face throbbed from several punches he had taken. He could feel the stinging of the scraped and bleeding knuckles on his right hand. But he took smug satisfaction in knowing that he had also dealt his enemies a few good blows. The door flew open, and the rabbi briskly entered the room, saying in a frustrated and angry voice, "So we've been fighting again!" The rabbi spoke in Russian.

Lev responded in unaccented English, but the rabbi cut him off. "Please don't talk that language!" he shouted. His own English skills were minimal, so he felt his son mocked him by speaking in what to him was a foreign language. "I don't understand you! We've had this discussion many times. It is very improper behavior for a yeshiva student. Oh, the goyim! Why the fighting? Why do you go near them?"

"Father, I did nothing to provoke the goyim. They were teasing me, taunting me, and that was all right. That didn't bother me. But then one of them punched me. What else could I do? I had to defend myself." He looked down at the floor and continued in a low voice. "There were simply too many of them."

"Lev, when I was a boy in the Pale of Settlement, the goyim, the Cossacks, they all taunted us, they all beat us." The rabbi began to relate the same story he always told about how badly the Jews were treated back in Perm, his home city in Russia. He and his family were forced to move to the Pale of Settlement, the only area in Russia where the Jews were legally allowed to live; otherwise, they would continue to face terror attacks by the goyim. His brother, Chaim, chose to stay in Perm, and Zvi was certain that he and his family had perished. To young Lev, the anecdotes seemed pointless. His father suggested that always turning the other cheek and letting people persecute and beat you was a reasonable course of action. Lev couldn't stomach another such lecture. "Father, this isn't Russia. This is the United States. The main reason we moved here was to avoid persecution, wasn't it?"

That question just fueled his father's tirade. After the rabbi was finished with the subject of Lev's fighting, he shifted to the boy's seeming lack of interest in his studies. It certainly wasn't for lack of intellect. The boy not only spoke Hebrew and Yiddish, but also spoke flawless, unaccented English. He seemed to learn the language effortlessly in the first several months that they lived in the United States. The obviously bright boy seemed to be bored by his studies. The rabbi came to the point. "Lev, you are expected to take my place as the community's rabbi. Your people need you. Your grandfather was a rabbi, as is your father. It is your destiny. Your dearly departed mother, God rest her soul, would be so disappointed in you. Yet you seem to take this responsibility very lightly. You are too easily distracted. I don't understand. What is going on in your head? You always say nothing after we have these talks. You just glare at me with those angry eyes. What is going on in your mind, in your heart? In many ways, you seem a stranger to me!"

Lev just stared ahead for a minute. Then he looked his father in the eyes and began talking very calmly. "Father, I don't know if it is my destiny to become a rabbi. I don't feel it in my soul. You may not want to hear me say this, but I am not you. I am not growing up in Russia. This is America, and my thoughts are different from yours. My dreams are different. I don't wish to live your life."

"How can you say these things?" replied his father. "You see how the goyim treat us Jews! Do you think it will get better as you get older? You will always be fighting and always be an outsider, even in America! They will never let you belong." The rabbi took a minute to regain his composure. His son just stared at him with those angry eyes. "What have you been thinking about? What kind of a future have you been envisioning for yourself, if not the rabbinate? What do you think you will do with your life in a world that doesn't really want us? We are different, you know."

The boy's eyes softened, and he stared off distantly as he slowly and methodically answered. "The sea. I would like to sail around the world and really experience the world. The water, well, you have no idea how it calls to me. Papa, did you know that our very street, Ludlow Street, was named after a United States naval officer, Augustus C. Ludlow? I think I was born to travel, to sail to places, to—"

"Listen to me, sailor boy!" thundered his father. "I can't believe what I'm hearing. Get these ideas out of your head! You will never fit in their world; you can only belong in our world! We are different, Lev. Don't you understand that?"

The boy looked up and said, "Maybe we're different because you make us different." He looked back down at the floor. Neither spoke for a few minutes. Finally, in a quiet voice, the rabbi spoke to his son while slowly shaking his head side to side. "Lev, you will always be my biggest disappointment."

***

Lev knew that his father was an honored man in their community. He had been greatly respected back in Odessa. Shortly after the first wave of immigrants from the Pale of Settlement had arrived in New York, the community elders felt the need to have a strong rabbinical presence to serve as the pillar of their religious life. Rabbi Kambotchnik was chosen and invited to emigrate from Russia to assume the post of Chief Rabbi. Although the title was largely a symbolic one, Kambotchnik accepted and immigrated to the Lower East Side with his only remaining family member, his son, Lev.

The rabbi was fifty years old at the time. He was also an increasingly morose man. His beloved wife had died giving birth to Lev. The boy always sensed a feeling of distance from his father, even as a youngster. As he grew, he began to believe his father blamed him for his mother's death. Shortly after their arrival in New York, Rabbi Kambotchnik sent for his spinster older sister, Sara, who moved in with them and ran their household. She, too, was entirely indifferent to her nephew. Her indifference evolved into growing resentment as she observed the constant feuding between father and son. She could see that the tension was taking a toll on her brother's health. He appeared more ashen and weaker. He napped more frequently. His behavior began to alarm her, although she would not discuss these concerns aloud.

In fact, the rabbi was not a well man. For the past several years, he had noticed a tightening sensation in his chest when he walked ever-shorter distances or exerted himself. In their New York apartment, climbing the stairs would sometimes cause this sensation. The rabbi was getting increasingly winded with less effort over the past year. At the end of the day, his legs were swollen, and he needed to rest in bed all night for them to return back to normal size. The rabbi didn't believe in doctors and felt they had little to offer him. He suffered in solitude. He noticed that his fights with his son also provoked his worsening symptoms. "Dear God," he prayed, "give my son the wisdom. Show him the light."

***

The rabbi had his hopes pinned on his son's upcoming bar mitzvah. Lev would be thirteen years old in a month. The rabbi hoped his son would embrace the Hebrew ritual that signified the transition into adulthood. Perhaps he would finally see himself as a man, a man who would dedicate his life to Judaism. Perhaps he would see the error of his undisciplined youth. In his heart, the rabbi was counting on the bar mitzvah, even though the he felt that young Lev hadn't applied himself adequately to his lessons.

Others in the neighborhood also noticed. Lev seemed so different from the other young Jewish boys who took their studies very seriously. They never strayed out of the neighborhood, and certainly, none of them would ever be involved in episodes of fighting with the goyim. It pained the members of his synagogue to know that the rabbi was having such heartache with his only son. So smart, yet so undisciplined, was what the neighbors said of the young boy. Everyone hoped he would grow out of this phase. After all, he had a legacy to continue.

Yes, thought the rabbi, *the bar mitzvah will produce the change.* All of his hopes for his son depended on the upcoming bar mitzvah. The responsibilities of becoming a man would make the difference in Lev.

Z

The New York and Brooklyn Bridge
Manhattan Approach
May 31, 1883

Young Lev could not wait for the opening of the new bridge. The Eighth Wonder of the World, the newspapers called it. Imagine, a bridge that connected the cities of Brooklyn and Manhattan! For the past two years, ever since his family had arrived in the United States, Lev often had gone to the waterfront in Manhattan and watched the construction. As ships sailed up the East River, Lev dreamed that one day he would travel the world aboard various ships. He felt a sense of tranquility as he watched the ships, and watching the bridge construction fascinated him. Now, finally, the bridge was complete. He heard that on the night of the official dedication, even the president of the United States had attended. From the steps of his tenement building, Lev could see the fireworks in the skies.

The following week, Lev had been able to borrow three pennies for the required toll; he actually planned to walk across the new bridge!

On Thursday, May 31, Lev left the apartment on Ludlow Street and headed west toward Broadway. As he walked, he noted the throngs of people all walking in the same direction with him. All of New York City seemed to be heading toward the new bridge. Upon reaching Broadway, the crowds headed south toward City Hall Park and the Manhattan approach to the bridge.

As the crowds formed into several huge lines to pay their tolls, like everyone else, Lev felt himself being literally hemmed in and could barely move. As he approached the tollbooth, he felt a sharp jab in his back and heard, "Hey, guys, look who's here with us! It's that damn kike we had to beat the crap out of last week! I guess he just loves us!" As Lev turned, he saw it was the same five boys, the goyim, with whom he had fought the previous week. Their leader was a redheaded boy with freckles whom Lev referred to in his mind as Irish. The leader cut in front of Lev as the others laughed and continued to poke at him. Staring straight ahead, Lev said nothing. A tall man in the crowd next to them looked at the rowdy boys and said in a firm voice, "Leave him alone!" The gang backed off, for the moment.

The crowd inched forward on the bridge approach, and he could see the looming granite towers of the suspension bridge ahead. Lev had the same crowded, packed-in sensation he often had felt during the transatlantic crossing two years ago. All the while, the gang behind him managed to get assorted jabs into his back and shoulders. He said nothing, but continued moving slowly forward with the crowd. In front of him, Irish purposely stopped short and tried to step on his feet. Lev could hear the redhead and his friends laughing as he continued the harassment. At this point, the movement of the crowd had slowed to a crawl, and Lev felt himself tightly pressed against Irish's back.

Unbeknownst to them all, at the center of the bridge, the crowds from Manhattan and Brooklyn had begun to converge. Many of the tightly packed people literally found it difficult to breathe. Movement in any direction became impossible. To accommodate the anticipated crowds, the Bridge Authority had opened the carriageways, as well as the central pedestrian promenade, to pedestrian traffic. Lev struggled in the center of the central promenade, just beyond the Manhattan Terminal Building of the bridge. Simultaneously, crowds pushed forward attempting to access the promenade via the stairwells from the north carriageway, while throngs of people approached the Manhattan terminal from the Brooklyn side of the bridge.

The crowds, heading in opposite directions, now found it almost impossible to move, yet the people kept plodding forward. No one had moved for nearly a minute, and the multitude became more compressed against one another. Panic set in. With the crowd compressing more and more, screams of terror erupted. The more people began shouting and screaming, the more agitated the crowd became. Then the cry began, "The bridge is unsafe! It's collapsing!" With that cry, all havoc broke loose. As the rumor quickly spread, people attempted to escape and began surging in all directions, shoving violently against each other.

Lev sensed something terribly wrong when he heard the shouting, which seemed to be coming from all around him. People were being knocked to the pavement and trampled by the panicking crowd. As the hysteria set in, Lev felt himself being pulled forward and then to the left by the surging crowd.

In a few seconds, the momentum had pushed him to the promenade railing. He saw several people being shoved over the railing onto the carriageway fifteen feet below.

"Help! Oh Jesus, help me!" screamed Irish, his back against the railing as he began to fall over backward. Lev reached out and grabbed Irish's left hand with his own and then held on with both hands. As the hysterical crowd seemed to be swarming in every direction, Lev held on and kept his nemesis from falling over the railing. Pulling the boy toward him, he was now face to face with Irish, who seemed to be in a state of shock. All Lev could think of was to shout, "Let's turn around and get off this bridge, or we will die!" Just as he finished his warning, the surge of the crowd knocked him forward on top of Irish. Both boys fell to the bridge surface as people around them continued to claw and scream at each other. Lev struggled to regain his feet, pushing another frantic pedestrian off of Irish, who lay face down on the pavement. As Lev struggled to his feet, he steadied himself and reached around to Irish's chest with this right arm. Pulling hard on Irish's lapel, he quickly brought him to his feet. The two struggled for a half-hour to get to the terminal building, moving over and around squirming, prostrate bodies.

Lev could barely comprehend the scenes around him. Children, old men, and women—all were being trampled by fellow citizens. As he struggled, he held on to Irish, pulling the boy behind him. He had to react, not think. It took over an hour to make it off the approach to the bridge on the Manhattan side

Lev's muscles ached all over, especially his arms. He tried catching his breath as he pulled Irish over to a bench at City Hall Park. They both sat down, totally exhausted. The young redheaded boy could barely speak; he was so winded from the struggle. Every breath hurt, and he wondered if he had broken a rib or two. As ambulances rushed by to assist the crowd, the two just sat there staring at each other, unable to speak. They made a very odd couple, the red-haired, freckle-faced Irishman and the orthodox Jew wearing a frock coat and broad-brimmed hat. At last, the redheaded boy spoke.

"You saved my life. I could have been trampled to death. I've done nothing but fight with you, attack you, and yet you saved me," he gasped, with tears forming in his eyes. "Why the hell would you do that?"

"I don't know why," replied Lev. "Are you complaining?" he asked rhetorically, staring straight ahead.

"Of course not!" snapped the redhead. "I mean, after all, all I've ever done is pick on you and make your life miserable." Staring at the ground, he continued. "Now I feel like a fool," he said somberly. "It's really ironic, you know? I mean, where the hell were my four other buddies? I'm sure they took off like bats out of hell. Yet you're the one who risked his life to save me. Not those worthless, jerk friends of mine."

"Tell me," asked Lev as he turned to face him. "What makes you feel worse; the fact that your friends deserted you or that you were saved by a kike? I'd really like to know."

"No, well ... I don't know," said Irish softly as he stared at the ground. "Look, maybe what's bothering me is that I'm forced to admit to myself, if I'm in any way honest at all, that maybe that kike is a better person than I am." He looked directly at Lev. "I never would have done the same for you, and we both know it. I would have let you die. Damn it, I feel so lousy admitting that!" Looking up at Lev he said, "Thank you; thank you very much. I mean that. And I apologize to you for everything, even though I know I don't deserve your forgiveness." After a few minutes of silence, he finally spoke again asking, "What's your name?"

"Lev, Lev Kambotchnik. What's yours?"

"Joseph, Joseph Morrison. My father is Congressman Caleb Morrison of Manhattan. Tell me, Lev, why are you always at the waterfront? I mean, I never see you Jews outside of your neighborhood. I know that's no reason to be picking fights with you, but you don't seem to stick to your kind."

"Is it so shocking to you that I should enjoy the waterfront? You seem to enjoy it, and that doesn't seem so shocking to me."

"I know, I know," replied young Morrison. "But, I don't know, you seem so strange in that outfit you people always wear. Always with those long coats, wide-brimmed hats, and those funny-looking hair curls next to your ears. Yet talking to you now, you seem … like, you know, … normal. I mean, you speak perfect English. I didn't even know you could speak English at all." He seemed a little embarrassed with his choice of words as he looked back at Lev.

"I know we look different," Lev acknowledged. "We have our ways, brought over from the old country. And you're right. We mostly stay in our own areas and don't interact with others. But let me ask you this, did it ever occur to you that maybe you make us different, too? I wonder, how many Jews have you ever even spoken to before me?"

"None."

"I think I've made my point," replied Lev as he gingerly rose from the bench. Amid all the shouting and chaos, they could see hundreds of people scurrying by.

"Lev, I've got to go and see if my friends survived this and are all right. Yeah, my great friends! Again, thank you for what you've done." Young Morrison turned slowly, his aching body ached covered with fresh bruises. His chest hurt with every breath he took. As he walked away toward the bridge, he turned back to his rescuer and said, "Lev, thank you again. I'll never forget what you did for me. You are a very brave individual."

As Lev slowly began to head home, he had trouble erasing the images of the unruly crowd from his mind. The following day, the New York newspapers reported that twelve people had died when the rumor that the new Brooklyn Bridge was collapsing had started the panic. Twelve people had been trampled to death by fellow New Yorkers.

3

Aboard the SS Corinthian
One Day from the Port of New York
June 1883

Captain Andrew McGowan yawned and rubbed his eyes as he fidgeted in his desk chair. It had been a long day and a long voyage. That evening, he had attended the formal dinner for the first-class passengers. He never tired of the opulent dinners with the cream of society. Ever charming and perpetually witty, attending these functions made him feel like royalty in spite of his humble origins. When he wore his captain's uniform, especially the dinner dress uniform, he felt such pride in his work. Sitting in his swivel chair at his writing desk, he remained in his dinner dress for now. The next day, they would arrive in New York after nearly a month at sea. A thrifty Scotsman at heart, it pleased him that operations aboard the *Corinthian* had gone smoothly. He was certain that the owners of the Anchor Line of London would also be pleased that he would be arriving with a full passenger roster. He concerned himself mainly with the twenty first-class passengers and made sure that the 1,250 steerage passengers were overseen by his ship's purser, James Talbott.

The ship had picked up the bulk of the steerage passengers in Marseilles. McGowan had heard that the owners of the Anchor Line, ever eager to keep the passenger beds filled, had made an arrangement with the wealthy Baron de Hirsch. De Hirsch, the noted philanthropist, had been financially sponsoring many Russian Jews in their quest to emigrate from Russia to South America, Palestine, and the United States. He had paid the passage for 268 of these refugees to sail to New York City. While loading these passengers, McGowan had also received instructions to sail on to Naples to pick up 470 Italian immigrants. After weighing anchor in Naples, the *SS Corinthian* departed for New York at its maximum speed of eleven knots. That was the last time that McGowan had given any thought to the passengers who would be jammed into steerage.

As part of his nightly ritual, the captain retired to his cabin and recorded in the ship's log all the important events of the day. By and large, it had been a routine, uneventful voyage. He had requested that his purser do a health, safety, and comfort inspection of the steerage spaces in anticipation of their arrival in New York the following day. The new United States Immigration Act weighed heavily on McGowan's mind as he wrote in his journal that night. The act required that all immigrants undergo a medical examination at the port of departure to the United States. The law mandated that the steamship companies vaccinate, disinfect, and medically examine immigrants to certify their health before departing from ports such as Marseilles. Those immigrants arriving at the United

States too sick to be admitted to the country would be returned to their ports of origin at the expense of the steamship company. This possibility had been worrying McGowan as they approached New York.

McGowan knew that these steerage passengers had not undergone any real medical evaluation and that some of them appeared very unhealthy as they boarded the ship in both Marseilles and Naples. Before departing Europe, he was also acutely aware that the sanitary conditions in steerage were suboptimal. Anchor Line simply did not believe that any appropriate budgeting for steerage was cost effective, and all of the line's captains lived with this reality. His concerns had always been the first-class passengers, and he could readily attest to the fact that these passengers had been more than pleased with both the accommodations and the pandering courtesies that had been extended to them by the crew of the *Corinthian*. Hopefully, the results of Talbot's inspection wouldn't be anything out of the ordinary for steerage.

McGowan had just poured himself a glass of sherry when he heard a polite knocking on his cabin door. "Come in," he ordered.

James Talbot entered, closing the door behind him as he saluted. "Good evening, Captain," he said. McGowan could see a look of concern hidden beneath the smile on his purser's face.

"Sit down, James," he ordered, as he proceeded to pour a glass of sherry for his assistant. He went back to writing in his log and assured the young man that he would be with him shortly.

"There!" he said, slamming the log shut and turning in his swivel desk chair to his purser. "I would like to propose a toast to a successful voyage, James," he said as he raised his glass.

The two men clinked their glasses together and downed the sherry. "And now, how did your inspection go?"

Talbot straightened himself in his chair and cleared his throat. "Well, sir," he began, "they are a filthy lot indeed. The conditions down there are appalling. The sanitary buckets are overflowing, and I don't know when most of them last bathed. Of course, they look so funny the way they dress. I don't know who is more bizarre, the Jews or the Italians."

"All that aside, James, you probably know I have one concern. Are any of them too ill to pass a medical exam? I don't want to be responsible for having to ship anyone back to Europe. Tomorrow, we anchor in the harbor in the quarantine station, and I'm told that three medical inspectors will come aboard for the exams. All those cleared will have to undergo another exam at Castle Garden when the ship disembarks. Are there any surprises I should know about now?"

Talbot stared at the deck for a few seconds before answering. "A few of them appear sickly. They have a fever, and the translator told me that they are complaining of headaches. Having said that, they all look so scruffy and dirty that the sick ones may not stand out, unless the medical examination is very detailed."

After he spoke, Talbot again stared at the deck. McGowan got the distinct impression that his young assistant had more concerns than those he had already addressed. Talbot had always been loyal to his captain and he found it almost painful to be the bearer of bad news. After looking at the young man for about a minute, McGowan stood, put his hand on the purser's right shoulder, and patted it gently. He then walked over to his bedside safe and began turning the tumblers. In a few seconds, the safe door opened, and the captain pulled out a small strongbox. He proceeded to count out five hundred dollars in United States currency. He placed it on the table next to the purser's folded hands.

Seeing the money, the purser looked up at his captain and noticed his rueful expression. After what seemed an eternity, the captain spoke. "James, you control the ship's finances as purser, but I have a discretionary fund that Anchor Line provides each of its captains. Take this money. When we arrive at the quarantine station tomorrow, use it to ensure that the medical examinations aren't too detailed. Do you understand what I'm telling you?"

At first, the young man didn't reply. Finally, he uttered a weak, "Yes, sir." Although he was a realist like his captain, he was also a devout Christian and felt conflicted over the plight of these immigrants. While he had no particular affinity for the Jews, he did pity them and ultimately prayed that they would accept Jesus Christ as their savior. The Italians- they were Christians, though papists. Still, Talbot understood what needed to be done. He nodded in assent once more.

"Good then," said the captain. "Now leave me while I finish my paperwork. And thank you, James."

***

The next day, shortly after the *SS Corinthian* anchored in New York harbor in the quarantine station, two medical examiners came aboard. Theirs would be an overwhelming task, even under the best of circumstances. They also had another ship to inspect that day, and at the last minute, the third member of their inspection team sent word that he had suddenly become ill and wouldn't be able to work that day. The other two medical examiners silently cursed him. They knew that his absence would make their efforts nearly impossible.

They did the best they could, but in reality, they performed only a cursory examination of the over one thousand steerage passengers. In due time, they issued the medical clearance papers. The *Corinthian* was authorized to proceed and anchor at Castle Garden, the final disembarkation point. There would be one more medical clearance once the passengers came ashore before they would be allowed to enter the United States.

Castle Garden was a massive structure, originally built as a fort to protect New York harbor. It was constructed on a small island adjacent to the southern tip of Manhattan Island. In 1855, New York State took over Castle Garden for use as an immigration processing center. A harsh environment for the new arrivals, it didn't seem much different from the steerage conditions that they had just left. When they finished their processing, they slept on hard floors, were poorly fed, and often had to pay twice for their baggage. Once outside the Castle Garden complex, thieves and moneychangers waited, ready to prey on them.

Fortunately, for the *Corinthian* steerage passengers, the entire processing procedure proved to be surprisingly cursory. The medical inspectors failed to notice the passengers who were sweating profusely and appeared ill. After several days, the immigration bureaucracy cleared the entire complement of Italians and Russian Jews for entry into the United States. Later that day, officials herded all 268 of them into one of Castle Garden's great rooms. There, at the front of the room, stood a solitary well-dressed man holding a sign. It read, "Welcome to the United States of America," in large Russian letters.

Abraham Glasser looked out over the crowd of immigrants assembled before him. He was born and raised in New York, and whenever he met a crowd of newly arrived Jewish immigrants, he always thanked God for the circumstances of his birth. He was from an upper middle class family and fluent in several languages. While he wasn't an overly religious man, Glasser had great empathy for his fellow Jews. It was this sense of ethnic pride and identity that had led him to assume chairmanship of the United Hebrew Charities in New York City. The assembled crowd appeared to him to be a ragged-looking lot. The men all wore beards and frock coats, their hair about their ears rolled into curls, called payis. The women all wore scarves covering their hair. In contrast, Glasser was clean-shaven and dressed in a three-piece suit with a high-collared shirt. A golden watch chain went from his left vest pocket to his right. He looked every inch the successful American businessman.

Shortly after the buzz from the assembled crowd died down, Glasser cleared his throat and began to speak in perfect Russian. "Ladies and Gentleman, *landsmen,* welcome to New York City and welcome to the United States of America! I am Abraham Glasser of the United Hebrew Charities, and it is my pleasure and honor to be the first of our people to welcome you to your new home. You may have heard the streets are paved with gold here. Well, they're not, but they are paved with something you've never experienced before today. They are paved with freedom and liberty. We do not have pogroms in America!" At this point, loud murmurs of assent rippled through the crowd. The new arrivals were obviously pleased with the remarks.

"Our first order of business will be to get you all settled into housing here in Manhattan. The United Hebrew Charities has arranged for you to be boarded in eight boarding houses located in the Lower East Side of Manhattan. You will be among fellow Jews, among friends. I will now proceed to divide you into eight groups corresponding to your boarding house assignments." At this point, several of Glasser's assistants entered the room, each bearing a sign listing an address. Although the signs were in Russian, Glasser also knew that a few of the new arrivals were illiterate. "When I call your family name, please proceed to the gentleman holding the first sign."

Before long, the new immigrants had been arranged into the eight housing groups and were ready to be transported to their new homes. Glasser beamed with pride as he watched them leave the front of the great hall, each of them ecstatic to be in their new country. However, he couldn't help notice that some of them did not appear healthy. In fact, a few appeared to be acutely ill.

4

Bank of the East River, Manhattan
New York City
June 1883

Lev felt relaxed and at peace, lying on his back, with the sun beaming down on his face. He always felt good to be here at his favorite spot on the waterfront, a couple of blocks north of the Manhattan tower of the great bridge. He never tired of looking at the bridge. Now that it had been completed, the crowds appeared slightly smaller. It didn't matter to Lev. Sitting on the embankment and watching the ships go by let him escape from the dingy life of the Lower East Side. Down river, directly under the bridge he could see a large crowd, apparently involved in some sort of ceremony.

Each day, the conflict within him grew more intense. In a little more than two years, they had moved from the grinding poverty of Tsarist Russia to the land of opportunity, the United

States of America. However, it just didn't seem right to Lev. They had left Russia because his people were treated as second class scum. The very fact that the Jews had been exiled and confined to the Pale of Settlement by Tsar Alexander was unpalatable enough. On the ship over to America, Lev felt a rush of hope and pride when they entered into New York Harbor. This is the new world, the elders would say. This is the land of equality. The very thought of becoming an American thrilled young Lev. Sadly, after two years in his adopted country, things had improved only marginally.

True, there were no pogroms, and they didn't live under the threat of daily violence, but to him, it seemed that nothing was significantly different. Their lives revolved around their neighborhood, and they were still in a ghetto—an American ghetto. Once he left the confines of the neighborhood, anti-Semitism reared its head, and he was often physically attacked. Once again, they were second class scum. This continuous discrimination is what bothered him the most. He thought that his life in his new country would be different. It also bothered him that perhaps the outward appearance of Judaism—the frock coats, the beards, the skullcaps—marked them as different. We're the Chosen People, he had been told all of his life, yet it seemed to Lev that they were chosen to forever be hated, ridiculed, and scorned. He resented the fact that his family seemed to have transplanted their closed life to America; what he really wanted and hoped for was to be an American. He wanted no part of an orthodox life in his future. He wanted to travel across the oceans and experience life. He was both proud of his heritage and resentful at the same time. This inner conflict intensified as time went on.

These feelings were compounded by his stage of life. Approaching the age of thirteen, he was beginning to go through puberty and growing physically. His voice was changing, which made the chanting of his bar mitzvah lessons, his haftorah, sound especially awkward. He was already taller than all of the other boys in the yeshiva and was developing a lean and muscular physique. In his frequent fights with the goyim, he could more than hold his own against any of them, a point that made him proud. The problem was that there were always several of them and the group overpowered him. He hated to run from these small bands of enemies, but he had no choice.

He sat up to admire a large steamship heading up the East River when he felt something suddenly strike his upper back. Instantly turning around, he saw a group of several boys pointing and laughing as they picked up more stones to throw at him. Lev didn't recognize any of these tormentors, but his sixth sense told him that a very dangerous situation could be evolving. He quickly stood up as two more stones stuck him in the chest and abdomen, and he heard the usual taunts. "Kike! Jew boy!" they yelled with delight as they began trotting toward him. Lev knew he had to escape, and he began running along the water's edge. Looking back over his shoulder as he ran, he saw that several of his pursuers were carrying knifes. His heart pounded as he tried to outrun them, thinking he could escape to safety with his long, sure strides.

Suddenly, he felt stunned and saw flashes of lights. A large stone had hit him on the back of his head, just below his left temple. He felt his legs go wobbly, and he began to stumble. Lightheaded and nauseated, he started to collapse to his knees. As he fell, he pulled his right hand from his head and could see the blood dripping from his fingers. His head throbbed violently. He tried to get up, but his wobbly legs would not support him. While he was struggling on all fours, the others arrived at his side. The leader kicked him viciously in the ribs, and Lev collapsed flat on the ground. Barely conscious, he heard their leader speak.

"Look what we got here, boys! I've seen this fucking Jew hanging around here on occasion. I don't know about you guys, but I think the kikes should stay in their own neighborhood." His friends all agreed with him in mocking tones, as he continued. "You know, kike boy, if you're going to be among decent people, you have to at least try and not look like some old-country trash. Don't you know how to dress? Don't you know how to wear your hair? You are pathetic!" he shouted, again kicking him.

"We're going to do you a favor. We're gonna get rid of that stupid hair of yours so you'll be a little less pathetic. Hey, don't thank me," he laughed. "There's no charge for this!" he said as he bent over his prostrate victim, a sharp knife glistening in his hand. He took the long curls next to Lev's right ear and cut them off with his knife. "There! Looks better already." He proceeded to repeat the procedure with the curls over Lev's left ear. "Hey, why stop here?" he laughed as his friends pinned the helpless boy on his back. He continued taking clumps of Lev's hair and methodically cutting them off until Lev was left with very short hair over his entire head. "Say," he laughed, "you look almost human. Christ, if I didn't know better, I would swear you don't look like a damn Jew at all! What do you think of that?" he asked, leaning over Lev's face.

Still very groggy, Lev didn't think to talk. With his tormentor inches from his face, he could only think of one thing.

He spit a large wad of phlegm directly into the face of his knife-wielding assailant.

The furious attacker reacted instantaneously. He pummelled Lev furiously with everything he had while his friends held him down. Lev quickly lost consciousness.

The boys dragged the limp body of the boy in the frock coat up to the corner of Suffolk Street and left him behind a mound of dirt and trash.

***

The steady clip-clop of the horse's hooves on the pavement served to make Joseph Morrison drowsy. As their family carriage made its way up the street along the East River, young Joseph took satisfaction in knowing that seemed to be quickly recovering from the injuries he sustained on the bridge. In fact, the bridge catastrophe was what brought Congressman Morrison and his son to the base of the Manhattan Tower approach that afternoon. As the extent of the carnage became public knowledge, it also became apparent that virtually all of those killed on the bridge were constituents of the congressman. Joseph had told his father that had it not been for the actions of the orthodox Jewish boy whom he and his friends used to torment regularly, he, too, would have been one of the victims. He could only remember the boy's first name, much to the chagrin of the congressman, who personally wanted to thank the boy for his actions. Congressman Morrison found the story of the rescue nearly unbelievable. "Imagine that," he had said aloud when he first heard of it, "that you would owe your life to a Jew."

The ceremony under the Manhattan approach to the bridge had been arranged by the congressman's staff. It began with prayers for the dead led by the priest from St. Anthony's Roman Catholic Church where the Morrisons worshiped. Next, Congressman Morrison spoke for about fifteen minutes, exhorting the crowd to honor the memory of their fallen neighbors. He reminded all of the indomitable human spirit that always triumphed over adversity. The congressman even related how his son was nearly killed that day, adding that it was only because of the kindness of a fellow human being that he escaped death. He did not go into any details about the rescue or the rescuer. When he finished, he signaled to one of his staff members to remove the sheet that covered the newly installed plaque. The simple bronze plaque read:

In memory and in honor of those who met their God
New York and Brooklyn Bridge
May 31, 1883

Overall, the ceremony went very well, and its success pleased Caleb Morrison. His heart went out to victims of the tragedy and all their families. As their carriage rounded onto Suffolk Street, Joseph blurted out, "Father, what is that?" as he pointed to a trash heap on the corner. There appeared to be something moving behind it. The elder Morrison tugged back on the reins and brought the carriage to a halt. Both of them quickly climbed down and ran over to the trash heap. "Sweet Jesus!" exclaimed the congressman when he saw the body of a young boy. "Quickly, Joseph, let's get him into the carriage."

They quickly lifted the unconscious boy and carefully placed him in the back of the carriage. As they wrapped a blanket around him, Joseph looked carefully at the boy, sensing that there was something familiar about him. The boy was bare-chested and wearing torn clothes, and the bruises on his face and chest indicated an obvious beating. As Joseph climbed back into his seat next to his father, he suddenly realized who it was. "Father, I think it's him!" he shouted with disbelief.

"It's who?"

"It's the boy who rescued me from the bridge. Lev! I'm almost sure."

"I thought you told me he was a Jew. This boy doesn't look like a typical Jew," replied the congressman. He snapped the reins, and the carriage began moving north rapidly on Suffolk Street.

"I'm almost certain. It looks as if whoever assaulted him cut his hair off. That's what looks so different. Really, Father, I know it's Lev! Who would do this sort of thing?" As he finished speaking, he felt a pang of embarrassment over his past behavior. He looked back at the beaten boy in the back of their carriage and asked his father, "What shall we do with him?"

"Son, we're going to take him home with us. We'll get Dr. Walsh to come over and see what he can do. If this is the boy you told me about, we are indebted to him." The congressman turned the carriage toward their home on Union Square.

***

After a thorough cleansing, they took Lev to the guest bedroom on the second floor. Dr. Walsh arrived soon after and examined the boy for a half hour. When he finished, he descended the large spiral staircase and went into the drawing room where Congressman and Mrs. Caleb Morrison and their only child, Joseph, anxiously awaited him. As he sat down, the portly doctor removed a handkerchief from his pocket and ran it over his sweating face. Mrs. Morrison offered him iced tea, which he readily accepted. He began to speak. "The boy has been severely beaten. I believe he has a concussion, and his nose appears to be broken. In addition, I suspect he may have a couple of broken ribs."

"Is he going to live?" asked the congressman.

"Yes, I believe so. However, some of those cuts and lacerations appear to be infected. Considering the trash you found him in, it's not surprising. He has a fever, and that's not a good sign. I cleaned and dressed his wounds, which should help. Caleb, are you going to notify the police?"

"No, we don't even know his identity. Joseph thinks he may have met him before today. Hopefully, when he wakes up, he'll be able to help us get him home. Can I count on your discretion, my good doctor? Also, can you stop by daily for the next few days? I think it's a blessing that I don't need to be back in Washington for several weeks."

"Of course, Caleb. I'll be back tomorrow afternoon. I'll leave some written instructions for the housekeeper to help with the dressing changes."

***

For four days, Lev lay in bed, unconscious and burning up with fever. The afternoon of the fourth day, the fever broke, and he began to stir. He opened his eyes, looked around, and saw that he was alone in the room. Looking at the beautiful furnishings in the room, he wasn't certain if he was alive or had died and gone to heaven. Certainly, such opulence could not mean anything else. He had never seen such a beautiful room, and the bed on which he found himself was so soft that the bruises on his body seemed almost tolerable. However, he also had a terrific headache. The door suddenly opened, and there stood a boy who appeared to be about his own age. "Mother, Father!" the boy exclaimed, "He's awake! Come quickly!" The sudden loudness of the boy's voice made Lev's head throb even more.

The three Morrisons entered the room and went to the bedside of their guest. At first, they just stared for a few seconds, but their expressions revealed both joy and relief that their guest seemed to be on the road to recovery. After looking at the three visitors, Lev spoke in a weak voice. "Where am I?"

"You are a guest in our house, and you are safe. I am Congressman Caleb Morrison, and this is Mrs. Morrison and my son, Joseph. I believe that you and Joseph have met."

Lev looked at the boy, at first not recognizing him. Suddenly, he remembered. "You were the boy on the bridge that day. I do remember you." His head throbbing, he paused a second and briefly shut his eyes.

"Do you remember what happened? How were you hurt?" asked the elder Morrison.

"I was attacked by five others." Father and son looked at each other and then back to Lev. "I can handle myself, but not against five others," he said, with a touch of disappointment in his voice.

"Young man, I personally want to thank you for saving Joseph's life. It was an incredibly brave thing you did that day. Certainly, Joseph's prior behavior toward you didn't merit it. Nonetheless, we are forever indebted to you. Tell me, what is your name?"

"Lev Kambotchnik. My father is Rabbi Zvi Kambotchnik. He is a distinguished and revered rabbi, a leader of our people. He is the Chief Rabbi of New York City."

"Where do you live?"

"On Ludlow Street, on the corner of Canal."

"When you are better, we'll be taking you home, and I will be thanking the rabbi personally. I must say, Lev, you speak excellent English. Were you born in the United States?"

"No, sir, we've been in America a little over two years. We came over from Odessa in Russia."

"Lev, we're going to leave you and let you get some more rest. Joseph will check up on you a little later. You must be getting hungry." Morrison was impressed with this well-spoken young man. He couldn't believe that he was an immigrant Russian Jew. He also couldn't help noticing a smoldering anger in the boy's eyes. "Is there anything we can do for you now?"

Lev thought for a minute. He ran his hand over his head and felt that most of his hair was shorn off. He could also feel that his face was puffy and swollen. "Do you have a mirror?" he asked. "Also, what day is this?"

Joseph fetched a hand mirror from the dresser on the right side of the bed and handed it to Lev, replying, "It's Sunday, June 24."

Lev held the mirror up and saw the bruised face looking back at him. His brown hair was short, and he looked disheveled. He was amazed that he looked so different. The light through the curtains reflected off the mirror, and as he stared at his image, tears formed in his eyes and began rolling down his face. The Morrisons remained silent, feeling the pain of the young man who looked at his battered image. They could only imagine how both the humiliation and degradation of his appearance could be affecting him.

However, they were wrong. Young Lev Kambotchnik did not cry over his appearance.

The day before, June 23, was the day of his bar mitzvah. He had missed it.

***

At the very moment Lev peered into the mirror, Rabbi Kambotchnik also lay in bed. He was heartbroken. His worst fears had been realized. He had been concerned when Lev wasn't home on Friday evening for the lighting of the Sabbath candles. It was then that he realized that this might be the ultimate act of rebellion by his son. He actually feared that the boy had run away.

His small congregation was both shocked and confused. Everyone knew that Lev was to be a bar mitzvah that Saturday morning, yet he hadn't shown up. The rabbi had led the services as usual, but it was obvious to all that he appeared both angry and weak. He left the synagogue at the conclusion of the service and went straight home without speaking to anyone. There, Sara noticed him sitting in the kitchen looking very pale and sweating profusely. She did not even want to bring up the situation with Lev; she was already so angry with the boy for the effect he was having on her brother. She finally spoke. "Zvi, you need to get into your bed. You appear quite ill. You are not well." She helped her brother stand and get into his bed. *How he has aged since coming to America,* she thought to herself.

Lying on his bed, the rabbi felt a heavy pressure in his chest. With sweat pouring down his neck, he suddenly turned his head to the side and vomited. The pains had been coming and going all morning. At one point at the synagogue, he wasn't sure he would be able to continue the ceremony. All he could think about was Lev. How could his son do this to him? How could he mock his father, his heritage, and his God? The rabbi's frustration and anger continued to swell. His own son did not attend on the day he was to be a bar mitzvah! With each labored breath, he recalled the difficulty he had with his only son and the shame that the boy now brought to his entire family. The chest pains continued. He felt as if an invisible vise had clamped around his chest, making it almost impossible to breathe. "Sara," he asked weakly, "please bring me some water and a towel."

Sara stood up and walked to her brother's beside. She then understood, for she always felt she could read into her brother's soul. She knew he didn't want her to see him suffer like this at the very end. She gently put her hand on his shoulder, and with tears in her eyes, she bent forward and kissed his forehead. Walking over to the window, she pulled the dark curtains shut to cut down the bright sunlight that entered the room. In darkness, she walked out of the room, closing the door behind her.

Rabbi Kambotchnik closed his eyes as tears rolled down his face. "Shema Yisrael, Adonai eloheinu," he quietly chanted, reciting his affirmation to God. He knew death was near, but he wanted to say the prayer for someone else who was also now dead to him. "Adonai ehad." He finished and closed his eyes. The breath left his lungs for the last time.

The Chief Rabbi of New York City was dead.

Office of the Health Commissioner
City of New York
July 1883

Dr. Cyril Elson sat at his desk in lower Manhattan and began to sip the cup of hot tea that his secretary had just brought to him. A meticulous man, he believed in process and order, and he ran the Office of the Health Commissioner accordingly. He did not suffer fools lightly and drove his staff to the maximum limits of their abilities. A graduate of the Columbia University College of Physicians and Surgeons, he was an acknowledged authority on the burgeoning specialty of infectious diseases. Arriving punctually at the office every morning at 8:00 A.M., he expected his newspaper to be on the left side of his desktop and the daily field reports to be in a neat stack on the right side of the desktop. After perusing *The New York Times* that morning, he turned his attention to the daily field reports.

His office organized the reports by sections of Manhattan. He always started with upper Manhattan and then worked his way down to midtown. The reports showed nothing out of the ordinary, and using red ink, he marked his initials on the reports with his fountain pen. The staff knew that he considered the report acceptable if the red initials appeared and if there were no questions written at the bottom of each page.

A gentle rain began to fall, and the rhythmic beating of the raindrops against his office window provided a soothing background of sounds as the doctor pushed aside the just-read reports and turned his attention to the reports from lower Manhattan.

The report from the lower Manhattan suddenly caught his attention. A report of four new cases of typhus, all from the same address, immediately caught Elson's eye. He had been worrying about this sort of situation ever since the large influx of immigrants to New York began over two years ago. From Elson's perspective, there could be no greater recipe for a public health disaster that the combination of overcrowding and grinding poverty. He had warned the mayor, as well as the local congressman, who happened to be a great personal friend. He removed his eyeglasses and breathed a mist onto the lenses. After wiping the moisture off with his silk handkerchief, he placed the glasses back on his nose and looked at the address: 40 East Twelfth Street. *Lower East Side,* he thought to himself. *The Jewish district.* He took another sip of his tea and then walked out of his office to a cubicle of desks in the adjoining large room where his field investigators worked. He looked around the room for the originator of the report, Dr. Gerald Rose, who just happened to be walking into the room at that very moment.

"Dr. Rose," said the health commissioner to his young agent. "I would like to speak with you in my office immediately." A formal man, Elson never addressed any of the other staff by their first names. Although the entire staff, including the doctors, feared him, they also regarded their boss as a brilliant and eminently fair man.

"Yes, sir, coming right now!" answered the younger doctor. He appeared slightly winded and excited as he followed his boss into his office and closed the door behind him. He sat down in the chair facing Elson's desk as the elder doctor had motioned him to do.

"Dr. Rose, I've just read your report of four cases of typhus from the same address. Is the diagnosis firm?"

"Yes, sir, but there is more."

"Go on," instructed the health commissioner.

"Well, as my report indicated, all four cases were from the same address, on Twelfth Street. Just as I wrote the report early this morning, we got wind of two more cases from another boarding house in the Lower East Side. They were located at 31 Monroe Street. Also in the Jewish section."

"I assume that all the victims are Jews, yes?"

"Yes, sir. I checked the papers of all the victims from the Twelfth Street boarding house. We noticed something both curious and alarming that I was just rushing into the office to tell you." The young doctor had an almost smug expression on his face, like a child who knows a secret and yearns to tell someone.

"Go on then. Don't keep me in suspense. What is it?"

"All four victims, sir," he said and then paused for dramatic effect. "All four victims—they've all just very recently arrived in the country, less than a week ago, and all on the same ship, the *SS Corinthian*!"

As the younger doctor sat back in his chair, reveling with pride in his investigatory work, Cyril Elson sat expressionless, his hands folded on his desk in front of him. His blank expression disguised his deep concern over the news that he had just heard. He picked up his teacup and took another sip, slowly placing the cup off to his right. He looked at his younger colleague with a grim expression.

"Dr Rose," he began, "the news you've brought is most distressing. Four cases from a recently arrived ship! I want you to go out immediately and check the situation at 31 Monroe Street. If they, too, recently arrived on the *Corinthian*, we may have a burgeoning epidemic on our hands. One imported from a foreign shore. Report your findings to me immediately. If the two new cases are also from that ship, we'll need to find every person on that ship that was in contact with these cases. Every last one. You do understand what that will mean?"

"Yes, sir, I do," replied the young doctor. "Quarantine," he said somberly. *Quarantine,* he thought to himself, *of a whole lot of sorry-looking Jewish immigrants.* Even as he thought this, he was almost amazed at what little pity he actually felt for them.

***

Dr. Rose quickly ascertained that they indeed had a problem on their hands. The landlord at 31 Monroe Street spoke little English, and none of the newly arrived sick immigrants spoke English at all. After taking their names, the landlord explained in fractured English that all of the new arrivals had come from a ship. He had a receipt for the rent, prepaid by the United Hebrew Charities, indicating that all the new arrivals at 31 Monroe Street had sailed aboard the *SS Corinthian*.

Dr. Rose next took a carriage to the offices of the Anchor Line near the waterfront piers on the Hudson River. After showing his City of New York Health Department credentials to the receptionist, he was escorted to the operations room that housed the ship's scheduling and passenger archives. He asked for the ship's manifest for the *SS Corinthian* and for the date when the typhus victims had arrived. Wiping his brow as he tallied the numbers, he noted that 268 of the steerage passengers were Russian Jews who had embarked in Marseilles. The documents also indicated that the bills for the transatlantic passage had been paid for by the United Hebrew Charities. The person who signed for the arriving immigrants was one Abraham Glasser. *My next stop,* he thought to himself.

It frustrated Dr. Rose to find the office of the United Hebrew Charities closed. He had to report to Cyril Elson by the end of the day, but he could do nothing more now. Frustrated by his inability to locate all of the contacts, he directed his carriage to the home of Cyril Elson to report his findings, as directed. Elson had told him to report to his house that evening because he had to prepare for a dinner party at a friend's house.

The Elson's eldest daughter greeted Dr. Rose at the door. "Father is expecting you," she announced formally. "Please come in and have a seat in the parlor." Rose entered as directed and sat down in a dark green chair with a velvet seat. He had only been in this home on occasions like this when the boss would insist on updates. Never had Dr. Rose or his wife been an actual guest in the Elson home. Rose, along with most of the staff at the Health Commissioner's Office, always resented Elson's social aloofness. Ruefully, Rose recalled that in similar visits, he had never been offered any food or drink. Elson would take his report and then dismiss him like a servant.

The sound of Dr. Elson descending the large curving staircase from the second floor of his townhouse interrupted Rose's thoughts. "And so, Dr. Rose, what information did you obtain? Do we have a public health crisis developing?" He sat down in the identical green chair and faced his young staff physician directly.

"Well, sir," Rose began and stopped to clear his throat. He definitely felt uncomfortable delivering the news. "We located the typhus victims, and they, too, arrived on the *Corinthian* along with the others. Both boarding houses had documents that indicated that these immigrants were sponsored by the United Hebrew Charities. I went to the offices of Anchor Lines, the steamship line that owns the ship, and examined the passenger manifest. Sir, they picked up 268 of these Russian Jews in France. All of them were crammed together in steerage."

"My God!" interjected Elson. "Two-hundred sixty-eight! Where are the rest of them? Did you find out?"

"Sir, I went to the offices of the United Hebrew Charities. The official who signed for these immigrants is a man named Abraham Glasser. When I arrived at the office a short while ago, it was closed. And I'm afraid they will be closed again tomorrow. You see, it's their Sabbath, the Jews' Sabbath, that is. A sign in the front window said, 'Closed for Shabbat,' which is what I believe they call their Sabbath. Tomorrow is Saturday."

Elson stood up, signaling that the visit would end shortly. As Rose stood, Cyril Elson gently tugged on his lapels and looked the younger man directly in the eyes with frosty distaste. "Dr. Rose," he began, "find this Abraham Glasser tomorrow. I don't care where you look or what you have to do to locate him. Find him and get us the locations of the remainder of the Russian Jews. I want the answers tomorrow. Am I being clear?"

"Yes, sir. Very clear indeed."

"Good then," Elson replied, taking the younger man by the elbow as he escorted him to the front door. "Excellent! Now you'll excuse me. Mrs. Elson and I are due shortly at Congressman Morrison's home. Our host likes his guests to be punctual."

***

By the time the dessert was served, it was well past 9:30 P.M. As was his custom, Congressman Morrison invited his guest to his library where brandy and cigars would be served. Their wives were never part of this gentlemen's bonding experience. As the butler lit their cigars, Cyril Elson walked over to the far wall to admire a new painting that the Morrisons had recently acquired. Although he had few hobbies or interests outside of medicine, Elson considered himself a knowledgeable art critic. He complimented his old friend on his recent purchase, and then both men settled into the plush chairs of the library. Their brandy glasses charged, they toasted each other's health.

Morrison had noticed that his guest seemed distracted during the dinner and asked, "Is it my imagination, Cyril, or is something bothering you tonight? You seem a little detached this evening."

"I'm sorry, Caleb. I should be more of an appreciative guest. As always, the dinner and the company were superb. A matter we're working on has me a little anxious. I hate talking business in a social setting."

"Well, if it involves health issues in my district, perhaps I should hear about it," replied Morrison, shifting in his seat as he crossed his legs. He could sense the anxiety that his guest tried to conceal.

"We've got an outbreak of several cases of typhus in the Lower East Side. So far, I've got six cases at two different addresses, tenements that house immigrant Jews. We've determined that all six cases recently arrived on the same ship, and we've been able to check the passenger manifest. Over 250 of these Russian Jews were crammed together for the voyage across the Atlantic. At the moment, we don't know where to find the others." Elson downed his brandy and paused for a few seconds. "Caleb, we need to find these people and quarantine them."

"You must know who brought these people over and arranged housing for them. There are records for these sorts of things."

"Their sponsor was this United Hebrew Charities, but their office is closed for their Sabbath. My staff is attempting to track down a man named Abraham Glasser, the man who signed for the refugees. We've dealt with him in the past, and unfortunately, he's been less than cooperative. I don't wish to appear melodramatic, but we've got to locate the rest of the passengers before we have an epidemic here in New York. Every minute we delay increases the danger."

Morrison sat back. Neither man spoke for a few minutes. Taking in the impact of what the Health Commissioner had just told him, Morrison knew that he had no answers for him. Then it hit him—Lev! Perhaps Lev would know where to find these people. After all, he had told them that generally he and his father, the Chief Rabbi, visited the homes of newly arrived Jews. It certainly seemed worth trying. "Cyril, let me tell you about a guest we have staying with us." He described the episode of how the boy had saved Joseph's life on the new bridge, how they later found the boy beaten and unconscious, and how they had brought him home with them to recover. Dr. Elson was suddenly very eager to meet this mysterious guest.

Outside the door of the guestroom, Morrison rapped on the door and they heard, "Come in, please," from inside the room. Entering, they found Lev sitting at a desk reading. The clothing that Joseph had given him appeared to fit very well. Although recovering nicely, as he stood up, Lev still felt the bruises from the beating he had received.

Lee Mandel

"Lev," announced Morrison, "I'd like you to meet Dr. Cyril Elson, the Health Commissioner of New York City."

The boy walked up to Elson and firmly shook his hand. "Nice to meet you, sir," he said, looking the doctor in the eye.

The boy's appearance surprised Elson. He didn't look at all like he would have expected. The boy wore his brown hair in a typical fashion and stood a bit tall for a boy of thirteen. He seemed well built and already Elson could see that he was well-spoken. He didn't have a trace of an accent. *Never would have suspected that this boy was a Jew,* Elson thought to himself. With some of the bruising on his face still present, Elson had a very hard time picturing the boy in the strange garb that the Jews wore. After formally introducing himself, Elson asked the boy to sit down and he pulled up a chair opposite him. "Lev, Congressman Morrison told me all about you and how you've come to be here. I understand that you are the son of Rabbi Zvi Kambotchnik, correct?"

"Yes, sir, that is correct. He is a man of great respect in our community."

Before continuing, Elson thought for a second. He could have sworn that he heard that this prominent rabbi had just died earlier this week. This must be his son. *My God,* he thought to himself, *the boy had been unconscious at the time and probably doesn't even know!* Elson didn't want to even bring the topic up. Not now, when he needed the boy's total attention. "Lev, I have to ask you something very important. A ship arrived in New York over a week ago, the *Corinthian,* the one that had over 250 Jews from Russia aboard. The congressman said that you often visited new arrivals with your father. Did you go with him? Do you know where they live now?"

The boy said nothing, appearing hesitant to answer. Elson told him about the outbreak of typhus. He emphasized the importance of locating the other *Corinthian* passengers. He stressed that time was of the essence and that if Lev did know where they lived, he had an obligation to help his fellow Americans.

The word American resonated in Lev's ear. It was the first time anyone had used that term and applied it to him. Lev felt a surge of pride and purpose. Now he, an American Jew, could help other Jews like him.

"What will happen to these people?" asked Lev earnestly.

"What will happen to them? Why young man, they will all get medical treatment so that they won't get sick. You will really be helping them and fellow New Yorkers as well." Elson felt only a twinge of guilt with his white lie.

"Okay then," said Lev hesitatingly. "I'll take you there, so that they can get help. I remember they were sent to eight or nine boarding houses. I can show you where, but I don't remember the exact addresses."

"Excellent, Lev, excellent! We'll go first thing in the morning," said an ecstatic Cyril Elson.

***

The following morning, Lev rode in a carriage with Cyril Elson and several other members of his staff. Several New York City policemen rode in the carriage that followed. At the first stop, 82 Norfolk Street, Lev acted as a translator for the police as they interrogated the landlord. They learned that fifteen *Corinthian* passengers lived there. Elson directed the policemen to have the residents brought down immediately so Elson's staff doctors could interview them. As they assembled, Elson turned to Lev, saying, "Come, young man, we must hurry to all the homes as fast as possible." He thanked the boy for his excellent work as they climbed back into the carriage and sped off for the next boarding house. Another carriage carrying several more police officers followed them.

When the interrogations of the Norfolk Street immigrants ended, another large police wagon pulled up in front of the tenement. Armed police officers emerged and forced the fifteen immigrants into the wagon at gunpoint. The terrified Jews had no understanding of what was happening to them. In fact, they would be taken to North Brother Island to be quarantined along with the other 253 passengers who had arrived in America with them from Russia. For weeks, they would be isolated and cut off from any contacts or social support. The New York City newspapers would soon bemoan the fact that such undesirables had been let into the country in the first place.

Among the quarantined Jews, word spread quickly about how the health authorities had been brought to their residences by a young boy who spoke perfect Russian, promising medical help for them all. Rumors began to fly that the boy, who at first glance seemed to be a goy, looked exactly like the Chief Rabbi's son, the son who reportedly had run away before his bar mitzvah ceremony. The rumors soon mingled with accounts in the Yiddish press that, in addition to the death of the beloved rabbi, the family had also sat shiva for his son, who was now considered dead to the family.

***

After two more days, Lev prepared to go home to Ludlow Street. He profusely thanked the Morrisons for all they had done for him and, wearing some of Joseph's clothing, he departed by carriage to his neighborhood. As they waved goodbye, the Morrisons agreed that, much to their initial surprise, they really enjoyed having the young boy as their guest. He and Joseph had certainly enjoyed each other's company. But now, it was best for him to return to his own world.

Lev asked the carriage driver to drop him off a few blocks east of his neighborhood. As he began walking home, he became aware of the odd looks he was getting from the local residents—the same looks they showed to all strangers. He quickly realized that his short hair and American-style clothing gave him the appearance of an outsider. With his head uncovered, he looked like a typical goy to all of the Lower East Side residents he passed. The hostile looks gave him a surprisingly uncomfortable feeling in the pit of his stomach.

At last, he reached his home and walked up the stoop. As he entered the front door, he noticed wooden boxes on the floor of the small, dark sitting room. "Father, Aunt Sara!" he called out, but his voice only echoed slightly in the emptiness. He walked into the front rooms and, finding neither his father nor aunt present, he headed to the back hallway where he saw a very faint light flickering from under the closed door. An uneasy feeling crept over him as he slowly opened the door. Something seemed desperately wrong in the house.

As he fully opened the door, he could see his aunt sitting in a chair in the flickering candlelight. She was dressed in black and didn't seem to notice that he had entered. "Aunt Sara?" he said as he walked up to the woman who continued to stare straight ahead. She slowly turned toward Lev and stared at him with a startled look. Then a look of recognition appeared on her lined face, and her eyes glinted with anger as Lev began to speak. She quickly interrupted him.

"You! We believed that you had run away before the day you were to celebrate your bar mitzvah. Oh, you horrible boy, you disgrace!" Stunned, Lev could only listen in shock as she continued. "And look at you. What are you now, a shaggitz? Are you one of *them* now? Why are you here? Haven't you caused enough misery in this family?" Tears of anger now rolled down her cheeks, and she began sobbing.

"Aunt Sara, where is Father? I need to tell you both what has happened to me. You see-"

"Your father is dead!" his aunt interrupted, shouting the last word. "We just completed sitting shivah for him, and we also sat shivah for you, too. You killed him! You killed my brother! You are dead to us, Lev," she said, turning her head away from him. "You are dead to me."

For a minute, the boy could not respond. The shock of what he had just learned started to hit him. His eyes began to well with tears, and he tried to speak, but he couldn't find the words. He had sensed that his father had not been in good health, but this news devastated him. Had the anger and heartbreak of seeing his only son miss his own bar mitzvah service, believing that his son had run away- could that have been the final strain his father's health could not endure? That thought crushed Lev, and he, too, began sobbing. He attempted to speak, when his aunt looked up at him and said, "Your father always told me that you were the biggest disappointment of his life. Look at you now. You don't belong in our world. You are dead to us. Go to the goyim, where you belong. Leave me; leave this place!"

Lev turned and walked down the hallway, his eyes burning. As he slowly walked out the front door, he heard his aunt cry out, "Damn your soul to hell!" The last words he ever heard in his home as he closed the door behind him would be his aunt again crying out, "Damn your soul to hell!"

***

The boy walked listlessly through the streets of lower Manhattan. He wandered in a daze, trying to absorb the news that his father was dead and buried and that his only living relative had disowned him, considering him figuratively, if not literally, dead. He had no idea what to do next. As tears streamed down his face, he walked aimlessly for hours. He had wanted so much to come to America, to be an American, and now it seemed to him his life was shattered and without purpose. He belonged nowhere. He was no longer part of the Russian Jewish immigrant community of the Lower East Side, and he certainly was not part of the rest of New York. *I'm a person who will never fit in anywhere in this country*, he thought to himself as he continued to walk, heading north.

As the afternoon blended into the early evening, he continued to walk without a purpose, or so he thought. He finally tired, his feet were aching, and he knew he had to stop. Looking up, he saw that he was on a familiar street. With amazement, he realized that he now stood in front of the Morrison residence. Subconscious instinct seemed to have brought him back to a place where he had felt safe and protected. A place where he wasn't second class scum and wasn't treated as a subhuman curiosity. A place where he was called an American for the first time. He sat down on the front steps of the Morrison home, placed his face in his hands, and began to cry uncontrollably.

Residence of Congressman Caleb Morrison
Union Square, New York City
July 1883

Mary Morrison returned home first to find Lev on the front steps. Bringing the nearly hysterical boy inside and taking him to the living room, she immediately tried to question him to find out what the problem seemed to be. He kept shaking his head from side to side, refusing to even speak. She finally brought down a blanket, wrapped it around the boy's shoulders, and sat down beside him. Placing her arm around him, she whispered into his ear, "When you're ready, Lev, when you're ready." She stood up as she heard the front door open and heard Joseph call out. Rushing into the foyer, she placed a finger over his lips and quietly told him of the return of their guest.

Only after Caleb Morrison returned home did Lev finally calm down enough to talk. Sitting at the kitchen table with the three Morrisons in rapt attention, the boy slowly began to tell them of the complex relationship he had endured with his father. They had never heard of a bar mitzvah ceremony, so Lev explained in detail the significance of the transition into manhood that it represented. Lastly, he told them of his father's death, the death he wasn't even aware of, and how he had missed it. With obvious pain, he repeated his aunt's accusations that he was responsible for his father's death. He again broke down crying when he finished. Just as Mrs. Morrison began to speak, he blurted out "And now I'm dead to them! They sat shivah for me. I don't know what to do."

Dumbstruck, the Morrisons looked at each other. They couldn't conceive of the idea of this bright young boy being discarded by his family, being treated as if he had died. The concept seemed so foreign to them, so unjust.

"Lev," the congressman said softly, "you'll stay with us while we figure out what needs to be done. Please don't worry. You won't be hungry or alone." He got out of his chair, walked around the table to him, and put his hand on the back of the boy's neck. As he did, Lev stood up, put his arms around the older man, and buried his head in the man's chest. Morrison looked at his wife and son. His wife motioned with her hand, pointing up. "Lev, let's go upstairs to your room." As Lev and Mr. Morrison slowly began to walk out of the room, Mrs. Morrison walked along side Lev, and she too put her arm around him.

***

The Morrisons weighed their options as they surveyed the situation. They genuinely liked the boy, as did Joseph. He was a perfect houseguest, and he was very intelligent. He was well-read and seemed to have a surprisingly diverse set of interests.

The boy's obsession with the sea and ocean travel seemed odd to them. He also impressed his hosts with his fluent Russian, his knowledge of the strange Yiddish language that they had heard babbled in the streets, and most of all, his flawless, unaccented English. They found it difficult to believe that a little over two years ago, he had lived in Russia. The Morrisons sensed the boy's feelings of rejection, not belonging, and isolation. That seemed to be a large facet of his personality. They could see it reflected in his sad, angry eyes.

After a week, Caleb Morrison came to a decision that he presented to his wife and son. He noted that Lev was legally an orphan and that his only surviving family member wanted nothing to do with him. He also pointed out that he and Mary were unable to have any more children. To him, the course seemed obvious; they would adopt the boy. The family agreed, and Joseph was especially pleased. He and Lev had become good friends and were intellectual equals. The following night at dinner, Caleb Morrison told Lev Kambotchnik that they were considering adopting him and wanted to know what he thought about the idea. They could tell by the look on his startled face that he was ecstatic. *Maybe God hasn't abandoned me,* he thought to himself as the family all gathered around hugging him and kissing his forehead. *Maybe there is to be a purpose to my life after all,* he thought.

Several weeks later, after petitioning the courts, the Morrisons officially adopted Lev into their family. At the same time, he had his name legally changed. With his new family's approval, he had selected the name Stephen. As they departed the courthouse, the boy who had been born Lev Kambotchnik in Russia in 1870 emerged as Stephen Lee Morrison.

***

The Morrisons enrolled Stephen in the Prentice School, an exclusive private school just north of Madison Square. He and Joseph became classmates, as well as best friends. Academically, Stephen excelled in his new school. His life had almost become a dream. He rarely thought of his old life at this point, until one night Caleb called him into the study and asked him to close the door. "Stephen," he began, "it is time to consider your future. There is something we need to discuss."

"Yes, Father," he replied, pulling up a chair. He always called Caleb 'Father' now, and it gave him much joy to do so. The warm feelings between the father and his new son were mutual.

"Stephen, you know we go to Mass every Sunday. We are Roman Catholics. My family came to America after the potato famine in the late 1840s. In those days, the Irish were considered trash and in many ways, today they still are. But those days are changing. Irish Catholics, like me, are working our way up the ladder toward the American dream." He paused for a second to study the boy's face, to see if he was following the discussion. "As you know, this is a Christian nation, and the day is coming when all followers in Christ will join together. Do you understand what I'm saying?"

"Not exactly," replied Stephen, feeling a little uneasy.

"Stephen, I have some books here on Roman Catholic doctrine, our catechism. I think you should start to study these, to learn about Catholicism. I was going to start having you take lessons with Father Coyle. I believe—"

"You want me to become a Catholic, to convert to Christianity?" interrupted the boy, somewhat incredulously. "I am a Jew. That's what I am."

"Stephen, you've left that life behind you. I want you to fit in without any additional burdens to bear. This is Christian nation. You know that. What would be the point of remaining a Jew when you have a new life? You don't go to the synagogue. You don't dress like you did." The elder Morrison paused for a second and continued. "You don't look like a Jew. No one would ever know."

"Father, are you ashamed of me?"

"Of course not! You know that, Stephen. I'm your father now, and I love you unconditionally. I'm just thinking of your future. As a Catholic, I also worry about your soul. But I fear that people will always use your religion as an excuse to hate you, the way Joseph once did. Why give them the chance? Don't you want to completely come into our world?"

The boy just stared ahead for a minute and then slowly began to talk. "Sir, I appreciate your wanting to help me in this manner. I really do, but don't you see? I was born a Jew, and I'll die a Jew. I can't change who I am. Even though I don't practice it as I once did, I still believe. Deep down, I do. I don't have the desire, or the belief, to change who I am." He could see that his father didn't comprehend what he was telling him. "I know you're thinking only of my well-being, but this is something I must decide for myself. I will read the books you want me to read out of respect and deference to you, but I can tell you, I'll always be a Jew, a Jew who is also an American."

Caleb looked at his son with a cautious smile and sighed. Although surprised by his son's response, his conviction also impressed him. He handed the boy the books on Catholicism and stood up. "Stephen, I can only encourage you to not wear your religion like a chip on your shoulder, daring people to hate you for it. This is a cruel world, my son. A cruel world that may always keep you out on the fringes just because you are a Jew. Just consider what I've suggested."

"I promise, Father, I will. For your sake."

They never discussed religious conversion again.

***

As the years went by, Caleb took great pride in his sons. They both excelled in their studies at the Prentice School. Both were natural athletes who competed fiercely on the newly formed Prentice baseball team. They grew very close and often had philosophical discussions while sitting on the bank of the East River. Their favorite spot was near the Manhattan base of the new bridge, which was still being touted as the Eighth Wonder of the World. On occasion, the topic turned to religion, and as usual, Joseph emerged from the conversation both confused and impressed by his brother. Stephen, obviously an expert on Judaism, also proved very conversant with the tenants of Christianity. "I read the books that Father asked me to read," he explained with a twinkle in his eye.

Early in their senior year at Prentice, the congressman returned from Washington after a congressional recess with an important announcement. "I have wonderful news, boys!" he began. "I had a long discussion with Dean Ferguson at Princeton. He's seen your academic records, and he assures me that there will be a place for both of you in next year's entering class at Princeton! How does that strike you future senators? Excuse me, future presidents!" The infectious delight in his demeanor was undeniable. Caleb Morrison was one of the first Irish Americans to graduate Princeton, and he was totally dedicated to the school.

Mary jumped up and kissed her two sons, exclaiming, "I knew it! Congratulations! This calls for celebrations!"

While Joseph seemed delighted, the elder Morrison noticed a less-than-enthused look on Stephen's face. "What is it, Stephen? Are you speechless with joy, or are you disappointed? I'm having a hard time reading your expression." After an awkward silence, he continued. "As you know, Princeton is very important to our family."

"Yes, sir, I know. Please don't get me wrong. I am grateful to Princeton and for all of your efforts on my behalf."

"Goodness, Stephen, you did all the work. You earned the right to attend."

"I know, but ... I really don't want to go to school there."

"But why not?" asked his exasperated father. "Where were you planning on going to school?"

"My heart is set on going to Annapolis, to the United States Naval Academy. It's been my dream since I was a child. You see, Father, I want to serve my country, to travel the world. I don't mean to disappoint you, but it has been my goal, my constant dream to become an officer in the United States Navy. "

The other three Morrisons stared at him for a minute saying nothing. Finally, Joseph broke the silence, saying, "Well, heck, I'm not surprised! You've always talked about it. Ever since I've known you, you would hang around the waterfront, staring at the ships. Father, you can't really be that surprised, can you?"

"No, I suppose not," he replied, sighing. "Well, there's certainly a lot of honor in what you plan to do. You've got the grades and the athletic abilities. And," he added with a wink, "I have a feeling that one of my colleagues can be bribed for a congressional recommendation from New York to the Academy. Stephen, you never cease to amaze me." He raised his glass and proclaimed, "I propose a toast!" They all raised their glasses, and the congressman continued, "To my sons and their quests to be great Americans!"

The loudest "Here, Here!" came from a delighted Stephen Morrison.

**

The graduation from the Prentice School was a triumph for the Morrisons. The salutatorian was Joseph Morrison, and the valedictorian was Stephen Morrison. Caleb and Mary couldn't have been more proud. That night at the party thrown at their home, Caleb took his sons aside individually to speak to them about graduation presents. He was convinced he had the perfect present for Stephen, and as they walked into the study, he asked his son to sit.

"Stephen, I've thought hard about an appropriate graduation present for you. Your mother and I have wracked our brains and spent many a night pondering this dilemma. Just what do you get for a son who came into our family so abruptly and added so much to our lives? Even though I don't understand you at times, I do feel that I can see into your soul. In many ways, we are very much alike." As he spoke, Stephen noticed his father's eyes moistening. He sat down next to his son. "Stephen, I've spoken with the Superintendent of the Naval Academy, and he has agreed to allow you to begin your studies a year from this fall." Noting the look of surprise and confusion on his son's face, he continued. "Stephen, as your graduation present, I'm sending you on an around-the-world tour, beginning with Russia."

A stunned Stephen Morrison stood bolt upright, unable to speak. His father could not have picked a better present for him. To go back to Russia as an American! It was a dream come true for him. "I, I … don't know what to say, Father," he exclaimed, embracing the older Morrison, "other than thank you, thank you! Oh, thank you!"

"Easy, Stephen," cried out the elder man, "you are breaking my ribs!" They both laughed. Caleb told his son that the rest of the family had known about the present for weeks and had been dying to tell him. But they had kept the secret, bragged his proud father. He showed Stephen his itinerary. Stephen would be visiting Russia as part of Senator Straythorne's Trade Subcommittee delegation, beginning with a reception to be held at St. Petersburg's Winter Palace. It would be hosted by Tsar Alexander III himself! Afterward, Stephen could tour Russia and then travel to the Orient and across the Pacific, back to the United States. "In fifteen months, you will begin his studies at the United States Naval Academy."

As the rest of the family and guests rushed in to congratulate him, Stephen Morrison sat back in his lounge chair, taking in the moment. He, a Jewish immigrant and son of a rabbi, would be going to Russia as a guest of the government and would be going to the Winter Palace! To a reception hosted by the Tsar himself! The whole concept seemed surreal. Only five years before, he nearly became a homeless street urchin, and now this honor. As the guests kept coming over to congratulate him on his academic achievements and his upcoming journey, all he could think to himself was, *Only in America, only in America!*

7

The Winter Palace
St. Petersburg, Russia
July 1888

Eighteen-year-old Stephen Morrison fidgeted nervously as he waited in the receiving line with Senator Straythorne. He and the Senator, both dressed in black-tie formal wear, blended in with the many colors of various military uniforms worn by the other guests in line. They looked to young Stephen as if they, with their gold braid and epaulets, had stepped right out of a meeting of one of Napoleon's war councils. Looking forward to the front of the line, he could see their hosts, the Tsar and Tsarina, greeting the guests, while their names were loudly announced. *This building,* he thought to himself, *makes the United States Capitol building look very ordinary!* It was with a combination of anticipation and excitement that he arrived at the Winter Palace, an official member of the United States Congressional delegation.

The trip from New York to London was the first treat for the young man. He was officially listed as a member of the trade delegation, one of fifteen members of the group. Compared to his last voyage across the Atlantic as a steerage passenger, the difference as a first-class passenger on the steamship contrasted like night and day. Senator Straythorne liked Stephen and had personally took him under his wing since their departure from New York. Also traveling with them was Sergeant Amos Johnson, recently retired from the New York City Police Department. When the rest of the delegation returned to the United States, Johnson was to be Stephen's bodyguard and traveling companion once the left St. Petersburg.

The remainder of the journey to St. Petersburg was all in first-class accommodations befitting their congressional status. Their hotel in St. Petersburg, the Grand Hotel Europe on Mikhailovskaya Street, was the most luxurious hotel that the young man had ever experienced. But when they arrived at the Winter Palace for the state dinner, the son of the United States congressman was truly astounded.

Built in the mid-1700s, the first royal resident of the Winter Palace was Catherine the Great. The front of the magnificent structure faced the massive Palace Square. The opposite side of the palace sat on the bank of the Neva River. As they entered the palace grounds, the guest coach carrying the American delegation in fell in line with the other diplomatic, military, and industrial guests approaching the Ambassador's Entrance on the side of the state courtyard. The entrance overlooked the Neva. Uniformed liverymen in red velvet coats assisted them from the coach and escorted them into the ground-floor entrance. From there they were ushered into the main vestibule.

"Have you ever seen anything so magnificent, Stephen?" whispered the senator to his young charge. They had just entered the Jordan Gallery with its massive marble columns and works of sculpture, following the escorted line of guests to the most beautiful staircase they had ever seen. This main staircase, also called the Jordan Staircase, was a marble structure covered with red carpet. Stephen engrossed himself in the wonderful details, the gold-inlaid royal crests featuring the double eagle of the Romanov dynasty, as well as the marble stair rails and royal blue columns supporting the vaulted arches of the first floor.

The opulence of the ground floor of the Winter Palace continued on the first floor. Arriving at the top of the Jordan Staircase, the uniformed staff escorted the guests down a lengthy cream-colored hallway, the portrait gallery of the Romanov dynasty. All of the guests walked slightly slower as they studied the fine oil portraits of Alexander III and his Romanov predecessors. The irony of this moment was not lost on Stephen. *Wouldn't you bastards all be surprised if you knew that one of the Jews you despised was now here as a guest in your palace?* he thought to himself. Midway down the hallway, the escorts led the guests through a double door on the right into their final destination, the Great Hall.

Marble, crystal, and gold defined the ambiance of the massive hall. The floor appeared to be inlaid parquet or a high-gloss tile; Stephen couldn't actually tell. Huge Corinthian columns lined the perimeter of the massive hall and numerous gigantic crystal chandeliers hung from the ceiling. At the far end of the room, many tables were set with gleaming crystal stemware and fine china. There appeared to be hundreds of guests as the receiving line moved forward toward the host and hostess. Soft music filled the room, provided by the orchestra at the far side of the hall. Finally, the Senator and Stephen reached the front of the receiving line. There stood Alexander III, wearing a blue military tunic with gold embroidery.

"Senator Samuel Straythorne, United States Senate!" barked the Tsar's aide as the Senator did a polite bow to the Tsar, who spoke one word in English, "Welcome." He moved on and bowed politely to the Tsarina and to the young man also in military uniform standing next to his mother, the future Tsar, Tsarevitch Nicholas.

"Master Stephen Morrison," announced the aide and the Tsar repeated his one word greeting. As he bowed, Stephen said, "Your Majesty," as had the senator. He repeated the bow and gave the salutation, "Your Highness," to Tsarina Marie and to the young man at her side, the Tsarevitch Nicholas. Stephen, at six-feet tall, towered over the Tsarevitch. A slight man, he appeared to be about Stephen's age. He also seemed to be very bored with the whole affair.

After all the guests had been formally received, the two Americans, along with the other members of the delegation, meandered across the hall to the tables and were taken to their assigned seats for the dinner. Seated in between the Senator and Stephen was Ptior Kodarov, owner of the Putilov Metal Works in St. Petersburg. He would be hosting the delegation the following day. The primary reason for the delegation's visit was to meet with Kodarov and tour his plant. The Putilov plant had submitted an incredibly low bid to the United States government to manufacture munitions in order to secure a long-term contract. Senator Straythorne and his group were there to see if the Putilov offer was feasible and to check out the manufacturing capability of the plant. Seated on Stephen's other side was Kodarov's son, Yuri, who seemed, like Tsarevitch

Nicholas, to be about Stephen's age, perhaps slightly older. The younger Kodarov leaned forward in front of Stephen and began to speak to his father in Russian.

"These Americans, they dress up well!" he quipped.

His father smiled in return. "I hear that they are somewhat naïve in foreign affairs and European culture."

"I also hear," interjected Stephen in flawless Russian, "that they don't have a talent for foreign languages." He smiled at the young man.

At first, Yuri Kodarov stared at Stephen, unable to speak. He then burst into uncontrollable laughter that proved infectious to Stephen. Senator Staythorne, who did not speak a word of the Russian language, smiled, thinking that at least some people seemed to be enjoying an inside joke. In excellent, slightly accented English, Yuri Kodarov said, "I'm sorry, my friend. Stephen, isn't it? That was extremely rude and undiplomatic of me. Please forgive me for my naivety."

"Please, think nothing of it," replied the young American. He liked the young Russian's forwardness and his candor. "Are you going to be at the Metal Works tomorrow, Yuri?"

"Yes, I am. In fact, I was supposed to act as interpreter for your group. It now appears that my services in this regard will not be needed. I don't think that Papa will mind me being there anyway. I know the factory and the people well."

Suddenly, the room grew silent and the Tsar began his formal welcome to the guests from many countries. During the Tsar's speech, Stephen acted as the interpreter for the delegation. Among the many treats in store for the guests tonight, the Tsar announced that they would be enjoying a short performance by the St. Petersburg Symphony Orchestra, and some performances of the St. Petersburg Ballet. "That is," the Tsar reminded his guests, "after everyone consumes mountains of food and oceans of drink!" The appreciative audience laughed and applauded their host's concluding remarks.

Halfway through the multi-course dinner, Yuri turned to Stephen and asked, "Where did you learn to speak Russian so well? You speak it like a native. I would have sworn you were born in Russia!"

"Actually, I studied the Russian language all throughout my schooling." It was a white lie that Stephen felt was appropriate for the situation. "I've always been interested in the Russian language and Russian culture. This trip to Russia is actually part of a graduation gift to me from my father, Congressman Caleb Morrison of New York. I'm traveling on to the Orient after my stay in Russia is concluded. I'll be back in time for my college studies next year."

"What will you be studying? I am currently a student at the University of St. Petersburg, studying politics." He seemed especially proud of his chosen field of study.

"I'll be going to the United States Naval Academy. I'm going to have a career as a naval officer."

Yuri had an astonished look on his face for a minute. "My God," he said, "you are possibly the most interesting and unique individual I have ever met! I expected you to be a bland, pseudo-educated, nouveau-riche American. You are anything but that!" He shook his head in mock disbelief. "I think I need another drink of vodka!" he joked and feigned chugging a drink from an empty glass. After a moment of silence, he turned serious. He had taken a liking to this interesting young American. "Stephen, tomorrow why don't I give you a personal tour of the Putilov Metal Works? The Senator and the rest of your delegation will be in meetings hosted by Papa all day. I think you'll find my tour much more interesting. You'll get the real insider's tour."

"Well, I don't want to … I mean it might not be, eh, appropriate. And I certainly don't want to burden you with—"

"Nonsense!" replied the young Russian. "It would be my honor. You, of all the people I've met recently, should see what I will show you. It will open your eyes. After all, you said you really want to learn about Russian culture, my friend."

***

The following morning, several carriages departed from the Grand Hotel Europe for the Putilov Metal Works. The factory was located in the Vyborg section of St. Petersburg, an area quite different from the elegant section from which they departed. Vyborg was largely an industrial area with a myriad of factories. The skyline was studded with chimneys belching black smoke and industrial gases. The streets were grimy and dark. On the streets were many peasants seemingly without a place to go. The scene reminded Stephen of his youth in Odessa.

Much to the relief of the passengers, the entire caravan of carriages soon arrived at the gates of the Putilov Metal Works. Most of the Americans had been appalled by the contrast of the opulence they had enjoyed the night before and today's traveling conditions. One of Kodarov's assistants waited inside the gates to take them all to the executive offices where Kodarov and his senior management staff were all assembled and waiting for them. A long table featuring vodka, caviar, and blinis, had been set up in the conference room, awaiting the arrival of the Americans. Gleaming copper samovars placed throughout the room featured freshly brewed tea for the guests. Looking at the bottles of vodka, Straythorne thought to himself, *It's nine o'clock in the morning! My God, can these people drink!*

As Kodarov welcomed the Americans, Yuri did the translating, since his father's English was not nearly as good as his own. He explained that the delegation would take a tour of the factory and then receive a lengthy presentation on the proposed munitions contract. When Yuri finished, he walked over to Stephen and said, "Of course, I will be giving you a private tour, my friend." Stephen agreed, having obtained the senator's permission the night before. "Come, Stephen, let's put on some coveralls. I don't want us to ruin our clothing. Where we're going it is grimy and beastly hot!" He handed his American friend a tan set of coveralls as he donned his own.

Yuri proceeded to take his guest all over the factory. They began at the loading docks where the deliveries of iron ore and other raw materials stood stacked in large piles. Stephen watched the surprisingly old men lift the loads of metals over and over with their bare hands. It appeared to be backbreaking work, and some of the workers did not appear to be in very good health. Next, they went to the smelting area to watch the metals being processed and melted down. The temperature, Stephen observed, had to be over one hundred degrees at several locations on the smelting area floor. Workers who had apparently passed out from the intense heat lay prostrate, largely ignored. The workers appeared to be wearing little in the way of any protective clothing or gear. Many appeared cachectic and dehydrated. The whole scene appalled Stephen, who looked over at Yuri and was surprised by the expression on his Russian friend's face. Yuri seemed to want Stephen to see the barbaric conditions under which his father's employees worked.

Next, they toured the munitions assembly area. The huge unventilated room contained what seemed like endless rows of long tables. Many women sat working in this area as their children toiled alongside them. They had the same look- dirty and malnourished. The men all had their hair parted in the middle, differing from the European style of parting the hair on the side, which the Russian aristocratics, as well as most Americans, such as Stephen himself, preferred. Instead of shirts tucked into their trousers, all the men wore a peculiar-looking tunic. Their pants were tucked into high black boots, unlike the western style favored by the aristocrats who wore cuffed trousers out over their leather shoes. *Mostly,* thought Stephen, *it's that hopeless look in their eyes, as if they are simply going through the motions of life.*

After several hours of touring and observing conditions throughout the plant, Yuri suggested that they go up to his office for some lunch. He had invited one of the floor foremen, a man named Vassily, to join them. Yuri explained that, like most of the workers, Vassily was a peasant and, in his case, raised near the Ural Mountains in Perm where the Kodarovs had a mountain dacha. Russia was primarily a rural country, but with the oncoming of the industrial revolution, many people like Vassily, people of the land, were migrating to the cities. They were largely uneducated and illiterate. "Take Vassily here. He was illiterate when he arrived in St. Petersburg two years ago. I arranged for a tutor for him because I saw potential in him. Now he is teaching several of the people who work under him to read. A chain reaction has started," said Yuri, beaming with pride in his successful attempt to educate the masses.

Vassily smiled back at Yuri with a look of genuine appreciation. "You may go now, Vassily," instructed Yuri. The peasant, wearing the common tunic of the worker, stood, thanked Yuri, and bade good-bye to the American visitor. He pulled the door shut behind him. Stephen immediately turned to Yuri and shot out a question. "Why are you showing me this, Yuri? It's as if you want to impress me with how miserable life can be in Russia, and how miserable this company—your father's company—treats its people. I'm not certain why you are showing me these things."

"You're right, my friend," replied the young Russian with a sly expression on his face. "I wanted you to see all of these conditions, and I wanted you to meet Vassily. We need to discuss many things about Mother Russia. You are an extremely intelligent foreigner, and your father is a man of influence. I feel that someday you yourself will be a man of influence. Stephen, in a few minutes, the rest of your delegation will be returning here for the production presentation and, unfortunately for us, we must sit through this boring part. But tonight, my friend, tonight, let us dine together in one of my favorite restaurants in all of St. Petersburg. We have much to discuss. You have much to learn."

***

That evening, Yuri's carriage arrived at the hotel to take the two young men to Yuri's favorite restaurant in St. Petersburg, located on Liteyny Prospekt. They had returned to the world of champagne and caviar, a world far away from the grimy factories that they had visited earlier in the day. As he entered the restaurant with his host, Stephen marveled at the red silken wallpaper, along with the gleaming crystal chandeliers. It occurred to the young American that he had one foot in each of the two St. Petersburgs: one a world of privilege and the other a hell hole of poverty. Their maitre d' escorted them through several rooms, each of which had a separate theme. He seated his young guests in a room where musicians playing balalaikas strolled among the tables. At the end of the room, a large stage promised more live entertainment.

As they looked at their menus, Stephen had the feeling that this dinner would be very important. He sensed that Yuri had a message to convey to him that night, and he suspected that his new Russian friend would be confiding in him about a very important matter. He would let Yuri set the tone and lead the discussion. After ordering and filling their champagne glasses, Yuri finally spoke. "It is quite disgusting, is it not?" he stated, with a forlorn expression.

"Isn't what disgusting, Yuri?"

"The conditions of the workers. How we treat them, how we pay them a wage on which they can barely exist. How the chasm in Russia between the fortunate, such as me, and the accursed, such as them, widens and continues to widen more." He sighed and lifted his champagne glass. "I propose a toast to a dying culture, to a dying empire!" he suggested sarcastically.

"Yuri, I don't understand. This is your father's factory. It's as if you are speaking against your own family."

"Not against my family, but against my family's way of life, what they stand for, what they are doing to Russia. The Putilov Metal Works is typical of all the factories in the Vyborg district. There is much discontent in Russia now. The Tsar and his bureaucracy continue their ways, and the country continues to fragment. They are either blind or stupid." As he spoke, anger clouded his face.

"It surprises me to hear you talk this way. I mean, where and when did you learn to feel this way, given your privileged background? Why should you care?"

"You'd be surprised, my friend. There are many like me at the university. We are children of privilege who disagree with the monarchy and its autocratic ways. A revolution is needed to change the Russian way of life. It will come in the future, and hopefully, I'll still be alive when it comes. I don't expect you, a son of an American aristocrat, to totally understand all of problems that plague Russia."

Stephen kept his sarcasm to himself. *Yes, you should only know about my aristocratic background*, he thought.

"It's a matter of justice, purely justice," continued Yuri. "You know, my colleagues and I at the university are exposed to great thoughts, great ideas. Most of my colleagues are from the moneyed class, the aristocracy, as I am. We had a greatness in Russia, you know. Alexander II, ah, yes, now that was a great Tsar, a visionary! After the debacle of the Crimean War, he knew that Russia needed to modernize, to adopt Western ideas. The civil servants in his reign saw their duty as public service. Yes, many of them were children of privilege as I am. Alexander's great reforms, such as freeing the serfs and the establishment of the zemstvos—the local assemblies in the provinces—were so inspired! This was the start of a great Russia. My God, Stephen, he was even planning a limited constitution before those reactionary bastards assassinated him!

"And look what we have now! His son, Alexander III, is a reactionary, an autocratic tyrant of the worst kind. He has undone all the good that his father had accomplished! And he's only in his forties, so I fear he'll be around for a long time, God help us!"

It surprised Stephen to hear such emotion from his friend, who had seemed so easygoing when they first met. The idealistic convictions that this wealthy young man held seemed both noble and, at the same time, overly idealistic. They left Morrison both fascinated and slightly dumbstruck. Multiple questions sprang to his mind. He began with the royal family. "Tell me, Yuri. We met the Tsarevitch Nicholas. What is he like?

He looks quite different from his father. Compared to the Tsar, he is physically unimpressive."

"I know Nicholas fairly well. To be honest, he's a zero, a nothing. Intellectually, he is like his father, a mediocrity at best. His father is outgoing and buoyant but, at the same time, is an intimidating man and a bully by nature. Nicholas is shy and soft-spoken. He carries the same autocratic airs that his father does. He's my age exactly but, don't even give him any thought; I assure you his father doesn't. The Tsar is sending him on a tour of Europe and the Orient next week, and I suspect it is just to get him out of his sight. As I said, the Tsar is a young man, so Nicholas' day won't be coming for many years."

Both men paused as their entrees arrived. The excellent pheasant and caviar provided a break in their serious conversations. For several minutes, the boys just enjoyed their food and listened to the traditional Russian folk music. Finally, Stephen again began to question his friend. "What are your thoughts for the future of your country, Yuri? Where is all of this discontent heading? I can see that you have given this a lot of thought, and I suspect that is why you've invited me to dinner. Am I correct?"

"You are indeed, my friend. The future, you ask. What is the answer? Well, the answer is populism; this is our credo."

"Populism? What is that?"

"Our concept of populism has several facets that will bring about the salvation of Mother Russia. First and foremost, we believe in freedom and democracy. This is our ultimate goal. But, we are not the United States of America, Stephen. The path to our goal will not be like the paths your Founding Fathers chose in 1776 and 1787. Yes, I've studied American history, and I can tell you that you Americans are a truly unique people to have created the country in which you live. On the other hand, Russia is primarily a peasant nation, an uneducated nation, ruled by an autocrat for hundreds of years. Our path will be different from yours. Our path will be a different type of revolution."

"How will you achieve your dreams? What will be your means? Armed revolution or a coup d'état?" asked the young American, as he leaned forward on his elbows, entranced by his friend's theories.

"The key to our revolution is the peasantry. They are so numerous and have been denied basic rights for so long. They are like diamonds in the rough. They will be the source of our revolution, but they must be prepared for this role. This revolution will come from the will of the people, the noble peasantry of Russia. Many of them have migrated to the cities, to work in our factories. That is why those of us with the means must educate them and help them. Don't you see, Stephen, that the basis of all freedom is the people? As an American, you must understand this reality."

"Is that why you wanted me to meet Vassily?"

"Exactly. He is a typical example of what we are trying to do. Uneducated and illiterate when he arrived in St. Petersburg, he is now becoming a leader. The truth be told, many of us at the university have established underground study circles where we educate the workers. It was through one of these groups that Vassily learned not only how to read and write, but also about social justice and revolution. Now he is becoming a teacher himself. You see, it is like a chain reaction that is unstoppable!

"Again, I tell you this, Stephen, because I sense you are not only capable of understanding it, but perhaps you are also a man of destiny. Maybe in your capacity as an American admiral, the son of an American congressman, your destiny will be entwined with the new Russia, should the revolution occur in our lifetimes."

"You flatter me and perhaps overestimate me, Yuri," replied Stephen with a chuckle. "As I told you at the Winter Palace last night, I've always been interested in Russia, and you've given me quite an education tonight." He paused to think and then asked, "Is this revolutionary feeling widespread throughout the country?"

"Yes, in various forms, it is. The government continues its self-indulgent ways and ignores its people. The discontent is growing, slowly growing. When things go bad, they blame things on the usual scapegoats, like the Jews, and think that people with real minds will believe it."

"You must be referring to the infamous pogroms that I've heard about. A number of Russian Jews have migrated to America, and many of them live in my father's congressional district. The stories I've heard from them are beyond belief." He looked his friend in the eyes and then asked, "What do you think about the pogroms?"

Sighing, Yuri replied "Believe me, my friend, I have no particular concerns for the Jews as a people. It's the concept of shifting the blame for one's own ineptness to a totally innocent group that grates against my sense of justice. To be perfectly honest, I don't know much about the Jews other than they look funny and have some strange customs and beliefs. I don't believe any of the garbage that the government likes to promote about Jews. I don't believe that they kill Christian babies so they can use their blood for religious rituals. I think it's a lot of nonsense."

"I agree," replied Stephen. "I don't believe any of that nonsense, either."

Before their after-dinner drinks, more lanterns were lit, illuminating the stage at the end of the room. A row of dancers clad as gypsies entered the spotlight to the wild applause of the audience of diners. Yuri enthusiastically applauded and shouted encouragement to the dancers. *He's a little drunk,* thought Stephen to himself, but he realized that the champagne had also made him slightly giddy. He joined in the applause. Eventually, the audience joined the dancers in singing traditional Russian folk songs. Yuri remained highly impressed with his American friend's ease with the language and his knowledge of the songs. He could have sworn that this young man was a native Russian.

After dinner, during the carriage ride back to the Grand Hotel Europe, both young men sprawled out on the seats. They were tired and slightly drunk. Stephen had thoroughly enjoyed himself and felt he had discovered a new and important friend. The feeling was mutual for Yuri, who felt that his new American friend would play an important part in his future. Yuri reached into the leather attaché case that he had stashed on the floor of the carriage and pulled out two books. He turned to Stephen and said, "My friend, I have a gift for you. Please take these books. They will give you some insight into the mind of Russia. I don't totally agree with all of what they say, but these types of works are providing the spark for the coming revolution."

In the dim lighting of the carriage, Stephen could barely read the titles. The first book, entitled *What Is To Be Done?*, was written by a man named Nikolai Chernyshevsky. The other book, entitled *Revolutionary Catechism*, was written by a man named Sergei Nachaev. Stephen had not heard of either book, nor did he recognize the authors. "I'm not familiar with these works," he told his friend as he leafed through the pages.

"I didn't suspect that you might be. This is not light reading fare. It is deep and dark, almost like discovering a new form of life on the planet. These are influential works among the people of Russia. Perhaps on the rest of your trip, you'll have time to read them." He rubbed his eyes and yawned. "This is my gift of learning to you, Stephen Morrison, and it comes from the heart."

Stephen thanked his friend as they turned onto the street where the hotel was located. "When do you leave on the rest of your journey?" asked Yuri. Stephen replied that he would be breaking off from the American delegation in two days to travel with Sergeant Johnson across Russia and the Orient, before sailing back to the United States. Yuri's face lit up, and he blurted out, "Stephen, I have an inspired idea! A truly brilliant idea!" His sudden animation startled his friend.

"My God, Yuri, are you all right? What is it?"

"Stephen, remember I told you that the Tsarevitch, the idiot Nicholas, is being sent on a trip to the Orient? My father is haranguing me about going to meet Nicholas in Japan. He thinks it would help him even further in his business ventures with the government. Apparently, the Tsar has been somewhat impressed with me on the few occasions that I've met him. He even made a comment that he wished that Nicholas could be more like me. Father has sent word word to the Tsar through the prime minister offering my services as an escort for Nicholas for part of his trip."

In his slightly drunken state, Stephen, a bit confused, replied, "I'm not following you, Yuri."

"Don't you see? Why don't I travel across Russia with you and Sergeant Johnson? Then we'll go on to Japan and continue our talks. I can take you to our dacha in Perm in the Ural Mountains and really show you Russia. What do you think of that plan, my friend?" he said, looking for the response on the young American's face.

Stephen broke out in a wide grin. "I think it is an excellent idea. Let me run it by Senator Straythorne and Sergeant Johnson. I know that they'll think it's a great idea, too. The son of a Russian industrialist and the son of an American congressman traveling together. What an odd pair!" Both young men laughed at the thought as the carriage pulled up to the front of the hotel. As Stephen stepped out of the carriage, he thanked his host for a memorable evening. He could sense that the last twenty-four hours had initiated a lifelong friendship.

"Oh, Stephen," Yuri called out of the carriage window as his friend walked toward the hotel entrance. "There is another book I have to get you. I'm sorry, I don't have a copy of it at my house. Are you familiar with *Das Capital* by a German writer named Karl Marx?"

Perm, Russia
August 1888

As the sun set over the city of Perm, Stephen Morrison, Yuri Kodarov, and Sergeant Amos Johnson sat on the long porch of the Kodarov dacha. The beautiful house, located north of the city on the northernmost bend of the Kama River, was their final destination of the day. Even the normally taciturn Johnson had loosened up on the journey thus far and seemed to be enjoying their travels immensely. They sat in wicker chairs, drinking vodka delivered to them by the servants who attended to their every need.

The journey to Perm had begun with a long train ride on the newly constructed first leg of the Trans-Siberian Railroad. It afforded ample time for Stephen to read, and he and Yuri had lengthy discussions over the merits of the books that Yuri had given him. Morrison found it ironic that when he challenged

Yuri on various points, invariably Yuri would return to the concept that, as an American, Stephen had no idea what it was like for the average Russian peasant who lived constantly under the boot of tyranny. The looming revolt of the workers always dominated Yuri's rhetoric. His passions had only been reinforced by their visit to his family's mine earlier that day.

Perm was a burgeoning industrial center at the foot of the Ural Mountains and was also the local seat of government. The first phosphorus mine in Russia had been recently developed there, and the Kodarov family was the major shareholder in the venture, but Yuri didn't hesitate to point out the appalling conditions under which the miners worked. "Disposable human capital," was what he cynically called the mine's employees. In addition, most of them lived in squalor near the mine. They were the uneducated descendents of serfs, people that Yuri and his kind so desperately strove to educate. At one point, when Yuri was called away from their tour of the mine complex, Sergeant Johnson whispered into Morrison's ear, "He sure complains a lot for a wealthy young man! Would he rather switch places with all these poor bastards? Seems to me that he's got a guilty conscience." Morrison only nodded in response.

As the warm sun continued to set, the three men sipped their drinks in silence as the servants began to bring out trays of food. When they began to eat, Yuri started to speak. "Gentleman, I hope your visit here has been instructive. Here, as in St. Petersburg, you see the two Russias: the Russia of the sun and the Russia of the shadows. When true justice will prevail, only God knows!" Finishing his vodka, he looked at his two guests. "Our train leaves the day after tomorrow. I thought we'd spend tomorrow here relaxing, unless you have any other places you'd like to see. We can even go sailing on the river, if you like."

Actually, Stephen did have something in mind. He had been thinking about it since they left St. Petersburg, but he wasn't sure how to broach the subject. Now seemed like an opportune time. "Yuri, I do have something I'd like to do tomorrow. It's a bit of an unusual request, but since we are in Perm, I really would like to locate a family if I could."

"Stephen, who could you possibly know in Perm?" asked the somewhat bewildered Russian.

"Actually, I don't know anyone. It's a favor for someone in my father's congressional district. He's a fairly influential rabbi in New York City who emigrated from Russia. His family was from Perm, and my father promised him that, if I could, I would check on his surviving relatives. If it is at all possible, I'd like to try, Yuri."

"But Stephen, there are no Jews left in Perm. I'm almost certain of it. After the last pogrom, it would be suicidal for any Jews to remain. They have all been banished to the Pale of Settlement. Really, I think the vodka has gone to your head, my friend."

Morrison turned and looked his friend straight in the eyes. "You asked, Yuri, and I'm answering. I want to track down this family, if possible. I am trying to honor my father's request, a United States congressman's request. I realize that the effort may be in vain, but I do want to try. Now, will you help me or not?" he asked, with a bit of annoyance in his voice.

The young Russian looked down at his dinner plate and sighed. "Of course, Stephen, of course. Tomorrow we will try to track down these mysterious and likely nonexistent Jews. I promise we'll make a noble effort to do so."

That night, Stephen lay in his giant bed in one of the huge guest rooms on the second floor of the Kodarov mansion. Finding it difficult to fall asleep, he kept going over details in his head. What were the exact details of his family history that his father had told him so long ago? He found it somewhat humorous that for all the times he had been annoyed by his father's frequent reminiscences about his family in Russia, now he was here trying to recall exactly what his father had said. His mind drifted back to his father's lectures.

The rabbi had said that they had left Perm in 1872 when Stephen was an infant. According to the rabbi he had left behind a younger brother. Stephen struggled to remember his uncle's name, and then it came to him: Chiam. There perhaps had been some sort of falling out between the two brothers. The rabbi never talked about the cause of the rift, but something happened, apparently long before the Kambotchniks had left for America. The rabbi hinted that his brother had never left Perm, but he never elaborated on his circumstances. On the one occasion when young Lev Kambotchnik had asked about his uncle and his family, the rabbi had ended the conversation abruptly. Stephen thought it very odd that his uncle would even attempt to remain in Perm under the Tsarist policies, but he couldn't know for sure if in fact he had remained. He hoped he would soon be able to resolve this longstanding family mystery.

The following morning after a sumptuous breakfast, Stephen and Yuri headed out by carriage for Perm, destined for the government record house located in the midst of the city. In this building, the young men felt they had the best chance of locating the fate of a man named Chiam Kambotchnik. As their carriage headed up the long dirt trail leading from the dacha, they looked back and saw Sergeant Johnson sitting on the front porch with his legs up on the railing, an ever-present cigar lodged in the side of his mouth. The boys laughed to see him staring at a Russian language newspaper. Johnson didn't speak a word of Russian.

The Kodarov family name opened all doors in Perm, and before long, they sat opposite the head bookkeeper in the government record house. Stephen outlined his request: to locate, if possible, one Chiam Kambotchnik and any of his relatives. To assist the bookkeeper, Stephen added the facts that the man was a Jew and that he had a brother who had left Perm after a pogrom in 1872. The bookkeeper seemed a bit puzzled that this young, well-dressed American who spoke Russian so well could possibly be interested in a Jew. Going through the archives of the municipal registries that had been used to collect taxes from the early 1870s, the bookkeeper announced, after an hour-long search, "I found him! At least, I found out what happened to him."

"Is he still alive?" asked Stephen.

"No, there was a reference to his death in 1872. I looked into some of the police reports that matched the dates referenced. It appears that he was a victim of that last pogrom. It was pretty gruesome reading," replied the bookkeeper. "You don't want the details, do you?"

"Yes," replied Stephen. "I do."

"Well, it appears from the report that this Jew you were looking for had a big mouth and a lot of nerve. When they were interrogating him, he refused to cooperate and, in fact, became belligerent. Apparently, they wanted to know where to find his brother and his family. Seems the brother was some sort of influential rabbi and was trying to flee."

"And?" inquired Stephen.

"Well, not only did he refuse to cooperate, but he spit in the interrogator's face. The report states that they took him outside to the center of the village and tied him to a tree. They doused him from the waist down in kerosene and set him on fire. Just before the flames reached his chest, they slit his throat." The bookkeeper looked at the stunned Stephen Morrison and said, "Anything else you need to know?"

"No. No, thank you. I'll just have my father inform the family that he died of natural causes." Stephen Morrison suddenly felt slightly nauseated.

"Just glad I could help," replied the bookkeeper with a smile.

***

Shortly after learning about his uncle's fate and on their journey to the next major Russian city, Ekaterinburg, Stephen's nightmares began. The rhythm of the train's rocking motion had gently lulled the three travelers to sleep. As usual, when he slept, Sergeant Johnson snored like a buzz saw. Stephen smiled as he removed the cigar from his bodyguard's mouth and extinguished it. He laid his head back, closed his eyes, and soon fell asleep.

In his dream, Stephen found himself in a dark room tightly bound to a wooden chair. He had no idea where he was or how he got there. There suddenly appeared the image of a menacing man whom Morrison didn't recognize. The man brandished a large knife, walked up to his captive, and lowered his face to the young man until he was just inches from him. At the same time, he held the blade of the knife against Stephen's throat as he whispered, "Make your choice." After a pause of a few seconds, he repeated, "Make your choice." Morrison had no idea how to reply to this threat and felt too paralyzed with fear to attempt to reply. The assailant then slowly sliced his blade deeply across the soft tissue of the young man's throat.

As the warm blood spurted onto his chest, pain seared into his brain. Morrison awoke with a start, blurting out, "No!"

Yuri looked over at his companion and noticed that the young American was sweating profusely. He had been awakened by Stephen's scream, and Sergeant Johnson also began to stir. Johnson looked at Morrison, who was seated in the middle between himself and Yuri. "You all right, Stephen? You look as if you've just seen a goddamn ghost!"

"I'm ... I'm fine. I just had a strange nightmare, that's all. Really, I'm fine," he replied. Before long, the three men again drifted off to sleep. The porter had to awaken them when the train pulled into Ekaterinburg station.

They had a one day layover. Yuri again proved to be an excellent host and tour guide, taking the two Americans all over Ekaterinburg. That night, they dined as the guest of the local governor, and, by the time the dinner had ended, all three of them were slightly intoxicated and bone tired. They were lodged in the city's finest hotel, one reserved for government aristocrats and foreign dignitaries. Stephen was so exhausted when he finally got back to his hotel room that he quickly undressed and went right to bed. Within seconds of his head hitting the pillow, he was sound asleep.

He again found himself bound to a chair by thick ropes, tied so tightly that he couldn't move at all. He also found it difficult to breathe. In the corner of the dark room flickered a solitary candle that provided the only source of illumination. Suddenly, a door opened. The rays of light that entered the room momentarily blinded Stephen. As his night vision slowly returned, he could see a man, a total stranger, walking toward him. The man, garbed in formal dinner dress, held what appeared to be a machete in his right hand. Morrison's heart started racing with fear. He felt totally powerless, totally at the mercy of this stranger walking toward him.

The man in the dinner dress stopped in front of the young man and smiled. He bent over, placed the machete blade at the base of Morrison's throat, and held it there. Leaning over until his lips practically touched the young man's left ear, he whispered, "Make your choice." Terrified, Stephen opened his mouth in an attempt to answer, but no words came. Again, the stranger whispered, "Make your choice," and waited for some reaction from his young captive. Hearing nothing, the stranger said, "Very well then," and slowly began a sawing motion, pushing the machete blade deeper into the young man's neck with each swipe of the blade.

Blood spurted onto the floor in front of the chair, and suddenly Morrison found his voice. "God, please help me. Please, dear God, help me!"

In the adjoining room, the screaming awakened Sergeant Amos Johnson. He reached for the Colt revolver on his nightstand, leaped out of bed, and ran into the hallway. Hearing Morrison's cries, the bodyguard kicked down the door and rushed in. He found his young charge screaming in his sleep.

He rushed over to the bed and began shaking the young man vigorously. "Stephen, wake up! For God's sake, wake up!" He continued shaking Stephen, and the boy's eyes flew open. For a moment, he appeared totally disoriented and too upset to speak. The older man again saw his charge bathed in sweat. As the young man struggled to sit up, the bodyguard softly said, "Stephen, I think you just had another one of those nightmares. They must be real beauts!" He sat on the side of the bed, as the young man calmed down and tried to get a grip on his emotions.

"I'm really sorry, Sergeant. I don't know what the hell is going on with me. I almost never have nightmares. Now, two nights in a row." The older man handed him a glass of water, and Stephen eagerly drank it down. "They are so vivid, too," he continued. "Someone is trying to kill me. Do you ever have nightmares, Sergeant Johnson? I mean, these lifelike, vivid ones, where someone is trying to do you real harm?"

"Oh, well, let's see," replied the older man, scratching his chin for effect. "Maybe, say, like every night," he said, winking at his young friend. "Let's face it. In my line of business, I make a lot of enemies, so there are many people who would like to see me dead." He started chuckling, and his humor brightened Stephen up considerably. They both start laughing, and the bodyguard tousled Stephen's hair. "You'll be the death of me yet. Don't worry Stephen, it's probably just a phase you are going through. It'll pass." Johnson stood up and looked at the clock ticking away on the wall. "Jesus, Stephen, we better get some sleep. We have to make a 7:00 A.M. train." He was walking toward the door when the young man called out.

"Sergeant Johnson?"

"Hmm?" Johnson replied, turning around to face the young man.

"Thanks for being such a good friend. I mean it."

The older man smiled at Stephen and then continued out the door. *Christ*, he thought to himself. *I'm gonna have to pay for that broken lock. Oh well, the congressman won't mind.*

Stephen Morrison laid his head back on his pillow. He knew that the story about his uncle had seriously affected him, but the sergeant was right. This was just a phase, and he would soon get over it. Within minutes, he was sound asleep and snoring loudly.

He couldn't know it yet, but for the rest of his life, he would be plagued by these recurrent nightmares. They would always be variations of the same concept. He was bound in a chair, and a stranger was placing a knife at his throat, ordering him to make a choice. He would never clearly understand what choice he was being asked to make, but he often thought about these dreams. *Ironic,* he would reflect, *that I've been making choices all my life: immigrant Jew or modern American, to run from conflict and humiliation or fight back, Princeton or the Naval Academy. I've always had to make difficult choices, and I've made them. Probably more so than most people. Will I ever stop having to make these choices? Will I ever have to make a choice to live or to die?*

9

Kyoto, Japan
Fall 1888

Tsarevitch Nicholas Romanov had been bored with the entire trip since leaving Russia several months before. The countries he had visited in Europe and the Orient held no particular interest for him, that is, until he reached Japan. He had fallen in love with the vibrant, colorful society. At last, he seemed to be enjoying himself. His two traveling companions contrasted with the introverted Nicholas; his brother, Grand Duke George, and his cousin, Prince George of Greece, were both extroverts who seemed to enjoy themselves wherever they went. As much as he liked Japan, Nicholas remained very angry with his parents for sending him on this prolonged trip.

The fact was, Nicholas was in love. He had decided on a bride for himself, and his parents did not approve. He had first met Princess Alix of Hesse in 1884 at the wedding of Alix's elder sister, Princess Elizabeth of Hesse, to Nicholas's uncle, Grand Duke Serge. He was smitten with the sixteen-year-old girl at first sight. They corresponded regularly, and when occasions such as marriages of European royal families brought them together, they were inseparable. Related through the House of Hesse, they were, in fact, second cousins. Alix's grandmother was Queen Victoria of England.

The Tsar and Tsarina had several reasons to dislike young Alix of Hesse. First, she was Lutheran and had displayed no interest in converting to the Russian Orthodox faith. That issue had been the source of several disagreements with young Nicholas. Knowledge that her older sister had converted to the Russian church to marry Grand Duke Serge offered hope to the lovesick Nicholas. The other reason for the Tsar's dislike of Alix was her dour disposition. In spite of her nickname, Sunny, the girl rarely smiled and seemed socially awkward. "She's just shy," argued Nicholas to his parents, but to no avail. The princess was also very educated and cerebral, and at times, this quality intimidated Nicholas. Nicholas was never a scholar, so this aspect of her personality was something else the Romanovs' seemed to resent. Nicholas had no doubt that his current trip abroad, arranged by his parents, had been largely designed to cool his ardor for his young princess.

Nicholas had been so angered by his parents' interference that, to provoke them, he chose as his traveling companions the two Georges, who were both known and indiscreet homosexuals. The Tsar was infuriated when he found out, and Nicholas was glad. There was much to resent about his domineering father. In Nicholas' view, his father was more proud of his son for his affair with the famous ballerina, Mathilde Kschessinka, than he was about anything else Nicholas had done in his life. The only thing that seemed to please his father was Nicholas' military service. At age nineteen, he had entered the military and soon was commanding the Hussar Guards. Much to Nicholas' surprise and delight, he very much enjoyed many aspects of military life. The pageantry, the pomp and circumstance, and the camaraderie all appealed greatly to the Tsarevitch. This part of his life appeared to be the only one that Nicholas ever heard his father speak of with great enthusiasm and pride.

The tour of Japan had been spectacular for the three royal travelers. The architecture, the teahouses, and the geishas had dazzled them all. The previous night in Kyoto culminated in a banquet at the governor's palace where the young Russians had been fawned over by several geishas. Much saki had been consumed, and when the banquet ended, Nicholas returned to his room quite intoxicated. His brother and cousin, he was certain, had gone on to explore the underside of nightlife in Kyoto. Now, this morning, Nicholas felt slightly hung over as he arose to bathe and dress. He looked forward to the day's journey. The governor had recommended they visit the picturesque town of Otsu, not far from Kyoto. The three royals and their bodyguards would be departing after breakfast.

Oh shit, he thought to himself. He had forgotten! Today he was supposed to link up with Yuri Kodarov for the rest of his journey. Just when he was really beginning to enjoy the trip! He never felt comfortable around Kodarov, whom he viewed as one of those smug intellectuals who liked to think deep thoughts. For some reason, the Tsar really liked young Kodarov and thought he would be a good influence on Nicholas. No doubt, that was why the heir to the Putilov Metal Works would now be accompanying him. *I'm sure,* thought Nicholas, *that Father can't stomach the thought that I might be traveling with my brother and cousin.* He had often heard Alexander III privately refer to both of them as 'reprobates.' Sure, Kodarov could be very pleasant at times, but he always seemed so condescending to Nicholas. Kodarov managed to bring out Nicholas' insecurities about his own intellect, the way that his beloved Alix did at times. Nevertheless, Nicholas consoled himself. It was he and not Kodarov who would someday be Tsar. And, oh yes, he recalled, Kodarov was traveling with a young American he seemed to recall meeting back in St. Petersburg. *Wonderful*, he thought derisively.

Before leaving for the banquet the previous night, a message arrived informing him that Kodarov, his America friend, and a bodyguard would be arriving in Kyoto the next morning to join them. With his typical distain for others who were not of royal blood, Nicholas decided not to wait in Kyoto for them to arrive, but instead, left instructions for them to meet him in Otsu. After all, he reasoned, spotting three royal Europeans and their bodyguards shouldn't be too difficult in a small Japanese city. After breakfast, the three royals departed in a carriage for Otsu, followed by their bodyguards in a second carriage.

***

Reading the message left at their hotel in Kyoto, Yuri Kodarov was clearly annoyed. Typical Nicholas Romanov behavior, he observed to Stephen Morrison and Amos Johnson. "Why am I not surprised by this behavior?" he asked himself rhetorically. Without even checking into their hotel, the three arranged for a carriage to take them to Otsu, where hopefully, they would link up with the Tsarevitch without too much difficulty. As they set out on the journey, Kodarov thought to himself, *This is the last full day I will get to spend with my American friend.* The following day, the two Americans would be heading for Tokyo, where they would begin their voyage back to the United States. Kodarov had very much enjoyed the company of this new intellectual American friend, and he remained confident that they would always be lifelong friends. As far as Morrison was concerned, the feeling was mutual.

They arrived in Otsu around lunchtime, and their guide took them to a little restaurant where they dined and formulated plans to link up with the Tsarevitch's entourage. Nicholas had actually been accurate in his assessment; the royal entourage was not hard to find. The town was abuzz with news of the visiting Russian dignitaries, and on many streets where the Tsarevitch travelled, residents had lined up to greet them.

Kodarov's guide inquired at the local police station and discovered the proposed route of the Russians. After finishing their lunch, the three travelers set out on foot for the street nearby where they knew the three royals would be arriving. After a short walk, they came to a corner and turned into a narrow street.

Small shops lined the street, with throngs of townspeople standing in front. At the far end, Stephen could see a carriage with three passengers coming toward them. "There they are," exclaimed Yuri, recognizing the three Russians. He waved to them as he and his American colleagues walked toward the approaching carriage. "That's odd," said Sergeant Johnson, taking note of the lone carriage in the street. "Don't those dumb-asses know they gotta have bodyguards in a foreign country?" The two young men nodded in agreement, as they strode toward the carriage. The crowds waved and, in some cases, women threw flowers at the carriage. Finally, Nicholas deigned to recognize them and waved with a smug look on his face.

Kodarov, Morrison, and Johnson were standing about twenty-five feet from the carriage when all hell broke loose. Nicholas, who was sitting on the right side of the open carriage, had turned to his left to speak to his brother when a man leaped from the crowd and, with a blood-curdling scream, attacked him. The man wore the uniform of a policeman and brandished a large saber in both hands. To all the spectators, it appeared that time moved in slow motion as the man ran to the carriage and brought his saber down on the Tsarevitch's head. The hilt of the sword crashed against the right side of Nicholas' forehead, and blood immediately began to spurt. The stunned Nicholas cried out, "What? *What* do you want?"

When the assailant raised the saber again for a second blow, Prince George reached for the bamboo cane he had purchased that very morning and struck it across the attacker's face, temporarily stunning him. The delay proved to be enough. Sergeant Johnson had begun running toward them when the attacker had first emerged from the crowd, and after Prince George struck the man, Johnson tackled the assailant to the ground and began pummeling him. "Get them the hell out of here!" he ordered, as he continued to punch the policeman until the man lost consciousness. At this point, the Tsarevitch's bodyguards finally appeared. Several of the crowd descended on the attacker after Sergeant Johnson left him unconscious.

Johnson looked up and saw that Nicholas was surrounded by Morrison, Kodarov, and the other two royals, who formed a protective ring arounbd the Tsarevitch. Nicholas appeared very groggy, with his face dripping blood. Morrison reached into his jacket pocket, pulled out one of his handkerchiefs, pressed it against the Tsarevitch's wound, and applied pressure to stop the bleeding. By now the local police had arrived on the scene to take the assailant into custody and disperse the crowds around the foreigners. They indicated that the Tsarevitch should be taken to the local governor's home. The Russians and the Americans were loaded into the carriages and driven to the governor's residence.

Morrison assisted Nicholas into the house. Supporting the Tsarevitch with his arm under his left armpit, he held the handkerchief against Nicholas' forehead with his right hand. The governor directed the entourage to a room in the back of the house. As they seated the Tsarevitch on a large cushion, Morrison could hear Johnson screaming at the Russian bodyguards, "What kind of worthless assholes are you? Why the hell weren't you doing your damn jobs? I've got a good mind to kick all of your asses right now!" Morrison smiled, knowing that the Russian bodyguards obviously didn't speak English and had no idea why the older American was ranting at them.

Morrison settled Nicholas down into the cushion and then sat down on his left; Kodarov sat on the Tsarevitch's other side. Nicholas trembled slightly and seemed to be getting his wits back. In a hesitant voice, he asked, "What in God's name was that all about? I … I have never seen anything like this!" He looked at Kodarov and then Morrison. "Thank you both for saving my life." He motioned to Sergeant Johnson, who was still engaged in a one-way shouting match with the bodyguards, and said, "And thanks to that brave man also." With a wry smile, he looked at Kodarov and quipped, "And so, Yuri, how have you been? It is good to see you again."

"I'm doing well, Your Highness, especially now that you're safe," replied Kodarov. "I'm very much looking forward to the remainder of our trip together. I trust your brother and cousin have been keeping you on your toes!"

"Indeed they have," chuckled Nicholas. He turned to Morrison and asked, "And who might this young man be?"

"My name is Stephen Morrison, Your Highness. My father is United States Congressman Caleb Morrison of New York City. I actually met you at the Winter Palace last July. Yuri has been traveling with Sergeant Johnson and me."

"Will you be accompanying us on the remainder of our tour?"

"No, Your Highness. We leave for Tokyo in the morning and I must catch a ship back to the United States later in the day."

"That's too bad," replied Nicholas with feigned sincerity. He reached up and took the handkerchief from Morrison's hand. "I'm sorry I ruined your handkerchief." About to re-apply it to his wound, he stopped when he noticed that it had colorful embroidery in the corner. He unfolded the bloodstained handkerchief and saw a pair of gray, crossed anchors embroidered in the corner with the letters USNA in blue under them. "This needlework is exquisite! What does USNA stand for?"

"It stands for United States Naval Academy. I'm going to begin school there next summer. My mother had several of these embroidered for me."

"I'm so sorry this one was ruined!"

"Please, Your Highness, I have several others. The point is that you are safe, and this gift from my mother helped you. That's all that matters."

"Well, thank you for your kind words," said Nicholas, whose demeanor quickly changed. He seemed sincerely interested in the young American. "Do you know that I am a military man, too? I am leader of the Hussar Guards of St. Petersburg." He suddenly judged the American worthy enough to talk to and began an animated description of his military ventures. After ten minutes of a one-way dialogue on military life, the local doctor finally arrived and through a translator explained that most of the people should leave the room because he would now be suturing the wound on Nicholas' head. As he was being escorted from the room, Nicholas looked back at Kodarov and his two American guests and said, "Once again, gentlemen, thank you for your valiant efforts in saving my life from that madman. I will never forget you."

As the door shut, Stephen looked down at the blood-soaked handkerchief. To himself, he thought, *My first military mission.*

***

That night, Yuri, Johnson, and Stephen arrived back in Kyoto. After a large Japanese meal, Morrison and Kodarov sat out on the veranda of their guesthouse. They had arranged for a large bottle of saki to be delivered to them, and the young Russian pulled out several excellent cigars. "If Sergeant Johnson knew I was hoarding these, he'd probably have me shot!" quipped Yuri. They lit the cigars, charged their glasses, and sat back with their feet up on the railing. The clear, starlit night provided a most enjoyable environment.

Stephen spoke first. "Yuri, I just want to tell you how much I've enjoyed your company these past several weeks. I feel like I've not only seen Russia, but also I now understand the country a lot better. I'll be forever indebted to you for this trip. I mean it. I'm not trying to be some sort of sentimental bore or something like that. I really mean it."

"I know you are sincere, Stephen. I feel the same way. You know, until I met you, I had the same opinion of Americans that most Europeans do, that you're all loud, crass, nouveau riche cowboys. You have provided quite an education to me, my friend." Yuri puffed on the cigar and paused to take another swig of his saki. "Stephen, do you remember what I told you the first time we dined together?"

"No, not really. We've talked about many things."

"Well, I told you that I detected greatness in you. You strike me as the kind of person who can make a difference, who can change the world. That feeling has only been strengthened these past several weeks. Stephen, you are a man of destiny!"

"Please, Yuri, you are starting to embarrass me. I think you're hitting the saki a bit too hard." Stephen leaned over with his glass extended and said, "To friendship everlasting!" Yuri raised his glass to his friend's and repeated, "To friendship everlasting!" as they clinked their glasses together and downed the contents.

Yuri refilled their glasses and continued. "I mean it, Stephen. I've been thinking about this. Fate is at play here. The stars have lined up a little for this one. Here you are, the son of a congressman, a most influential American, and instead of becoming the typical rich playboy, you chose a life of military service. Instead of going through the motions of an education, you have become a real scholar, a multilingual scholar. An upheaval is brewing in the largest nation in the world, and you have come here to study it firsthand.

"I really believe that God has a great purpose for you, my friend. Continue to study, become a fine officer in the navy, and become a leader who will change the world!" By now, Yuri's speech had become slightly slurred from the saki. He started to speak again. "Promise me this, Stephen Morrison. Promise me that we will always be friends. Promise me that we will write to each other and keep each other informed of our worlds and our achievements. Promise me that we will never lose touch with one another."

Stephen looked over at his friend. "Yuri, I promise. Our friendship is too important not to sustain it. Besides, should you lose touch with me, I'll have Sergeant Johnson come to

Russia and kick your ass, as he threatens to do with everyone else in the world!" Both young men erupted in laughter. Stephen extended his hand and Yuri took it in a firm handshake. Yuri impulsively pulled his American friend over to him and embraced him in a firm bear hug.

With tears in his eyes, in a low voice Yuri said, "God bless you and your journey through life, Stephen."

The following morning, Stephen Morrison and Sergeant Amos Johnson left for Tokyo to catch their ship back to the United States. It would be seventeen years before Morrison would set foot in Russia again and under very different circumstances.

10

December 20, 1891
Naval Cadet Second Class Stephen L. Morrison
United States Naval Academy
Annapolis, Maryland
United States of America

My dear Stephen,

It has been months since I last wrote you. I truly apologize for this delay. I trust your studies continue to go well. I am glad that you are enjoying your chosen studies and seem to be excelling in them. My friend, I am not surprised at all!

I am now the assistant director of the Putilov Metal Works, a job I despise. My father and I disagree on just about everything, especially the treatment of our workers. I was finally able to convince him to let any of our workers who are ill see a doctor without the threat of being fired. I consider it a big victory for the Russian working man; my father considers it a foolish business practice and a sign of weakness on my part. Other than business, my father and I do not talk at all. It's funny, but I don't care. He has become a stranger to me. Ever since he was unable to get that munitions contract with your government, he has been bitter and seems to resent the entire world, myself included. It is sad, but he needs to face reality. I feel I cannot help him.

Things in Russia have become grave over the last several months, and I have been extremely busy. This is the reason I haven't written to you in many months. We are in a crisis the likes of which Mother Russia has never experienced before in history. It began over a year ago after the autumn crops were planted. We had an extremely early frost and late snows. All of the young seedlings and plants were unprotected from the frosts. These events were just a harbinger of the disasters to come.

Stephen, there has never been anything like the weather conditions that we have suffered from! This past spring brought nothing but dusty winds that eroded the topsoil throughout much of the land. This was bad enough, but the summer was one of the driest in memory. We went weeks without rain in many parts of the country. You can imagine the resulting harvests from late summer and early fall. A disaster! A catastrophe! As a result, there is famine throughout Russia.

Unfortunately, my friend, it gets worse, much worse. A natural disaster such as this famine is hard enough to comprehend. A manmade disaster superimposed on this is unthinkable and unforgivable. Yet this is exactly what has happened because of the Tsar's government and its bureaucratic incompetence! I, and many others like me, am absolutely livid over the actions of the government, and we can only pray that its downfall is hastened. It is almost too unbearable to tell you because I seem to fly into a rage when I even think about it.

The famine began in the Volga region and now has spread from the Urals to the Black Sea. There is widespread starvation in many parts of the country. And how has the government responded? They deny its existence! Instead, officials refer to it as a poor harvest! The newspapers are not allowed to print any reports on the famine, although many do; they are just not using the word. Some of the more reactionary elements are claiming that it would be an act of disloyalty to talk of a famine. Pathetic!

Do you remember, Stephen, when I last wrote, I profiled for you some of the government bureaucrats? Well, the Minister of Finance, that bastard Vyshnegradsky, propagated the greatest outrage of them all. In the spring, the government was going to ban all exports of grain abroad so that our peasantry could be fed. Vyshnegradksy—God damn him!— blocked the ban until late August. He did this so that all of the grain merchants, who no doubt give him bribes and kickbacks, could sell their grain abroad for a hefty profit while Russians starve to death! Rumor has it that Vyshnegradsky himself made a tidy profit by delaying the ban. I am also most distressed to tell you that my father, Ptior Kodarov, the distinguished owner of Putilov Metal Works, also made a nice profit because of the actions of the Minister of Finance. I am totally disgusted by all of this.

Last month the government realized that its house of cards was crumbling. With people starving to death all over Russia, they could no longer pretend that there was no famine in the country. Alexander III issued a decree calling for all Russians to form volunteer groups to help with famine relief. Mind you, Stephen, this was months after people began dying in the streets! Still, do you realize what a milestone this is in Russia's history, in the history of the Romanov dynasty? With this seemingly well-intentioned decree, the Tsar has acknowledged to the country that his government has failed its people miserably! Never before has there been such a public admission on the part of the government! My colleagues and I believe that this signals the beginning of the end for the Tsarist tyranny.

There is much revolutionary activity amongst my colleagues. We have worked so hard to bring up the peasantry. We believe that *transforming the peasants into workers will create the capitalist stage required to bring about the socialist revolution. I must admit that the docility of the peasantry to the famine crisis has been a great source of disappointment to me and to all of my populist colleagues. Are they truly immutable to the forces of social change? They have responded like passive lambs to the slaughter. As a result, we have been working very closely with the Marxist factions to effect social change.*

As you must recall from our discussion and your reading of Das Kapital, the Marxists views are similar to our populism but with a major difference. These revolutionaries do not feel that a capitalist stage of enlightened peasantry is necessary to achieve the socialist revolution. They favor the jump to the immediate overthrow of the government by the working class in order to spark the revolution. They have some great and original thinkers, but they are very impatient. Although I am very disappointed in the peasantry at this point, I am not quite ready to give up on them. We will continue to work with the Marxists, but only up to a certain point. They can be so overbearing, with their insistence that Marx's theories offer the only scientific solution to Russia's problems.

I am leaving tomorrow with a number of my colleagues. We are going to the Volga, where the problem originated, to work on famine relief. Many of Russia's greatest thinkers and activists have volunteered for the cause. Some of our greatest writers, including Tolstoy himself, are volunteering. The playwright, Chekhov, is working in the famine-stricken districts near Moscow. Were you aware that Chekov is also a medical doctor? Oh, Stephen, when I think of the talent and the greatness that resides in the Russian people, and how their lives are being destroyed by a despotic system that abuses them instead of serving them with equality and justice, my heart simply breaks. But as my heart breaks, my anger rises inside. I can only hope that the revolution comes in my lifetime.

Well, I've been quite wordy and I hope I haven't bored you to tears or depressed you. Please stay well and continue to excel at Annapolis.

Lee Mandel

Remember, your fate is to become an admiral and a great leader in the cause of world justice. Again, I will pray for all things good for you and your family. Please enjoy the upcoming holiday season. I think of you frequently.

Your friend always,
Yuri

11

United States Naval Academy
Annapolis, Maryland
May 1892

Stephen Morrison reported to the United States Naval Academy in the summer of 1889, traveling by train with his father. As they parted at the front gate, the congressman embraced his son tightly and whispered into his ear, "Make us proud, son. Become a leader of men." Stephen promised that he would put forth one hundred percent effort and reiterated to his father that becoming a naval officer would be the fulfillment of his life's dreams. A short time later that day, after completing all of the in-processing, he became Naval Cadet Fourth Class Stephen L. Morrison, Class of 1893. There were fifty-five other members of his class, an impressive-looking group of young men from all over the country. At six-feet tall and one-hundred-eighty well-muscled pounds, Morrison appeared to be the typical naval cadet.

During the in-processing that day, Jared Russell from Minnesota, another new arrival in the Class of 1893, also became a naval cadet. He was a strapping young man at six feet three inches who was handsome enough to be an actor in the Broadway theater. Outgoing and with an extremely confident air about him, it became apparent to all that he would be a charismatic leader of men in the future. *He seems like a great guy*, Morrison thought to himself. *They all do.*

One of the first tasks for each newly arriving cadet was to officially sign himself into the academy ledger, listing name, home town, address, birth date and birthplace, religion, and father's occupation. Morrison felt enormous pride as he listed his father's occupation as United States congressman. He felt somewhat amused when he listed his birthplace as Perm, Russia. In the religion column, he wrote Hebrew. Looking down the column, he noticed that all of the twenty-five cadets who had signed the register thus far had written Protestant or Episcopal, except for one who had written Roman Catholic. In the end, once all of the fifty-six new cadets had signed the ledger, only Stephen had listed his religion as Hebrew or Jewish.

***

Always an excellent student, Morrison immediately took to the academic environment. After only one semester, it became apparent to all that Jared Russell and Stephen Morrison were the top two students. After their first year, both were wearing stars above the anchors on their collars, signifying academic excellence. Although both were fine athletes and public speakers, it was Russell who had the more charismatic personality which contrasted to Morrison's more reserved and, at times, sullen one. It seemed logical that two evenly split groups of followers would form around the two class leaders, but this arrangement was not to be. Stephen Morrison became a pariah shortly after his arrival at the Naval Academy.

After settling into in his dormitory room in the New Quarters, Morrison learned that he was the only cadet who didn't have a roommate assigned. Because he was by nature a private person, a single room really didn't bother him, nor did he assign any sinister meaning to his dormitory situation. But at the end of the first week, certain things became apparent to him. Chapel attendance was compulsory for all cadets, and the academy chapel was for Protestants only. Catholics and Jews were not allowed to attend religious services on the grounds and had to attend church or synagogue in town. The rest of the class noticed when Morrison did not attend the academy chapel services, attending instead Temple Beth Elohim in Annapolis. In reality, Morrison didn't particularly want to attend any religious services, but academy policy mandated attendance. The idea that they had a Jew among them was anathema to many of the new class, especially Jared Russell.

Russell organized and dominated several dormitory study groups in which Morrison was not allowed to participate, and was very vocal in his disapproval of the New Yorker. In the small Minnesota town where he had grown up, Russell had never seen a Jew, but he had read all of the popular dogma about them. As a child, he had grown up believing that Jews had horns, which was not an unusual belief in certain regions of the country. What especially irked him was that Morrison "didn't look like a kike." Russell spread the word that Morrison was trying to pass for a Christian in a Christian world. He couldn't possibly fit in. One of Russell's colleagues pointed out that Morrison never claimed to be anything but Jewish and was extremely well qualified for the Naval Academy. Russell's retort was, "It doesn't matter; you're missing the point!"

Russell's father was an attorney and the mayor of their hometown of Elkerton, Minnesota. For Russell, life had been a most pleasant journey. A superb student, he graduated first from the private school that he had attended in New England. He was class president and the school's star athlete. He was also admired by his friends for his prowess with the ladies. His good looks and his charismatic charm were a magnet for attracting young women. Jared Russell excelled in anything he attempted, and life responded to him, as it should, with all the accolades of a favored son.

Every member of the fourth-year class knew that Russell and Morrison were the top two students. The very fact that he suddenly had competition for top academic honors ground away at Russell's soul. Especially since his competition was a Jew! The situation didn't make sense to him, it offended his sense of right and wrong, and it insulted him. Early in their four-year tenure at Annapolis, Jared Russell decided that he would make life miserable for this undeserving competitor. His solution was to send Morrison to Coventry.

Being sent to Coventry at the Naval Academy meant being shunned. Although not officially acknowledged by the Naval Academy, the policy was unofficially tolerated. This practice was routinely inflicted on the rare Jews who attended the academy. Other students had minimal conversations with Morrison, and he received no invitations to participate with any other cadets in any endeavors. The organizer of this banishment was Jared Russell, who had quickly become a favorite among the faculty because of his academic brilliance. It was Russell and his roommate, Derrick Parsons of Pittsburgh, Pennsylvania, who provided the most active harassment.

Studying in his room at night, Morrison began to receive notes that were slipped under his door. The first one he received said, "Drop dead, Christ killer!" and the next night it was followed by, "Leave here, and go back to kike-town, you Jew bastard!" Nearly every night thereafter a similar note followed. The first night, Morrison was infuriated, but he convinced himself to swallow his pride and ignore it. *They are trying to provoke me into a fight so that I'll get expelled,* he reasoned to himself. Certain that this was the work of Russell and his kiss-ass roommate Parsons, he chose to ignore the taunts. If no one wanted to talk to him, all the better. Nothing would stop him from succeeding at the academy.

As soon as the evening meal ended, he always went back to his room. Before studying, he performed a ritual of physical fitness activities to maintain himself in top physical condition. In addition to the required sports activities he participated in every afternoon, he developed a nightly ritual of situps, push-ups, and running in place. Then he hit the books. He became accustomed to the absence of another human voice from the time he departed the dining hall until breakfast. Not that anyone spoke to him during mealtimes, either.

Morrison's strategy to withdraw unto himself in response to his banishment to Coventry also worked against him. He soon developed a reputation as a *grind*, a striver of excellence. Grinds were considered loners and intellectual elitists. In addition, he was perceived as less-than- honorable because he wasn't helping the students who were struggling academically, known as *woods* in Naval Academy parlance. On the other hand, Jared Russell became well known for his tutoring efforts to help the woods. Because of this, his prestige among his peer group grew even greater.

Another fact of life at the Naval Academy was hazing by upperclassmen. All of Morrison's classmates received their share of hazing and torment because of this unofficially condoned practice. The hazing that Morrison received was especially brutal and virulent. Russell had sent anonymous messages to several upperclassmen informing them that a Jew lived among them, and as a result, he was singled out for more than his share of hazing. Demerits were given to him for petty offenses while other students received no demerits for similar infractions. His rare liberty times off campus were often cancelled due to his demerit totals. His treatment only made him more determined to succeed. He would not be provoked into doing anything that would get him kicked out.

His parents had no idea of the treatment he was receiving. He never told them. In a letter written shortly after the beginning of his second year, he reported, "As usual, things are fine here at the Academy. It's great to be back with my friends, whom I really missed. The collegiality of this place is what makes it so great. I'm really going to miss the guys when we all graduate."

Many a lonely night he remembered his father's words to him from so many years ago. "Stephen, I can only implore you not to wear your religion like a chip on your shoulder, daring people to hate you for it." *Is there a chip on my shoulder just because I am not ashamed to say who I am?* he asked himself. The shunning he received made so little sense to him that he would dismiss it from his mind. *Better to concentrate on my studies and on the future. Better to beat them at their own game, to show them that I can be just as good, if not better, than they are. Then, they will have to accept me.*

Morrison's stressful existence was significantly worsened one evening in March 1891 when he heard an unexpected pounding on his dormitory room. As he opened the door, the duty upperclassman handed him a telegram from the House of Representatives that had been sent to the superintendent, Captain Robert Phythian. Closing the door, he sat at his desk and stared at it for a minute before removing it from its envelope. The cable stated that Congressman Caleb Morrison had suffered a major stroke and had been hospitalized. The envelope also contained a handwritten note from Captain Phythian, allowing him a week of emergency leave to be with his father.

When he finally got to his father's bedside, he found out that as a result of the stroke, his father had a dense hemi-paresis and was unable to move the right side of his body. In addition, Caleb Morrison could not speak. The doctors explained to Mary Morrison and her two sons that the congressman's condition seemed to have stabilized, but that he would require much physical therapy. In addition, they were not optimistic about his chances of recovering the use of his right arm and leg, and they were uncertain if he would ever speak again. It tore into the soul of Stephen Morrison to see his father as an invalid, trapped in a flawed and unresponsive body. When he said good-bye to his father at the end of the week, tears were rolling down the congressman's cheeks as he tried to form words that never came. Naval Cadet Third Class Morrison departed for the Naval Academy only to return to Coventry.

***

In the fall of 1891, Morrison learned that a guest lecturer was scheduled for his physics class. It was Dr. Albert Michelson, the distinguished head of the department of physics at the University of Chicago. Michelson was also a graduate of the Naval Academy, Class of 1873. After graduation and his midshipman cruise, he had returned to the academy where he remained on faculty until 1882. He had received world recognition for his 1879 achievement of accurately measuring the speed of light while on faculty at the academy. That semester, Morrison and Russell were running neck in neck for the honors in physics. Morrison eagerly awaited the opportunity to meet the famed scientist.

The following week, after completing his lecture on optics, Professor Michelson promptly dismissed the class for the noon meal. As Michelson descended the steps of the Natural Philosophy Building, Morrison called out to him and the professor turned around. Morrison approached, extended his hand, and asked if he could speak to him for a few minutes. Observing from the doorway, Russell quipped to his roommate, "He may think he can kiss a famous professor's ass, but I'm still gonna take the physics prize."

Morrison walked alongside of the professor. "Sir, I really appreciate you taking a moment to talk with me. I know you're very busy." Short and sturdily built, Michelson had a thick moustache and appeared to be about forty years old.

"Not at all, young man. Come, let's walk along the seawall. I know you have to be in the dining hall shortly."

"Sir, my name is Naval Cadet Second Class Stephen Morrison. I wanted to tell you how much I enjoyed your lecture and what an honor it is to speak with you."

"Mr. Morrison, I'm flattered but I don't give you your grade!" quipped the older man as he smiled at the cadet.

"Oh, no sir, I know that," replied the flustered Morrison at the professor's unexpected joke. "I just wanted to ask you a question, one that can help me. I mean no disrespect, but I understand you are Jewish, isn't that right?"

The surprised professor looked at the younger man with suspicion in his eyes. "What kind of a question is that to ask? Why are you asking me that question?" This unexpected query into his private life had caught Michelson completely off guard.

"Well, sir, you see, I'm Jewish too. And I know you are an alumnus. I wanted to ask you if … if, when you were a cadet, did they, uh … were you …"

"Was I banished to Coventry?" Michelson interrupted, looking at the young man next to him. *I would not have guessed he was Jewish,* thought Michelson to himself. "Yes, I was. It was four very long years here. In fact, when I was on faculty here for six years, in each class, there were one or two Jewish students. Most of them were in Coventry also. The academy—and I love this place—pretends it doesn't know that this goes on. How are you handling it?"

"Well, sir, it is rough. I have few friends here, and I almost think that the silent treatment is starting to get to me. But I will get through it. I'm in my third year, and I am in the running to graduate first in the class. I guess I just needed to hear it from someone like you, someone who has experienced it also. God! At times I feel so alone!"

The two men sat on a bench at the sea wall. They could see the sailboats out on the Severn River on that crisp fall day. "Where are you from, Mr. Morrison?" asked the professor.

"I'm from New York City. I was born in Perm, Russia. And you, sir?"

"I was born in Streino, Prussia. My family came to the United States when I was two years old. I was raised mainly in San Francisco." Both men stared out across the clear blue waters and said nothing for a couple of minutes.

Finally, Morrison stood up and said, "I must be going, sir. Thank you so much for your time. It means a lot to me." He shook the professor's hand and then saluted him.

As he walked away, Michelson called out after him. The cadet turned around to the professor. "Stephen, you are what you are, and you can't be anything else. The key is to believe in yourself and beat them at their own game. When you do that, you will win their respect, which is all that they can offer. You will never win their friendship, and they will never accept you as an equal. Win their respect and consider it a monumental victory. That is the best you will be able to do."

12

The physical fitness trainer at the academy, a retired gunner's mate named Ralph Breckenridge, enjoyed inspiring both fear and respect in the entire corps of naval cadets. He still insisted on being called "Chief," and he believed in the concept that a sound body was equally as important as a sound mind. He had been retired for five years when the class of 1893 arrived on campus.

Most of the physical fitness training centered on calisthenics, which many of the cadets found boring. Chief Breckenridge had an amazing ability to do pushups and had a longstanding challenge to anyone who felt that they could do more pushups than he could. No one ever challenged him, even though several cadets probably could have bested him. They feared that if the Chief lost, he would make the physical fitness program even more onerous to them. The one activity that he wanted to have the cadets engage in was boxing, but the Academy had a ban against this sport. It disapproved of bare-knuckle fighting, as was the custom in the United States at the time.

Lee Mandel

One morning in May 1892, Chief Breckenridge had nearly finished reading the sporting section of the morning newspaper when an announcement caught his eye. The heavyweight champion of the world, John L. Sullivan, had announced he would be defending his title that September against the challenger James J. Corbett. The fight would be held in New Orleans. Significantly, this fight was going to be the first American championship fight to be fought under the Marquis of Queensbury rules, which would change the face of boxing in America. This event provided the incentive for the chief to schedule an appointment to speak with the superintendent the next day.

A week later, when the second class naval cadets reported to the gymnasium for physical fitness, they found the Chief beaming with enthusiasm and standing in the center of a twenty-four-foot square surrounded by ropes. A layer of canvas mats covered the floor of the square. In his hands, he held what appeared to be oversized gloves. He studied the cadets, clad in the blue gym shorts and gold T-shirts that reflected the academy's recent adoption of blue and gold as its official colors. After blowing a short blast on the ever-present whistle that hung around his neck, he instructed everyone to be seated. "Gentlemen, welcome to the world of modern boxing. I don't know if any of you has access to a newspaper, although I'm told naval cadets can read and write!" Several of the cadets burst into laughter. "Anyway, the great John L. Sullivan, heavyweight champion of the world, has announced that he is going to defend his title against Gentleman Jim Corbett this fall in New Orleans. What is significant about this news is that the great John L. has agreed to fight using the Marquis of Queensbury rules. You must realize that this changes boxing in America forever!

"I realize that some of you may not know about the Queensbury rules. Well, I'm gonna give you the skinny. First, no more bare-knuckle fighting. This style of fighting is gone forever. Fighters will now wear gloves like these," he said, as he held up the boxing gloves. "Each round will last three minutes, with one minute between rounds. A few other rules go along with this style, and we'll cover them as we go. Last week, I met with the superintendent. He gave me permission to add boxing to our curriculum, seeing as it's now more civilized than bare-knuckle brawling. So guys, we're going to take up the art of boxing and self-defense. As a baseline, I wanna see what you guys got. I want a volunteer … say you!" He pointed directly at Jared Russell. "Get your ass up here, Russell!"

Jared Russell jumped into the ring as the other cadets applauded. As Breckenridge tied the boxing gloves on him, he instructed, "Pick an opponent of equal size."

Russell scanned his fellow cadet until he found Morrison. "You, Morrison, let's see what you got! Are you up for it, or are you too scared?" The other cadets hooted as Morrison slowly came to his feet and entered the ring. As the Chief helped Morrison on with his gloves, Russell danced around, holding his gloves over his head like a victorious warrior. Finally, the Chief called them both to the center of the ring and gave final instructions. "Okay, you guys, I want a fair fight. No hitting below the belt. When I blow the whistle, you both stop fighting and go to a corner of the ring. You got that? Okay, so touch gloves, and when I blow the whistle, begin this fight!"

As they touched gloves, Russell growled in a low voice, "You're going down, Jew-boy!"

The shrill whistle blast initiated the bout. Immediately, the other cadets erupted into catcalls and shouts. "C'mon Russell, kick the kike's ass!" Other similar taunts filled the air in support of the popular Russell.

Russell slowly approached Morrison with his arms bent at the elbows and his gloved fists in a cycling motion typical of most bare-knuckle fighters of the day. Morrison came toward him with light, nimble steps, his left hand in front of his right. To Russell, he almost appeared to be dancing, and this greatly annoyed him. "C'mon, you cowardly fuck, stop the—" A sudden crashing jab from Morrison's left gloved fist hit Russell in the face, sending him reeling back a few steps and stunning him. "What the fuck?" he cried out, as he realized his lower lip was cut and bleeding.

Russell stood three inches taller and had nearly twenty pounds on his opponent, but he didn't realize that Morrison had many advantages over him. First and foremost, he had been fighting his entire life and often against more than one opponent. He had learned to be very mobile when fighting because he often had to flee when multiple assailants assaulted him. Also, Morrison's personal physical fitness regimen of nightly calisthenics, in addition to his required physical fitness classes, had resulted in his well-muscled and very powerful build. Lastly, he had his inner rage. Morrison had repressed his fury during his tenure at the academy because he realized that he could be expelled for fighting, even if he was in the right. But now, for the first time, he was being encouraged and authorized to fight, and with the one cadet who seemed to be the source of most of his torment at the Naval Academy. Russell's invitation to fight was Morrison's chance to vent his rage.

As Russell approached with his gloved fists again in a cycling motion, Morrison quickly jabbed Russell twice in the face with his left glove. Russell swung wildly with windmill-like punches that missed his opponent and exposed his own head. Morrison countered with a quick left jab to the head and followed with a devastating right hook to the side of Russell's head, dropping him to his knees. Stunned, Russell remained on his knees while the Chief blew his whistle. As Morrison backed off, he softly taunted his opponent, saying, "You weak little prick!"

Meanwhile, the cadets observing this battle roared with excitement. Most shouted encouragement to Russell, but a number of them began to support Morrison, shouting things like, "You show 'em, Morrison!" and "Go, Morrison, go!"

The Chief began to count to ten; by eight, Russell rose to his feet. Livid that this Jew seemed to be humiliating him, and he knew he had to regain the initiative. As they approached each other, Russell grabbed his opponent and hugged him in what almost appeared to be a bear hug. The Chief pulled them apart, shouting, "Cut that shit out, Russell. This ain't wrestling!" Russell unleashed another windmill-like blow that caught Morrison on the left shoulder and threw him back a step. In response, Morrison rushed in with right hook that caught Russell in the left side of his ribcage. It knocked the wind out of Russell, just enough so that he momentarily dropped his gloves. That mistake proved to be the opportunity that Morrison needed.

First he hit Russell with a right hook to the head and then a left hook. The wobbly Russell again began to drop to his knees. Before his knees hit the canvas, Morrison delivered another right and left hook in quick succession to Russell's head. His eyes glazed over as the shrill sound of the Chief's whistle rang out. As Morrison began to back off, in a loud voice, the beaten Russell spat out, "You fucking Jew bastard!"

The comment infuriated Morrison, and he lost control. He proceeded to deliver three more crashing blows to Russell's head, and his opponent collapsed to the mat while the Chief grabbed Morrison from behind, shouting, "It's over Morrison, it's over! Back off!"

Several cadets rushed to the ring, some of them to help Jared Russell to his feet. However, others ran over to Morrison to congratulate him and slap him on the back. Finally, several of his classmates lifted Morrison onto their shoulders and carried him around the ring like a conquering hero. Some proclaimed him "The Joltin' Jew" in an odd compliment showing their admiration. He looked back over his shoulder and saw two of his classmates helping Russell slowly to his feet. He also could see tears of humiliation forming in his beaten opponent's eyes. Morrison felt absolutely no sympathy for Russell. Instead, Morrison felt a great deal of satisfaction as his classmates carried him victoriously around the gym. In addition, he felt oddly exhilarated to have administered a severe beating to another individual, a person whom he despised. Even so, in his moment of triumph, the words of Professor Michelson came back to him. He had won their respect, but he would probably never win their friendship.

***

That night, Morrison fell asleep in his dorm room with a sense of accomplishment and inner peace. He drifted off to sleep and began dreaming of his youth in Lower Manhattan. Suddenly, he was awakened by several intruders pinning his arms to his mattress while they stuffed a rag into his mouth. He started struggling against the intruders, but they easily overpowered him. They rolled him over and tied his arms behind his back. He could hear Jared Russell commanding the four others. "Tie a gag around his mouth! Put a blindfold on him, too. I don't want a sound from him." After two of them held his feet together and bound them, four of them lifted him off the bed. "Follow me," commanded Russell. Morrison, dressed only in his underwear, ceased his futile struggling.

The five assailants carried Morrison down to a basement room in the New Quarters. They pulled out a chair and sat their prisoner in it. They leaned him forward and unbound his hands. Pushing him against the back of the chair, someone grabbed a length of thick rope laying in the corner and wrapped it securely around his waist. The ropes bound Morrison so tightly that he could feel the circulation to his hands being cut off. They left his ankles bound together. After turning the overhead light on, the others stood back as Russell walked up to their prisoner and removed the blindfold and the gag. The sudden burst of light hurt Morrison's eyes. As he slowly accommodated to the light, he could see the face of Jared Russell in front of him only inches away.

"You think you won that fight, Morrison? Do you really think you won? Well, we all know that you used a bunch of dirty Jew tricks. Right, guys?" Among the affirmations of support, Morrison recognized the voice of the ever-present Parsons. "You know, you humiliated me in front of everyone else with your tricks. I don't like being humiliated. In fact, I don't like losing to anyone in anything, especially not to a Jew. You better believe it right now that I am going to be the top graduate in the class, not you. You're going to have to pay for this, Morrison. What do you think of that?" When Morrison just stared back at him without answering, Russell's anger seemed to increase. "Just look at those sad, angry eyes of yours Morrison. They speak volumes to me."

Parsons walked over to Morrison with a small can of blue paint in his hand. "You know, you're not in the appropriate uniform of the day, Morrison. Heck, we don't want you to get in any trouble, do we? After all, what are friends for?" He dipped a brush into the can and brought it to Morrison's bare chest. With great flourish, he painted the word *Kike* on his chest. "There! It's perfect!" he cried, as he began laughing uncontrollably.

Russell smiled and he walked over to the corner of the room where he picked up a pair of canvas working gloves from the floor. He slowly pulled each one onto his hands while staring directly at Morrison. With dramatic display, he began his cycling motions with his fists, just as he had in the boxing ring earlier that day. Standing in front of his victim, he began to gently swipe his fists along the side of Morrison's face, as if to taunt him further. He stopped and put his hands on his hips. "You know what I can't stand about you, Morrison?" He paused for a moment, but received no reply to his question. "Well, I'm going to tell you." With that, he delivered a punishing blow to the side of Morrison's face. "I hate you because you're a fucking Jew who doesn't look like a Jew." He then smashed his right fist into the left side of Morrison's ribcage, knocking the wind out of him. Russell stood back and watched his victim cough up some blood-tinged mucous and gasp for air. After a moment, Russell continued his tirade.

"I hate you because you're taking up a place here at the academy, a place that belongs to a real American, a Christian." Again, he threw a crushing blow to the center of Morrison's face. Morrison started to lose consciousness. Russell leaned over and placed his face inches from Morrison's face. "And you know what else I hate about you, my silent friend? It's the fact that you don't know who you are or who you want to be. Are you a goddamn Jew, or are you an American? You don't seem to know where your place is in this world. What the hell are you?" Seeing Morrison beginning to slump over, Russell grabbed his hair and jerked his head up. "Don't pass out on me now! Answer my question! What are you? Are you another one of those fucking Jews who wants to take over the world or just a fucking Jew who is pretending to be a Christian? Tell me right now, you piece of shit!"

Morrison's swollen lips seemed to be moving, attempting to form words. "That's good Morrison, tell me," taunted Russell in a patronizing tone. "What did you decide?" He placed his ear up to Morrison's lips so he could clearly hear the answer. His colleagues had also gathered around and bent forward to hear the answer.

In a weak but clear voice, Morrison spoke so that all in the room could hear his reply of three words: "Go fuck yourself!"

Russell stood up in a fury and drew back his right fist. Suddenly they all heard the sound of the outer door to the basement being slammed shut. "Oh shit," cried Parsons, "it's the duty upperclassman making rounds. We gotta get out of here!" He grabbed his roommate's arm and screamed, "C'mon Jared! If we're caught, we're screwed. Just leave him here!"

Russell looked at his colleagues and then looked at the window in the back of the room. "There!" he cried as he pointed. Parsons ran over and turned off the light. Within seconds, the five cadets had climbed out the back window. Russell was the last one out the window. Just before he shut it, he stuck his head back in and spoke. "Fuck you, Morrison!" he said with a smile. He slammed the window behind him shut.

Naval Cadet First Class Neville Anderson had the duty that night. He despised these watches just because they bored the hell out of him; nothing ever happened. He had been walking around the periphery of the New Quarters when he thought he heard some noises coming through the basement window. He had to walk around the front of the building and go in the main entrance to access the basement stairs. He slowly checked the doors of each room; they all seemed to be locked. It startled him when he came to the final room found the door unlocked. Turning the knob, he slowly pushed open the door and shined the beam of his lantern into the room. His eyes focused on the back of a chair in the center of the room where someone appeared to be sitting. "All right, what's going on here?" he asked, as he walked around to the front of the chair. The shock of what he saw when he flashed the light beam on the seated man's face caused him to drop the lantern. He, too, spoke three words: "Oh, my God!"

***

The following afternoon, the superintendent, Captain Phythian, arrived at the Naval Academy Hospital. "Attention on deck!" shouted by the corpsman at the ward desk brought the entire staff to attention when he walked out of the stairwell. He informed the corpsman that he wanted to speak to the attending physician, Commander Claude Fitchett, immediately. Within a minute, Commander Fitchett arrived at the nurse's station to meet with Captain Phythian. "I want to know exactly what happened, Commander," barked the superintendent.

"Well, sir, it appears to be a rather nasty case of hazing, one with some pretty serious religious overtones." He explained about the painting on the patient's chest. Phythian had heard about the boxing match that had taken place earlier that day. Most people on campus had heard about Morrison's humiliating defeat of the popular Russell. Phythian had a good idea what the whole incident implied, and it made him livid. "What is the extent of Cadet Morrison's injuries?" he inquired.

"He has a broken nose, which I was able to set without much difficulty. His face is a mass of bruises. And he has bilateral periorbital ecchymoses; that is, black eyes. His eyes are almost swollen shut. The left side of his jaw is swollen and tender, but I don't think it's broken. In addition, he may have a cracked rib or two on the left side. He was unconscious when he was brought in here last night, but he's beginning to come around now."

"His father is a United States congressman. At least he was until he had a stroke recently," said Captain Phythian, thinking out loud. "When can I speak with him?"

"Sir, I'd recommend no sooner than tomorrow. Let's give him a little more time to wake up. Say, tomorrow afternoon, if that's okay."

"Tomorrow it is. I'll be back at 1300 sharp!" Phythian paused for a second and looked at the doctor. "He is going to live, isn't he?"

"Yes, sir, but he's going to be pretty sore for a while."

The following afternoon, Captain Phythian returned and the Command Senior Enlisted Leader escorted him to Morrison's room, along with Commander Fitchett. Seeing the superintendent enter, Morrison made a feeble effort to get up before they ordered him to remain in bed. Phythian asked the doctor to leave them so they could speak privately. The doctor walked out of the room and closed the door behind him. The superintendent pulled up a chair next to Morrison's bed and sat down. He studied the young man lying in the bed who stared back at him through bruised, swollen eyelids. He had heard unofficially that Morrison was having a tough time throughout his academy tenure, despite his excellent academic record. Phythian had turned a blind eye to the harassemen, but one look at the brutalized cadet told him that he could no longer ignore the hazing. It had to stop.

"Cadet Morrison, I can't tell you how sorry I am, and how disgusted I am, that this happened to you. I want you to know that this type of hazing, no, this torture, is going to end at the Naval Academy. Can you understand me? Can you speak? Dr. Fitchett says you may have a broken jaw."

In a soft voice, Morrison replied, "Sir, I can both hear you and speak." Phythian could see that it was painful for the young man to move his jaw. "But please don't ask me to box with you."

Phythian smiled at the young man's cynical sense of humor. "All right, Cadet Morrison, we'll cancel tonight's bout." He leaned forward and lowered his voice. "Cadet Morrison, I want to know who did this to you. I think I have an idea. Give me the names. There's going to be hell to pay." He scratched his chin and repeated more forcefully, "Hell to pay!"

Morrison looked directly into the captain's eyes and stared for a few seconds. "Sir, it was too dark, and I couldn't see who it was. I really couldn't." Through his swollen eyes, Morrison saw the stunned look on the captain's face when he finished speaking.

At first, Phythian was speechless. Morrison could see his face redden with anger. Finally, he spoke again. "What do you mean it was too dark? Didn't any of them speak? I can't believe you. In fact, I don't believe you. Cadet Morrison, this is serious business, and I expect your full cooperation! Do you understand me?"

"Yes, sir, I do," replied the young man. "I am just not able to identify my attackers. It was dark, they had me blindfolded, and they didn't speak to me. That's all there is to it. I can't give you any more details. I'm sorry, sir."

Captain Phythian leaped up from his chair, barely able to control his anger. "Young man, this is a violation of the honor code here at the Academy! You are not cooperating with an official investigation, and that is a serious honors violation. I can have you expelled for this behavior. I will have you expelled for it!" He paced back and forth along the side of the room. "Unacceptable! I will have you expelled if you do not give me some names!"

"Sir, I don't think you really want to expel me," replied Morrison in a quiet voice. "I've had a bit of trauma to my head, and I believe that Dr. Fitchett will tell you that sometimes amnesia can occur after head trauma. Perhaps that explains why I can't recall who the attackers were, or maybe it was just too dark. In either case, you'll be left to explain why you had a beating victim at the Naval Academy and why you decided to expel him when you couldn't identify the perpetrators. I don't think that will be easy to explain.

"Also, the cadet you decided to expel happened to be the son of a very popular and influential congressman. Even though he is ailing, he still has a lot of influence on Capitol Hill, as well as friends on the Military Affairs Committee. So you see, I just don't believe that you will be expelling me. I'm sorry I can't help you identify any attackers. I'm afraid it was just too dark."

Captain Phythian stood up and looked at the battered young man in the bed. He had to admit, the kid had guts. He was right. There was no way he could expel Morrison for not cooperating with his investigation. He sighed and cleared his throat. In a calm and reasonable tone he said, "You realize, Morrison, that unless someone confesses to this beating, I can't charge anyone without your identification of them. Your attackers will get off scot-free. I can't believe this is what you want. I really can't. I'll ask you one last time. Who did this to you?"

Through his swollen eyelids, Morrison looked at the superintendent and replied, "Captain, I'd like to help you, but it was too dark."

"Very well, Morrison," he said as he walked to the door. "I'll check on you in a couple of days. I hope you feel better." As he pulled the door shut behind him, he thought to himself that this Morrison was one stubborn, unreasonable young man. He really wanted to help him, but Morrison didn't seem to want his, or anyone else's, help. Phythian just didn't understand.

The following morning, Captain Phythian ordered Cadet Russell to report to his office at 1000 sharp. Before calling the young man into his office, Phythian pondered his dilemma. Without a doubt, Russell was an outstanding cadet and had tremendous potential for a great naval career. In addition, he liked the young man, as did everyone else at the Academy. He did not look forward to this session. With a sigh, he stood up, opened the door, and ordered the young man to enter and sit.

"Cadet Russell, I'm sure you heard about what happened to Cadet Morrison the other night," he began. "What do you know about all of this?"

"Sir, I first heard about it this morning, and I was quite shocked. In fact—"

"Don't you dare insult my intelligence, young man!" shouted the superintendent, rising from his chair. "Do you think I didn't hear about the boxing match? Do you think I really didn't know about the harassment over the past years? Do you know that I can have you thrown into the brig for a long, long time? Now, what do you have to tell me?"

The young man just hung his head and said nothing. The superintendent slowly walked around the young man, who continued to stare at the floor saying nothing. "Jared," said Phythian softly, "you're off the hook. Morrison is refusing to identify who administered the beating to him. I have no idea why, but he insists that it was too dark, and he flat out refuses to identify his assailants. Without his testimony, I am powerless to do anything. This is purely his choice and certainly not mine.

"You're getting the rare second chance, Jared. Make the most of it. You have a brilliant career ahead of you, an absolutely brilliant career. Even though I can't prove you did this, I'm telling you, no, I'm ordering you, to cease and desist. Leave Morrison alone. If there are any further incidences of violence, if anyone lays a hand on Morrison, I will blame you. I know the influence you have over the rest of the cadets. As much as I admire you, consider this the final warning. Am I perfectly clear, Cadet Russell?"

In a faltering voice, Russell replied, "Yes, sir."

"Good. Now get out of here and get back to class."

That evening, when they returned to their dorm room, Parsons immediately began questioning his roommate. "How did it go? What did he say? Are you in a boatload of trouble? C'mon, tell me, Jared! Quit screwing around!" He watched with irritation as Russell just stared out the window. Finally Russell sat down with a grin on his face and folded his arms.

"The truth is, I got off kinda easy. The old man chewed my ass a bit, but there will be no charges against me or any of us. The damnedest thing is—and this I can't really figure out—we're getting away with it because of Morrison! Can you believe it? He refuses to rat us out! Captain Phythian told me that Morrison steadfastly refuses to identify anyone. Says it was too dark to see who assaulted him."

The astonished Parsons sat there with his jaw dropped. "I don't get it. Why isn't he pressing charges against us all?"

"Hey, who the hell cares?" snapped Russell. "The truth is I thought that Phythian would have turned a blind eye. I mean, who the hell cares about a lousy Jew? He surprised me. He must know what's been going on and, by his inaction, I say he's condoned it. I'm disappointed with Captain Phythian, my friend. Very disappointed."

"So I guess we cease and desist," sighed Parsons.

"Well, maybe not," shot back Russell. "I've been ordered to refrain from any physical harm or harassment in regard to Morrison. And I will obey that order explicitly, but I'll tell you this, roomie, I will be the top graduate in our class. You can bet on that! Yes, I'm going to lay off Morrison for now. You know, I've been thinking of a way to get the upper hand and still obey Captain Phythian's edict. Rest assured, Derek, your roommate is a genius!"

13

Stephen Morrison's final year at the Naval Academy proved to be relatively uneventful. After he was released from the hospital, he reported for his summer cruise and, upon returning to Annapolis in the fall, he noticed that life had definitely improved. Although still in Coventry, most of his classmates were actually more respectful and, even to a small degree, friendlier toward him. From his first day back, he noticed that the anonymous notes with the religious epithets had ceased. He also learned that his boxing match with Russell had become something of a legend at the Naval Academy. His classmates would frequently refer to it as if it were a pivotal event in the school's history.

One thing that hadn't changed was the academic competition between him and Jared Russell. Both young men were vying for the top spot in the class. As they entered the final weeks of their last semester, it still wasn't clear who would emerge as the class valedictorian. Morrison remained a loner, while the ever-popular Russell continued to cultivate a following among his classmates and among the faculty. It was obvious to all that Russell was considered by the faculty to be the student with the greatest potential for a brilliant naval career.

Russell had remained much more engaged in extracurricular activities, unlike the shunned Morrison. Ironically, one of the extracurricular tasks given by Captain Phythian to Russell because of the Morrison beating incident proved to be the instrument of ultimate vengeance for the young man from Minnesota. A faculty decision in Spring 1892 led to the creation of a yearbook to be issued for each Naval Academy graduating class. The first class to have a yearbook, named *The Lucky Bag*, would be the class of 1893. Captain Phythian decided that the editor of the first yearbook would be Jared Russell.

In June 1893, all of the cadets could feel the excitement in the air. Not only had President Grover Cleveland been invited as the commencement speaker, but equally as titillating for all of the First Class Cadets remained the question surrounding the top two graduates. Who would emerge as first in the class? The academic grade point averages of Russell and Morrison remained so close that the superintendent decided to delay the announcement until the top two graduates actually received their diplomas. The night before the commencement ceremony, the families of the graduates arrived in Annapolis. Stephen spent the night with Mary Morrison and Joseph at the hotel. The only disappointment for the family this day would be that former Congressman Caleb Morrison had been judged too frail to travel by his doctors in New York.

The following morning, the cadets reported to the administration building to pick up their copies of *The Lucky Bag*. Eagerly anticipating its release, the class had been assured by the editor, Jared Russell, that it would be a monumental and unforgettable tribute to their years at the academy. Like his classmates, Morrison could not wait to pick up his copy and share it with his family. Everyone lined up in alphabetical order and entered the building one at a time to sign for and receive their yearbook. After being given his copy, Morrison strolled out to the quadrangle, sat alone, and began leafing through the pages.

The shock of what he saw in the book stunned him. He quickly thumbed through all of the pages to make certain he hadn't missed anything or misinterpreted what he had seen. But he had not been mistaken. It was all there in black and white. Each page of the yearbook featured two graduates per page, but on the page with Morrison's picture, his was the only picture and the back of the page was blank. His page was not numbered, but the pages preceding and following his page were consecutively numbered. To complete the insult, his page was perforated near the binding to allow for easy removal, the only such page in the entire yearbook.

Underneath his photograph was his biography, but it was not the one he had written for the yearbook. Instead it read, "Born in the town of Hebrewville, on the fifteenth day of June, 1870, in Tsarist Russia, thrown out of Russia due to incompatibility; educated in the Son of Abraham Academy; expert in history and self-advancement; destined for a short-term tenure in the United States Navy before returning to Russia where he belongs." Morrison flushed with anger as he stood up. His family waited for him to return so that they could see his yearbook. He turned slowly toward the pathway near him to begin the walk back to the hotel. As he reached the corner of the quadrangle, he walked by a trash can. Without breaking his stride, he dropped his copy of *The Lucky Bag* into the trash.

Later that morning, Captain Phythian perused his copy of the yearbook. When he came to Stephen Morrison's page, he froze. Trembling with anger, he ordered his yeoman to bring Jared Russell to his office immediately. Minutes later, Cadet Russell stood in front of his desk. Barely able to control his anger, Phythian blurted out "What the hell is this?" as he pointed to Morrison's page.

"Well, sir," began Russell very methodically, "I did follow your orders as I understood them. If you recall, you told me that if there were any other incidences of violence or harassment against Cadet Morrison, I'd be in trouble. As you plainly observed, no one laid a hand on him this past year. I followed your orders to the letter.

"Also, sir, you were the one who assigned me to be the editor of *The Lucky Bag*. I thought that it would be a gentlemanly way to end our stay at Annapolis with a little good-natured fun and satire. If anyone is offended by my humor, as you can see, they can easily remove that page and it will be as if it never existed."

Phythian managed not to raise his voice as he ordered Russell to, "Sit down and shut up!" The young man sat down with just a hint of a smile on his lips. "Listen to me, Cadet Russell. I've told you before that you have a brilliant career ahead of you because you are a leader and you're very smart. Well, you're a little too smart and a little too cute for your own good. The graduation ceremony starts in just over an hour, and you'll be graduated. Your timing is very clever." He reached into his desk drawer and removed a folder. Opening it up, he removed what appeared to be a certificate. "Do you know what this is?" he asked.

"No, sir," replied Russell, eyeing the ornate certificate with raised engraving.

"It's a certificate that we were going to inaugurate with your class for the graduating cadet who is considered to be the most likely to achieve the rank of admiral. This is to be presented at the graduation. This certificate has your name on it Cadet Russell." With that, he stood up and ripped the certificate to shreds. "Now, get the hell out of here!" he shouted.

***

The sun shone brightly, adding to the splendor of the important day in Annapolis. President Cleveland had been speaking for about twenty minutes when his speech drew to a close. "And so," he concluded, "I will end my remarks and wish all of the graduates of the Class of 1893 fair winds and following seas!" Thunderous applause erupted and the president received a standing ovation from the audience.

Captain Phythian rose and shook the president's hand as he escorted him back to his seat. He returned to the podium and announced, "We will now call the graduates up individually to receive their diplomas. Guests, proud parents, when these fine young men return to their seats, they will no longer be Naval Cadets. They will be Passed Midshipmen, awaiting their orders to their first ships, the initial step on their paths to long and proud naval careers. I will now start calling the cadets up to receive their diplomas in the reverse order of their class rank."

He called up the class anchorman, the graduate who finished last in the class academically. Many good-natured catcalls arose from the graduating class as he walked up to the stage to receive his diploma. Captain Phythian continued calling up the fifty members of the graduating class, and the process went very smoothly. Finally, only two graduates remained: Jared Russell and Stephen Morrison. The rest of the student body and faculty sat on the edge of their seats with anticipation. Among both groups, betting pools had emerged so that everyone could wager on who would be the top graduate. Now the moment had arrived.

"Ladies and gentleman, I now call up the number two graduate in the Class of 1893. He is the winner of the bronze telescope for excellence in navigation. It is my pleasure to call up ... Naval Cadet First Class Stephen Morrison!" As Morrison rose, walked up the steps, and crossed the stage to receive his diploma, Mary and Joseph Morrison applauded enthusiastically. They were joined by several other graduates. Captain Phythian shook Morrison's hand as he gave him his telescope and diploma and whispered, "Well done, Stephen."

Facing the audience again, Captain Phythian announced, "Ladies and gentlemen, I present the top graduate in the class, winner of the trophy for seamanship, Naval Cadet First Class Jared Russell!" As Russell strode up the stage, thunderous applause broke out among the graduates, guests, and faculty. Shaking hands with Captain Phythian, who gave him the trophy cup and his diploma without saying a word, Russell stopped and faced the audience and held the cup up over his head, like a conquering hero. The crowd roared its approval, and as Russell walked by Morrison on his way back to his seat, he winked at him and smiled.

***

The two rivals would never meet again. Upon graduation, Morrison received orders to the *Atlanta,* and Russell received orders to the *Boston.* Both were part of the U.S. Navy's ABCD fleet, since the four ships were named *Atlanta, Boston, Chicago,* and *Dolphin.* Although these ships were the navy's first steel warships, they were a curious combination of old sailing ships and the first steel warships of the day. In addition to steel hulls, each had two large masts forward and aft for the canvas sails that they sometimes used for propulsion.

Both men excelled at their assignments. For Morrison, being at sea was exhilarating. It was the ultimate fulfillment of his boyhood dreams. He knew that United States Navy was to be his life's work. He quickly gained a reputation in the wardroom as a serious and highly competent young officer. The enlisted men under his authority held him in high regard. Although he was very demanding, he was also very fair. During his first sea tour, it became obvious he had tremendous potential.

Russell, too, excelled aboard the *Boston*. His dominating personality clearly marked him as a leader, and he showed no lack of self-confidence. In his interview with the commanding officer shortly after reporting aboard, he was asked what his career goals were. He replied without hesitation, "To be the senior admiral in the United States Navy, sir." Russell joined the ship in San Francisco shortly after its return from the Hawaiian Islands, where it had participated in the overthrow of the Kingdom of Hawaii.

The ship remained in overhaul at the Mare Island Navy Yard at that point. The athletic Russell decided that he would begin each morning with an invigorating, brief swim in the cold waters of San Francisco Bay. In no time at all, his charismatic leadership resulted in what became known as "Russell's Polar Bears," a group of twenty officers and men who would also take part in this daily ritual. Russell led this daily swim until the following spring when, one morning, he announced that he would skip the swim. He felt unusually tired and wanted to rest.

A few days later, he developed stabbing pains in his legs and lower back. He reported to sick bay, and the ship's doctor diagnosed lumbago and prescribed heat and gentle massage to the muscles. The following day, Russell attempted to swim again, but could only last a minute before he came out. By that night, he became nauseated and began to shiver. The next morning, he reported again to sick bay and complained of weakness and diffuse muscle aches. He was febrile, and the doctor recorded a temperature of one hundred and two degrees. He also complained of having difficulty swallowing. The doctor ordered him to lie down on one of the exam tables. He had to help the young officer get up on the table, lifting his legs, because they had become so weak. Jared Russell never walked again.

The doctor arranged for Russell's transfer to the base dispensary and called in a specialist in infectious diseases. By this time, Russell had begun to have difficulty breathing. The specialist did a detailed physical examination of the young man and then went out to the waiting room where the commanding officer and the executive officer of the *Boston* waited. They stood as the doctor entered the room, but they could see by the stern look on the doctor's face that the news would be grim.

"Gentlemen, I'm afraid I have some bad news for you. After examining Mr. Russell, I'm pretty certain of his diagnosis." The doctor paused for a moment before he cleared his throat and continued. "I'm afraid he has poliomyelitis. I'm truly sorry. There's nothing that anyone can do for him."

The next morning, Passed Midshipman Jared Russell died. He was twenty-three years old.

14

December 3, 1896
Ensign Stephen L. Morrison, USN
United States Cruiser Brooklyn
FPO 46
Philadelphia, Pennsylvania
United States of America

My dear Stephen,

I can't begin to tell you how much your last letter cheered me! I wish it wasn't a matter of months between the time we write to each other and the arrival of the letters. Nonetheless, it delights my soul to hear from you. You certainly sound as if you are doing well and that a career in the United States Navy agrees with you.

How exciting it must be to sail on a brand new ship like the Brooklyn! And how proud you must be to be a commissioned officer! When are you next slated for a promotion? Remember, I will not be content until you are an admiral and are well on your way to becoming the American president!

How did you like South America when you were there earlier this year? You never told me whether you behaved like an officer or not. I'll take it as a matter of faith that you represented your country well. How proud your father would be if he were alive to see how you've grown and developed into the man I knew he hoped you would be. As for my father, we barely acknowledge each other's existence. I believe our relationship is a metaphor for the relationship between the Russian government and the people it supposedly serves. Yes, my friend, things continue to deteriorate here.

I know you are aware that Nicholas has been Tsar since Alexander III died over two years ago. Yes, he's now Tsar Nicholas II, a lofty sounding title for such an unworthy individual! I can't recall if I told you that in his first public speech after the death of his father, what does he choose to talk about? His right to an absolute autocracy! He and the state are one. My God, Stephen, he sounded like Louis XIV: "L'etat, c'est moi!" What a message he picked to begin his reign! He merely gave Russia a preview of things to come. But I must tell you about his coronation.

As per our church protocol, there was a mourning period for Alexander for over a year. No official state celebrations of any kind were observed. It was finally decided to have Nicholas' coronation last May. Russian tradition, going back to the start of the Romanov dynasty, has dictated that the Tsar will be formally anointed in Moscow. My family was invited to attend all of the coronation proceedings and, of course, we attended. The crowning ceremony took place on May 14 at the Assumption Cathedral, and I must admit that it was a beautiful ceremony. My family was in the third pew and, due to my father's distinguished position, we were invited to attend the Bolshoi that evening along with the royal family and several other prominent families. As is tradition, they performed the first and last act of "Life of the Tsar," as well as a new ballet called "The Pearl." It was a pleasant, if not over-indulgent, evening.

The next several days were endless parties and balls. Remember, dear friend, virtually all of the crowned heads of Europe were in Moscow for the festivities. It was quite a spectacle, and I suppose the royal family was quite pleased. The final day of the coronation festivities was to be May 18. That day, Stephen, was a day of horrors that will live in my mind forever. I almost cannot describe to you the terrible events of that day. I get furious even thinking about it. Again, it has to do with our Russian traditions.

I know it probably sounds somewhat quaint to a world-traveling American such as yourself, but after a coronation in Russia, it is customary for the peasantry to gather in tribute to the new Tsar, and for the Tsar to have a celebration for the masses. Hundreds of thousands of people, mainly peasants, gather on the outskirts of Moscow for the gala where the Tsar provides them free food and beverage, as well as ceremonial mugs. It was arranged for them on the Khodynka Field where tents were set up for the festivities. Khodynka Field was not a wise choice. It was not quite big enough to accommodate the huge crowds. In addition, there are several ditches in the terrain in between where the crowds were assembled and where the tents were set up. I understand there were over a half million people present.

No one knows exactly how it all started. Some suspect that rumors were starting to circulate that they were running out of food, mugs, and beverages. The crowd started surging forward and people began to be knocked off their feet to the ground. The people on the edge of the ditches lost their footing and fell into the shallow little valleys as the waves of people moved forward and trampled them. A general panic soon broke out, and the crowds became uncontrollable. Men, women, children—hundreds were crushed to death by the crowds. I later saw a police report, and it was shocking. They estimated that nearly two thousand people were trampled to death on the Khodynka Field that morning. I am told that the grounds looked like a battlefield with broken bodies, shattered limbs, and blood everywhere.

This shocking tragedy would seem to be the sad but logical end of the coronation ceremonies. Incredibly, this was not the case! The government decided to go on with the festivities! Broken bodies were discretely removed in wagons so as not to disturb the gaiety of the evening where the royals danced at their opulent balls! His people are crushed to death, and yet the Tsar and his fellow oppressors dance on! Stephen, you can't imagine my horror—no, my shame—at this spectacle! I have never been so ashamed to be a Russian as I was that day. And yet, the story gets worse.

Romanov family politics and squabbling soon took over the situation. Nicholas' mother, Empress Marie Feodorovna, knowing what a weakling her son is, insisted on the immediate creation of a commission of inquiry with the purpose of punishing the guilty parties. She knew full well that her brother-in-law, Alexander's brother Grand Duke Sergei Alexandrovich, as Governor-General of Moscow and organizer of the coronation ceremonies, would shoulder the blame. She also demanded that Nicholas cancel the remaining coronation festivities. I am told that he initially agreed to do this.

But as you can see, dear Stephen, nothing in Tsarist politics is simple. Apparently, there is much bad blood between the empress-mother and the new Tsarina. Alexandra forbade Nicholas to cancel the remaining balls and receptions. As if this weren't enough of a conflict for the spineless Nicholas, there was another factor in play here. Grand Duke Sergei Alexandrovich is husband of Alexandra's sister! There was absolutely no way that she would allow her brother-in-law to become the scapegoat for the Khodynda debacle. Needless to say, Nicholas changed his mind and sided with his wife, much to the fury of his mother. That night, they danced and celebrated as if nothing had happened. This resulted in much gossip throughout Russia about the new Tsar's lack of compassion, as you can well imagine.

The final farce to the whole Khodynka incident was the commission of inquiry that Nicholas finally did appoint. I learned that the empress-mother personally picked its figurehead leader, another sycophant, Count Pahlen. Apparently, the commission wanted to at least give the appearance of a genuine investigating authority that was interested in getting to the truth. Again, Romanov politics intervened. Two of the Tsar's uncles threatened to resign from the court if Grand Duke Sergei Alexandrovich was harmed because of the investigation. So the entire affair was whitewashed, and some minor bureaucrat took the fall. A disgusting resolution to a horrid affair!

It has been months since this event occurred, and do you know what galls me most, Stephen? The total lack of response by the peasantry! They turn the other cheek and do nothing, except to virtually invite the Tsar and his cabal to strike them again! As you no doubt have detected by the tone of my past several letters, I have been coming to a sad but necessary conclusion. That is this: the philosophy of populism, bringing up the peasantry to lead the revolution, is flawed; it is wrong. The peasants are not the answer- they are only interested in increasing their status to become capitalists, not revolutionaries. It pains me to think of the hours, the years, I have spent on this quest, only to learn that it is not the right way.

I now believe the answer lies with the workers to lead the revolution. My colleagues and I are enthralled by the writings of Georgii Plekhanov. This visionary of a man has elucidated the tenets of Marxism to the Russian revolutionary activists such as myself. Although he is in exile, his work, "On the Question of Developing a Monistic View of History," is sheer brilliance and has galvanized us! Yes, we will continue our two-phased strategy as before. First, the establishment of a "bourgeois democracy" to prime the revolution. But now, it is the workers of Russia, not the peasantry, who will accomplish this goal. The second phase will remain that of a socialist revolution that will seize power for the workers and all the people of Russia! To further my participation in this great endeavor, I have joined with the Marxists in St. Petersburg.

Already we are making a difference. We Marxists are not only spreading our message with propaganda, but we've also resorted to mass agitation in the form of labor strikes. You would be amazed, Stephen, but last year we actually organized a massive labor strike in St. Petersburg. We had over thirty thousand workers in the streets protesting. The price of our success was high. Two of my esteemed colleagues, Julius Martov and Vladimir Ulyanov, were arrested and jailed. I myself barely escaped the authorities. But we all realize that the cost of freedom is high, and we are willing to pay the price.

I'm not sure how long I can remain at Putilov. My revolutionary activities are becoming a full-time job, and I have more disgust each day when I see our workers toiling under such exploitive conditions. I believe my father will be relieved to see me go.

So, Stephen, the hour grows late, and I must prepare for a meeting. Forgive me for venting so to you, but you know that it is therapeutic for me to share all of these things with you. You will never know what an important thing your friendship is to me. I am longing for the day when we can get together for dinner in a free Russia. I pray it happens in our lifetimes! Remain safe, my friend, and know I am thinking of you.

Your friend always,
Yuri

15

*Aboard the United States Monitor Monterey
Yangtze River, China
November 1901*

Despite the late evening hour, Lieutenant William Sims continued to write by the dim light in his cabin. His ship, the monitor *Monterey*, had left Shanghai earlier that day to begin a slow patrol up the river. He never tired of his writing ritual, and when his watches ended, he would frequently be found putting his thoughts to paper. His thoughts always involved the navy. For Sims, the navy was his life. A bachelor in his early forties, he had no outside interests and considered himself married to the service. Tall, handsome, and articulate, his brilliance was somewhat contradicted by his middle-of-the-class graduation standing in the United States Naval Academy, Class of 1880.

Considering his junior officer status, Sims was both pleased and flattered that he had a growing reputation and a fairly large following in navy circles. He was representative of the new breed of naval officers; those who sought true reform and improvement in many facets of the navy. The young reformers found themselves opposed by the inertia of the establishment—the old school senior officers who tended to stifle innovative thought and seemed to be content to grow old in their admirals' uniforms. Despite these obstacles, Sims had become the voice of the younger generation. This status resulted largely from the frequent airing of his ideas and impressions in the form of lengthy letters not only to the Navy Department, but to many of his colleagues as well. He had returned to sea duty only the year before after having served as naval attaché in Paris, Madrid, and St. Petersburg for a three-year period. During that tenure, he had ample time to write and send a voluminous amount of reports on a myriad of topics. These reports were widely read, and he had developed a cult following of officers who looked forward to reading the latest report of Sims' impressions. Among those who had been impressed by his reports was the Assistant Secretary of the Navy, Theodore Roosevelt, who took the time to send an occasional short letter to the observant naval attaché. After three years in Europe, Sims received orders to the battleship *Kentucky* in Gibraltar and sailed to the Far East, where he joined the *Monterey* on China Station.

It was not in Sims' personality to remain an underground icon. He freely acknowledged that he was an extremely opinionated officer and was especially passionate about two issues: naval gunfire marksmanship (or rather, the lack thereof) and battleship design. His main fear was that he might be destined to remain only an idea man who was a prolific letter writer; one who, in the end, would not make a difference in his beloved navy. In September 1901, an event occurred that was to change the lives of many people, including the life of Lieutenant William Sims. An assassin's bullet took the life of President William McKinley, and on September 19, Vice President Theodore Roosevelt was sworn in as president of the United States. Roosevelt, an avid naval historian and former assistant secretary of the navy, was also a reformer and innovative thinker. When Sims learned that Roosevelt had taken office, he realized that it was time to gamble, and he was ready to roll the dice.

As he finished the lengthy letter that evening, he knew he would be violating naval protocol. He was about to correspond directly with the president of the United States. Doing so was unheard of. All such letters had to be vetted through the chain of command and, ultimately, through the Navy Department before they would even be sent to the White House. Once there, the odds of penetrating the White House bureaucracy were indeed slim. It was highly unlikely that Roosevelt would ever see the original letter. However, Sims felt that he had a kindred spirit in Roosevelt, and, if he read the man correctly, the letter just might bypass the White House bureaucracy and make it to the president personally. If Roosevelt did receive the letter, Sims was confident that the president would give a fair hearing to his ideas. The issue that Sims wrote about that particular November evening was the horrendous state of affairs in naval gunfire, and his ideas on how to remedy the problem.

Although he was in Europe during the Spanish-American War, Sims had become extremely knowledgeable about all facets of the war. He had studied the gunnery results extensively and was mortified, although not surprised, by the results. He had been disgusted to read that in the battle of Manila Bay, Admiral Dewey's ships had fired about six thousand projectiles and recorded fewer than 150 hits on target. The Battle of Santiago produced even worse results. He had recently read the results of a special target practice by the North Atlantic Squadron during which all five ships managed to hit their target a total of only two times! These dismal results seemed to be the standard for the United States Navy and for many of the world's other naval forces as well. The old guard was content to live with this reality. William Sims was not, and he had an answer.

During his time in Far East, he had befriended Captain Sir Percy Scott, commanding officer of HMS *Terrible*. Scott himself was a known naval innovator and a rebel like Sims. Scott had heard about his writing exploits and felt an instant kinship for the young American officer. "You know, Lieutenant Sims, to our respective navies, we are both royal pains in the arse!" Scott had expounded over dinner in the *Terrible*'s wardroom. The effect of several brandies made that comment outrageously funny to both of the officers, as well as the other British officers dining with them. It was at that dinner that Scott got the idea to have Sims go out to sea with them. "Why not see a demonstration of real gunnery instead of the rot that passes for it in the British and American navies?" offered the enthusiastic commanding officer. Sims eagerly accepted the offer after receiving permission from his own commanding officer.

At sea the next week, Sims watched the *Terrible* demonstrate its skill at naval gunnery. The results astounded him. Round after round was delivered right on target with deadly accuracy. Scott had shown Sims that this accuracy resulted from a system that he had developed called "continuous-aim firing." Sims realized that he now had the answer he had been seeking. He became determined to introduce this innovative idea to the United States Navy. Scott taught him all facets of the new technique. Sims knew that the old guard would oppose any such innovations, but he had the support of a very influential officer, Rear Admiral George Remey, Commander in Chief of the Asiatic Fleet. Remey had liked Sims' ideas and promised a strong endorsement of his letter. Sims also believed that if he could just get the letter to President Roosevelt that he, too, would support his ideas on gunfire.

Sims finished his lengthy letter and folded it neatly. He would arrange to have it delivered to Rear Admiral Remey as soon as possible for his endorsement. He stretched, yawned, and then thought to himself, *I have the watch from 0400 to 0800, and it is nearly midnight. I had better get some sleep.* He undressed to his underwear and climbed into his rack. In his mind, he replayed the sight of round after round hitting its intended target. It proved to be better than counting sheep. He fell asleep in minutes.

***

On an unseasonably warm January afternoon, Lieutenant William Sims stood on the bridge of the *Monterey*. He was assigned as officer of the deck for the 1200-1600 watch as they began to make the first approach to Shanghai. As he looked out over the forward turret that housed two of the *Monterey*'s twelve-inch guns, he could see the sun first beginning to set as his watch drew to a close. He reflected on his tour aboard the *Monterey*. Surprisingly, he had enjoyed it tremendously, much more that he had expected. The four-thousand-ton ship actually handled quite well, although speed was a definite problem. The ship could only make six, perhaps seven knots at best.

Sims had become very well respected among the other eighteen officers and 136 enlisted crew of the *Monterey*. Best of all, he had ample time for his writing.

His watch relief, Lieutenant Junior Grade Ellis Hansen, had just reported to the bridge for their turnover. After relaying all of the relevant data, they saluted each other and Hansen crisply barked, "I've got the conn." Returning the salute, Sims replied, "I stand relieved." As Sims began to walk out of the bridge house,

Hansen called after him, "Mr. Sims, I almost forgot. The skipper wants to see you in his cabin as soon as you come off watch."

"Any idea what it's about?" asked Sims.

"I really don't know, sir. I was just told to give you the message."

"Very well then," Sims replied as he exited the bridge and headed for the captain's cabin. After knocking on the door, the captain ordered him to enter. The commanding officer of the *Monterey* was Commander Eugene Luetze, a pleasant man whom Sims greatly admired. "Please sit down, Mr. Sims," he offered, "I have something for you." As Sims took a seat at the table where the skipper was seated, Luetze handed him an envelope. "It's not every day a member of my crew gets a personal letter from the president of the United States! Congratulations, Mr. Sims," he said, beaming with pride.

Sims stared at the envelope, which had a White House franking insignia in the upper left corner. It was addressed to "LT William S. Sims, USN, c/o Commanding Officer Monterey, FPO China Station Shanghai." The next line read, "Personal and Confidential." Sims began to open the envelope and then looked up at his skipper. "Go ahead, if you like," assured Commander Luetze, "or, if you prefer to go back to your stateroom to read it, feel free to do so. After all, it is a personal letter. I only ask that you use your judgment to keep me informed on any of the contents that are germane to this command. You are dismissed, Mr. Sims." Sims promptly thanked his skipper and departed for his cabin.

Closing the door behind him, he sat on his rack and stared at the envelope. The very fact that he was receiving a personal letter from President Roosevelt told him that his letter had made it directly to the president as he had hoped. His gamble had been successful! Now to see what Roosevelt had written. *Let's see if I read this man correctly,* Sims thought to himself as he carefully tore open the envelope. He unfolded the short, one-page letter, noting the stationery head containing the engraved block letters PRESIDENT OF THE UNITED STATES.

"My dear LT Sims," it began, "I have read with great interest your letter dated 16 November 1901." It was a short, polite letter in which Roosevelt thanked Sims for his thoughtful letter and invited him to correspond again. He assured Sims that any further letters from him would be brought to his personal attention. That was the entire content of the letter. Sims pulled his legs up on the rack and stretched back, the letter face down on his chest. After staring at the overhead for a few minutes, he re-read the letter. The letter said absolutely nothing at first and second glance. His letter, it would appear, had no impact on Roosevelt.

But Sims began weighing the evidence before him. Why would the president of the United States even bother to write a personal letter to a lieutenant? Especially a letter that said nothing and yet invited him to write again and guaranteed that the president would personally read the letters? As Sims lay back with his hands behind his head, he suspected that perhaps he had succeeded in his gamble.

In fact, Sims was correct in his suspicions. Several weeks before, President Roosevelt had read Sims' letter and had been thoroughly impressed with the lieutenant's proposals. He had remembered Sims' informative letters from Europe, and when he received the November 16th letter, he knew he had a kindred spirit, and one he needed to cultivate. Never one to be satisfied with the status quo, Roosevelt had found the perfect man to whom he would entrust the modernization of the United States Navy, a rebel and reformer like himself. Interestingly, they were exactly the same age, and both young men were eager for the missions on which they were embarking.

Roosevelt did note one problem with his plans for Sims. He was still a junior officer. Throwing obvious support and responsibilities to such a junior officer could negatively affect the man's career. The entrenched bureaucracy would resent the younger man's influence and would work within the archaic status quo to diminish Sims' promotability and destroy his naval career. *No,* Roosevelt reasoned to himself, *I have to be subtle with this situation.* Instead, he ordered that Sims' report on the poor state of naval gunnery be printed and sent to every officer on active duty in the navy. The reports would be sent without any reference to Lieutenant William Sims. Roosevelt, determined to overhaul the navy, knew that Sims' letter would be his opening salvo. What the entrenched old-school bureaucracy did not know was that a junior officer, Lieutenant William S. Sims, had supplied the president's ammunition.

In late January, the *Monterey* tied up pier-side in Shanghai when a wagon arrived from the U.S. Consulate with mail for the crew. Mail call sounded with the usual trumpets and the administrative department handed out the sorted mail. Each of the officers that day received an identical official letter from the Navy Department. The title was: "On the State of Naval Gunnery," and the letter explained the poor state of marksmanship in the navy. It went on to state that improvement in naval gun accuracy would be a priority of the president. It did not describe a remedy, but it put the navy on notice. Change was coming.

That evening in the wardroom, his fellow officers congratulated Sims, for they all knew that this coming change was because of his influence on the president. Commander Luetze proposed a toast to Sims, and the wardroom downed several rounds in tribute to their outspoken rebel leader. Sims was euphoric. He had been correct. He had read Roosevelt correctly, and his gamble had paid off. Soon it would be time to begin his important work in earnest.

16

Aboard the USS Indiana
Brooklyn Navy Yard
March 1903

As Lieutenant William Sims walked across the officers' brow onto the large battleship, he paused at the summit, faced the ship's stern, and rendered a smart salute to the national ensign. Walking to the Officer of the Deck, dressed in his service dress blues with a telescope under his left arm, Sims approached and in a firm voice said, "Request permission to come aboard," as he saluted. The Officer of the Deck returned his salute, replying, "Permission granted. Can I assist you, sir?" he inquired.

"Yes, young man, you most certainly can. I have an appointment with the CO, Captain Robinson."

"I'll have an escort take you to his cabin, sir," the OOD offered and summoned an escort. The ship's secretary, an earnest young man who tended to the CO's daily schedule, informed Sims that the captain would be ready for him in about fifteen minutes and invited him to take a seat. Sims sat in one of the comfortable chairs in the CO's outer office and looked at the photographs of the *Indiana* that covered all of the bulkheads. Sims remembered that this very ship was another example of the innovation and creativity of his patron, Theodore Roosevelt. He recalled that, as assistant secretary of the navy, Roosevelt had pushed for funding of three battleships as his first step toward transforming the U.S. Navy into a blue-water sea power. The isolationist sentiment in the United States Congress was very strong at that time, and representatives opposed funding for long-range battleships, fearing they would be provocative to foreign powers. Roosevelt cleverly obtained the funding by assuring Congress that the new class of ships would be called "sea-going coast-line battleships," implying that their only role would be coastal defense.

As he sat patiently, Sims reviewed the events of the past year that had radically changed his life. The catalyst was his relationship with President Roosevelt. Interestingly, they had first met face-to-face only weeks before. Throughout the past year, his writings continued to be distributed navy-wide, all as a result of Roosevelt's endorsement. Although his name did not appear on any of these documents, all officers in the navy knew that William S. Sims was the author. Then, in September 1902, Sims had received orders to detach from the *Monterey* and proceed to the Navy Department in Washington, D.C. where his new job was to be "Inspector of Target Practice." Theodore Roosevelt had handed him the keys to the kingdom.

Shortly after his arrival in Washington, Sims had his first meeting with Roosevelt. The two men took an immediate liking to each other. The president's confidence in Sims was further reinforced by the plan that Sims proposed to him. With typical

Sims flair, the young officer proposed that he demonstrate his ideas in a headline-capturing fashion that would change gunnery practices overnight. After presenting his plan, the president authorized the new Inspector of Target Practice to proceed with presidential approval and arranged to have orders cut that, in essence, gave Lieutenant Sims complete authority over the project. Roosevelt also ordered all other officers, regardless of seniority, to cooperate with him.

Now, as Sims sat waiting to talk with the CO of the *Indiana*, he smiled, knowing that this ship would be perfect for his purposes. The *Indiana* had fought in the Battle of Santiago during the war and had generated a dismal record for marksmanship. It also had a reputation for being a difficult ship for gunners to fire from due to design flaws. The main gun mountings had not been constructed directly over the ship's keel. This lack of central stability caused the side of the ship where the guns were aimed to dip lower than the opposite side, thereby limiting the elevation that would be required for the guns to hit the target. The last advantage was the ship's mission itself. She was a training ship that performed training exercises and fleet maneuvers, as well as providing practice cruises for the midshipmen, as they now were called at the United States Naval Academy. The *Indiana* could effectively disappear, while Sims put his experiment into pratice. The ship wouldn't be missed.

"Captain Robinson will see you now," announced the ship's secretary, opening the door for the visitor. Sims thanked him and entered as Captain William Robinson greeted him with a firm handshake. He invited his guest to sit and rang for his mess steward. "Please bring the lieutenant and me some coffee," he ordered, as Sims opened his attaché case and began removing papers.

"Captain, thank you so much for this preliminary meeting. Are the arrangements still for us to get underway in a week, sir?"

"That is correct, Mr. Sims. Let me say that, for a lieutenant, you have an incredible amount of clout," he remarked with a touch of resentment in his tone. "Admiral Nixon contacted me and told me only that we are to make preparations to get underway for at least four weeks. Our destination and our mission would be brought to us by a Lieutenant William Sims, acting with full authority of the president of the United States. To date, I've received only one piece of communication from you. I sure as hell hope you are going to enlighten me now, Lieutenant."

"Yes, sir, that is why I'm here today." Pulling the operational orders from his case, Sims continued. "We will be proceeding down to the Caribbean operating area. There we will link up with some targeting drones that I've arranged for. Captain, we are going to revolutionize naval gunnery, and the *Indiana* is going to make history accomplishing this feat."

"Yes, I've read your writings, Mr. Sims. To be blunt, your proposal seems like a lot of theory to me. Can you really pull this off, whatever it is that you plan to do? Also, I assume this whole mission is top secret."

"Yes to both questions, sir. We will accomplish our mission. I guarantee it. And that, sir, leads me to my next question. You just mentioned my prior communication. Regarding the request in that communication, do you have the candidate for me?"

"Oh, that," replied Robinson. "That was easy. You asked me to select the smartest, most talented, and most respected junior officer on the ship. Piece of cake." The Captain smiled as he walked over to his desk and picked up a brown folder. Walking back to the table, he dropped the officer's service record onto the table directly in front of Lieutenant Sims. The name on the front of the service record read, "Lieutenant Junior Grade Stephen L. Morrison."

***

The following day, Lieutenant Stephen Morrison reported to William Sims' stateroom as he had been ordered. He had no idea with whom he would be meeting or why he had been ordered there. After he knocked on the door, a voice from inside ordered him to enter. Closing the door behind him, Morrison saw the tall lieutenant standing by the porthole, gazing out. The man turned to him and extended his hand. "Hello, Lieutenant Morrison, I'm Lieutenant William Sims. Thank you for arriving so promptly," he said as he shook the younger man's hand.

Startled, Morrison stared at the bearded, handsome officer, finally replying, "Yes. Yes, sir. I've read a lot of your writings. It's a pleasure, no, an honor to meet you. I had no idea you were aboard the *Indiana*."

"Well, it's a somewhat secretive mission that I'm on. Please, sit down. We have a lot to discuss. First off, let's dispense with the formalities. You are to call me William in private, and I'll call you Stephen. Understood? You see, Stephen, we don't have a lot of time to do what I'm here to do, and that is to alter the future of naval warfare. You and I are going to bring the United States Navy into the twentieth century, kicking and screaming if necessary!"

Morrison sat there, stunned to be hearing this statement from a man whose writings he so admired. But what did he have to do with Sims' plans? "Sir, I mean William, I'm confused. What is it exactly that you need me for?"

"In due time, Stephen," replied the energetic Sims. He had Morrison's service jacket in his hands. Thumbing through it for a few seconds, he looked up at the younger man. "I read through this last night. Very impressive. You've had excellent fitness reports, but I want to know a little more about you. Tell me about yourself, Stephen."

"Well, there's not really much to tell. I mean, I suppose I'm just a typical Naval Academy grad, Class of 1893. This is my third ship, and I love sea duty. Ever since I was a little boy, I've wanted to be a naval officer and to travel. That's really all there is to it."

"Stephen, where are you from originally?"

"I was raised in New York City."

"Were you born there?"

"No, sir, I was born in Russia. My family came to the United States when I was a youngster. I was orphaned, and my adoptive parents were New Yorkers."

"Interesting." Sims flipped a page in the service jacket and then spoke again. "They say you are quite an athlete. It says that you were the boxing champion on every ship you've served on." Looking up at Morrison, he quipped, "You certainly look fit! Where did you learn to fight so well? Are you aggressive by nature?"

"Well, I learned to fight growing up in New York City. It's almost a way of life there. Am I aggressive, you ask? I would say no, but I believe in standing up for principles, and I believe there is a line between right and wrong that I won't cross, and I won't allow others to cross it when that line affects me. I'm not sure if that answers your question or not."

"No, that's fine. Tell me, Stephen, it also says here that you're quite a linguist. You speak Russian fluently? I don't know if you know it, but I spent several months as the naval attaché to the American embassy in St. Petersburg. I wish I had your fluency for the language. Have you ever been back to Russia?"

"Yes, I have. I was there for several months in 1888. I hope to go back someday. It's a fascinating country."

"Lastly, Stephen, it says that on every ship you served on you volunteered to be the ship's historian and that you started a regular lecture series at sea. That's quite ingenious. Can I ask why you do this work? I mean, you have a reputation as a technical expert. Why history?"

Morrison couldn't understand why Sims asked all of these questions about his background, but he tried to answer as honestly as he could. Perhaps this was a test that had something to do with Morrison's fitness to work with Sims on his quest to—how had Sims put it?—bring the United States Navy kicking and screaming into the twentieth century. He looked Sims straight in the eye and spoke. "Why history? I would counter, William, why not history? Without a background in where we've been, we have no rudder to steer us, no chart to guide our way into the future. We have to learn the mistakes of the past so we don't repeat them over and over and over. Without knowledge and a sense of our American tradition, how can we know what we in the military are truly about? How can those of us in the military do our jobs if we don't know what George Washington, Thomas Jefferson, and Abraham Lincoln faced and what they stood for?" Morrison paused for a minute, seeing that Sims was staring at him almost transfixed. "I'm sorry, sir; it's a subject about which I am passionate."

"No, Stephen, that's fine, really excellent," he said as he closed the service jacket. *I've found the right man,* Sims thought to himself. Folding his hands on the table in front of them, Sims spoke again. "Stephen, let me tell you what the mission is, what we will accomplish on this cruise. Are you familiar with my writings on continuous-aim firing? I assume you are. Well, my new job in the Navy Department is Inspector of Target Practice. I have been given a mandate and a free hand by President Roosevelt himself for this venture upon which we are about to embark.

"We will be going to sea in six days. We will be steaming to the Caribbean operating area, and we will be maintaining strict emissions control—no messages to or from the ship. There we will be training continuously in the technique of continuous-aim firing, using the forward turret initially. If the training goes as I anticipate, we will also train the aft turret. I need someone to lead the turret teams, to train those men to act as a team and to perform their duties both expertly and expeditiously. Stephen, you will lead this team. I will, of course, oversee the project, but you will be the team leader. After all, I can't realistically expect that as an outsider, I can just come aboard a ship and win the respect and loyalty that you have achieved by your year aboard. Are you following me?"

"Yes, sir. And after we master the technique, what then?"

"Ah, yes, I was coming to that." A large grin spread across Sims' face. "I have scheduled a gunnery exercise off the Atlantic coast in the Philadelphia operating area. The *Indiana* will be one of five ships competing in this exercise. Here's the whole point of this project of ours. The other ships will manage their usual mediocre to dismal performance, which the senior admirals seem to be content with, while we will achieve a perfect score. Do you understand what I'm saying, Stephen? Not a good or great score, but a perfect score! That will change things overnight for the navy. And here's the beautiful part. You, Lieutenant Junior Grade Stephen Morrison, will have trained and supervised the gunnery team, not me. This will no longer be Sims' pet project that only he wants or understands. A very junior officer will have demonstrated it to the world! Pretty damn exciting, don't you think?"

"Yes, it is. I must admit I'm intrigued. And this whole at-sea period is some big secret?"

"It is. The CO has been instructed to accommodate all of my directives to complete this mission. That comes straight from President Roosevelt. You see, Stephen, we cannot afford to fail. We *will* not fail. There is too much at stake here."

Morrison current job aboard the *Indiana* was that of assistant navigator. He brought that up to Sims, who countered "Not a problem. That has already been taken care of by the CO. As of this moment, you are the gunnery officer. Any other thoughts, problems, or issues, young man?"

"Well, yes. I've read about continuous-aim firing, but there really hasn't been anything published that I've seen with enough detail on the process. I know that you'll teach me over these next few weeks, but it a nutshell, how does it work?"

Sims smiled at his protégé and laughed. "How does it work? Stephen, that's the beautiful part. It's really not that complicated, either the principle or the process. I know you worked for the gunner aboard the *Brooklyn* for a while, so I know you understand the current principles of targeting and fire control. Currently, all of our guns have those antiquated, worthless notched sights. As a result, our gunners only aim to fire at the target when the ship's rocking motion brings the target right into the notched sight.

"I was with Captain Percy Scott aboard the HMS *Terrible* in the China Sea and saw him deliver ordinance on target continuously. And here's how he did it. He had his gunners keep the gun pointed at the target at all times, regardless of the rocking motion of the ship. In addition, Captain Scott disposed of those worthless notched gun sights and replaced them with a modified telescope that he attached to the top of the gun. This scope really magnified the targets. Also, Scott had cross hairs installed into the telescope lenses. This modification made the targeting more precise. That's basically it, Stephen. It's that simple.

"Of course, when I first reported on this, the powers that be were unimpressed. Even the Chief of the Bureau of Ordinance opposed my concept. Do you know what that unimaginative idiot did? He claimed that he tried to duplicate the process, and it didn't work. Of course, what he did was use a gun that was mounted to one of the seawalls at the Washington Navy Yard. He claimed that the gunner, when targeting, had no way to overcome the resistance involved in raising and lowering the gun to simulate a ship's rolling motion. Case closed! You see Stephen, in the United States Navy, everyone thinks that continuous-aim firing is pure theory and will not work. I include your CO, Captain Robinson, in this group, by the way." Sims stopped and took a drink of water from the glass on his desk. "Now, Stephen, that is our mission. We will begin in the morning, after I unpack the new telescopes I mentioned. I had them custom-made in Washington. Any further questions before we break?"

"No, sir. I can't think of any at the moment."

"Then you're dismissed. We'll get together at 1000 tomorrow." The two men shook hands. Sims was delighted that Morrison appeared to be just as enthused about the whole project as he was. As Morrison walked out the door, he turned and said, "William, thanks for selecting me for this duty. I really am honored."

Sims' face beamed with a broad smile when he replied, "Remember, Stephen, we will be making history!" As the young man shut the door behind him, Sims thought to himself, *I have found the right man. He is an extraordinary individual.*

***

Sims knew he had to change the entire procedure of target practice, and he had prepared well for the exercise. He knew that resentment had grown among junior officers over the farce that gunnery practice had become. The results of the Spanish-American war still resonated in his mind as he developed his plan. He envisioned a new way of conducting gunnery competition that would shock the navy into the modern era.

Before the *Indiana* departed on its history-making cruise, Sims gloomily recounted to Morrison the current state of the art. Gunnery practice consisted of a ship firing from a prescribed distance of a thousand yards to an area between two buoys. Aligned with the buoys would be a boat containing the judges, who estimated where the ordinance landed and where it would have struck a ship had there been one between the buoys. The judges drew intricate diagrams to record their findings. The ship's gunnery proficiency was then evaluated on these drawings. It also galled Sims that the ship could take as much time as it wished before firing. That entire system was about to end.

Sims had brought aboard two twenty-foot by twenty-foot square wooden rafts, each with fifteen-foot high posts on either side. A thin wooden target featuring a large red solid circle would be installed between the poles. Sims intended to have these target rafts towed by a small surface craft and for the *Indiana* to practice its gunfire on these targets. He had arranged for small boats from San Juan to rendezvous with the battleship off the coast of Puerto Rico to perform the towing duties. The ship would drill daily in secrecy until Sims felt the results he desired had been achieved. Only then would the *Indiana* proceed to the Atlantic coast for her final examination: the next gunnery competition for the North Atlantic Squadron.

***

On the transit down to the Caribbean, Sims and Morrison installed the telescopic sights on the two thirteen-inch guns in the forward turret and attached two small caliber rifles with telescopic sights to the two thirteen-inch guns in the aft turret. Shortly after the installations, Morrison mustered both of the turrets' gun crews. After introducing Sims to his men, Morrison explained their assignment. He would personally oversee the operations in the forward turret, and Ensign Jack Harramore would be his assistant supervising the aft turret operations. He began describing the basics of continuous-aim firing and concluded by informing the men of the upcoming gunnery competition. He summed up by announcing, "Men, we will be firing ordinance every fifteen to twenty seconds while we are running at full speed, and we will achieve one-hundred-percent accuracy. Make no mistake about it, we will hit the target with every round!"

The stunned gun crews just looked at each other in disbelief. The Leading Chief Petty Officer of the gunnery department, Chief Thad McFadden, finally broke the silence. "Sir," he said cautiously, "that ain't possible!"

Sharply, Morrison replied, "Yes, it is possible, and we *will* achieve this goal! Am I clear on this to all of you? Now, let's muster on the enlisted mess decks for some didactic lecturing on the technique by Lieutenant Sims. Dismissed!" Grumbling, the men fell out and headed for the mess decks.

Each turret on the *Indiana* had two gun crews. Each gun crew consisted of a gun pointer who actually aimed the gun, the gun captain in charge of the overall operation of the gun, a loader who opened and shut the breech of the gun, and the rammer who rammed the powder and ordinance into the breech. Morrison explained that they would work solely with the forward turret initially. Chief McFadden would be his assistant. Sims used a chalkboard to explain the principles of continuous-aim firing. "To give the pointers the feel of what we are trying to achieve, Mr. Morrison and I installed small rifles parallel to the guns of the rear turrets. The triggers of the thirteen inch guns have been modified so that when you sight your target through the telescopic lens and fire the thirteen-incher, it will fire the small rifle. That way, we can sight your guns by checking the results of the rifle hits on target and, at the same time, introduce you to the technique. Men, from now on, Mr. Morrison is in charge. Tomorrow, we do our first drills. Good luck and remember, we are going to change history with our efforts!"

***

The next day's initial practice rounds did not go well. Old habits proved hard to break, and the pointers had difficulty with the new concept of using the telescopes continuously. Learning to adjust for the rolling of the ship added to the frustration levels. At the end of the session, Morrison tried not to be overly critical of their performance, but he informed them that each day, he would expect a measure of improvement. This approach did not sit well with Chief McFadden. He had been a gunner's mate for over twenty years and was very set in his ways. He resented this outsider Lieutenant Sims coming aboard and imposing this new nonsense on his gun crews. This new technique couldn't possibly work.

At the next morning's muster, the temperature already exceeded eighty degrees, and the tropical sun brutally beat down on the assembled gunners. As Morrison walked up to them, Ensign Harramore shouted, "Atten-shun!" The two rows of men smartly snapped to attention. Morrison ordered them at ease and began to go over the plan of the day. When he finished, Chief McFadden requested permission to speak before they left to man the turret. Morrison granted permission and McFadden began.

"Mr. Morrison, this new stuff ain't practical. I've been firing these guns for a long time, since you were in toddler's britches, and I know guns. This is too hard, and it don't work. I respectfully recommend, sir, that we go back to the way we always done things." A few murmurs of assent arose from the assembled gunners.

At first, Morrison just stared at the chief. The men could see the anger in his eyes as he began to speak. "Is that so, Chief? Well, consider yourself relieved. Get the hell out of here. You're no longer involved in this exercise, and I'll ask the XO to have you transferred out of the gunnery department for the duration." The stunned sailor started to speak, but Morrison cut him off. "Get the hell out of here now before I have you charged with dereliction of duty and failure to obey a direct order!"

McFadden realized that the conversation had ended and broke ranks to leave. He had already been sweating from the morning sun, and now his face reddened with anger. Over his shoulder, he sent a frosty look of hatred back at the new gunnery officer.

"Any others of you care to comment?" challenged Morrison. The assembled crew remained silent. "Good. Then let's get to work! Oh, yes, Gunner Trask, you will assume Chief McFadden's former duties. You are now my assistant."

Gunner's Mate First Class Peter Trask, who greatly admired Lieutenant Morrison, replied enthusiastically, "Aye, aye, sir!"

Smiling at the men, Morrison finished relating the plan of the day to them and announced to Ensign Harramore, "Dismiss your troops, and carry out the plan of the day." Harramore and Morrison exchanged salutes, and as Morrison left, Harramore faced the men and bellowed, "Dismissed! Men, target practice in ten minutes! Let's go make history!"

A cheer broke out amongst the gunners as they scurried to the turrets.

***

After the first week of daily, repetitive drills, the teams in the forward turret learned the rhythm and teamwork that would be necessary for continuous-aim firing. Morrison supervised all of the sessions while Sims remained in the shadows. Each night, he was debriefed by Morrison, and they critiqued the day's results together. As a courtesy, both men briefed Captain Robinson intermittently. By the end of the second week, Morrison felt that the teams had become very proficient. He could sense their growing confidence. He felt confident that the time was right to shift his attention to the aft turret and its two teams.

For this work, he let Ensign Harramore supervise the two aft teams. Each morning Morrison went over the day's gunnery plans with Harramore, who would be directing all the turret activities. Although occasionally present in the aft turret during operations, Morrison acted solely as an observer. It was Harramore who was in charge and to whom the men responded in the aft turret. The situation was precisely what Morrison wanted. After three weeks of daily drills, the aft turret had become as proficient as the forward turret.

Their time in the Caribbean rapidly drew to a close. That final evening, Sims and Morrison prepared to debrief the Captain Robinson. Morrison reviewed all of the activities of the previous three weeks. Robinson listened intently, occasionally stroking his Vandyke beard. When Morrison finished, the CO looked at the two younger officers and asked, "Well, gentlemen, are we ready? Are we going to achieve what you claim, or are we going to return to base with our tail between our legs?"

Sims started to respond when Morrison inadvertently interrupted him. "Not only are we ready, sir, we are prepared to teach the United States Navy what naval gunfire is all about. Nothing will ever be the same when we are finished with our shooting demonstration."

Robinson looked at the young man and sighed. "I'm glad you are confident, Mr. Morrison. How about you, Mr. Sims? Are you as confident as your colleague?"

Without hesitation, Sims replied, "Captain, I not only totally concur with Mr. Morrison, but I guarantee that the results will be perfect."

The commanding officer of the battleship *Indiana* smiled at the two young officers. "I suppose we'll see, won't we? Gentlemen, tomorrow we head back to the Atlantic Coast. I only hope we can deliver on your promises."

17

Admiral Roland Cathcart stood on the bridge of his flagship, the battleship *Massachusetts*, enjoying the cool spring breezes that traversed the open bridge. With his binoculars fixed on the two buoys, he awaited the first salvo from the cruiser *Philadelphia*, the fourth ship to participate in the annual gunnery competition. The two boats carrying the scorers for the competition, called raking crews, had signaled their readiness so that the *Philadelphia* could commence firing at will. A moment later, a thunderous boom erupted from the cruiser's eight-inch gun. The ship remained dead in the water, and it fired its second round five minutes later.

Cathcart remained miffed that afternoon as the competition progressed. He knew that the *Indiana* had been off on some sort of secret training mission, and no one had heard from her since she got underway weeks ago. What exasperated him even further was the fact that the *Indiana* was scheduled to be the fifth and final ship to take part in this gunnery competition, and there was no sign of her. Cathcart had heard rumors that the famous Lieutenant Sims had been working with the ship in his capacity as the Inspector of Target Practice. If the rumors were true, it would seem highly irregular, if not blatantly insulting, for the ship to fail to show for the competition. As Cathcart watched the *Philadelphia* prepare for its third salvo, he heard the officer of the deck announce, "There is a small ocean-going tugboat approaching the port buoy!"

The commanding officer of the *Massachusetts* raised his binoculars and scanned the area indicated by the officer of the deck. He, too, saw the small boat, and it appeared to be towing a raft behind it. "Signal that damn fool to stay away! Does he want to get killed?" shouted the CO. "What in the name of God is going on here?" he shouted rhetorically.

Cathcart observed this dilemma, cynically thinking to himself that, in fact, the tug would be in little danger of being hit by any of the projectiles fired that day. After all, there was so much chance involved in gunfire. Suddenly, the bridge speakers exploded with the shouting of the lookout who announced, "Ship approaching from starboard bow! Approaching at flank speed! It appears to be a large warship!"

"Identify immediately!" bellowed the CO.

"Sir, it appears to be … yes, it is. It's a battleship! It's the *Indiana*!" The ship rapidly came into view just as the *Philadelphia* fired its last salvo and signaled that it was withdrawing from the firing line.

"Sir," shouted the lookout, as all binoculars now focused on the approaching ship. "The *Indiana*'s signal flags indicate that she is about to fire!" Just as the *Indiana* was raising her guns, the tugboat positioned the target raft near the port buoy and slowly began to tow the raft across the target area.

Aboard the *Indiana*, Captain Robinson ordered the ship to remain at its maximum speed of fifteen knots as it knifed in front of the other ships, which remained two thousand yards from the targets. The sea state remained calm, with an occasional five-foot wave under bright and sunny skies. The target sat off the ship's starboard bow, and both of *Indiana*'s turrets were aimed directly at it. With Sims beside him on the bridge, Robinson saw that the ship was now in position and called down to Morrison who stood in the forward turret. "Mr. Morrison, the show is yours. Commence firing at will!"

Hearing the CO's order, Morrison turned to Gunner Trask, whose eyes remained glued to the officer's face. All of the other men concentrated intently on their jobs. Morrison grinned at Trask and spoke, "Petty Officer Trask, commence firing!" Trask turned to gun team number one and screamed, "Fire! Fire at will!" Immediately, the first salvo from the thirteen-inch gun erupted with a roar as the gun captain pulled the lanyard. Then, what Morrison called "the coordinated ballet" began. Once the big gun had recoiled, the breech man slammed open the breech to expel the shell casing, and the loading crew immediately followed with another thirteen-inch shell. Then the rammer shoved the powder bag in while the breech man rammed the breech shut. All the while, the pointer never took his sights off the target, the large plywood wall between the two posts on the raft with the large red circle. Trask again yelled out, "Fire!" and the gun captain again pulled the lanyard, hurling another projectile into the clear sky. The whole process took less than twenty seconds. The ballet continued for several minutes.

Aboard the *Massachusetts*, Admiral Cathcart, along with all of the other observers, watched in stunned silence. The *Indiana* had rapidly fired off twelve rounds from its starboard gun of the forward turret, and it hit the towed target every time! The accuracy was beyond belief. To their further amazement, all twelve salvos had been fired in under five minutes. Adding to the astonishment of all was the fact that the target was moving and the *Indiana* was sailing at flank speed! While the speechless observers tried to understand what they had just witnessed, they didn't notice that the *Indiana* had changed course, right full rudder, and was approaching the firing line from the opposite direction. Her turrets now turned full port to the target. This time, the forward turret's port gun fired twelve times and duplicated the feat just accomplished. All twelve projectiles successfully hit the target.

Almost to emphasize the point, Sims had convinced Robinson to repeat the demonstration. This time, with the target still off the starboard bow, the starboard gun of the aft turret would now provide the firepower. "Mr. Harramore," ordered Morrison, "You've got the conn. Show them what you can do!" Immediately Harramore ordered the aft teams to commence firing, and once again, twelve rounds sequentially hit the target. It seemed almost anticlimactic when the *Indiana* had again reversed direction and allowed the port gun of the aft turret to deliver twelve rounds on target.

There was total silence aboard the bridge of the *Massachusetts*. All binoculars now focused on the target raft that had recorded forty-eight direct hits. Almost symbolically, as they all counted the hits for themselves, the wooden target crumbled into pieces and fell into the sea around the raft. Finally, Admiral Cathcart broke the silence. Gentlemen," he began softly, "I am nearly sixty years old, and I am set in my ways. I have always thought that I was too old—you know, you can't teach an old dog new tricks, that sort of thing. I hope you realize the importance of what we've all witnessed today. Nothing will ever be the same. The performance of our ship today was a disgrace compared to what we've just seen. And I, along with many other people in the navy, am to blame for this disgrace.

"It's a new day, gentlemen, and let us adjust accordingly." He turned to leave the bridge, but when he reached the door, he stopped and said loudly enough for all to hear, "Lieutenant William Sims, you are a genius," and left the bridge.

Aboard the *Indiana*, Captain Robinson called down to the turret. "Mr. Morrison, congratulations and well done! Bravo Zulu to your gun crews!" He turned to the Officer of the Deck. "OOD, plot a course for the Philadelphia Navy Yard. We're going home." He also sent word for every officer not on duty to assemble in the wardroom at 1800 that night.

***

To describe the mood in the wardroom that evening as jubilant would have been a gross understatement. All of the officers beamed with pride, ecstatic over the *Indiana*'s history-making performance that afternoon. They all realized that they had just set the standard for the United States Navy. They would now be the model of the can-do team that the rest of the navy would strive to emulate. At 1800 sharp, the cry, "Attention on deck," rang out and the officers snapped to attention. As Captain Robinson strode into the wardroom, he ordered them at ease and requested that they all be seated. He stopped in the front of the room and simply smiled at his men. "Gentlemen, I can't tell you how proud I am of every single one of you!" Cheers and applause erupted from the wardroom. "I want to thank all of you, and I personally want to shake hands with every man in this room. But first, let me acknowledge the real heroes of the day's events. On your feet, Lieutenant Sims and Lieutenant Morrison!" As the two officers stood, the applause grew. Soon, the entire wardroom was on its feet, cheering wildly. Sims and Morrison faced each other and embraced in a bear hug. They gave each other a Russian-style kiss on both cheeks, as the other officers roared their approval.

As Captain Robinson moved to the wardroom door, the men formed a line so he could shake every officer's hand as they departed the wardroom. Just as he began, he announced, "I almost forgot! We'll tie up at pier-side in Philadelphia about 1500 tomorrow. Every one of you is invited to have drinks with me tomorrow evening at the officer's club. The first two rounds are on me!" Once again, the wardroom erupted into cheers.

***

By the time the *Indiana* docked at Philadelphia, they had been at sea and anchor detail for several hours as they transited up the Delaware River. The men, excited and thirsty, finally departed the ship and headed for the officer's club. In the words of the executive officer, "We have some heavy-duty partying to do tonight!" Before departing the ship, Lieutenant Sims had said his good-byes to the gun crews and had personally thanked each of them. Shortly afterwards, the officers, dressed in their choker white uniforms, departed the ship.

The officers of both the *Philadelphia* and the *Massachusetts* had already arrived at the club and had a head start on the festivities. As soon as they saw the *Indiana*'s officers arrive, they swarmed around them to offer congratulations. They seemed just as jubilant as Captain Robinson's officers were, and it obviously pleased them to be a part of the history-making event, even if their competition had gotten the glory. The most commonly asked question to the *Indiana* officers was the obvious, "How the hell did you guys do it?" This was always asked in tones of awe and envy. Shortly thereafter, the officers of the other two ships, the battleship *Texas* and the cruiser *Raleigh* arrived, adding to the party-like atmosphere. Nonstop toasting, singing, and sea stories soon wafted through the club. True to his word, Captain Robinson bought the first two rounds of drinks for the entire assembly of officers in the club.

One officer present wasn't feeling particularly jubilant. He had heard about Admiral Cathcart's comments from the day before and had taken them as a personal affront. As gunnery officer aboard the *Massachusetts*, he had fine gun crews and he had trained them well. How could anyone have anticipated the new tricks the *Indiana* had developed? Why hadn't Lieutenant Sims come to his ship so they could have gotten the glory? As he downed his third drink at the bar, *Massachusetts*' gunnery officer, Lieutenant Junior Grade Derrick Parsons, sat there, determined to get very drunk, to ease the pain and humiliation he now felt. It only exacerbated his humiliation when he heard the *Indiana* officers over in the corner of the club loudly toasting themselves. Parsons ears perked up when he heard the toast, "To the man of the hour—the finest gunnery officer and leader in the fleet—Lieutenant Stephen Morrison!" Thunderous applause and shouting immediately followed the toast.

Both Morrison and Captain Robinson had become slightly tipsy at that point. Robinson tousled the young officer's hair and then playfully grabbed him in a mock headlock, proclaiming, "See, I can still lick this tough guy!" The men roared with laughter, and Robinson whispered to Morrison in a low voice, "Stephen, let's go to the bar and buy another round!" Grinning widely, Morrison replied "Aye, aye, sir! I would never disobey such a brilliant, well thought-out order!" The two men strolled over to the bar, and the captain informed the bartender that he wanted to order another round for the entire bar. As Stephen Morrison leaned against the bar, he didn't notice that sitting next to him was his Naval Academy classmate, Derrick Parsons.

Morrison had his elbows on the bar and his right foot up on the bar railing when he heard a voice next to him say, "You fucking kike." He immediately turned his head to the right and recognized Derrick Parsons, who appeared to be drunk.

"What did you say?" demanded Morrison.

"Still up to your dirty Jew tricks, aren't you, Morrison?" asked Parsons, his words slightly slurred. In a single motion, Morrison grabbed Parsons' choker whites with his left hand, spun him around, and then delivered a solid blow to Parsons' face with his right fist. Parsons sprawled backward, knocking over several other officers as he hit the floor.

Although slightly drunk himself, Morrison immediately pounced on his old adversary and began delivering devastating blows to the man's face. The other officers, well on their way to becoming drunk themselves, reacted slowly. As Morrison repeatedly smashed his fists into Parson's face, he taunted him, "This is for four years at the academy! Why not share this with that prick, Russell, you spineless little bastard?"

By this time, the others had overcome their shock and descended on Morrison, pulling him off the prostrate Parsons, who lay on the floor unconscious, his face a bloody pulp of torn flesh and broken bones. As they pulled Morrison away, Captain Robinson, who had overheard the entire exchange, stood there with a puzzled expression on his face. *Why,* he thought to himself, *did that other officer call Morrison a Jew?*

***

As the ranking officer present, Captain Robinson convened an investigation into the fight that had erupted at the officer's club. Fortunately for Morrison, his commanding officer not only was there, but had overheard the remarks that had provoked the incident. When the investigating officer took Morrison's statement, Morrison decided to relate the entire story of the harassment he suffered at the Naval Academy. He also revealed the facts of the beating he had received at the hands of Jared Russell and his cronies, including Derrick Parsons. All of this factored into Captain Robinson's decision to give Morrison a non-punitive reprimand.

On the other hand, when he recovered from his injuries, Derrick Parsons went to captain's mast and received a formal counseling statement in his service jacket. Due to the unusual circumstances of the incident, Robinson referred the entire results of his investigation to the navy's Judge Advocate General, Captain Samuel C. Lemley who concurred with the findings and with the decisions rendered by Robinson. The matter was considered closed.

12

The White House
Washington, D.C.
December 1903

In December 1903, Lieutenant Commander William Sims met with President Roosevelt at the White House. A favorite of the energetic president, Sims had become a frequent guest, for Roosevelt truly enjoyed his company and valued his advice. Roosevelt recognized him as a kindred spirit and had been surreptitiously grooming him to become his naval aide. Toward the end of their meeting, Roosevelt decided to share a dilemma with Sims and ask for his counsel.

"You know, Commander, I've got a bit of a situation brewing at the Secretariat's office. Secretary of the Navy William Moody has tendered his resignation to me. It is to become effective this coming summer."

"I didn't know he was considering leaving, Mr. President," replied Sims. "He's a very decent man, and I shall miss him. I dare say that many in the navy will feel the same way once he leaves. Do you have a replacement in mind, sir?"

"Well, William, that's part of my dilemma. The man that I'm considering has an excellent business and administrative background. In fact, he is a former secretary of agriculture under President Grover Cleveland. I believe Paul Morton can do a solid, efficient job, and he's expressed his interest in the position to me. My only hesitation is that he is a businessman and an administrator, not a military man. And therein lies the problem. If I appoint him, I would like to appoint a naval aide to him to be his right-hand man, to be his resource on the ways of the navy, if you know what I mean. I wonder where I can find such a man?" he asked playfully as he grinned at the naval officer.

"Please sir," protested Sims, "this job is one that I'd just as soon avoid. There is much to do in the fleet and—"

"Relax, Commander," exclaimed the president as he burst out into laughter. "I've got bigger plans for you, William, believe me. You are way too valuable to me in your current position as savior of my beloved United States Navy. I think you'll agree that a naval aide will be necessary for Morton to be effective. I want to ask you if you have any suggestions about whom to assign the job. On matters such as these, I trust your judgment explicitly!"

Sims sighed with relief as he watched the president remove his pince-nez glasses and wipe them with his handkerchief. He immediately replied, "In fact, I have an officer who would be perfect for the job. He is very intelligent, squared-away, and a fine leader. I may have mentioned him to you in the past."

Lee Mandel

"Pray tell, William, who is this man? My God, it didn't take you much thought to come up with a name. He must be outstanding."

"His name is Lieutenant Junior Grade Stephen Morrison, and he's currently aboard the battleship *Indiana*. He was the gunnery officer that trained and led the gun crews at that famous competition earlier in the year."

"Ah, yes, I do remember this lad. Quite a bully, impressive performance as I recall. Tell me a little more about this young man," demanded Roosevelt enthusiastically.

"He's in his early thirties, and he's single. Ruggedly good-looking. He's a linguist and is fluent in Russian. He also happens to be a superb boxer; he's been the boxing champion on each of the three ships on which he's served. I think he's your man, Mr. President.

"Hmm, fluent in Russian," Roosevelt murmured to himself. Looking up at Sims, he said, "That could be very useful in this job, especially considering the ongoing tensions between Russia and Japan. Tell me, Commander, are there any Achilles' heels we should be aware of before making a decision? He almost seems too good to be true."

"Not really, sir. If anything, at times he can be quite intense. Sometimes he looks like he's angry at the world with the way he looks at you straight in the eyes. Mind you, though, he is cultured and a gentleman. Definitely not a grinner or a jovial person."

"Then it's a good thing that the job doesn't require a grinning idiot!" retorted Roosevelt, laughing at his own humor. "Thank you, William, for your assistance. I think Stephen Morrison will do quite well as a naval aide to the secretary of the navy. I'll arrange for his reassignment."

19

April 3, 1904
Lieutenant Stephen L. Morrison, USN
Office of the Secretary of the Navy
Washington, D.C.
United States of America

My dear Stephen,
I must begin my letter with an apology. I realize that it is well over a year, possibly two years, since I last wrote to you. I have been traveling extensively, and I am rarely in the same spot for very long. Your last two letters were forwarded to me by my sister because I no longer have anything to do with my parents, Putilov Metal Works, or my former life. I now devote all of my energies to the revolution. It is truly a full-time life's work and, for me, there is no turning back. As always, things in Russia turn from bad to worse.
Before I continue, let me congratulate you on your new assignment. An aide to the man who is in charge of the United States Navy!

Stephen, from the day we met I knew that you had the potential to be the sort of man who could change the world. It certainly appears that you are on your way! My pride in you is only surpassed by my expectation that you would be selected for such an important job. The world needs great men, men of destiny such as yourself, for without you, there will be continued chaos.

You are no doubt following Nicholas' latest blunder. Oh, this senseless war with Japan! Why must Mother Russia continue to suffer under the likes of that stupid, insensitive excuse for a Tsar? Good Russians are dying every day, and for what? Many people are asking this question, Stephen, and they see the injustice of it all. The government is reaching into its quiver and pulling out its usual pathetic tricks. They think they can distract the people from its own incompetence by throwing the blame for everything on the Jews. The government is encouraging a new round of pogroms in an effort to divert the public's attention, but it is pathetic and ultimately futile. But even though the incompetence is obvious, as always, the Russian people act as passive children. They need focus. They need a leader to show them the way. As I've learned, it will not be the peasants who will transform Russia. It will be the workers. But even they have no collective sense of how to bring about this needed transformation.

In my last letter, I believe I told you how the workers were being seduced into the concept of "Economism" - they work to improve their lives by concentrating on improving the capitalist system and achieving economic aims. Here we are, trying to overthrow the system, and the very people we're counting on to do it are trying to become better capitalists! That is when I realized that the revolution needed to happen as soon as possible. The Tsar and his government need to be overthrown as the first and final step. No longer can we count on a transitory process. No longer can we strive for the establishment of a bourgeois democracy as the first step. We need to go directly to the overthrow of the status quo.

We Marxists have been organized as the Social Democratic Labor Party and formally codified our status with our first meeting, the one I wrote to you about in my last letter. My God, Stephen, it seems like a lifetime ago that we met in Minsk, even though that was only four years ago. Much has occurred since then. There is a philosophical rift within the group. One faction favors a more democratic approach to party matters. Given conditions in Russia, the other faction is demanding strong centralized control to run the party with an iron fist and an iron will. This is my belief, and I have allied myself with the faction's leader, Comrade Vladimir Ulyanov. I believe I have written to you about him. As is becoming fashionable for revolutionaries in Russia, he has adopted a nom de guerre and is now known as Comrade Lenin.

Quite frankly, Lenin is a genius. He so eloquently stated the case for strong centralized party control and discipline in his brilliant pamphlet, "What Is To Be Done?" You no doubt recognize that title- he adapted it from Chernyshevsky's book. In addition, he has established our revolutionary newsletter, Iskra. I have enclosed the latest issue with this letter. I will send you as many future issues as I can. Stephen, the man's writings are truly inspiring! I realize that many of our tenets go against American ideals, but you must always remember that we are not the United States of America. We have not evolved as you have evolved. We do not have a George Washington or a Thomas Jefferson to lead our masses. Russia needs discipline. Russia needs the whip, and we Marxists will provide it.

Comrade Lenin exhibited his brilliance last year at our second party congress in Brussels. As was to be expected, Comrade Martov, who leads the democratic faction of our party, was debating the wording of Article One of the Party Statute. I won't bore you with the details of this, but Lenin was steadfast in his opposition and refused to compromise. You see, Stephen, he was displaying an iron will, the kind of iron will that will be necessary for our views to triumph. Lenin prevailed by the narrowest of margins, but he proclaimed our faction the Majority Men (or

Bolsheviks, if you have not kept up with your Russian language skills!) and Martov's faction the Minority Men, you know, Mensheviks. These names have stuck to each faction even after a year. You see the public relations genius of Lenin? Always fight, always lead, and never compromise! These are his strengths; these are our strengths. We have a long road ahead of us, but we will never surrender or compromise. We will prevail in our revolutionary struggle.

No doubt I am boring you, Stephen, and I know that certainly you have many problems and issues that you face in your new job. Please never forget that we are brothers—brothers who only want justice and liberty for both of our peoples. Pray for us, Stephen. There are difficult times ahead for Russia. Pray we can extricate ourselves from this pointless, accursed war. Pray for the overthrow of the Tsar. Please continue to write, as I get much comfort from your letters. God bless you. I wish you much success in your new endeavor.

Your friend always,
Yuri

20

The White House
Washington, D.C.
November 1904

Lieutenant Junior Grade Stephen Morrison, naval aide to Secretary of the Navy Paul Morton, hated wearing his mess dress uniform, but for a White House reception, it was mandatory. He had been warned that formal dress functions would become part of his job, and tonight would be the first time he had to attend such an affair. Standing near the far corner of the East Room, he surveyed the throng of guests, all elegantly attired. As the orchestra played quietly in the background, the guests mingled as waiters offered both drinks and heavy hors d'oeuvres to them. On the far side of the room, Morrison could see President Roosevelt engaged in animated conversation with a small crowd of admirers who gathered around him.

Although Morrison had not personally met the president, he greatly admired the man for his intellect and his energy.

When he first reported to his new job the previous May, the incoming Secretary Paul Morton proved to be an eager student of naval affairs. He and Morrison became nearly inseparable. Morton insisted that his new aide accompany him to Chicago for the Republican Convention held that June. The entire train ride from Washington was filled with briefings. "Heck, Lieutenant, let's call this remedial education!" was how Morton jokingly put it. Morrison was both glad and honored to accompany his new boss. They quickly developed an excellent working relationship, despite Morton's relative lack of knowledge concerning the day-to-day operations of the United States Navy.

That evening at the East Room, as Morrison watched several couples take to the dance floor, he chuckled to himself about his increased competence as a dancer. His boss had insisted that he learn how to waltz, stating, "Stephen, as a bachelor, you will likely be attending White House functions. No doubt, you will be tasked with escorting young guests and dancing with them. Let's not embarrass ourselves, shall we?" Soon afterwards, Morrison enrolled in dance classes, in addition to his other duties. On one prior occasion, he had escorted an ambassador's daughter to a ball at the British Embassy, and he surmised that his dancing had been adequate. Tonight, feeling fairly bored and wishing that the evening would end, he suddenly saw the most beautiful girl he had ever seen. Like a bolt out of the blue, her beauty struck him, and he couldn't take his eyes off of her. She stood nearby, surrounded by several admiring men.

She looked to be in her twenties, and all of the tuxedoed admirers appeared to be middle-aged. She seemed to be regaling them with a story, and all of them laughed, obviously enjoying the entertaining presence of such a beautiful and vivacious young lady. Her dark brown hair, pulled up in the fashion of the day, highlighted her porcelain skin and sparkling green eyes. To Morrison, she looked just like the famous socialite Consuelo Vanderbilt or even the fictional Gibson Girl. He was absolutely mesmerized by her beauty. He found himself walking toward her until he came to a stop in front of the small crowd that had formed around her.

"Gentlemen," she purred, "it appears that the United States Navy is about to make an official port call. Am I right, Lieutenant?" The other gentlemen around her broke into laughter as a smile played upon her lips. She looked directly into Morrison's eyes. He was captivated.

"Ma'am, I am under direct orders of President Roosevelt," he began. "I have been directed to rescue you from this distinguished throng and escort you to the dance floor where I will proceed to dazzle you with my waltzing abilities." The other men burst into laughter, yelling "Bravo," and slapping Morrison on the back for his effort. They grabbed his arms and brought him closer to the beautiful young girl, who smiled broadly. "Well, Lieutenant," she replied, "I always obey orders!" He offered her his arm, and she took it as he led her to the dance floor.

They began waltzing and she complimented him, saying, "I must say, for a navy man, you are not a bad dancer. Tell me, Lieutenant, do you have a name? Are you John Paul Jones? Or are you perhaps the Flying Dutchman or some other figment of my imagination?"

"Actually, I do have a name, ma'am. I'm Stephen Morrison, naval aide to Secretary of the Navy Paul Morton. Also, let me say that I can't believe the line I made up to get you to dance with me! That really isn't like me. It just happened."

"Please don't apologize, Stephen Morrison. You actually rescued me from a bunch of stuffy old men. Nice, but stuffy, you know." She looked into his eyes, and decided that he was fairly handsome. "Tell me, Lieutenant, do you always look so serious?"

He smiled at her. "Only when I don't know the name of the woman I'm dancing with. That just drives me crazy. If I didn't know better, I would say I'm dancing with Consuelo Vanderbilt. Is that who you are? Or are you the original model for the Gibson Girl?"

She threw her head back and laughed heartily. "I'm so sorry, but thank you for that nice compliment. I'm Helen Leavitt, and I must say, Lieutenant, that it is pleasure to be with someone under the age of fifty. I really do thank you." She was beginning to find this mysterious naval officer intriguing and sensed that there was perhaps much about him that she wanted to learn.

"Please, call me Stephen, and I'll agree to call you Helen. Tell me, how does a lovely young girl like you end up at the White House?" The music stopped and all of the dancers offered polite applause as the musicians left for a break. "May I get you some punch?" She nodded, and they strolled over to the serving tables.

"My father is in government," she explained. "He was the United States minister to the Ottoman Empire for two tours. Now he is a consultant to President Roosevelt. He is also very active in B'nai B'rith. You've probably never heard of that organization." Morrison nodded, indicating that he hadn't. "It's an organization dedicated to the betterment of world Jewry. They do great work," she said, pausing to lift her cup of punch. "I propose a toast. To the dashing young naval officer, who rescued a damsel in distress with the worst line ever uttered in the history of the United States."

Morrison raised his glass as he grinned and clinked it to hers. "I'll drink to that!"

The couple sat down. "Tell me about your father, about you, about, well, everything about you," Stephen encouraged.

"Well, let's see. I'm twenty-five years old. I was born in Philadelphia but I've lived all over the world. I'm a graduate of Swarthmore College. My father is Oscar Leavitt, and he was born in Germany. He is a genius and the love of my life. Most recently, he is active in B'nai B'rith. Earlier this year, Father was one of several key officials of B'nai B'rith that petitioned President Roosevelt to protest that terrible pogrom in the Russian city of Kishinev. They convinced the president to act, and he did lodge an official protest with the Russian government. That's the type of honorable and just man my father is. There he is! Doesn't he look aristocratic?" she proudly asked as she pointed to a group of distinguished looking gentlemen. "He's the tall man with the graying beard and moustache. And my mother, well, she's an angel. Now you know everything about me. So, what is the story of Stephen Morrison?"

He refilled their punch glasses and replied, "I was raised in New York City. My father was a United States congressman, Caleb Morrison. I'm a graduate of the United States Naval Academy, Class of 1893, and, well, that's really about all there is to know. I'm a really boring individual, I must warn you."

"Somehow, I rather doubt that, Stephen." As he handed her the glass, she wrapped her hand around his for a brief moment. Morrison felt almost giddy from her touch. This feeling was something new to him. He had been involved with a few other women in his life, but no serious relationships resulted. He had never felt a closeness to any woman and finally concluded that he would always be a confirmed bachelor. He was now thirty-four years old and too set in his ways to let a woman enter his life. There was also the question of his naval career. Like his mentor William Sims, he was also likely to be married to the sea. Looking at the lovely face that smiled back at him that night, Morrison wondered if perhaps it was possible that things were about to change.

At the end of the reception, he said goodnight to her and found himself saying, "I hope that sometime we may meet again. Nothing would give me more pleasure, Helen."

She smiled a mischievous smile at him and replied, "One can certainly never know, Lieutenant Stephen Morrison. One can certainly never know."

The next week, when Morrison returned to his room at the bachelor officers' quarters at the Washington Navy Yard, he found an invitation waiting for him to have dinner with Mr. and Mrs. Oscar Leavitt and family at their Georgetown home the following week. *Things are definitely looking up,* he thought to himself. He walked to the mirror over his sink and said out loud, "Stephen, old man, I do believe you're in love!"

***

The invitation for Morrison to join the Leavitts for dinner came after much discussion at the Leavitt home. Both of Helen's parents had typical parental concerns for their daughter. She was very bright and very beautiful, but she was a free spirit, and this quality proved to be a constant source of worry for them. She had no interest in marriage, despite ample proposals from the sons of the elite of the Jewish community from around the world. She seemed to intimidate and ultimately drive off any potential suitors with her wit, sarcasm, and directness. In an era when marriages were often prearranged by parents, Helen Leavitt would have none of it. She always had a criticism or complaint about any young man who attempted to court her. She seemed to be interested only in travel and government. In fact, she worked as her father's personal assistant.

She had shocked her parents when she asked them to invite the young naval officer to their house for dinner. This behavior was not at all typical for her, and this was what concerned the Leavitts. She seemed very interested in this man. With all the eligible young Jewish men she had met, she seemed interested in this naval officer—the son of an Irish Catholic congressman! Oscar Leavitt had spotted them together at the White House reception and could see the look in his daughter's eyes. He sensed the attraction. "Why do you want to bring home a shaggitz?" he demanded, using the Yiddish word for a non-Jewish male. "There aren't enough eligible Jewish boys for you to choose from?"

"Father, please!" she retorted. "I don't want to marry the man. For God's sake, I only met him once! He just happens to be a good-looking, very intelligent man whom I find very interesting. He's a nice change of pace from the other dullards you and mother seem to prefer for me. And I'll be honest, he reminds me a bit of you- intelligent, witty, and dedicated to his country. Is that so bad? I just want to introduce him to you."

In the end, their free-spirited daughter won. Her parents backed down and issued the invitation with the understanding that he would never be invited back again. To this stipulation, Helen agreed. Although she didn't express her intuition to her parents, she had the definite feeling she would be seeing a lot more of the handsome lieutenant in the future.

When Stephen Morrison arrived at the Leavitt home in Georgetown, the family butler met him at the door and escorted him into the foyer, instructing him to wait there while he summoned the family. In a moment, Oscar and Sadie Leavitt appeared, with Helen right behind them. Again struck by her beauty, Morrison could see that she seemed very pleased that he had come, as indicated by her radiant smile.

"So good of you to come tonight, Lieutenant. We've heard so much about you from our daughter," greeted Leavitt, as he and his guest shook hands. He introduced his wife and then stated, "I believe you and Helen have already met."

"Yes, sir, we have. Thank you so much for inviting me." He simultaneously handed them a bottle of expensive wine that he had purchased.

"Excellent! Thank you so much," said Leavitt. Turning to the butler, he announced, "James, we'll have a glass of wine in the parlor before we dine. Come, Lieutenant, I want to hear all about you." The four of them went to the parlor and sat down while James poured the wine. Leavitt proceeded to ask Morrison a variety of questions about his job, his naval experiences, and about his relationship with his late father, Congressman Caleb Morrison.

Leavitt and his wife had to admit to themselves that their guest appeared to be an impressive, articulate young man. He certainly cut a dashing figure in his dark blue naval uniform. *Damn it all,* Leavitt thought to himself, *I can see why Helen is attracted to this man!* He glanced over to his daughter, who seemed absolutely entranced by the young naval officer. For his part, Morrison was also impressed by Leavitt. The young officer could see that Helen was a reflection of this man's worldliness and intellect. Even though he knew he was being sized up, he felt comfortable being in the presence of the Leavitts.

Finally, James announced that dinner was ready to be served, and they all moved into the dining room. As they walked through the hallway from the parlor, Morrison noted the opulence of their home. It reminded him a little of his home in New York City. Momentarily, they all sat at the dining room table with Oscar Leavitt at the head of the table and Sadie at the opposite end. Morrison sat facing Helen. He smiled and gave her a wink when her parents weren't looking. She blushed slightly and looked down at the table, hoping her parents wouldn't notice. When the kitchen staff brought the first course and began to serve, Leavitt turned to Morrison and said, "As our guest, Lieutenant Morrison, I want you to feel comfortable and at home with us. Please feel free to say grace before we begin, if you'd like."

"Thank you so much, sir. I believe I will." He bowed his head slightly and spoke, "*Baruch atah Adonai, Elohaynu melekh ha-olam, ha-motzi lechem min ha-aretz.*" When he finished, he looked up and saw three looks of utter astonishment on the faces of the Leavitt family. Finally, Helen broke the silence after a few seconds. "You speak Hebrew? You know the blessing for bread?" she asked incredulously.

"Why not?" he replied, smiling slightly. "I'm Jewish." A few more seconds of stunned silence followed. Oscar Leavitt spoke first.

"But I don't understand! Your name is Morrison; your father was Caleb Morrison. I met him years ago. I know he was an Irishman. And if you don't mind my saying, you certainly don't look like a Jew. How is this possible? Are you joking, because if—"

"Sir," interrupted Morrison, "Caleb Morrison was my adoptive father. My actual father was named Zvi Kambotchnik, and he was a rabbi. I was born in Perm, Russia, and my family immigrated to the United States, to New York City, when I was eleven years old." He then proceeded to fill in several key details about his life.

As each course was being served, his hosts continued to pepper him with questions. He couldn't help noticing that they seemed to warm up to him immensely as the meal progressed.

Lee Mandel

Throughout the dinner, Helen Leavitt said practically nothing. Her father and mother did a fine job interrogating her naval officer. Intermittently, their eyes would meet, and she could sense the communication between them. She was absolutely ecstatic over the developments of the evening.

After dinner was over, Leavitt directed his butler to have dessert served to them in the parlor where the delighted parents continued to press Stephen with questions about his life. Ocasionally, they let their guest ask a few questions himself. "Tell me, Stephen, why would a young Jewish boy, an immigrant, want to be an officer in the United States Navy?"

"It's always been a dream of mine, a goal or a quest if you will," replied the young officer. "I suppose one could also ask why a Jewish immigrant from Germany would want to serve as a minister to a Muslim country not once, but twice." The young man's knowledge and wit impressed Leavitt.

"It would be hard to be a religious Jew in the navy, given the lifestyle. Are you a religious man, Stephen? Do you ever go to synagogue?" As Leavitt finished his question, Morrison could almost sense them all leaning forward in anticipation of his answer.

"No, I don't go to synagogue. That's a personal choice I made years ago. Am I a religious person?" He stopped and chose his words carefully. "Yes, I believe I am a religious person. I believe that the inner core beliefs are what make a person religious, not the outer or superficial trappings. I've seen too many people, Jews and gentiles, who think that showing up in a place of worship once a week cancels out the hypocritical lifestyles they live the rest of the week. God can't be so naïve that He accepts the idea that mere attendance in a church or synagogue constitutes a religious person."

"Hmm, interesting," mused the elder man. "Care to expound on that philosophy for us? I don't mean to put you on the spot, but you are certainly one of the more unique and interesting people I've met, Jew or gentile."

"I'm probably not that eloquent, sir. Are you familiar with the British poet, James Leigh Hunt, and his poem *Abou Ben Adhem?*"

"No, I'm not."

"Well, let me recite it. It's short, but I think it sums up my philosophy on religion better than I can express it."

"Please do," interjected Helen.

"All right, here we go then.

Abou Ben Adhem (may his tribe increase!)
Awoke one night from a deep dream of peace,
And saw, within the moonlight in his room,
Making it rich, and like a lily in bloom,
An Angel writing in a book of gold:
Exceeding peace had made Ben Adhem bold,
And to the Presence in the room he said,
"What writest thou?" The Vision raised its head,
And with a look made of all sweet accord
Answered, "The names of those who love the Lord."
"And is mine one?" said Abou. "Nay, not so,"
Replied the Angel. Abou spoke more low,
But cheerily still; and said, "I pray thee, then,
Write me as one that loves his fellow men."

The Angel wrote, and vanished. The next night
It came again with a great wakening light,
And it showed the names whom the love of God had blessed,
And, lo! Ben Adhem's name led all the rest!"

"Stephen, that is so beautiful," Helen said softly.

"Thank you," he replied.

"No, thank you," retorted Oscar Leavitt. "Thank you for sharing that with us. I think I understand now what your core beliefs are. A beautiful poem, Stephen. You are right. It really says it all."

By this time, the atmosphere in the room was much more relaxed. Morrison felt as if he was with his own family. Finally, as the evening grew late, he announced that he had better be leaving. He thanked his hosts profusely, and they invited him to return any time he wanted. After a firm handshake from Oscar, Sadie gave him a big hug. He then turned to Helen, took her right hand, and brought it to his lips. Kissing it gently, he announced, "Thank you, Miss Leavitt, for the pleasure of your company. I hope I can see you in the very near future."

With her eyes glistening with tears of joy, she replied, "You can count on it, sailor!" Her parents erupted into laughter as they escorted him to the door. James returned his cover to him, and with a final word of thanks to his hosts, he departed into the chilly night.

"Well, Mother, Father, what did you think of my naval officer?" asked the giddy daughter as they lingered in the foyer. She still hadn't come down from the euphoria of the evening. In response, both of her parents hugged her. "Helen, he's wonderful," said her father. "A dream come true," added her mother.

"Well, I'm glad you approve of him," she announced delightedly, "because he's the man I'm going to marry!"

"Really now, Helen," replied the amused Oscar Leavitt. "Don't you think you're being a bit premature with—" He was interrupted by a firm knocking on the front door.

Leavitt opened the door to find Lieutenant Junior Grade Stephen Morrison standing there. "Stephen!" exclaimed Leavitt. "Did you forget something?"

"Well, uh, yes, I did, sir." Clearing his throat, Stephen continued. "Mr. Leavitt, I forgot to ask you for the hand of your daughter in marriage."

21

Stephen Morrison and Helen Leavitt were married in March 1905. The wedding was orchestrated by Oscar and Sadie Leavitt. It was held in Temple Beth Israel in Washington, D.C., with a reception following at the Willard Hotel downtown. Oscar Leavitt beamed as he gave his daughter away to the dashing young naval officer. He noted with satisfaction that nearly one hundred guests attended. Although invited, President Roosevelt had been unable to attend. He was in New York City that weekend for the wedding of his niece, Eleanor Roosevelt, to his distant cousin, Franklin Delano Roosevelt.

Joseph Morrison served as best man for his brother's wedding, feeling somewhat awkward at the Jewish ceremony. Both of the Morrison brothers wished that their mother could have been there. She had died several years before. Joseph, now a highly successful attorney in Boston, had taken the train down to Washington to be in Stephen's wedding. When it was time to toast the newlywed couple, Joseph instructed the guests to raise their glasses. "To my brother and his beautiful new wife.

May they always remain as young and as happy, and as in love, as they are today!"

A resounding chorus of "Here, Here," resonated from the guests.

Not to be outdone, Oscar Leavitt, already slightly tipsy from too much champagne, stood up, and proposed his own toast. "Honored guests! Your attention please! I propose a toast to my wonderful daughter and my magnificent new son-in-law. Just look at my daughter. Have you ever seen a happier or more beautiful bride? God gave her the intellect to complement her beauty, both inside and out. I couldn't be more proud of her!

"Now, look at my son-in-law, Stephen. Notice he's wearing a uniform, the uniform of an officer in the United States Navy." Tears rolled down his cheeks as he continued. "Stephen, I know I don't have to ask you to make my baby happy in life. I know that you will because you just took an oath to God, just as you took an oath to your country when you put on that uniform. After all, Stephen, you are a man of honor. And if we have honor, we can live and die with dignity. And so, beloved guests, raise your glasses! A toast to Lieutenant and Mrs. Stephen L. Morrison! *L'chaim!*"

The guests enthusiastically responded, "*L'chiam,*" as they downed their champagne, and rose to give Oscar Leavitt a standing ovation.

The newlyweds spent their first night as man and wife at the Willard, leaving early the next day for their honeymoon. Stephen had only been able to arrange for a week of leave, so they decided to go to New York City. They departed by train from the Pennsylvania Railroad Station on the Mall, with Oscar and Sadie Leavitt enthusiastically waving good-bye to the young couple.

Stephen had originally apologized for the fact that they could take only a week off and could only go to New York rather than travel to Europe. "Nonsense!" replied Helen. "I love staying in New York. Besides, I want to see where you grew up, what your life was like. I love you, Stephen Morrison, and I want to know everything about you. You see, you're stuck with me so you better get used to having someone love you unconditionally for all eternity. Got It, Lieutenant?"

As part of their wedding gift, Oscar Leavitt had arranged their honeymoon accommodations in New York with his business acquaintance, the famous financier John Jacob Astor. "I don't want my baby and her husband to be staying just anywhere!" explained the proud father; ergo, the Morrisons would be staying at the famous Waldorf Astoria Hotel on Fifth Avenue and Thirty-fourth Street.

After arriving at Grand Central Station on Forty-Second Street, the newlyweds took a hansom cab to the Waldorf Astoria. As they entered the opulent lobby, the sheer beauty of the place awed them both. The wine colored carpeting perfectly complemented the rich mahogany furniture and fine artwork on the walls. Crystal chandeliers studded the ceiling and uniformed bellmen stood by to assist guests. "God, Helen, I'm sure glad that your father is paying for this! I don't think a flag officer could afford to stay here," gasped Stephen.

"Ah, ha!" she replied. "Now I know it! You only married me for my money! You sailors are all alike. I suppose I ought to see if I could get an army officer to marry me."

She hugged him tightly, and as he kissed her forehead, he retorted, "Just you try and run off with an army guy, Mrs. Morrison. I'll make sure that it will make the annual Army-Navy game look like a picnic in the park!"

With a flourish, he announced to the desk clerk, "We are Lieutenant and Mrs. Stephen Morrison."

The clerk responded, "Oh yes, honored guests, you are expected. Welcome to the Waldorf Astoria." Hitting the well-polished silver bell near his hand, he called out to one of the bellman. "Robert, please escort Lieutenant and Mrs. Morrison to the bridal suite on the seventeenth floor." Turning back to Stephen, he said, "Welcome again, sir. Your bags will be up shortly. If you need anything, Mr. Astor himself has left instructions that New York City is to belong to you and Mrs. Morrison while you are our guests."

The elevator whisked them to the seventeenth floor where the bellman opened the door to the bridal suite. They entered the huge outer sitting room that reminded Helen of a French chateau. On the far side of the room stood a grand piano. On the other side of the room, they noted a bar and a large polished mahogany hutch, upon which sat a huge basket of fruits and flowers with a note attached to it.

"Please, follow me," the bellman instructed as he opened the double doors to the bedroom and led them in. On the far wall, a king-sized, four-poster canopied bed with blue silk runners dominated the room. A large mirror that appeared to be rimmed in gold hung over the highly polished dresser. The bellman sat their luggage on a small rack. "If there is anything you need during your stay, please ring for me." Stephen thanked him and gave the man a generous tip.

Walking back into the sitting room, Stephen exclaimed, "Can you believe this place! It's incredible!" Pulling Helen into his arms, Stephen tipped her chin up, gazed into her green eyes, and kissed her passionately.

"Are you glad you married me?" Helen playfully asked.

"What do you think? Point of order, young lady. You are the best thing that ever happened to me. From now on I will live only to make you happy."

Helen rested her head on his shoulder and kissed his neck. "Look, Stephen, there's a note on that fruit basket. Let's see what it says." She walked over and opened the envelope. In a moment, her eyes widened with delight. "Look at this, darling! It's an invitation!" she exclaimed as she handed it to him.

Morrison gazed at the engraved invitation that read:

Colonel and Mrs. John J. Astor IV
Request the pleasure of your company tomorrow
night for dinner and theatre.

Hand-written on the bottom of the letter was, "Meet you in the Waldorf lounge for drinks at 6 o'clock, show at 7:30, then dinner at Delmonico's." It was followed by the initials JJA.

"I cannot believe this! Dinner with the Astors! I've heard that he is the richest man in America." Still staring at the note in his hands, Stephen hadn't noticed that Helen had gone back into the bedroom. From behind him, he heard his wife's sultry voice. "Hey, sailor," she murmured. Turning slightly to his right, he saw her silhouetted in the doorway to the bedroom. And she was totally naked.

"Lieutenant Morrison," she began, "yesterday I became your wife, and last night you gave me the experience I've only dreamed of. Look behind me. That is, if you can take your eyes off of my voluptuous body! Note the exquisite canopy bed. Darling, I am delighted that we'll be dining with the Astors tomorrow night, but tonight you are mine alone, and right now I just want you to make love to me." With a twinkle in her eye, she smiled demurely. "And that's a direct order!"

***

Stephen and Helen Morrison arrived at the cocktail lounge of the Waldorf Astoria just before 6 o'clock. Morrison felt uncomfortable in the civilian formal attire. It was a gift from his in-laws, and Helen had to reassure him that he looked devilishly handsome. As he admired his beautiful wife, a sudden commotion arose in the lounge as the Astors arrived. The Morrisons stood up as Colonel and Mrs. Astor approached their table. All around them, people stared and acknowledged their presence. Astor thrust his hand out to Stephen, exclaiming, "Hello, Lieutenant. J.J. Astor, and this is my wife, Ava."

"So pleased to meet you, sir and ma'am," replied the impressed young naval officer as he shook their hands in sequence.

"Please, call me John or J.J., and I'll call you Stephen." Turning to Helen, he proclaimed, "And this must be the beautiful Mrs. Morrison. Helen, I believe." Kissing her hand, he exclaimed "You are even more ravishing than everybody says, including Oscar." Blushing a bright red, Helen thanked him as they all sat down.

A waiter appeared instantaneously to take their drink orders. Morrison looked at the multimillionaire. Astor didn't appear to be that much older than himself. A handsome man with piercing dark eyes and a thick black moustache, both he and Mrs. Astor were elegantly dressed for a night on the town. They were the epitome of the moneyed people of the gilded age. Astor spoke very highly of Oscar Leavitt and of his dealings with him, referring to him as a first-class gentleman. Ava Astor inquired about their wedding and Helen gladly provided the details of the event, leaving Stephen to embellished the details.

"I'm fascinated that you are in the navy, Stephen. Wasn't your father Congressman Caleb Morrison?" Astor asked him about the navy and his job as the naval aide to the secretary of the navy. "Sounds like a damned important job," said Astor as their drinks arrived.

"Oh, it is. It's really important," interjected Helen before Stephen could even respond. The newlyweds looked at each other for a second, and then they both burst out in laughter.

Ava complimented the young bride, adding, "Helen, dear, there is nothing wrong with singing the praises of your spouse, especially when he has such a noble calling as military service! J.J founded a volunteer military battalion during the war with Spain, you know."

"Oh, please, Ava. I was just doing my patriotic duty," protested her husband. The couples' light discussions continued for about a half hour more as they consumed their drinks, with the Astors toasting to a long and happy marriage for the Morrisons. The evening had begun delightfully for the young newlyweds, who were made to feel comfortable and at home with the Astors.

"By the way, about our theater plans for tonight," interjected Astor. "I saw this play when it opened last November, and it was absolutely sensational. Ava wasn't able to make it that night, and I promised her I'd take her. When Oscar told me you were coming to New York for your honeymoon, I thought this would be the perfect opportunity. It's called *Little Johnny Jones* and stars this incredibly talented showman named Cohan, George M. Cohan. He and his show are the toast of Broadway. It's a really unique musical show and actually has a plot around which the songs are built. I really think you all will enjoy it." Astor pulled out his pocket watch and said, "In fact, we'd better be going. My carriage is waiting outside for us."

In front of the hotel, Astor's private carriage waited for them. The driver assisted the Astors and the Morrisons into the carriage, and moments later, they departed for the Liberty Theater on Broadway. Arriving a few minutes before the 7:30 P.M. show time, the foursome entered the theater as the crowds gazed with recognition at the Astors. An usher and the theater manager escorted them to a private box where they were seated in comfortable chairs with plush red velvet cushions. Ava Astor handed a small pair of binoculars to Stephen and Helen just as the theater lights dimmed. The orchestra began its overture, and moments later, the curtain went up.

The performance of *Little Johnny Jones* thoroughly mesmerized the Morrisons. As a child from a privileged background, Helen had received piano lessons as a young girl and was a gifted musician. She had attended the symphony regularly with her family and had an appreciation for fine music. Stephen, on the other hand, was tone deaf and had never developed much of an appreciation for music or the arts in general. He had never shown any interest in theater before this evening. It was a revelation to him to discover that he absolutely loved the performance.

The musical story of American jockey Johnny Jones, accused of throwing the English Derby, totally captivated the young naval officer. He found his foot tapping to the music for each song, and he especially loved the show-stopping number "Yankee Doodle Dandy".

During the intermission between the second and third acts, the foursome left the box and stretched their legs. The theater manager had provided champagne cocktails for them, and as they relaxed, Astor asked his wife and guests, "Well, what did you think?"

"It's sensational, J.J.! An absolute delight!" gushed Ava.

"Oh, I definitely agree!" concurred Helen. "I've never seen a musical show quite like this one. What did you think, Stephen? I swear I thought you were going to stand up and start dancing yourself!"

Morrison buoyantly replied, "It is absolutely wonderful! I can't get that "Yankee Doodle Dandy" number out of my head.

What talent! That fellow Cohan is incredible. Tell me, J.J., did I read the theater marquee correctly? Cohan also wrote and directed this play?"

"Yes, that is true. He certainly is a multitalented dynamo, isn't he?"

"I'll say. What energy! What talent! He must be an incredibly interesting individual," exclaimed Morrison, shaking his head with a sigh.

"Well, Stephen," grinned Astor, "you'll have a chance to judge that for yourself. Mr. Cohan and his wife, Ethel, who, by the way, is also in the show, will be dining with us at Delmonico's after the performance."

When the curtain came down on *Little Johnny Jones,* George M. Cohan received five curtain calls, with thunderous applause coming from the appreciative audience that delivered a standing ovation. Once the houselights came up and the audience began departing, the Astors and the Morrisons left their box and the theater manager arrived to escort them backstage. After a knock on the dressing room door, the manager escorted the foursome into the dressing room where they were greeted by Mr. and Mrs. George M. Cohan. Astor had actually met Cohan the previous November when he requested to go backstage to congratulate him the first time he had seen the show.

"George, another spectacular performance! You and your lovely bride brought down the house again!" thundered Astor enthusiastically. He then began the introductions. "George, Ethel, I'd like you to meet my wife, Ava. And this is Lieutenant Stephen Morrison of the United States Navy and his lovely wife, Helen. They're here in New York on their honeymoon." Cohan enthusiastically shook all of the visitors' hands and introduced his wife and co-star, Ethel Levey. Shortly after, the six of them departed in Astor's carriage, and headed east along

Forty-Fourth Street toward Fifth Avenue. In a few minutes, they reached their destination—Delmonico's Restaurant.

Delmonico's had been a favorite of the Astors, ever since it had moved to its present location in 1897. Its three floors of dining rooms provided a lavish ambiance for fine dining. The first few times he had dined there, Astor preferred one of the private dining rooms, but the management had made a recent change to its dining experience that Astor enjoyed even more. In the main second floor dining room, an orchestra now played music gently in the background so that diners could enjoy the music while dining. Astor had arranged for a table off to the side for his dinner party. The owner, Josephine Crist Delmonico, ebulliently greeted the Astors at the door and welcomed their party. Calling over the maitre d', she commanded him to escort the Astor party to their table immediately.

As they departed the elevator to the second floor dining room, heads began to turn. Word had already spread that John Jacob Astor and company would be dining there tonight. As they walked to their table, people also recognized another famous guest in the entourage, many of them pointing at Cohan. As the maitre d' escorted them individually to their seats, the orchestra suddenly began playing 'Yankee Doodle Dandy,' and the rest of the diners began to applaud.

"Come on, George, your fans await you!" kidded Astor. Smiling, Cohan stood and bowed in acknowledgment of the applause. As he sat down facing the Morrisons, Stephen studied the man. He appeared to be in his late twenties and had an impish Irish rascal charm about him. With a pleasantly handsome smile, he was possibly the most extroverted person that Morrison had ever met. His wife, Ethel, was a true beauty. She was more reserved and appeared more refined. *They seem like a somewhat oddly matched couple,* thought Morrison.

As the headwaiter and his team fawned over them and recited the bill of fare, Astor recommended to his guests, "Try the Lobster Newburg tonight if you'd like seafood. It's a real delight. Of course, if it's beef you want, there is nothing better on this planet than a Delmonico steak!" After they all made their selections, Astor motioned for the maitre d'. "Please request Chef Monsieur Grevillet to perform his usual culinary miracles for my guests and me." As the first of many courses arrived, the conversation stayed lively, even when interrupted by an occasional autograph seeker.

"George," confessed Helen, "I have to admit I've never seen you or the Four Cohans perform before tonight. You see, my father always considered vaudeville 'vulgar,' even though I would beg him to take me to shows. But I had my revenge. I played all of the latest tunes on the piano, and he'd just shake his head. If he could have seen *Little Johnny Jones* tonight, I believe he would have seen the error of his ways."

"Helen's father is Oscar Leavitt, the former Minister to the Ottoman Empire," interjected Astor. "He's active in the Roosevelt administration."

"Oscar Leavitt?" asked Ethel Levey. "Then you must be Jewish. My stepfather is Jewish, and he always speaks highly of your father and his accomplishments.

"I was wondering about your name," replied Helen.

"My birth name is Ethelia Fowler, and now my name is proudly Levey. Well, now it's legally Cohan, of course. How do you like that! A WASP girl with a Jewish name, married to a smiling Irishman! How original can one get?" They others raised their glasses in toast to Mrs. Cohan for her originality.

Before the entrees arrived, Astor announced to the group, "Dear guests, I would like to announce that I have wedding presents for the honeymoon couple."

"Oh no, J.J.," blurted out Helen, "you shouldn't have. This wonderful dinner and company is gift enough! Really, sir, you are spoiling us. We'll never want to return to Washington, will we, Stephen?"

Morrison smiled at his wife as Astor continued. "Nonsense, young lady, a special occasion calls for special gifts. When Oscar told me several months ago that you would be honeymooning in New York, I sent a cable to an associate in Paris and had these made." He reached into his coat pocket, produced two small boxes, and gave one each to Stephen and Helen. The gold embossing on the red box cover said *Cartier*. They each opened their boxes and removed a beautiful gold Cartier watch. They looked quite different from any watches that the Morrisons or the Cohans had ever seen. There was no watch chain or fob. On each side of the watch was a leather strap, the ends of which fastened together.

"It's called a wristwatch," explained Astor. "My friend Louis Cartier designed the concept himself. You see, an aviator friend of Louis' complained to him that he couldn't pull out his pocket watch when he had his hands on the controls of the aircraft. Hence, Louis designed this watch to be worn on the wrist. I think it's quite unique, and it is becoming the rage of Europe. They are beautiful, aren't they?"

"Thank you so much, J.J.," replied Stephen, quite touched with the thoughtfulness and generosity of Astor. "This watch is so beautiful and so unusual. I'll treasure it always."

"Yes, thank you," added Helen. "I will never look at this and not think of this wonderful night and the wonderful people with whom we spent it." With smiles of satisfaction, J.J. and Ava Astor watched the Morrisons place the watches on their wrists.

As the dinner progressed, Stephen decided to make a confession. "George, J.J., I have to admit to both of you that I have never seen a vaudeville show or had any interest in the performing arts. Tonight has really changed my perspective, and, I suppose, my life. I guess I always deluded myself into thinking there would never be time or a place in my life for things like music and dance. But being with three distinguished, creative individuals tonight—"

"Two, Stephen, just George and Ethel," interrupted Astor.

"No, I do mean three, sir. I've read your science fiction book, *A Journey in Other Worlds*, and found it fascinating. I also know that you are an inventor with several patents. You see, you are a creative genius, as is George. George, you, and Ethel have such incredible talent, talent that moves and inspires people. You're so blessed. It's just, well, it's a thrill and an honor to be with you tonight."

Astor broke the silence that followed. "Stephen," he began, "you have nothing to be envious about. As an officer in the United States Navy ... well, a lot of people, myself included, would say that what you do is more important than making millions or anything like that. I know you're proud of what you've accomplished thus far, aide to the secretary of the navy, among other things."

"Well, yes, I am proud, but it's really not quite the same thing. I've always had a calling to do this work. You creative achievers, though, are what make America great."

Cohan added, "Stephen, you look at me and see a successful song-and-dance man who happened to hit it big. You look at Mr. Astor, and you see a premier businessman who is transforming life in the United States, if not the world." He looked across the table at Astor, who began to smile. "Mr. Astor and I like to think we are the movers and shakers who love America, create things American, and make it great. Please let me say something, as the youngest man at this table. Stephen, whatever anyone else is doing to make this country great, you are

Lee Mandel

the one who is making it safe, allowing the Cohans, the Astors, the average public to try to make America greater. We can only do this because men like you are out there, putting your lives on the line and protecting us. Any greatness we will ever achieve will only be possible because of men like you.

"I've never met you before tonight, Stephen, but I've written a song about you. You just didn't realize it. It's 'Yankee Doodle Dandy.' Sure, they call me the Yankee Doodle Boy, because I play him every night on the stage, but you live the life twenty-four-hours a day. My God, Lieutenant Morrison, don't you see? An officer in the United States Navy- that's really the sort of thing that the song is about. You are the Yankee Doodle Boy!"

Helen Morrison had tears running down her face as Cohan finished. She leaned over and kissed her husband on his cheek. Astor nodded his head in agreement, and Stephen was at first speechless. Finally, he spoke. "George, I am so honored by what you just said, and I really don't know what to say, other than thank you."

Cohan smiled broadly and announced, "Stephen, you do have a lot to learn if you're going to ever enter show business! The appropriate response is 'My mother thanks you, my father thanks you, my sister thanks you, and I thank you.' Believe me, it has worked wonders for the Four Cohans!"

22

*The White House
Washington, D.C.
March 1905*

President Theodore Roosevelt believed that the twentieth century would become, as he called it, "America's time." He believed that the era of the United States isolating itself behind two ocean barriers had ended and that he would be the president to bring the United States to prominence on the world stage. He had an avid interest in international affairs, and his background as Assistant Secretary of the Navy served to fuel this interest, as did his passion for history. At the age of twenty-four, he had published *History of the Naval War of 1812,* which had become the definitive book on the subject. His interest in naval affairs had only heightened since then.

He intended to convert the United States Navy into a true "blue water" navy, and he eagerly sought the council of advisors, such as William Sims, for his naval planning. He had successfully pushed legislation through a reluctant Congress to fund the construction of several new battleships, and his ultimate intention was to have his new fleet sortie on an around-the-world deployment to show that the United States had indeed become a world-class naval power.

In early 1905, he asked William Sims to brief him on the new super battleship that the British were constructing. The briefing on this new class of battleship, the *Dreadnought*, deeply disturbed Roosevelt. It already made obsolete the new American battleships that had been proposed. He asked Sims for his recommendation, to which his advisor replied, "Mr. President, we need to send someone to England to work as a liaison officer specifically on this project for a few weeks and learn all about this battleship. From what I've heard, this is the future of naval warfare. I know from my British counterparts that they would welcome the opportunity to show off their technologies." Roosevelt agreed with Sims and assured him that he would arrange this with the highest levels of the British government.

Roosevelt had also been closely following the war between Japan and Russian, even tracking the progress of the war on a large wall map using colored pins. He made no secret to those in the administration of his admiration of the Japanese fighting men and their successes. He had little regard for the Russian government or its policies, and he felt that their expansionist policies in Manchuria would serve only to provoke the Japanese into action. His analysis had been correct. On February 8, 1904, the Japanese had staged a surprise attack on Port Arthur and virtually destroyed the Russian Oriental Fleet. The audacity and ferocity of the Japanese action stunned the rest of the world.

As impressed as Roosevelt was with the Japanese military actions, he became equally disenchanted with the leadership of the Russian government. *Couldn't they see this coming,* he wondered to himself? He had heard about their autocratic mentality, and he totally disapproved of their use of anti-Semitism to divert the public's attention away from governmental failures. The pogroms were an abomination to the young president. He was proud to have worked with the B'nai B'rith to lodge his formal protest over the Kishinev pogrom. In addition, he intensely disliked the Russian Ambassador to the United States, Count Cassini, whom he regarded as a pompous fool.

Each day, the war continued to bleed both countries dry in terms of manpower, resources, and morale. Roosevelt reasoned that both countries must be tiring of this senseless war and just might be looking for an honorable way out of the conflict. Specifically, he thought that peace negotiations mediated by a third party could possibly get the warring enemies to sit down and negotiate a truce. However, all the informal feedback that he had received indicated that the Russians were too proud or, as Roosevelt feared, too stupid, to allow this to happen. Roosevelt knew very little about Tsar Nicholas II, but he remained unimpressed by his actions, both militarily and politically.

Just before leaving for New York City for his niece's wedding, he had received a military briefing from Commander Sims on the massive battle in Manchuria that had just been concluded. The Battle of Mukden, the largest land battle in history, was a humiliating defeat for the Russians, who suffered nearly one hundred thousand casualties combining killed, wounded, and losses as prisoners. It had also cost the Japanese seventy-five thousand casualties. Both sides had been stretched beyond the breaking point. The death toll of the horrific battle convinced Roosevelt that even the Tsar could no longer ignore the reality of the situation. The time to act was now.

Roosevelt consulted with Secretary of State John Hay and proposed that they let the Japanese government know that Roosevelt would be willing to help facilitate a peace conference. The president specifically instructed Hay to coyly inform the Japanese that he would be willing to help as a facilitator if they requested his assistance. He did not want to give the Russians, specifically the Tsar, the impression that he had solicited the job. After the Battle of Mukden, Roosevelt felt confident that the Japanese would be grateful for such an offer. He remained hopeful that even the Russians would now come to their senses and face reality.

Hay cautioned Roosevelt not to be overly optimistic about the Russians. Earlier that day, he had met with Count Cassini, who "proceeded to cry in his beer to me about the cross that the Russian people were bearing after Mukden."

"For God's sake, man," retorted Hay, "why the devil don't you try and negotiate a settlement with Japan?"

Shaking his head slowly and unable to look Hay in the eye, Cassini responded, "We are condemned to fight. We cannot honestly stop."

"My opinion of the Russian leadership has fallen ever lower, John. I didn't think that was possible," responded the grim president. "In any event, I'm off to Eleanor's wedding. Let's proceed with our plan to try to engage the Japanese. What other choice do we have?"

23

Waldorf Astoria Hotel
New York City
March 1905

"Oh, my God, help me! Please help me!" screamed Stephen Morrison, his arms bound and unable to resist as the blade slowly sliced into his neck. Blood spurted out onto the assailant in the black suit as he continued screaming.

The screams awakened his wife, Helen, who looked over and saw that her husband, drenched in sweat, was obviously in the throes of a nightmare. "Stephen!" she shouted as she began shaking his shoulders, "Stephen, wake up, wake up!" After a few violent shakes, Stephen Morrison's eyes flew open with a terrified look.

"Jesus, Stephen. You scared the daylights out of me." Helen placed a gentle hand on his forehead.

"Sorry, it was just a nightmare."

"Some nightmare! You screamed loud enough to wake the neighbors."

"Yeah, well ..." He watched her face in the moonlight. The darkness felt like it was closing in, obscuring her face. He reached over and turned on the light.

Helen squinted against the harsh light. Stephen expected her to complain, but she didn't. Instead, she asked, "What was it about?"

"Same damn thing as it always is, ever since I was a teenager," he began. "It started when I was traveling through Russia in 1888." He told Helen about the gruesome death of his uncle that he learned about when they visited Perm. "I don't get them nearly as often as I used to get them, but they are terrifying. It's always a variation of the same thing. I'm sitting in a room somewhere, tied up. I haven't a clue where. Then some bastard walks up to me and tells me to make a choice. I don't know what the hell he is talking about; I never know what choice he wants me to make. Then he proceeds to slit my throat. Pretty delightful stuff, eh?"

"It's horrible. It's grotesque!" Helen whispered as she laid her head on his shoulder and began rubbing his back. "Whatever can it mean?"

He kissed her forehead. "I'm afraid it may mean that I have a screw loose," he teased. "I really don't think it means anything," he added seriously. "After all, I've been having variations of this stupid dream for seventeen years now." He faced her and smiled. "Well, now you know my deepest, darkest secret, Mrs. Morrison. Sorry you married me?"

"Hey, sailor, it's going to take a heck of a lot more that an occasional nightmare to get rid of me, you know! Look around us, Lieutenant Morrison. We're in the bridal suite at the Waldorf Astoria, and we have one full day left on our honeymoon before we leave tomorrow. The sun has just come up, and a beautiful day is beginning in New York. I'm the happiest girl in the world, married to the most wonderful, honorable man in the world. Am I sorry I married you? You must be joking, you silly guy!"

He hugged her and kissed her again. "I think you're stuck with me, Helen Leavitt Morrison. I can't believe that God was kind enough to me to bring you into my life. I really love you, Helen. I will thank God every day of my life that you're mine."

"I love you right back, Stephen. I just hate to see you so distraught by that nightmare." She got out of bed and stretched. "Say, what would you like to do today?"

He smiled at her and replied, "Whatever you want to do. Just name it."

"I'll tell you what I want to do. I want to see where you grew up, where you lived when you were a young boy. Will you take me there?"

"Are you sure you want to do that? We only have today, and then it's back to Washington."

"Stephen, I want to learn everything about you, how you became the man that I love. Yes, I do want to see where you grew up. Please, let's go."

After finishing their breakfast at the hotel, Stephen announced to his bride that she was about to experience a surprising thrill. "But you promised me we were going to visit your old neighborhood," she protested.

"Oh, we're going there," he reassured her, "but how we get there, that's the treat. We're going to get there in the new underground train system that opened last year, the one that they call the subway. Can you believe it? We're going to travel there under Manhattan!"

The hotel concierge directed the excited couple to the nearest subway station at 33rd Street and Lexington Avenue. There they saw the subway sign above a set of concrete stairs leading below street level. At the bottom of the platform, they followed the sign to the tollbooth, where Stephen purchased a few tokens, and they entered the turnstiles. Following the sign that said "Lower Manhattan, " they walked to a train platform where numerous other people stood waiting for the train to arrive. Clinging to her husband's arm, Helen whispered, "This is kind of creepy, isn't it? I mean, we're actually underground, like moles." They looked around at the handsomely tiled walls of the station, impressed not only with the engineering concept of an underground train system, but also at the clean and pleasing appearance of the station itself. He smiled back at her as they peered over the platform and down the darkened cavern to see if they could detect a train coming.

After a few minutes, they felt a rush of air on the platform, and looking down the darkened tunnel, Stephen announced, "I see a light! This must be our train." The tiny pinhole of a light rapidly enlarged as the train arrived, and the noise level rose dramatically as the train pulled into the station, generating a sensation of gusting wind that died down as the train slowed. After the train stopped, the electric doors on the side of the subway cars slid open, and passengers disembarked before the new passengers boarded. The Morrisons entered and sat down near the door they had entered. A subway system map covered part of the opposite wall of the car.

"Do you know where we should be going?" asked Helen.

"We're going to start at the beginning," answered Stephen. "We're going to the last stop in southern Manhattan, Bowling Green Station, according to the map."

The train continued on southward, stopping at about ten more stations along the way before arriving at Bowling Green Station. The Morrisons departed the train, followed the small crowd to the stairs, and exited the station at the southern tip of Broadway. Across the street was Battery Park, which contained several large buildings. "We're here," announced Stephen, as he looked across at the park.

"It looks like a fortress or something like that," noted Helen.

"Actually, you're quite right. You're looking at Castle Garden, and it was built as a fort during the War of 1812. The army eventually sold it to New York City in the mid-1800s, and it became the main immigrant processing center for the state of New York. I read somewhere that over eight million people have entered the United States through Castle Garden." He turned to Helen, smiled as he bowed formally, and added, "and that includes yours truly!" He held her hand as they crossed the street and entered the compound which had been closed for over ten years. Opened by the federal government in 1892, Ellis Island had taken over immigration processing from the states. However, the deserted buildings remained open to the public without charge.

The main hall struck them both as cold and dreary. Most of the furniture had been removed and despite this emptyness, it still exuded a feeling of crowded conditions and cold, impersonal interactions. Looking around the great hall, Helen asked, "Stephen, do you remember this place at all?"

He nodded his head. "Yes, I was about eleven years old when we came through this place." Turning to face the doorway at the far corner, he pointed and noted, "This was where we entered the building." They walked over to a spot near the doorway and he said, "This was where there were aisles where we waited on line. We had to get processed in and then get a cursory medical exam. They were especially vigilant for trachoma and tuberculosis, which they called the 'Jewish disease.' We slept on the floor for three days while we went through more screenings. When everything was completed, we were instructed to go out the door where you and I entered the building. At that point, we became residents of America.

"Come on," he said, taking her hand. "Let's go to the back, to the piers." They hurriedly walked to the rear doorway and out into the light.

The bright New York sunshine provided a vivid contrast to the cold, dank building they had just left. The couple walked over to the edge of the compound to the waterfront. They stared out at New York Harbor. As they looked at the Statue of Liberty, Stephen said, "Do you have any idea of how excited I was when we first arrived in the waters of New York's harbor, when I knew we were actually entering America?"

"It must have been thrilling for you, coming from such a horrid place like Russia," she agreed.

"When I learned we would be immigrating to the United States, I was ecstatic." They had walked over several yards along the waterfront when he stopped. He looked at her and said, "It was here, right here. The boat was tied up here, and this was where I took my first step in the United States. Funny, but I remember it like it was yesterday, not twenty-four years ago." A few feet away stood a rotting bench where they sat as they continued looking out on the harbor. For several minutes neither of them spoke.

Helen suddenly asked him, "Stephen, how did it feel to be a new American? I was born in the United States and have always been a child of privilege. What was it like for you? This seems like such a cold, impersonal way to first see one's new home."

He continued to gaze out at the Statue of Liberty as he answered. "Helen, your father emigrated in a different era. The Jewish immigrants from Germany that preceded us were self-sufficient and had trades and professions. They were largely welcomed in this country. I later learned that, even though we were fellow Jews, the previous Jewish immigrants, mainly from Western Europe, weren't exactly thrilled to have us join them in the United States. We represented an embarrassing burden to them."

He paused a few seconds, deep in thought, as he remembered. "When I first learned we would be immigrating to the United States, I was absolutely thrilled. I hated Odessa, I hated Russia, and I was delighted that I was going to become an American. As I told you, my father was a prominent rabbi in Odessa. He had actually been recruited by several of the immigrant Jewish groups in New York to serve as a de-facto 'Chief Rabbi', hopefully to organize the Russian Jewish community. He was an honored, important man in our community circle.

"You see, my father and I were two totally different people. His vision of being an American was to continue the old ways in America and live a life isolated from the outside, non-Jewish world. I couldn't have disagreed with him more. Hell, we could have stayed in Russia for that kind of life. I've always wanted more—I wanted to become an American, to blend in with my Russian background, not to isolate myself because of it. I always wanted to belong, not to be an outsider. My father could never understand that. We frequently quarreled over my future. Did I tell you that he wanted me to become a rabbi?"

Helen looked at him incredulously. "I'm sorry, but I can't picture you as a rabbi, darling."

"That makes two of us!" He laughed at the thought. "I knew from the time I was a little boy that I wanted to travel and see the world. I used to watch them build the Brooklyn Bridge, dreaming that one day I would be sailing in one of the many ships I saw sail by me. God, how that infuriated my father! He always said that I needed to stay with my own people and that even though this was America, people would always hate the Jews. I think it would be a slight understatement to say that my father was opposed to my dream of a career in the navy."

"Did you hate him for it?"

"No, not really. I resented him for the way he looked at being an American. He felt that people would hate him because he was Jewish, and he chose to isolate himself from the anti-Semitism by hiding in his community. I refused to live that way. I wanted to become an American, and if people chose to hate me because I was a Jew, fine. I wouldn't be hiding in a Jewish ghetto. I'd compete and beat them at their own game, so to speak."

He sighed before continuing. "You know Helen, my father was not exactly wrong in what he was trying to tell me. I think in his way he was trying to protect me. He was right in many ways. The streets here aren't really paved with gold. Even though this is America, a nation of immigrants, and Lady Liberty welcomes us with open arms, there is still much anti-Semitism here, even if it's not sanctioned by the government as it is in Russia.

"I remember as we walked out the door of Castle Garden and into Battery Park, there were many carts with people talking in all languages, yelling at us. We were new immigrants and we didn't speak a word of English at that point. One of the carts had a sign in Russian that said 'Rubles converted to dollars'. Father had been given rubles by the community in Odessa to help us get started with our life in America, so we went up to the cart, and they gladly exchanged all our rubles for dollars. They laughed as they gave us our money. We, of course, didn't understand the English that they spoke, and shortly thereafter, we learned that they had given us counterfeit money. I learned English pretty rapidly after that. I remembered the words that those moneychangers said to us as we walked away from their cart. They called out, "Welcome to America, you stupid fucking kikes!"

"That's just so terrible! That was your welcome to America? It's absolutely disgusting that people would take advantage of others that way!" The more Helen learned about her husband's past, the more she began to understand why he had such serious eyes, as she called them. He had a dark, angry part of him that he kept repressed, deep inside of him. She laid her head on his shoulder, and nestled in the crook of his arm. "Does it hurt you to talk of these things, to relive them like this?" she asked.

"No, not really. These are the bits and pieces of my life that made me who I am today. Darling, you wanted to see these places, and I'm willing to show them to you. Maybe in the end you'll have a better understanding of the man you married."

After a half hour of cuddling in his arms as they stared out onto the harbor, Helen asked, "Can we go now, Stephen? Take me to your old neighborhood. I want to learn more about you. You see, it gives me more reasons to love you. Even more than I already do!"

The couple entered the subway station and rode it to the City Hall Station. As they exited the station and headed east, Helen could see the Brooklyn Bridge looming several blocks ahead.

"Did you live this close to the bridge?" she asked.

"No, but I spent a lot of time here as a child. I was fascinated by the bridge, and I spent the first two years of my life in this country watching them finish it. There's something I want to show you." As they walked along the underside of the Manhattan tower of the bridge, they crossed over, and several blocks north of the bridge, Morrison led his wife onto the waterside park area where he had spent so many days as a youth. They sat down on the grass right next to the waterfront.

"Here it is, Helen, the very spot I used to visit. I'd watch the workers on the bridge and, more importantly, I'd watch the ships sail by me. Oh, how I used to dream and pray that one day I would be on one of the ships. That's how I first got the idea to become an officer in the navy. I believe I've already told you how that made my father feel!

"This is also where I learned how to fight. It wasn't unusual for the goyim to attack me when they saw me here. In retrospect, I suppose it was pretty stupid, an orthodox Jewish boy all by himself and somewhat out of his neighborhood. But I always felt it was my right to be here, and the river always had a magical effect on me. I was willing to fight for that right. Unfortunately, fighting occurred fairly frequently."

"That is so horrible, Stephen!"

"It's not that horrible. It taught me some good lessons about the person I wanted to be. I watched our people be treated like dirt in Russia, and even though I was only a boy when we came to this country, I had already decided that I wasn't going to stand for the mistreatment and humiliation anymore. I was tired of being a Jewish punching bag. So many in our neighborhood acted as if they were back in the *shtetl;* America was just a continuation of their second-class life in Russia. I was one Jew who wasn't going to sit back and turn the other cheek. I was going to become an American and on my terms. My God, Helen, I got so sick of seeing weak, passive Jews. I was determined that I wasn't going to be one of them."

"Besides, in a way, all of the fighting was the best thing that happened to me. It's how I met my brother, Joseph. Look here," he said as he stood and took her hand. He pointed over to a weathered plaque on the ground near them on a low granite pedestal. Walking over to it, Helen saw the bronze plaque that had turned green with age. She read the inscription dedicated to the memory of the people who died on the New York and Brooklyn Bridge on May 31, 1883.

"What is this about, darling?" she asked. Stephen explained the terrible story of the people being crushed to death on the bridge a week after it opened. "You see," he said proudly, "I rescued Joseph that day from being trampled to death. I know this will seem strange to you, but he was one of the tormentors who used to attack me on a regular basis." Noting the astonished look on his wife's face, he said, "I'll explain it to you while we walk back to the subway station. It takes a while to tell this story and to do it justice."

The Morrisons strolled back to the City Hall Station and rode the subway two stops further north, exiting at the Canal Street Station. Climbing the station stairs to the street level provided a bit of a jolt for Morrison. He felt that he had almost stepped back into time. He had not been in his old neighborhood in over twenty years. Seeing the tenements immediately brought back memories he had long since repressed. Almost to himself he muttered, "This seems like a lifetime ago." They continued east on Canal Street, heading toward the river.

Pushcarts laden with different foods, clothing, and dry goods lined the street, which seemed alive with people hawking their wares. Morrison could discern Yiddish, Hebrew, and Russian being spoken. To his surprise, he also heard a lot of English being spoken. Trash lined the streets. He saw a striking difference from two decades ago.

"In those days, all you saw in the neighborhood were orthodox Jews in frock coats and broad-brimmed hats. Now it looks as if many people are dressed like, well, like Americans. My father never would have approved." As they strolled down the streets, heads turned, and people gazed at them. The well-dressed Morrisons gave off an air of money and sophistication. Stephen could swear he heard a few people mumble *goyim* as they walked by.

Occasionally, a beggar stopped them with outstretched hands. Helen would reach into her purse and give the poor soul a quarter. The beggar expressed appreciation in excited Yiddish. Stephen could sense that his wife felt uneasy being around the poverty that she had never experienced. "It's hard for me to believe that you grew up here," she said. "Believe me," he replied, "I've known worse. I spent my first decade in Tsarist Russia," he reminded her. Soon they reached the corner of Ludlow Street. "We turn here, Helen," he instructed. "We're almost there."

Walking north on Ludlow Street, Stephen stopped in front of the third building. "Here it is," he announced, "Six Ludlow Street. We lived in this building in a small apartment on the first floor." Helen gazed up at the six-story tenement. The dreary, dingy-looking building looked identical to the other buildings that lined Ludlow Street. The Morrisons noted that many people were walking north on Ludlow, and a crowd had begun to form at the far corner of Ludlow and Grand Street.

A young boy sat on the stoop of the building, watching the crowds forming down the street. His clothes were frayed and old, but he wasn't dressed in clothing from the old country. On his head he wore a cap, not a traditional Jewish yarmulke. Stephen asked him, "What is going on up the street?" as he pointed to all the people walking north.

The boy looked suspiciously at the strange couple and answered in accented English, "He died last night."

"Who died?" asked Helen.

"De Rabbi! Rabbi Skolnik, he's de Chief Rabbi. Dey be carrying him to the cemetery to bury him now. All de people come to watch him go to God. He a great man!"

The Morrisons watched the crowds beginning to line the edge of Grand Street. It brought back an eerie feeling for Stephen, recalling how he had missed his own father's funeral so many years before. Now another Chief Rabbi was being laid to rest. "Come on, Helen," he said taking her hand, "let's watch the procession." They followed the crowd to the end of Ludlow Street and stood among the throngs that had assembled along Grand Street. Gazing westward, they could see the procession coming up the street.

The funeral procession consisted of a mass of people following the coffin of the late Chief Rabbi who was being carried by several pallbearers. The crowd swelled as the procession wound through the streets of the Lower East Side, passing every synagogue along the way. By the time they had reached Grand Street, over twenty thousand marchers followed the coffin, almost all of them orthodox Jews. The Morrisons could hear chanting in Hebrew in honor of the departed leader of the Jewish community. All along the route, people had gathered along the streets. Many watched from the windows of the upper floors of the tenements and factories that lined their route.

Several factories lined Grand Street on both sides as it intersected with Ludlow Street. Just east of the intersection stood a five-story building that housed a furniture manufacturing company named L. Jones and Company. As in the other buildings lining the route, workers in the upper floors watched the curious procession as the crowds began to walk past. Most of the factory workers at L. Jones and Company were Irish and watched with disdain as the crowds marched past.

Suddenly, a wrench, thrown by one of the workers, flew out of a second-floor window and hit one of the marchers in the head. Immediately, several bottles rained down on the marchers in the street. As the Jews stopped, stunned by the violent

Lee Mandel

act of disrespect shown toward them and the late Chief Rabbi, the workers packing the windows of the upper floors of the factory began laughing and jeering at the crowd below them. Barely able to see this activity from their vantage point on the densely crowded street, Morrison began to feel a sense of rage. "Nothing ever changes here," he said to Helen, "not from the disgusting treatment of the Jews, to their lambs-to-the-slaughter passive acceptance of this kind of treatment! It makes me furious!" In a moment, however, even Stephen Morrison would be amazed by what he witnessed.

The pallbearers respectfully placed the rabbi's coffin on the ground and suddenly turned toward the factory and charged through the front doors. Immediately, the massive crowd stopped and picked up bricks, cans, and scattered debris from the street and hurled them at the windows of the factory. Hundreds followed the pallbearers through the front door as factory workers struggled unsuccessfully to close the doors. Inside, the Jews charged the workers they encountered, and the surprised factory employees realized that they had provoked a bloody confrontation that they hadn't counted on. All around them, the Morrisons could hear the shrill sound of police whistles blowing, as policemen who had been monitoring the procession realized that a riot had developed.

Helen grabbed her husband's arm and held it tightly. She looked up at his face and saw a smile slowly developing on his lips. Under his breath, she heard him mutter, "Well, I'll be damned!"

She tugged at his arm now, pulling him back from the street toward Ludlow Street. "Please, Stephen, let's go! Please don't get involved. The police are here, and they'll handle it. Please, darling. It's not your fight now!"

He looked at her and saw the terrified look on her face. He wrapped his arms around her and said, "No, you're right; it's not. Let's head back to the subway station and go back to the Waldorf. I think we've seen enough today." The couple walked south on Ludlow, away from the crowds and headed back to the subway station.

They barely spoke on the ride back to the station at 33rd Street and Lexington. Arriving at the Waldorf Astoria, Helen smiled at Stephen and said, "I think we should go to the lounge and relax a little. I certainly could use a glass of wine."

"Your wish is my command," he pledged as he offered his arm to her. Arm in arm, they entered the lounge and sat down.

Within a few minutes, their server brought them two glasses of wine. "Oh, this is so good!" she exclaimed as she took her first sip. She raised her glass and proposed a toast to her husband, proclaiming him the most interesting and most accomplished person she had ever met. He smiled and thanked her.

"No, it's I who should be thanking you," she countered. "Thank you so much for taking me to all these places today, Stephen. I think I understand you a lot better now."

"Do you really think so?"

"Yes, I do. You know, when I first fell in love with you, I told Father that you were one of the most distinguished, handsomest men I had ever seen. But there was something in your eyes that I saw, something very serious and perhaps also angry. After today, I think I understand some of that anger. A part of you is filled with so much anger that I think it even scares you a bit. You know, Stephen, it's almost as if you are a man between two worlds. The one you left behind makes you feel uncomfortable and different, yet it's one that you can't let go of."

He looked at her and smiled. "Maybe you do know me a little better than I thought you possibly could. Your description of me is probably pretty accurate, although I never thought of my life that way. You're right. I look at the orthodox Jews, and it's almost inconceivable to me that I was one of them. I look at how they cling to their little world and almost invite the world to abuse them, and it makes me sick. Yet today was the first time I ever saw them look the aggressors in the eye and say, 'Enough!' I was so proud of what they did to those factory workers." He paused to finish his wine and called their server over to order another round.

"You're probably right. I can't let go. My father, my stepfather that is, wanted me to convert to Catholicism, and I refused, telling him I was and would always be a Jew. Although I don't think he really understood me, not deep down inside, he respected my choices. He did give me some advice that I've never forgotten. He said something along the lines that I should not wear my religion as a chip on my shoulder, daring people to knock it off. Something like that. Maybe he was right. But you know what, Helen? I can't be anything but who I am."

She placed he hand over his. "You know what? I love you more now than I did this morning." She leaned over and kissed him. "I've got me a Yankee Doodle sailor boy who happens to be Jewish and, like my father, is a man of the world, a leader. Thank you, God, for giving me this naval officer." They raised glasses again and she chirped in, "I've got a great plan for our last night in New York!"

"And what might that be, Mrs. Morrison?"

"We are going back to our room. First, I'm going to bathe. Then we're going to get dressed to the nines and have a totally elegant dinner at the fine restaurant right here at the Waldorf."

"Sounds like a great plan to me!"

"But you haven't heard the best part! After dinner, we're going back to our room. And then you are going to make love to me all night," she said to him. "And that's a direct order!"

24

The White House
Washington, D.C.
May 30, 1905

After hearing the preliminary news of the naval battle in the Sea of Japan, Theodore Roosevelt requested a senior level briefing at the White House. If what he had heard was true, this battle may well have decided the outcome of this futile war between Japan and Russia. In addition to Commander William Sims, who would be doing the briefing, he requested Secretary of the Navy Paul Morton to be present, as well as his designated replacement, Charles Bonaparte. As Roosevelt bounded into the room, he directed, "Please be seated, gentlemen. Commander Sims, please begin."

"Thank you, Mr. President," Sims began as he stood. "As you know, sir, the Russian Pacific Fleet was essentially destroyed last year at Port Arthur. The Russians had intended to sail their Baltic Fleet to relieve the Pacific Fleet and engage the Japanese in their own backyard. Well, the Baltic Fleet encountered a myriad of difficulties. They left the Baltic last October and didn't arrive into the area of operations until this month. They had difficulties securing coaling stations, and the material condition of their ships was seriously deficient. In addition, Admiral Rozhdestvenski's forces suffered from extremely low morale and defeatism, not to mention having to deal with the general revolutionary fervor that has infected the Russian navy.

Sims continued to describe the decimation of the Russian fleet in the ensuing battle. "Sir, forty-five Russian ships entered the Straight of Tsushima. Only three of them made it to Vladivostok. We've heard that as few as six of their ships made it to neutral ports. The rest were either destroyed by the Japanese or captured by them." As he finished the sentence, he heard all three men literally gasp.

"Who is the leader of the Japanese fleet? He must be one hell of a leader to accomplish such a feat!" blurted out Secretary Morton.

"Admiral Togo was in command of the Japanese forces," replied Sims. "He is a supremely capable combat leader, and he certainly proved himself with this engagement. He was absolutely brilliant. At this point, there is no longer any Russian navy."

"What about Japanese losses?" asked the president.

"We've heard that the Japanese lost only three boats, all small torpedo boats. They suffered about six hundred casualties, in contrast to the Russians, who suffered as many as six thousand killed." Sims looked around at the three men facing him. "I think it is worthwhile to point out that this was the largest naval battle in history."

All four men remained silent. Roosevelt expressed the thoughts of the entire group when he spoke, almost as if he were talking to himself. "That's it then. The Russians are finished. They can't go on now. Oh, those damned Russians! When will that Tsar face reality? You know, one of the top members of our diplomatic corps, George Meyer, serves as our ambassador to Russia. I sent him to Russia in an attempt to get inside their leadership's mind, to learn what their war perceptions are. Turns out, no one there can figure out Nicholas, either.

"Gentlemen, earlier today the Japanese government contacted me and asked me to invite both the Japanese and the Russians to come together to negotiate the end of this senseless slaughter. After hearing these details of the naval battle that destroyed the Russian Fleet, the time for action is now. I will make a direct approach to that fool Nicholas and try to save him from himself. His people deserve compassion, even if he doesn't."

25

Catherine Palace
Tsarskoe Selo, Russia
June 6, 1905

George Meyer, United States ambassador to imperial Russia, had his instructions directly from the president of the United States. He carried a message for the Tsar's eyes only. Through the Russian foreign minister, Count Lamsdorff, Meyer had requested a private meeting with Nicholas. Lamsdorff balked at first, noting that the imperial family was at Tsarskoe Selo to celebrate the Tsarina's birthday the following day, June 7. Meyer convinced the foreign minister to allow him to visit the Tsar that very day.

Meyer traveled by train to Tsarskoe Selo and hoped that his mission would be successful, but he had his doubts. He had never been impressed with Tsar Nicholas, either as a statesman or as an intellect. He had warned the president not to get his hopes up. Nonetheless, he intended to deliver the president's proposal as forcefully as possible.

Upon his arrival at the Catherine Palace, Nicholas kept him waiting for over an hour in his outer office. When he was finally admitted to the Tsar's office, Meyer presented President Roosevelt's proposal, reading the exact instructions given to him. Roosevelt stressed that the unanimous consensus of all the world leaders was that the war was hopeless. Its continuation would have disastrous repercussions for Russia and its foreign possessions. He emphasized the total secrecy of the invitation and expressed his belief that he could get the Japanese to agree to the meeting; the message did not reveal that the Japanese agreement had already been secured. The president proposed that the negotiations take place as soon as possible and at any location agreeable to the belligerents.

Meyer grew exasperated at Nicholas' rambling responses, which seemed both irrelevant and trivial. For minutes at a time, he simply stared at Meyer. The meeting evolved just as Meyer had feared it would. Meyer continued to play on his close relationship with the president and his knowledge of the man's great integrity. He expressed empathy for the Tsar, agreeing that decisions such as these were always difficult, but stressed that the ultimate good of the people must be the objective of any great leader.

At the end of the nearly hour-long meeting, Tsar Nicholas II of Russia instructed a surprised and delighted Ambassador George Meyer to inform President Roosevelt that he agreed to his proposal. He would meet with the Japanese. The war had to end.

26

State, War, and Navy Building
Washington, D.C.
June 1905

A few days later, the American press learned of Roosevelt's diplomatic triumph and widely praised him, as did the foreign media. Later that week, Roosevelt scheduled a cabinet meeting. When he arrived in the room, the cabinet rose to their feet and gave him a standing ovation. Roosevelt beamed as he raised his hands in the air, pretending he didn't care to receive the adulation that, in fact, he craved. He finally sat down, with the others following his lead, and the meeting began.

"Gentlemen, this is indeed great day! At least now, I believe we can be instrumental in ending this ridiculous war. And the world will see the United States is the active broker in bringing peace to the world. I've received some preliminary feedback from both the Russians and the Japanese. They are agreeable to having the peace negotiations take place here in the United States. We haven't determined a site for the peace talks yet.

"Here's a little background you should know. The Japanese readily agreed to peace talks a few weeks ago. They have proven to be very reasonable, and I have no doubt they will be approaching the negotiations in good faith." He poured himself a glass of water and drank deeply before speaking again.

"It's the Russians about whom I have questions. They have been unreasonable from the start. I find them a very difficult people to understand. I need to enter these negotiations with a much greater understanding of Russia than I have now. I've got to learn how they think, what drives their actions, and what their politics are really like. Hence, gentlemen, I have a request. Please search among your staffs and find me an expert on Russia. Find me someone who speaks the language, who is up-to-date on their internal politics, and who understands the Tsar. Find me someone who can think like a Russian. I can't stress how critical it is to find such a person. I need this man to prepare me for the peace talks, and I need him soon. Please notify me directly when such a man is identified."

BOOK THREE

1

*The White Sea
Approaching Solovetsky Island
May 1906*

The cold sea winds bit into Stephen Morrison's face as the prison boat headed eastward across Onega Bay in the White Sea. Dead ahead, he could barely see their destination—Solovetsky Island. The desolate island was the home of the monastery that served as a labor camp for convicted criminals and political enemies of the Tsar. Morrison felt glad to be finally going there, after having spent several months in the port city of Kem, which served as the debarkation point for the island prison. He had been imprisoned in a detention prison used mostly for prisoners bound for Solovetsky Island. "Enjoy your stay here this winter," his jailers taunted him. "The bay is basically impassable from October until May due to ice and treacherous seas." So, for several months, he had resided in a solitary jail cell, waiting for the weather conditions to improve.

As the small steam-powered boat proceeded eastward, the waters tossed the small boat with each rolling wave. Morrison actually felt a little seasick toward the end of the two-and-a-half-hour voyage, a sensation he hadn't felt since his first year at the Naval Academy. Through the morning mist, he now could discern the outline of their island destination. His nose continued to run, but he couldn't wipe it; his hands and ankles were tightly shackled together. *At least my face has stopped itching*, he thought to himself. He now had a beard, and when it had grown in, the itching nearly drove him crazy. He found himself scratching his face continually. "One half-hour to dockside!" shouted out the coxswain as the island loomed larger.

The walled monastery could be easily seen on the waterline at the edge of Prosperity Bay. Above the twenty-foot walls that appeared to be made out of large boulders, Morrison could see several buildings that featured impressive towers and onion-shaped domes that typified the Russian architecture of the 1600s. After a short while, the boat tied up at the piers, and the guard ordered the four prisoners on their feet. He then proceeded to remove their ankle shackles. A gruff man wearing a military-looking coat boarded the boat and assumed custody of the prisoners. He led them single file through a large entrance gate into the thick fortress-like walls.

"Stay in line, you walking dead! Single file! Follow me!" he barked, as he led them up the stone walkway to a large white multi-storied church-like building that looked to Morrison to be the monastery's main building. Once inside the building, their escort gave instructions. "Stand here and don't move until you are individually summoned by me. Do you understand?" Each of the prisoners nodded in assent. The escort disappeared behind a large wooden door, pulling it shut after him.

A few minutes later, he emerged and pointed directly at Morrison. "You!" he bellowed, "Follow me!" Morrison obediently followed him into the room and stood in front of a desk. The escort left, closing the door behind him. Seated at the desk was a monk, who did not look up from his paperwork or acknowledge the presence of his prisoner for several minutes. After a short while, he slapped shut the folder in front of him and looked up at Morrison. The monk's first impression of the prisoner was that he was probably a violent man, based on his angry eyes and what the monk had read about him in his dossier. Indicating the chair at the front of the desk, he directed, "Be seated."

The monk leaned forward with his hands folded on the desk as he began to speak. Looking at his graying hair and weathered face, Morrison judged him to be in his forties. "I am Father Gregor," he began "and I am in charge of this monastery. You may think it a bit incongruous that a man of God is in charge of your prison. It is not. Our monastery was founded here in the fifteenth century. This place of solitude has always been faithful to the Tsar, our leader and defender of the Russian Orthodox faith. Accordingly, we house within our walls persons judged to be enemies of the Tsar. It is a harsh place, but one where repentance is possible. Unfortunately, most people sent here do not repent, and they die here. That is your one way off Solovetsky Island alive, through repentance and rehabilitation.

"Your name is Anatoly Matushenko," he continued, reading from the dossier. "I see that you were the ringleader of the mutiny aboard the battleship *Potemkin* last year. A real anarchist and rabble-rouser, according to these records. All of this over some maggot-infected meat?" he asked wryly, as he looked up at the prisoner.

Morrison didn't know how to reply, so he remained silent. Rather than look at Father Gregor, he stared straight ahead. Finally, he said, "Well, Father, the meat was tainted, and the crew was hungry."

"I think that the government has been somewhat merciful to you, my son. I'm surprised you weren't executed. No doubt, they didn't want to create a martyr for the revolutionary element within Russia today. According to these documents, you have been sentenced to ten years at hard labor. You are to be in solitary confinement with no contact whatsoever with other prisoners." He smiled at Morrison. "Maybe that is a blessing when you consider what the rest of the prisoners are like. We have about one hundred prisoners here, who are one of two types. About a third of them are political prisoners like you. Most of these men are educated. The rest are hardcore criminals, and they are truly the scum of the earth, most reprehensible people. There is no hope for them. Each group is kept in a separate barracks. You will be in a solitary cell. Do not despair. You have a chance to repent, my dear Moryak," he said, using the Russian word for sailor or mariner. "I can end your solitary confinement after two years if you earn it. Stay out of trouble and work hard.

"I've initiated a program whereby a prisoner's rations are determined by the amount of work he does. More work will result in more food. Work hard, and your overseer will report your performance. Hard work shows me that you are sincere. Work less, and it indicates disrespect for the Tsar and, by implication, for God Himself. It is not impossible for one to starve to death here, Moryak. It all depends on your actions. Do you have any questions?"

"No, sir."

"From now on, your past life does not exist. Forget Anatoly Matushenko; he is dead. Earn a new life, my son. Earn a new life or end your current one here at Solovetsky Island," directed Father Gregor as he lifted a small bell off his desk and shook it. In response, the door opened and the escort entered. "Josef, take Moryak to his cell. That is to be his name from this point on. Instruct him in camp procedures along the way. Finish his in-processing." Josef nodded his head and indicated to his prisoner that he should stand. "Follow me," he ordered.

Exiting the main monastery, Josef led Morrison around the side of the building in the direction of three, oblong brick buildings. "Barracks," he said as they past each one. "First one is for the criminals," he sneered. "Be thankful that you won't have contact with these animals!" Morrison noticed several small windows about six feet off the ground that were crisscrossed with wire. When they approached the second barracks, Josef announced, "Political prisoners here, Moryak. Maybe if you behave, someday Father Gregor will let you move in here." The buildings looked identical, both constructed out of old stone bricks, weathered and faded with age.

They stopped at a brick building between the two barracks. "In here," ordered Josef. Inside the musty room, several people looked up at the two men who had just entered. "Here's a new one for you," announced Josef. "In that chair, Moryak," he pointed. Morrison obediently sat in the chair as one of the workers approached him with a scissors and began to cut his hair. He painfully cut it to the scalp as Josef laughed. "Hopefully that will keep the lice off, at least for a while."

Next, Morrison's beard was cut short to stubble. When the barber finished, Josef shouted to him, "Strip off your clothes!" Looking at one of the other workers, he barked, "Get him his suit!" Hearing this, one of the other workers rummaged through an old trunk and pulled out what looked like a burlap sack. "Your new uniform, Moryak. Maybe not as fancy as the Imperial Navy, but it will do. Also, pray your shoes hold up. They're in short supply here at the Solovetsky Monastery."

Departing the building, they turned right. Continuing toward the other end of the complex, they approached a third barracks building. Stopping at the large wooden door, Josef reached into his jacket and pulled out a large ring of keys. After fumbling with them for a few seconds, he unlocked the door and pushed it open. "Congratulations, Moryak! You are the only prisoner in solitary confinement." Pulling his prisoner by the arm, he led him into the open hall and toward the first steel door with the number one painted on it. He unlocked the cell door, opened it, and turned to his prisoner. "This shithole will be your home, possibly for the rest of your life! Take a good look," he ordered. The cell appeared to be about six feet by eight feet. On the far wall was a small window near the ceiling. The floor was a concrete slab, and in the far corner, was a filthy mat. A rusty pail containing dried human feces sat in the corner.

"Sorry, our maid service is a little slack here," laughed Josef. "Look, let me tell you how it is here. Father Gregor is strict, but he believes in rehabilitation, the goodness of man, and all that crap. I personally don't give a shit about you or whether you live or die. It makes no difference to me at all! You see, I've been assigned as your overseer, so piss me off, and I'll delight in taking you apart piece by piece. Do your work, and we'll get along just fine.

"Your routine is, well, routine. We slip a few slices of bread under the door," he said, as he pointed to the little sliding latch door on the cell door, "at five every morning. Then you are taken out to work. You'll find we have lots of marshes on this island, lots of trees that need to be felled, lots of vegetation that needs to be cleared, and plenty of open strip mines that need to be worked. That will be your job every day. Totally meaningless work. You will be doing it all by yourself. You will have no contact with any other prisoners. If I catch you trying to communicate, I'll crack you in the face with my walking stick. When you return to your cell, you'll have a meal slipped through the latch door. As Father Gregor said, if you work hard, your food ration improves. You'll see a lot of skinny prisoners working near you. That's because the worthless bastards are lazy. Hell, they may waste away to nothing! As I said, it doesn't matter to me at all. Now, any questions?"

"No, sir."

"Good," he said as he shoved Morrison into the cell and slammed the door behind him. "You'll spend the rest of the day in your new home. Enjoy it. This is the last time you will be in your cell during the day. Think of it as a welcome gift! Tomorrow, you go to work, Moryak. Your job will be trees. We have a forest that needs to be cleared. Have a pleasant day."

Staring at the closed door, Morrison sat on the mat and put his arms around his knees. *I've been gone from the United States for seven months,* he thought to himself. All things considered, he was still in decent physical condition, even if his weight had dropped by about ten pounds. The physical labor would not be the problem. It would be the boredom. He would have to keep his mind active while in his cell. Concentrate on his labor during the day and exercise his mind in the evenings. That would be his salvation. Tomorrow, he would review naval gunnery, every aspect of it until he covered the topic completely. Next he would review the new Bluejackets Manual from cover to cover in his mind. Then, the design of the *Dreadnought. Yes,* he thought, *I will keep my mind busy. I will try to live only one day at a time.*

He also knew that several other things had already been sustaining him. For months, he had thought about Sidney Reilly and wondered if he was the one who had betrayed him. Oh, how he would love to get his hands on Reilly! He had become increasingly bitter over his fate. At times, all he could think about was killing Sidney Reilly. Other times, his anger and bitterness shifted to himself for having accepted President Roosevelt's mission. He often thought, *What was I trying to prove?* When he thought of his wife, widowed as far as she or anyone else could know, he felt waves of self-loathing. Yes, anger, bitterness, and vengeance could also be very powerful sustaining forces for him, along with a strong dose of increasing self-hatred.

He stretched out on his back on the thin, lumpy mattress and stared at the ceiling of his cell. He took deep breaths to calm himself and to clear his mind. *This is what I have to do. Stay focused on survival, by any means. Let thoughts of vengeance and hate sustain me.* After a few minutes, a sense of near serenity engulfed him. He smiled and gently began singing "I'm a Yankee Doodle Dandy..."

Z

Catherine Palace
Tsarskoe Selo, Russia
July 1906

Tsar Nicholas II, Supreme Autocrat of Russia, sat at his desk in the formal study of Emperor Alexander I in the Catherine Palace, which served as the official residence of the Imperial family. As he arranged the papers on his desk, he knew that he was about to violate his own rule against conducting business while the family was in residence at Tsarskoe Selo. Today had to be an exception. Nicholas had summoned the Chairman of the Council of Ministers, Count Sergei Witte, to meet with him that morning. The train from St. Petersburg would be arriving shortly.

Nicholas fidgeted in his chair. He was furious with Witte. He had agreed to Witte's October Manifesto only to appease the revolutionaries. He thought about the situation as he waited.

Surely, the count must have realized my intentions. Could the count really have believed that I would retreat from the principles of autocracy? Already I have had to remove him as prime minister, and yet he persists in his democratic principles. Now his precious Duma does nothing but spew forth inflammatory rhetoric, in spite of the fact that I can dissolve the Duma at any time.

As he sat reflecting on the situation, he heard a knock on the door. His valet cracked the door open and announced, "Count Witte has arrived." Nicholas ordered him to be brought in, and the giant Witte entered with a flourish. Nicholas did not look up at his guest or suggest that he sit down. "Count Witte," he began, while he appeared to be writing. He looked up at the former prime minister and announced, "I am signing a document that proclaims the Duma dissolved, effective immediately."

"What?" blurted out the astonished Witte. "Your Majesty, you can't be serious! This would be a tragic mistake!"

"Watch your tone, Count Witte!" cautioned the Tsar. "I am supremely serious, and I am most certainly dissolving this joke of an organization. You know that I retain the power to do so."

"But the October Manifesto—"

"It is just a duplicitous document that you virtually shoved down my throat, playing on my concern over mob rule! Be assured that it was never in my thoughts to cede any royal powers of autocracy. I am astonished that you would actually think I would. Your thinking is contrary to all aristocratic thought! No, dear Count, the Duma is finished. By decree, it is dissolved today, July 8."

Witte stammered a little, not knowing what to say. Looking directly into the eyes of his Tsar, he realized how right he always had been in his assessment of this man. *What a shame,* he thought to himself, *that those Allied agents didn't remove him last year. This little man in the regal-appearing uniform was going to be the agent of demise for all of Russia.* "Your Majesty," he finally began, "I don't know if I—"

"Count Witte," interrupted the Tsar, "as of this moment, you are no longer the Chairman of the Council of Ministers. I have already signed the decree ordering your removal from that office. Out of deference to your past services to Russia and to my father in particular, I will allow you to remain a member of the Council of Ministers. I am also appointing Peter Stolypin as prime minister. Next year, I will allow the people to elect a new Duma if they wish. Hopefully, they will use a little more discretion and elect people who are not treasonous or unreasonable. People who realize, as they should, that my reign is a gift from God Himself."

Standing erect, Witte responded, "Your Majesty, if you are finished with me, I'll not take up any more of your time."

"That would be nice. You are dismissed."

Witte turned and walked out, livid over the indignity that he had just endured. All he could think about was Theodore Roosevelt, the American president he had met less than a year ago. *If only Russia had a leader like him. If only I hadn't interfered with the British-American plan,* thought Witte. The regret would haunt him for the rest of his life.

3

Nobel Prize Awards Ceremony, Norwegian Parliament
Oslo, Norway
December 1906

Theodore Roosevelt was absolutely delighted when the cable arrived at the White House. Rushing into their bedroom, he called out to his wife Edith as she was dressing. "Darling, wonderful news! The Nobel Committee in Norway has sent official notification that I have been selected to receive the Nobel Peace Prize for 1906! My God, isn't that wonderful?"

"That is wonderful, indeed!" Edith replied, smiling with pride.

"You know what I think I'll do with the prize money? I will donate it to establish an organization dedicated to world peace. Won't that be bully?"

"Yes, dear, it certainly would."

"Damn! The Nobel ceremonies are scheduled for December 10 in Oslo. I have other commitments then. Well, I'll just have Herb Peirce accept it for me."

United States ambassador to Norway, the Honorable Herbert H. D. Peirce, stood in front of the Norwegian Parliament on December 10, 1906, to accept the Nobel Peace Prize on behalf of his president. Radiating pride and confidence, Peirce announced to the audience that President Theodore Roosevelt intended to establish a foundation in Washington, D.C., dedicated to improving relations among all nations and to the maintenance of peace throughout the world. As the audience erupted into enthusiastic applause, Peirce could not hold back his tears of delight. "Good Lord," he said softly, "how they love the man!"

Several weeks later, the diplomatic pouch from Norway arrived at the White House. Its contents were brought to the president. They included an engraved certificate from the Nobel Committee, announcing the award of the 1906 Nobel Peace Prize "to Theodore Roosevelt, President of the United States, for his extraordinary efforts in promoting world peace by mediating the end of the Russo-Japanese War." Beaming with pride, Roosevelt removed a small leather case from the pouch and opened it to find a gold medal. The front contained a profile image of Alfred Nobel. The backside had the image of three men embracing in a fraternal bond, with the inscription, "Pro pace fraternitate gentium," meaning, "For the peace and brotherhood of man." Tears welled in Roosevelt's eyes as he held the medal in his hand. *This honor belongs to so many others,* he thought to himself. Lastly, the pouch contained a sealed envelope that he gently opened with a letter opener. It contained a check from the Bank of Norway, drawn on the account of the Nobel Committee, in the amount of thirty-seven thousand dollars.

The following week, Roosevelt scheduled a meeting with Calvin Briggs, his private attorney. He told Briggs in advance that he wanted to draw up papers for the peace foundation that he would be funding and, in addition, he had a private estate matter that he wanted to discuss. When Briggs entered the Oval Office, Roosevelt asked him to be seated, and proceeded to outline his vision for the peace foundation to be funded with thirty-five thousand dollars of the Nobel Prize. When he handed the bank draft to Briggs, the attorney noted the amount of the draft and said, "Mr. President, this check is for thirty-seven thousand dollars. You are earmarking only thirty-five thousand of it for the foundation. What is your intention for the rest of the money?"

Roosevelt sat across from his lawyer with his hands folded and stared down at his desk for a few moments before speaking. "Yes, Calvin, you are correct. The entire amount of the draft won't be used for the foundation." Looking up at the attorney, he continued by saying, "You know, as always, I expect strict attorney-client privilege to be the rule with this matter that we are about to discuss. No one other than the two of us must know about it. Do you understand?"

The president's demeanor puzzled Briggs. This sudden serious tone seemed so atypical of him. In addition, Briggs felt a little offended that the president thought it necessary to remind him of attorney-client privilege. "Of course, Mr. President," he replied. "That goes without saying. Now, what are you intending? What do you want me to help you with?"

"I want you to establish a trust fund with the remaining two thousand dollars. I want this funding to be anonymous. My name must never be linked to it. That is critical. Not even my wife must know about this trust, and you are to ask me no specifics or questions in regard to this trust fund. I just want to set these rules before we continue, agreed?"

"Yes, sir. Who is to be the beneficiary of the trust? What name will go on the legal paperwork?"

"The name of the beneficiary is Mrs. Helen Morrison. Her late husband was a naval officer, a Lieutenant Stephen Morrison. That is all you really need to know. Remember, Calvin, no one, especially Mrs. Morrison, must ever link this fund to me, even after my death. This anonimity is crucial to me. I never want this woman to want for anything. Now, if there are no further questions, we can end this meeting."

"I understand, sir. I will contact you when the paperwork is ready. And I guarantee you that no one will know who funded this trust, especially not Mrs. Morrison, when its benefits accrue. Thank you for your confidence in me, Mr. President."

As his attorney departed the office, Roosevelt remained very somber. *The memory of Lieutenant Morrison will cause pain in my heart as long as I live,* he thought.

4

Solovetsky Island
Summer 1907

The mid-afternoon sun beat down mercilessly on all of the prisoners, and Stephen Morrison, drenched with sweat, once again drew back his axe. The sunlight shimmered on the axe blade like the bright light from a lantern. With rhythmic precision, each arching chop bit deeper into the thick tree base until the tree finally fell. He had been chopping down trees since sunrise, just as he had done every day since arriving on the island prison over a year ago. Josef sat near him with his ever-present walking stick. His overseer had just taken a large draught from the ever-present bottle of vodka that he brought with him. His drinking capacity continued to amaze Morrison. He never seemed to be overtly intoxicated.

Nearby, about thirty other prisoners worked felling trees under the watchful eyes of several guards armed with shotguns.

As usual, Morrison noted that only a few of the prisoners seemed to be working hard. Some appeared not to be working at all. It seemed odd to Morrison that the guards were not bothered by the lack of work by these prisoners.

On his first day of felling trees over a year ago, Morrison noted the group of other prisoners working in the forest-like region not more than fifty yards away. After cutting down the first tree, he had paused for a second to look at the nearby group when suddenly he felt a searing pain in the backs of his thighs. Josef had just stuck him with a vicious blow to the hamstrings with his walking stick. "No staring, Moryak! You will have nothing to do with the other scum here. Rules of the house, you know. Now get back to work!" For a second, Morrison glared with anger at his guard, but he thought better of it and returned to his work. "That's right, Moryak, don't give me an excuse to kill you!" instructed Josef as he burst out into laughter.

The days were monotonous, and the routine rarely varied. Other than the occasional comment from Josef, Morrison had not spoken to anyone or heard a human voice in over a year. As the summer turned to fall and winter, the routine never varied. He was given somewhat warmer clothing and boots when the harsh winter set in, and he actually looked forward to his daily labor in the forests. At least the heavy physical labor would keep him warm. Regardless of the weather, to the satisfaction of his personal guard, he proved to be an excellent worker and, as a result, his evening food ration was the largest in the prison. Among the guards, Josef bragged that it was the prisoner's fear of him that drove him to be such a productive worker. Because of the hard physical labor, combined with the slightly increased rations he earned, Morrison managed to stay in very good physical condition. As an additional benefit of being the only prisoner in solitary confinement, he was not affected by many of the contagious diseases that ran rampant in the labor camp. He had no way of knowing, but the other three prisoners who had arrived at Solovetsky Island with him the year before had died of typhus.

His nighttime routine also never varied. About an hour after he finished his dinner, he did push-ups and sit-ups. He became accustomed to the filth and the ever-present hunger in his belly. His personal hygiene became abysmal. Once every two weeks, in the evening, the door would open and Josef would appear with a hose. "Bath time!" he would announce as he aimed the high-pressure hose at his prisoner, totally dousing him and his entire cell, including his mattress. The mattress soon became infested with roaches. Morrison learned to sleep with insects crawling all over him. He never really worried about his physical condition. His mind was what concerned him.

Nightly, he concentrated on his studies. He went into as much depth as his memory would permit. Gunnery, battleship construction, navigation—they all became part of his prison curriculum. He relived some of his favorite classes from the Naval Academy. He gave strict attention to anything that kept his mind sharp. The lack of companionship slowly began wearing on him, and he worked doggedly to fight it. *Don't give in,* he exhorted himself. *Keep plugging away. You will survive this! Remember, you have scores to settle! Let your hatred sustain you.* He set his first goal for survival after several months. It resulted from something that Father Gregor had said to him on the day he arrived. He tried to recall the monk's exact words, but he remembered the essence of what he had said. After two years, Father Gregor had the authority to move him out of solitary confinement. He had to get out of solitary, or he feared he'd go crazy. He would be a model prisoner and earn the right to leave the isolation that engulfed him.

Surprisingly to him, on some nights, he reminisced about his father, Rabbi Kambotchnik. He couldn't get the memory out of his mind when his father told him that he was the biggest disappointment of his life. *If you were disappointed by me then, Rabbi, you should see me now,* he mused. He relived many of the fights of his youth—the taunting, the epithets. "You fucking kikes!" resonated in his ears over and over. On other nights, he would wake himself up screaming as he felt the knife blade of his recurrent nightmare cutting into the soft tissue of his neck. The irony of his situation amused him. All his life he had worked to prove himself a worthy American; he had not allowed others to put him down or deny him the respect he was due. He would beat the world at its own game and distinguish himself. That was the way he lived his life, without any apologies to anyone, including Rabbi Kambotchnik. *And look where this has gotten me,* he thought. *To a Russian labor camp, living the life of a Russian naval mutineer. It's not over. I will survive this ordeal. I still have things to accomplish and scores to settle.*

***

In July 1908, the prisoners on the island began a new project: working on irrigation ditches and dams. The island was a combination of swampland interspersed among many lakes, and the administration of the prison camp had decided to harness the water into a series of small dams and levies. These, in turn, would create watermills to produce power for the buildings. As usual, Morrison remained segregated from the other prisoners while they worked. For weeks, he worked waist-deep in water as he shoveled mud and built dam fortifications.

One day when he finished his daily work, Josef informed him that they had a meeting scheduled with Father Gregor that evening. The announcement delighted Morrison. Anything that would break the routine and relieve some of the monotony would be welcome. When he returned to his cell, he was startled to discover that Josef wanted him to bathe, even allowing him to use soap after his usual cold water drenching. "Got to get you clean. You know, you stink to high hell, but I'm used to it. I don't want to sicken Father Gregor!" laughed the overseer. As the finishing touch, he handed him a brand new set of prison garb.

As he entered the main monastery building, Morrison was amazed by how much he enjoyed going there. Even this mundane walk was a pleasure after more than two years of his monotonous, unchanging daily routine. Entering Father Gregor's office, he saw the monk sitting at his desk much as he had been two years before, only now appearing older and grayer. Morrison suspected he might be ill, judging by his sallow appearance. "Sit down, Moryak," Gregor ordered as he pushed a small tray across the desk. The tray contained two cups of tea. "Please, take one," he offered.

"Thank you very much, sir," the prisoner replied.

"Moryak," began the smiling monk, "it has been over two years since you arrived at Solovstsky Monastery. Even though I haven't physically seen you since your arrival, I've been following your progress very closely. Josef has many good things to say about you. You have become the model prisoner. You are undoubtedly the hardest worker on the island. You never cause any trouble, and you appear to be in good physical condition. No doubt, that is also a reflection of the increased food rations that your hard work has earned you. You are virtually the only prisoner who has worked to earn those increased rations. I don't know why the other prisoners can't emulate the example you set. The others see you working all the time, rain or shine, hot weather or snowfall, and they wonder about you. I'm sure they have created some ingenious names for you! Being our only prisoner in solitary confinement makes you a celebrity no matter what you do.

"Now, as a reward for your excellent work, your status here among us is officially changing as of this moment." The monk stood and walked around his desk to Morrison who politely stood as the monk approached. "Please sit down, my son," ordered the monk as he put his hand on Morrison's shoulder. "You are proof that there is redemption with hard work, with personal sacrifice, with suffering in silence. I have the power to release you from solitary confinement, and, as of this moment, I am ordering your release. Josef will be taking you to Barracks Number One, the barracks for political prisoners. You will be among the rest of the political prisoners. There are currently about fifty of them. Congratulations, Moryak, you have earned this bit of freedom.

"For the remainder of your sentence, the next eight years, at least you will have company. Please remember, however, that the ban on communication with the outside world will remain for the rest of your stay here. You still cannot send any mail, and you cannot receive mail. I do not have the power to reverse that edict. Also, I will warn you that there is friction between the political prisoners and the hardened criminals in Barracks Number Two. You will have to deal with all of these conflicts. The road to redemption for all has many pathways. You all must find your own path. Now, please stand," he requested. He offered his hand and solemnly said, "Thank you for finding the road to God. Don't stray from the path, my son." He made the sign of the cross and said, "Go with God, my son!"

Morrison thanked the monk as Josef came alongside him. Josef ordered Morrison to follow him. As they left the building, Josef chuckled and said, "He really does believe in that redemption crap. I've been listening to it for years. I've heard rumors that he's dying. That's why he looks so terrible. But, he is correct; you've done well. When I met you, with that angry look you always have, I was sure I would have to kill you."

"Sorry to disappoint you."

"Look, Moryak," Josef said seriously, as they walked toward Barracks Number One, "Father Gregor hinted about the conflicts among the prisoners. He understated the issue. It's often a blood war. The guards rarely get involved because it's too damn dangerous. They'd rather let the scum prisoners kill each other than risk injury to save any of you. It's a genuine, full-time war. Watch yourself. I won't be there to protect you. Now that there is no one in solitary confinement, I'll be working full-time for Father Gregor."

"Thanks, I'll keep a close watch out."

"I'm not kidding!" Josef said, stopping to face his prisoner. "They all talk about you now already. Father Gregor only hinted about it. They call you 'the machine,' 'the crazy one'—all because they watched you working so hard for the past two years, all by yourself. You were the only prisoner in solitary the entire time. That alone was enough to create a mystique about you. Watch yourself, Moryak. You may wish you had never left solitary confinement." Josef smiled and said softly, "If any real problems arise, pass me a message through the guard in the barracks. They all work for me now."

Those words reminded Morrison of the final words that the warden at Peter and Paul Fortress had spoken to him before he left St. Petersburg over two years before. "Don't worry about me, Josef, I'll be fine," he replied quietly. He meant it. He was going to survive. He was strong. They approached the door of the barracks, and Josef pulled out his huge key ring and found the correct key. After opening the lock, he threw open the

MORYAK

large door and told Morrison to enter. As he walked through the door, he heard Josef softly say, "Good-bye, Moryak."

***

Upon entering Barracks Number One, the delight of seeing other people in such close proximity nearly overwhelmed him. As the door slammed shut behind him, the other fifty people in the barracks turned their heads to stare at him. A large rectangular room with individual cots for each of the prisoners, the barracks also contained several small tables in the center of the room, as well as a fireplace on either end of the building. Morrison noted that there appeared to be only one guard in the building who had a shotgun slung over his shoulder. The prisoners mulled about freely and seemingly were free to communicate with each other. As he entered the room, he could hear the hushed whispers, "It's him! It's the Moryak, the crazy one!"

Morrison had been told by Josef that he had been assigned to bunk number fifty in the corner, and he walked over to his new bed. He was delighted that he could actually sit on a cot with four legs, instead of a roach-infested straw mat.

As he sat and looked around, many continued to stare at the new member of the political barracks. Shortly, a small owlish-looking man with glasses walked up to him. Extending his hand to Morrison, he said, "Welcome to our barracks! You are the one they call Moryak. We heard about your exploits on the *Potemkin*, and we are honored to have you among us. My name is Alexandr." Morrison shook his hand and said nothing.

"I think you'll enjoy being among us, Moryak. We are all political prisoners of the criminal Tsarist regime, just like you. Our discussions nightly are very stimulating. I'm sure you'll enjoy them. We also have many books, should you desire to read them."

"They allow you books?" asked Morrison incredulously.

"Oh, yes," replied Alexandr enthusiastically. "We are also allowed to write home and to receive mail. Of course, they read it and censor it, but it's still mail! They didn't allow you mail in your cell?"

"No, nothing. I haven't spoken to anyone other than my overseer for over two years." Morrison stood up and looked around at the other faces in the room. Turning to Alexandr, he said, "Tell me something. I see you people working near me every day. It looks as if I see everyone from this room doing some sort of work every day. I see others sitting around on their asses doing nothing while you do all the work. Who are the others? I don't see any of them here."

"Oh, them," responded Alexandr with obvious disgust in his voice. "They are in Barracks Number Two, you know, the one that houses the real criminals. Murders, thieves, and the like. Quite a disgusting bunch of thugs—the dregs of humanity. Watch out for them, Moryak, and stay away from them. Unfortunately, they seem to run roughshod over this place, so their influence is everywhere. Unlike us, they will never leave this island, at least not alive."

Suddenly, Morrison tired of talking to this man. That surprised him. For two years he had been dying to hear a human voice and now he wanted the man to leave him alone. "Listen, Alexandr, I want to be alone now. Please leave."

Looking into the eyes of the one they called Moryak, Alexandr sensed that this was not a man to trifle with and certainly not one to challenge. "Of course, sir, I'll leave you alone. Again, welcome to our barracks. Perhaps we'll talk again tomorrow after our work detail."

Over the next several days, Stephen Morrison began to adjust to his new life. He reveled in hearing human voices again, even if they came from the mouths of political prisoners who seemed to discuss nothing but revolution and anarchy. Now he worked with the rest of the working parties, and, as usual, he worked hard and long. The other prisoners watched him with wonderment. Why would any prisoner work so hard? The prisoners talked freely, a luxury that took some adjustment. They often greeted him with his new name, Moryak, and spoke almost reverently of his actions aboard the *Potemkin*. As usual, Morrison noted that some of the prisoners just sat around, not working at all. They seemed to almost intimidate the guards themselves. They all resided in Barracks Number Two, home of the hardcore criminals. He often heard them spouting derogatory comments toward him, taunting him because he worked at all.

In the evenings after their dinner, the barracks residents always broke off into political discussions. The other prisoners, led by Alexandr, asked him if he wanted to take part in any of the discussions, but Morrison simply glared at them. They seemed intimidated by him, and that perception suited Morrison just fine. On his third night in the barracks, an incident occurred that would change the remainder of his imprisonment on Solovetsky Island. He woke at about three in the morning, hearing a prisoner yelling and screaming on the other side of the barracks. Morrison, who had craved the sound of another human voice for over two years, was now just annoyed to hear a human voice interfering with his needed sleep.

Sitting up, he could see another man standing over the prisoner in rack number one, and the prisoner appeared to be struggling as he screamed.

Morrison felt a hand on his arm as he was about to get out of his rack. "Don't get involved, Moryak!" whispered the prisoner in the next rack. "It will only make life worse for you. This is how things are here in the barracks."

"Who the hell is that?" demanded Morrison, pointing to the dark figure standing over the prisoner in rack number one. He appeared to be punching him.

"It's one of them, one of the *vors*, from Barracks Two. I'll explain it to you in the morning."

"Where the hell is the barracks guard?" demanded Morrison. "I don't see him."

"Look, they're as afraid of them as we are! Besides, the *vors* bribe them to step outside when they come over here. That way they can honestly say they didn't see anything. Not that there would ever be any sort of investigation. Please, Comrade Moryak, do nothing. Go back to sleep. I'll explain all of this to you in the swamp tomorrow."

Morrison laid back in his rack, wondering what this new development meant. *Who are the vors?* he wondered. *I sure as hell intend to find out.* He could sense that his growing bitterness and anger were about to be inflammed again.

***

The morning sun promised another scorching hot day as they returned to the swamp in the morning. Once again, nearly one hundred men worked at the site of the new levee. As usual, Morrison worked more diligently than the others did and sweat poured off him. The prisoner who slept in the rack next to him, Constantin, worked beside him. After working for about an hour in relative silence, Morrison finally turned to him and asked, "Well, what were you going to tell me about these assholes in the other barracks?"

"Sorry, comrade," Constantin sheepishly replied. "You didn't look like you wanted to talk, so I was afraid to—"

"Just tell me, okay? Who was that guy? What is a *vor*? Where was the guard, and why didn't he do anything?"

Constantin stood and wiped his brow. He began talking slowly and methodically, occasionally looking over his shoulder. "The *vors*. That is short for *vor v zakonye*, or *thieves-in-law*. They are the professional criminals in Russian society today. Almost the entire Barracks Number Two is filled with *vors*. Actually, Comrade Moryak, the *thieves-in-law* are not a new phenomenon. The *vors* have existed since the times of Peter the Great. I'm a little surprised that you haven't heard of them." Nodding subtly over his left shoulder, he continued. "See those prisoners just sitting there, not doing a lick of work? They're all *vors*. If they don't feel like working, they don't. And they never feel like working."

"How do they get away with it?" asked the incredulous Morrison. "Why don't the guards do anything about it?"

"As I told you last night, the guards are also scared of them, and, more importantly, they are on the take and they are bought off. They're no fools. They want to live as much as we do. It has to do with the philosophy of the government. To the Tsar and his gang, we're all the same. They view us political prisoners as being just as severe a threat as the real criminal dregs. If any of us live or die, it's of no consequence to the government. You see, they're delighted if each group kills one another. That leaves fewer problems for the government to handle. That's why the guards ignore all of this conflict. They couldn't care less if anyone is injured, and if someone is killed, well, that's one less prisoner for them to have to take care of."

"Some of these *vors* seem to do a little work. Why is that?" asked Morrison, as he motioned over to a group that was actually doing some light work.

"Those? They are petty thieves, safecrackers. Even though they're in Barracks Two, they are not *vors*. They are the *vors*' lackeys and servants. They actually do all of the *vors* bidding."

Morrison continued his work, shoveling the mud onto the levee as he thought of more questions. "Constantin, what was that guy doing in our barracks this morning?"

"More than likely just robbing him and beating him up. That prisoner is fairly new to our barracks, and I'm sure that the *vors* leaders ordered that thug to enter our barracks to take his possessions before he beat the shit out of him. Sort of a 'Welcome to Solovetsky Island' reception for newcomers. We have another new prisoner who arrived last week. I'm sure he's next. Incidents like this are not an uncommon occurrence, but there are even worse things than that," he said ruefully.

Morrison stopped shoveling and stood up, facing his fellow prisoner. "Like what?" he asked cynically.

"Most of the *vors* have been here for years. They have sexual needs, and there are no women on this island. The women are over on Anzer Island. Oftentimes, the *vors* come into our barracks for sex."

"Are you serious?"

"Quite serious. Rape is common in our barracks."

"Have you ever been raped?"

"Unfortunately, yes. Everyone gets his turn. Be careful, Moryak! Remember, you are new here also. However, I believe that they are a little intimidated by you and haven't quite figured out what to do with you. They see you working like a madman all the time. You're not quite like any of us. Please be careful!"

"I'm just trembling in my boots," he laughed as he returned to work. Morrison had not changed his work ethic at all since moving into Barracks Number One. He still wanted to keep in the best possible physical shape. He wanted those extra rations and he had a feeling he would need to be in good physical condition to deal with the *vors*. They were a facet of Russian life that he had never heard of or dealt with before now. *I've been fighting bullies all my life,* he thought to himself. *Looks like nothing has changed much in that regard.* Seeing the *vors* lying around while others worked did nothing but add to the disgust he already felt for these degenerates. Morrison could sense that he was on a collision course. *Good,* he thought. *I need an outlet.*

He would be ready.

***

As Constantin had predicted, three nights later, the sounds of scuffling and screaming again awakened Morrison. The sounds seemed to be coming from the middle of the barracks on the far wall. As he stood up, he saw what appeared to be a man struggling with the newest prisoner in the barracks. Morrison, angered that he had been awakened again, looked around and noticed that the guard had conveniently left the barracks. As he got out of his rack, Constantin pleaded with him in a whisper. "Please, Moryak, don't get involved!" Morrison ignored him and walked over to the source of the noise. He walked past all of the cots; all of the prisoners' eyes were upon him.

Morrison arrived at the rack to find a stranger, obviously a *vor* from Barracks Two, on top of the new prisoner, sodomizing him. The victim kept screaming as the attacker continued to thrust into him. Morrison reached down and tapped the assailant on the shoulder. Without breaking his rhythm, the attacker reached behind himself to swat Morrison's hand away. In a normal speaking tone, Morrison spoke. "You're making too much noise. I can't sleep," he said. The attacker continued to thrust into his victim, totally ignoring the intruder. Morrison reached over and roughly smacked the attacker on the back of his head with an open palm and repeated, "You're making too much noise. I can't sleep." The assailant stopped thrusting immediately. Registering fear and horror, the eyes of every prisoner in the barracks were fixed on the two men.

Livid with rage, the *vor* turned around and faced Morrison. "Who the fuck are you, you worthless bastard? I'm going to kill you right here!" he threatened as he stood up. Morrison noted he had several homemade tattoos on his arms, and his bare chest revealed a large tattoo of an eagle. He also had a slight potbelly and fleshy arms, indicating that he probably hadn't done any physical labor in a while. The *vor* reached into his right boot and pulled out a six-inch knife. Using the knife to arc circles in front of him, he announced, "I'm going to carve you up like a turkey and eat your entrails!"

Morrison stood impassive and announced, "I couldn't sleep with all the racket you were causing. I asked you to stop, but you didn't." Putting his hand on his chin as if he were thinking, Morrison calmly observed, "I suppose that's because you are an ignorant, disgusting, piece of shit. That's pretty accurate, wouldn't you say?"

Seeing the rage smoulder in the *vor*'s eyes, the other prisoners held their breath. Morrison just stared back at him with arms folded. After a few seconds, the *vor* let out a loud cry as he lunged forward with his knife. Morrison quickly threw his right arm up against the assailant's knife wielding hand, deflecting it upward as he slammed his left arm down on the *vor*'s proximal forearm. In the same motion, he charged forward, propelling his victim backward until he had him pinned against the wall. The overpowered *vor* cried out in pain as Morrison's left forearm crushed his neck. His right hand was painfully clamped over his victim's right hand, holding the tip of the knife blade directly under his jaw.

The *vor* began to turn blue from anoxia when Morrison gently said to him, "Let me take you out of your misery, asshole." He thrust his right hand directly upward, slamming the six-inch blade directly into the soft underside of the *vor*'s jaw, tearing through his tongue and hard palate and into the base of his brain. Blood spurted out, as the man gasped and then became limp. Morrison pulled the knife out and let the man collapse to the floor.

The other prisoners watched in disbelief as Morrison wiped the blade clean with the dead man's shirt hanging on the rack. He then walked over to the body that lay in an ever-expanding pool of blood and viciously kicked him in the head. As he began to walk back to his rack, he saw all the other prisoners in their racks staring at him. He grinned and announced, "I don't like it when people are noisy when I'm trying to sleep."

They all laughed as Morrison walked back to his rack and got in. He had just killed another man, and he felt just as he had when he killed the guard back in St. Petersburg. He felt absolutely nothing. If anything, he experienced the same emotional catharsis; a sense of halcyon, inner peace and righteousness. It was as if the injustices he had suffered at the hands of the goyim when he was young, at the hands of his Naval Academy tormentors, and at the hands of all of those who inflicted pain and humiliation on him were suddenly eased by his own act of violence. Within minutes, he was sound asleep.

Constantin stared at the man they called Moryak, sleeping deeply in the rack next to him. *What kind of a man is this?* he thought to himself. *He just killed a man and now he peacefully sleeps! Not only does he not seem to fear the vors, but he is actually more vicious than they are!* Laying his head back on his mattress, he concluded, *This man scares me.*

***

Word quickly spread throughout the prison about the exploits of the Moryak, who had coolly taken on a *vor* and without seeming to break a sweat, easily killed him. Constantin had been proven correct. In the morning, as the guard entered to awaken the prisoners for work detail, two other guards entered, picked up the dead body, and removed it without saying a word. To Morrison, it appeared as if they were just taking out the trash. It simply meant one less prisoner for the Tsar to feed. Before they left the barracks, all of the political prisoners walked over to shake Morrison's hand or to thank him. They had always been at the total mercy of the *vors*. No one had ever stood up to the *vors* before, and certainly no one had ever come to their aid the way Moryak had done earlier that morning. The dangerous-looking, mysterious Moryak had become their hero.

That night, Morrison relented a bit and actually talked with the other prisoners as they sat at their tables after dinner. He wanted to know more about the *vors*. He looked at Alexandr and said, "Tell me something about these *vors*. That pig was covered with tattoos. I noticed that some of the other lazy bastards who sit around also have them. What's the significance? Is it some sort of badge of honor?"

"One can definitely say that," replied Alexandr with deadly earnest. "Did you see that attacking eagle tattooed on his chest? My God, you couldn't have missed that! That's their symbol. That eagle is what the *vors* have tattooed on their chests to distinguish them. They love to have disgusting things tattooed on their arms. Things like people having sex, tattoos of sexual organs. You didn't get a look at his legs before they dragged him out of here, did you?"

"No. What about them?"

"If you had seen his bare legs, you would have seen tattoos on both of his kneecaps. The *vors* do that to symbolize that they bow down to no one."

"Gee, such tough guys," replied Morrison sarcastically. "I believe he collapsed onto those kneecaps just before he died."

"They are no laughing matter, Moryak!" Constantin chimed in. "They are a vicious criminal cabal. They literally have a code that they live by, every one of them. They are animals. Vile, disgusting animals."

"What code?"

"These savages—they never work or have any kind of job. Any income they get is from robbery, extortion, you know, all ill-gotten gains. They will never cooperate with any authorities, not the police and certainly not the government. They will never serve in the military. They abandon their families and certainly will never have a family of their own. Their loyalty is only to the *vors*."

"They sound like a charming bunch. I guess that's why they lie around on their asses all day."

"Correct, Moryak," replied Alexandr. "They have their servants, the lesser criminals, do their work and do their bidding. They call these underlings *the bitches*. The bitches also scout our new arrivals in Barracks Number One for their masters to rob and abuse. They also inform them of possible new sex partners. You know, Moryak, no one has ever resisted them, not anyone in our barracks."

"Why is that? Do you like being crapped on?"

"No, but how can we resist them? We're thinkers, intellectuals. We're revolutionary thinkers, not savages. We obviously come from a higher class of Russians, not the criminal class!"

"Yes, I see where your higher class got you all," Morrison smirked. "An opportunity to be raped on a whim."

The two fellow prisoners looked somberly at him. "You're different from us, Moryak. You are obviously very intelligent and well-spoken, but you've got a rough edge, an angry edge, and you are a very physical person. That is a feature that most of us don't have. It makes you sort of, like—"

"Like them?"

"I didn't mean it that way. I didn't mean to insinuate anything like that."

"That's okay. Don't worry about it. Maybe I am like them." Changing the subject slightly, Morrison asked his two colleagues "Why are you two here on Solovetsky Island? What were your crimes?"

Alexandr spoke first. "Our exploits do not compare with yours, comrade. Your actions aboard the *Potemkin* still inspire all revolutionaries! Me, I was there with Father Gapon in St. Petersburg."

"On Bloody Sunday?"

"Yes. I was arrested by the Okhrana, and that spring, I was sent here to Solovetsky Island. I am a Social Revolutionary, my friend. I am embarrassed that we didn't resist with violence that day. "

"What about you, Constantin?" inquired Morrison. "How did your invitation to this place come about?"

Constantin had a serious look on his face as he began. He began speaking almost as if he was reciting a holy litany. "Moryak, for years I was an active member of the Social Democrats. We believed, and still believe, that the workers will lead the revolution. Our party had fragmented over methods. I am now with the Bolsheviks, which is how I ended up here. We organized massive labor strikes in St. Petersburg and Moscow nearly two years ago. My colleague, Comrade Mozger, and I actually had a local printing press for our revolutionary newsletter *Iskra*. During the strikes, the police cracked down on us and through an informant, they discovered our printing press. I wasn't able to escape. Thank God, Mozger got away!"

"Mozger? The 'Brain'? That's your partner's name?" Morrison continued to be amused by all of the revolutionary names that he was learning. He didn't let on that he had read many issues of *Iskra* in the past. After all, he was the Moryak, a sailor in the Russian navy, not an American expert on Russian affairs.

"Yes, his name is appropriate; the man is a genius. He has become Comrade Lenin's right hand. I received a letter last month from Lenin. He's currently in Finland. Mozger continues as his organizer and strategist. Have you ever read any of Lenin's writings?"

"No," lied Morrison, "but I've heard of them, and I will admit they must be very good. Many of our sailors on *Potemkin* were inspired by his writings. I believe he wrote that masterful pamphlet, *What Is To Be Done?*, did he not?"

Constantin suddenly got very animated. "You know, I received a five-year sentence. Next year, God willing, I'll be released. Let me tell Comrade Lenin all about you, Moryak! Imagine—a man who is as tough and as violent as a *vor* yet with the mind and the soul of a revolutionary! When you get out of this hellhole, you must join us! Your talents would benefit us greatly."

"Well, if I'm lucky, I'll get out of here in about eight years," thought Morrison out loud. He looked up at Constantin, saying, "I wouldn't keep a candle burning for me, my friend."

"Do not worry comrade, I'll keep in touch. You can count on that!" He saw Alexandr shaking his head with amusement. "Don't be so smug, my friend. We are a small party now, but with each year, we grow stronger. We're not merely bomb throwers. We're thinkers! Moryak here would fit in well with us!"

The two prisoners began debating each other, and Morrison decided he had listened to enough. "Gentlemen, I'm going to bed. You two are getting a little loud." As he stood, he smiled at them and said, "And you know what happens when noise interferes with my sleep!"

5

Barracks Number Two
Solovetsky Island
The Same Day

Nikolai lay in his comfortable rack, quite upset. He couldn't believe the news when they told him that his underling, a *vor v zakonye*, a *thief-in-law*, had been murdered by one of the political prisoners. As the head of the *vors* at Solovetsky Monastery, he had total dominance over all of the prisoners. He was the most feared man on the island, and he was not used to having his will thwarted. Especially galling was the fact that one of his *vors* had been killed. The guards were out of the building, as usual, so they couldn't identify the killer. According to their reports to the guards, none of the political prisoners allegedly saw anything. Nikolai's fury grew as he lay there, and he had his suspicions about who the culprit was.

It had to be that crazy laborer, the one who was always working like a slave. That bastard who was in solitary confinement all those years. The one that everyone called Moryak. *I know Moryak did it,* he thought to himself. *That sailor boy must be taught a lesson in respect. No one ever defied Nikolai. Not back in Odessa, not in Moscow, and certainly not here. This Moryak would be taught a lesson. One he might not survive.*

The next night, the guard admitted one of the *vors* to Barracks Number One. After inquiring about Moryak, the guard pointed to the far table where several prisoners sat discussing politics. He walked over to the table and demanded to know where he could find the one called Moryak. One of the prisoners pointed over to the corner rack where Morrison lay on his back. The *vor* walked over to the side of the rack and announced, "Nikolai wants to see you."

Morrison remained stationary, lying with his hands behind his head and staring up at the ceiling. Without looking directly at the stranger beside his rack he replied, "Who the hell is Nikolai?"

"Nikolai runs things in this camp, and he wants to see you, *now!*" His shouting of the last word caused all the other prisoners in the barracks to look over toward them. Morrison looked over at him, slowly put his feet on the floor, and stood up. He and the *vor* were roughly the same height. Morrison looked him directly in the eye and said, "Tell Nikolai that I'm busy." Sitting slowly back down, Morrison reclined onto his rack, again resting his hands behind his head.

The *vor* flushed with anger, but he just stood there and did nothing. He had seen something in this Moryak's eyes that frightened him. *This man is crazy,* he thought to himself. *He's got the crazed eyes of a killer.* Never before had he feared any of these political prisoners. *This man is different,* he thought. *He is not at all like the others.* The vor stood there a minute and then stormed out of the barracks.

After returning to Barracks Number Two, he sheepishly walked over to Nikolai. "Where the hell is he?" demanded the *vor* leader.

At first, his underling couldn't look his leader in the eye. Head down and shoulders hunched forward, he mumbled softly, "He says he's busy."

Furious at what he had just heard, Nikolai grabbed his messenger by the shirt and jerked him up until his face was inches from his. "What the hell did you just say?" he roared.

His lower lip trembling with fear, the *vor* again softly replied, "He said he's busy." As soon as he finished speaking, Nikolai slammed his fist into his abdomen, dropping him to the floor. Writhing in pain, he gasped, "Please, Nikolai, that man is crazy! I believe he would have killed me! You should see the look in his eyes! I tell you he's a crazy killer."

"No, you stupid bastard, I'm a crazy killer!" roared Nikolai." I'm the one you should worry about killing you! I'll take care of this man tomorrow!"

The following day the prisoners resumed their daily routine of working in the swamp. As usual, Morrison worked the hardest and had his shirt off due to the heat. His muscular torso glistened with sweat. Out of the corner of his eye, he saw several *vors* sitting off to the side chatting and motioning toward him. After a while, one of them stood up, stretched, and yawned vigorously. His unbuttoned shirt revealed multiple tattoos all over his chest and arms. A large tattoo of an eagle adorned his chest, and his protuberant belly draped over his trousers. A large metal cross-like medallion on a chain dangled from around his neck. He smiled at his colleagues and sauntered over to where Morrison was working. Stopping at the edge of the swamp, he called over to Morrison. "Hey, you!" Initially, Morrison ignored him, and he repeated, "Hey you! The one they call Moryak!" His booming tone assured that all of the other prisoners heard him.

Morrison stopped and firmly planted his shovel into the mud as he straightened up. Looking over to Nikolai he responded, "What do you want?"

"I want to talk to you! Come over here, now!"

Morrison realized that this must be the infamous Nikolai. He also noticed that the eyes of all of the prisoners and guards now were trained on him and Nikolai. Obviously, this would be Nikolai's chance to demonstrate his dominance. Morrison purposely walked slowly over to the edge of the swamp. He stepped up onto the dry land and stood facing the *vor*. Nikolai looked over this political prisoner from head to toe. He appeared to be very fit and actually appeared somewhat muscular, an unusual characteristic in this environment. The underling didn't exaggerate—he did have the crazed, burning eyes of a killer. Finally, the *vor* spoke. "I'm Nikolai, you disgusting maggot, and I run things here. You understand?"

Morrison said nothing and just stared at Nikolai. *Another real tough guy,* he thought to himself. *Just a fat tub of lard, a blow hard. Another punk.* He just shook his head with disgust and turned to walk away. This act of disrespect infuriated Nikolai, who screamed, "Do you hear me? I run this prison! You and every other maggot in this camp will bow to my will!"

As he ranted, Morrison returned to his shovel and lifted a spadeful of mud out of the water just as Nikolai stopped yelling. Morrison smiled at the *vor* whose face seethed with rage and flung the shovelful of mud over to the edge of the swamp where Nikolai stood. The mud hit the water, splashing the dirty water all over Nikolai's legs. For a moment, the stunned *vor*

Lee Mandel

remained speechless. All of the prisoners collectively held their breath. Finally, Nikolai exploded. "You're a dead man, Moryak! Do you hear me? *You are a dead man!*" Turning on his heel, he stomped away and Morrison returned to his work.

When the tension finally dissipated, a very agitated Constantin scurried over to him. "Comrade Moryak, are you crazy? Are you insane? Do you not realize with whom you're dealing? Do you want to die? You must have a death wish!"

Continuing to shovel mud onto the levee, Morrison calmly replied, "No, Constantin, I don't want to die. I thought I made that clear to you. Please don't worry. I know how to deal with this Nikolai character. Just because he scares the shit out of everyone else on this island, I assure you, he doesn't scare the shit out of me." He stopped working and stuck his shovel in the mud. Facing his friend, he put his hand on Constantin's shoulder and smiled. "Look, don't worry. I've got a plan to deal with him and maybe make the lives of all the prisoners in Barracks Number One a little more bearable. Just trust me." Lowering his voice, he continued. "Spread the word to all members of our barracks. If any *vor* ever gets admitted to our barracks at night, make sure that I'm signaled and awakened if I'm sleeping. That's all I ask of any of our fellow political prisoners. Do you understand?"

Taking some deep breaths, Constantin began to calm down. "All right, comrade, all right. I'll trust you to do it your way." He smiled gamely and started to walk away when he turned and said, "In some ways, you scare me, Moryak. You know I am a friend and an admirer. I think the world of you, and I pray you'll make it out of this hellhole to join my comrades and me. But you scare me. You really do. There is a certain part of you that is dark and dangerous." He turned and continued to walk away.

***

It took two nights for Nikolai to make his move. One of his fellow prisoners awakened Morrison from a sound sleep, whispering, "Moryak, wake up! There's a small group of *vors* assembling near the door of the barracks and the guard just walked out to them. I think something is about to happen!" Morrison thanked him and quickly bolted out of his rack. From under his rack, Morrison pulled out two sacks full of rags and placed them under his blanket, which he pulled over the top of them. In the dark room, it would appear that he was still in his rack. He quickly stepped into the shadows in the corner of the barracks. In his hands, he held the knife and the small club that Josef had provided for him. *I owe Josef for this,* he mused to himself.

In less than five minutes time, the door to the barracks opened and with deliberate stealth, two *vors* entered and began walking toward Morrison's rack. The other prisoners lay still pretending to sleep, just as Morrison had instructed them to do. They all watched in the darkness as the two thugs made their way slowly and quietly toward Morrison. They both wore long overcoats and, as they approached Moryak's rack, they pulled out the long clubs they had hidden under their coats. At the side of the cot, they each held their clubs in the air as they looked down at the immobile body completely covered by the blanket. "This is a love letter from Nikolai!" shouted one of the *vors* as they began to smash their clubs down on the inert figure in the rack.

They had not seen Morrison maneuver behind them in the darkness. When the *vor* on the left lifted his club up for the third time, Morrison used his own club to block the attacker's weapon by hooking it over the *vor's* club. He simultaneously smashed his knee viciously into the small of the assailant's back. With an agonizing scream, the *vor* began to crumble. As he did, Morrison slammed his club into the side of the man's chest, splintering his ribs. The other assailant, realizing what had happened, pulled a knife from his belt. He lunged at Morrison, who swung his club at him but missed. The *vor* managed to stab him in the left shoulder, causing him to drop the club. "C'mon, Moryak! Let's see what you got! I've got permission, no, *orders*, from Nikolai to kill you if necessary!"

Morrison pulled his knife out of his belt, and the two men stood facing each other in the darkness. By the way he moved, Morrison could see that this *vor* was an experienced knife fighter. However, Morrison had anticipated a situation like this one, and he knew that his fellow prisoners would do what he had trained them to do. The two combatants lunged at each other and continued to jockey for position while the crowd of prisoners formed a circle around them. Facing outward from the circle, Alexandr picked up the edge of a blanket covering a large lantern on the floor in front of him. Lighting a match, he quickly lit the lantern and used the blanket to block the light. On the opposite side of the prisoner's circle, directly facing Alexandr, Constantin waited until Moryak had the *vor* in the correct position. After a series of jabs at each other and attempting to achieve favorable position against one another, Morrison's back was directly in front of Alexander, and his opponent now faced him directly. "*Now!*" shouted Constantin.

Alexandr immediately pulled the blanket off the lantern and the bright light blazed directly into the *vor*'s eyes, blinding him. Morrison lunged forward and smashed his fist into his opponent's face, knocking him off balance. The *vor* slashed out at Morrison, but his blade only caught Morrison's blouse sleeve. As his momentum rotated him slightly, Morrison plunged his blade deep into the *vor*'s lower abdomen. The man let out a scream of agony and froze, as Morrison grabbed him by the collar and pulled him close. The assailant's face, only inches from his own, had a wide-eyed look of shock and disbelief. With firm, steady pressure, Morrison pulled the knife blade directly up the man's abdominal cavity, effectively slicing apart his internal organs. As the man began to go limp, Morrison spit in his face and let go. The *vor* crumpled to floor and was dead before he hit it.

Morrison turned to the other *vor* who lay on the floor, gasping for breath. The man posed no further threat. He then looked up at his fellow prisoners who stood there, stunned at what they had just witnessed. "Thank you for your help, comrades," he offered, as he heard the small crowd begin to murmur.

"What happens now, Moryak?" asked one of his colleagues as he brought over some cloth strips to tend to Morrison's arm wound.

Morrison smiled and replied, "Now we send a message to these guys. They need to know who the real boss is. You see, a lot of this is all bluster and positioning. Power through intimidation. They aren't used to being intimidated. Believe me, they won't like it. Bullies always feel like tough guys when no one fights back. I've been fighting jerks like this all my life. I know what I'm talking about. Now, who has the ink that I need?"

Outside the barracks, five *vors* waited patiently for their partners to emerge with the one they called Moryak. Nikolai had been clear in his instructions: feel free to rough him up, bring him out, and tie him up. Then bring him to Barracks Number Two where he would be taught a lesson in submission and obedience. They hadn't heard any noise coming from the inside, and they certainly knew that the political prisoners—the ones that they referred to as the sheep—wouldn't lift a finger to help Moryak. It remained fairly quiet when the door slowly opened. Suddenly, a very bright light shining from three glowing lanterns blinded them.

They heard a loud *thump* hit the ground near them, followed by a second one and soon screaming and gasping could be heard. The lights were suddenly extinguished and all went black again. After about a minute, their eyes adjusted to the darkness. What they saw shocked them. Nearest to them lay one of their colleagues, naked and dead. His abdomen had been sliced open from his pubic bone to his breastbone and his bloody entrails protruded out. In addition, his throat had been slashed and blood had gushed out all over his torso. His wide-open eyes bore witness to his horrible death. One of the five *vors* immediately began to vomit.

Closer to the doorway lay the second attacker. He moaned and wailed loudly and could barely breathe. Tears streamed down his face. In a strained whisper he called out, "Help me, comrades, help me!" They rushed over and found him naked, but wrapped in a bed sheet that had been affixed to his chest with a knife that had been tunneled under the skin of his chest wall. Over the bottom part of the sheet, a message announced in black ink, "Tell Nikolai that I'm still busy. I'll meet with him tomorrow. Moryak." Totally shocked, the horrified *vors* looked at each other.

They had never witnessed anything like this carnage. This Moryak; how could one man be so ruthless and fearless? Was it possible that he was more intimidating than Nikolai? Each man mulled those thoughts over as they lifted the bodies of their two broken and dead comrades and carried them into Barracks Number Two.

***

Twenty-five *vors* lived in Barracks Number Two, in addition to twenty other petty criminals. It became obvious to Nikolai that each of them very much feared this Moryak. After they brought the two bodies back into their barracks, the ones who brought them in couldn't stop talking about the crazy and terrible Moryak. Nikolai soon realized that they seemed to fear this Moryak more than they feared him. *This is unacceptable,* he thought. This situation had rapidly spiraled out of control and had to be resolved rapidly. This intolerable dilemma became even more obvious to him when he ordered one of the bitches to simply deliver a written message to Barracks Number One for Moryak. "Please, Master," they each begged him, "don't make me go over there!" The last one got on his knees and started kissing Nikolai's feet. He savagely kicked him out of the way. After all of the *vors* expressed fear of confronting Moryak personally, Nikolai realized that the problem had become critical. They *did* fear Moryak more than they feared him. He had to act now. He finally bribed one of the guards to deliver the message.

When the prisoners returned from work the next evening, Moryak found the message that Nikolai had sent him. Most of the prisoners gathered around him as he read it, eagerly waiting for him to reveal its contents. He finished it and sat there deep in thought. Finally, Constantin could no longer take the suspense. "For God's sake, Moryak, what does it say?" he blurted out.

"He wants to meet me in Barracks Two at midnight. He wants to come to an understanding between us. He wants me to come alone."

"You are certainly not going to go, of course! That would be suicide!"

"No," countered Morrison, "I'll go. We might as well end this tonight. I'm getting tired of all of this, and I think you are, too. Even Nikolai seems to be getting tired of dealing with me, so I think tonight we'll get everything straightened out."

"You can't be serious!" blurted Alexandr. "You know it's a trap. How can you simply walk right into it? Please, Moryak, if something happens to you, we are all doomed!"

He looked at all of his colleagues gathered around them, touched by their genuine concern for him. "Please, comrades, I'll be prepared. Now, leave me alone so I can write a message. When I'm done, we'll need to bribe the guard to deliver it, so please gather up some bribe money amongst yourselves." The prisoners began to disperse, leaving Morrison to his writing.

Just before midnight, Morrison arrived at the door of Barracks Number Two. Two *vors* escorted him inside and ordered him to remove his coat. After complying, they frisked him. "He's clean," one of them declared. They then escorted him to the far end of the barracks. All of the residents' eyes remained fixed on this mysterious mad man that they had heard about, the one called Moryak. At the end of the barracks, Nikolai sat in a large chair, slapping a baton-like stick into his other hand. *Must think he's a king on his throne,* thought Morrison. Some ugly-looking henchmen flanked either side of him. As he arrived in front of Nikolai, Morrison said, "You wanted to meet with me? Here I am."

Nikolai threw his head back with laughter. "Moryak," he bellowed, "I can't believe you are so damn stupid to come in here alone and unarmed! You know that I am going to have you killed! You had to know that!"

"I don't think so," replied Morrison. Suddenly, the sound of breaking glass on either side of the barracks interrupted their conversation. Four rifle barrels protruded through the windows as Josef yelled, "All of you, back against the wall! *Now! Move!*" The surprised *vors* at first stood still until Josef fired a round into the wall over one of their heads. They moved as ordered against both walls, in perfect sight for all of the armed guards to shoot if necessary. Only Nikolai and Morrison remained in place. "All right, tough guy, let's end this now!" challenged Morrison. At first, Nikolai just sat there, turning purple with rage. This bastard Moryak had insulted him again. He had tricked him again. He had to die!

With a guttural yell, Nikolai leapt out of his chair toward Morrison, smashing his head into his chest and knocking him over backward. As Morrison hit the floor, he momentarily had the wind knocked out of him. Nikolai landed one good punch into the side of his head, but Morrison rolled away before the second one hit him. Nikolai's fist crashed painfully into the floor. Like a wrestler, Morrison quickly maneuvered free and sprang to his feet. He delivered a fast kick to Nikolai's flank that momentarily stunned him. Morrison pulled him to his feet, punched him in the abdomen, and then kicked him in the groin. As Nikolai doubled over in pain, Morrison clamped a hand around his throat and straightened him up to his feet. After delivering a punishing right hook to the head, followed by a left hook, Nikolai crumpled to the floor, lying breathlessly on his side. Morrison walked completely around him once and stopped to kick him in the ass. He then paused and appeared to be in deep thought.

Propping his nearly unconscious foe up on his knees, Morrison positioned himself behind Nikolai as he removed the *vor*'s leather belt. Wrapping it around Nikolai's neck, he began to pull it tight until his victim started to gasp. A few of the *vors* started to rush in, but stopped at the sound of the bolts of the guards' rifles depositing a fresh round into the chambers. Morrison continued to pull the belt tight as the struggling Nikolai started to turn blue and went limp. Suddenly, he let go of the belt and let Nickolai collapse in front of him, still alive.

Morrison stood up and straightened his shirt. He looked around the room at all of the *vors* and petty criminals assembled there. The silence in the barracks was deafening. "Listen up, you pieces of shit!" he announced. "I'm Moryak, and I run things in this camp now. *Do you understand me?*" he roared. The assembled criminals meekly nodded their heads. "Good. Let's understand each other. If any of you enter Barracks Number One without my permission, I will kill you. If any of you anger me in any way, I will kill you. In fact, I just may decide to kill you because you are each disgusting animals, and I can't stand looking at you. That is my prerogative, understand?" Hearing no response, he bellowed, "*Understand?*" Everyone again nodded.

"Should you ever want to speak to me, you have to ask my permission. God help you if you ever open your disgusting mouths around me without asking first!" He looked over at Nikolai who was now awake and starting to move. He watched as his beaten foe finally managed to sit up. Morrison looked up and continued. "That brings me to this guy, Nikolai. As far as I'm concerned, he is a fat, sadistic, sick bastard like all the rest of you. However, in spite of being a lowlife scumbag, he is my number two man. That should indicate to you how low all of the rest of you all are in my eyes. He is in charge of Barracks Number Two, and you will all obey him. If you don't, he has my permission to deal with you any way he sees fit. We will work out any other details later. Now, are there any questions, you disgusting maggots?" No one dared say anything. "Good!" Morrison said. "I didn't think there would be."

He reached down, took Nikolai's hand, and pulled him to his feet. Looking him straight in the eye, he stated, "I think I made myself clear, Nikolai. Don't make me come back here again. Understand?" The *vor* just nodded in assent, finding it difficult to look directly at Moryak.

He then turned and began to walk toward the door. As he passed each criminal, they looked at him with a totally new respect. He was in charge now. Once he walked through the door, the guards withdrew their rifles.

When he entered Barracks Number One, all of the residents mobbed him. Many hugged him, delighted that he appeared safe and unharmed. They started chanting, "Moryak, Moryak!" over and over. He finally sat down and they poured him some vodka that they had acquired recently from one of the guards. "Tell us Moryak, what happened in there?"

Downing his vodka, Morrison replied, "Nothing really, we just worked out a few details. Comrades, I think things will be just a little better for us all from now on!"

As he lay back on his rack that night, it occurred to him that he had achieved a goal that he had longed for all of his life. He was admired and accepted for his deeds. *You were wrong Professor Michelson*, he thought. *I have won their respect and their friendship. I did it by becoming a killer. A cold-blooded killer.*

Victoria Street
London England
November 1909

Mansfield Cumming already knew that his new offices at 64 Victoria Street were going to be inadequate. He would have to bide his time and lobby for more space in the near future. After all, he had been delighted to be named the man in charge of this latest evolution of the intelligence services for His Majesty's government: the Foreign Service Bureau, soon to be called MI6. The workload was astounding, but he also found it invigorating. It seemed that he was barely making a dent in his workload. Yes, lobbying for more space would have to wait.

    Now in his third week on the job, he noted that on this morning he had an appointment on his schedule with William Melville of the War Office Intelligence Division. Cumming knew that Melville had been running the majority of overseas intelligence operations for the past several years. Melville had, in fact, been instrumental in lobbying for the creation of a permanent intelligence office. He had continued as the head of the Special Section, whose specialty was pursuing German spies. This morning Melville was scheduled to turn over all of his files on foreign intelligence operations. Cumming, eager to review them and learn the breadth of England's overseas clandestine operations, had awaited this morning with great anticipation.

Precisely at 10:00 A.M., Cumming's secretary announced that William Melville was sitting in the foyer for his appointment. Cumming rose and walked into the foyer, greeting Melville cordially. One of Melville's assistants stood next to him, pulling a small cart carrying two packing crates. "My files," indicated Melville as the three men entered Cumming's office. After unloading the crates in the corner of the office, the assistant left and the two intelligence officers sat down. "How goes it, Mansfield?" asked Melville politely.

"Very well, thank you. I can't tell you how much I appreciate these files. It certainly looks like you have been quite busy these past several years."

"Indeed, I have," replied Melville. "I have a file for virtually every operation we've undertaken and even for planned operations that we considered but never carried out. You'll note that each folder has a code name and a date. The folders are in sequential order by date. Some of the agents listed in these files are still active with us and are indicated by an asterisk. When you read these, please feel free to give me a ring if you have any questions, and we'll discuss them."

"Excellent," responded Cumming as he stood up and walked over to his small bar located on top of a black safe. "Can I offer you a drink, William?"

"Have you ever met an Irishman who refused you yet?"

"You're quite right!" Cumming chuckled as he poured single malt whiskey into two tumblers. "A toast!" he proclaimed. "To the new Foreign Bureau!"

Melville stood up, his glass raised high. "After all the work, all the lobbying I did to help get this thing off the ground, I certainly will drink to that. Damn right, I will!" Both men downed their drinks and continued their visit, sharing tales of their past exploits as younger men.

Several weeks later, Melville received a phone call at his office from Cumming. The new head of the foreign service requested that Melville come to his office at his earliest convenience. A case file that he had just read had grabbed his attention, and he wanted to discuss it with Melville.

When Melville arrived, he and Cumming engaged in the usual small talk and banter. Finally, Cumming got down to business. "William, last night I read one of the old files. It was from 1905 and called Double Eagle."

At first, Cumming thought that Melville looked as if he had been shot in the back with a bullet from a high-powered rifle. After staring blankly for a few seconds, he finally spoke. "My God," he said, "I haven't thought about that for a while. I suppose you can say I put that one out of my mind."

"It is incredible that His Majesty's government would actually be involved in a plot to kidnap or kill a foreign leader," said Cumming as he looked down at the file in front of him. "President Roosevelt is the only American who knows about this mission, according to this file?"

"Yes, he personally authorized it. You know, I was with Prime Minister Balfour when Russian Prime Minister Sergei Witte pleaded with us to undertake the mission. Balfour would only consent if the Americans were in on it. You have to realize that the Tsar was going to sabotage the entire peace conference. The entire conference was set up, and there was great hope in the world that peace would finally be achieved. Witte told us that the Tsar was never going to agree to any peace plans. So, we had to act. It was only at the last minute, when the Tsar acquiesced, that the plan collapsed. We don't know exactly what went wrong. We suspected that an insider in Russia betrayed the mission."

"Interestingly, it was shortly after the whole affair that Witte fell out of favor with the Tsar, as I understand it. The American, this Stephen Morrison, was killed?"

"Yes. We learned that he was hanged at the Peter and Paul Fortress in October 1905. He apparently never cracked and betrayed his cover. A subsequent cover story was created by the Americans to explain his death, which stated that it occurred here in England. He was buried with full military honors at Arlington National Cemetery."

"What about this Sidney Reilly? It says he escaped. He has an asterisk next to his name. He's still active?"

"Yes. He's an incredible asset that I know you'll find very useful. He's a linguist, and he's well-traveled and very well-connected. The country doesn't matter—England, the United States, Russia—he's got the contacts. Currently he's got front businesses in St. Petersburg. He does have a weakness, though."

"What is it?"

"Women. He can't resist them. I believe he's been married three times already. He seems to have a proverbial 'wife' in every city in Europe. He definitely has trouble keeping his pants buttoned!"

"Interesting," mused Cumming. "I'm looking forward to meeting this character." Sitting back in his chair, he asked

Melville, "Is there anything else I should know about this Double Eagle case?"

Melville suddenly developed a deadly serious demeanor. "Mansfield, there are only six people in the world other than yourself who know about Double Eagle: King Edward, President Roosevelt, former Prime Minister Balfour, former Russian Prime Minister Witte, Sidney Reilly and myself. Not even Prime Minister Campbell-Bannerman knows about it. It is imperative that no else ever learn about it, ever! Can you picture the international ramifications? You must swear that the secret remains safe with you."

Taken aback by the melodramatics, Cumming noticed that Melville seemed uneasy even discussing this case, almost as if he carried a burden of guilt over it. *He was right though*, he thought to himself. *This whole affair is too dangerous ever to be revealed.* He smiled at Melville and sighed. "You have no worries in that regard, William. I will take this secret to the grave with me."

"Good!" blurted Melville. "How about pouring me another whiskey, and we'll drink to that!"

7

Rue Blanche
Paris, France
January 1912

The persistent, gentle rapping on the door continued until Vladimir Lenin finally reached the door and pulled it open. The light of the overcast sky silhouetted the small man in front of him, making it difficult for Lenin to recognize him at first. Then he smiled and offered his hand to the man he hadn't seen in nearly eight years. "Comrade Constantin Verontov! Welcome! Please come in!"

Lenin escorted his old colleague into his small apartment on Rue Blanche and called out to the other occupant of the apartment. "Comrade Mozger, look who just showed up at our door." Mozger arose from his seat and went to shake the newcomer's hand. "By God, it is you! We got your letter weeks ago! When did you get out of prison?" he asked.

"I left Solovetsky Island about three months ago. My God, it is good to be free! Nearly eight years in that godforsaken place! I hope I don't look as bad as I fear I do. Believe me comrades, as often as my body felt broken in the prison camp, my spirit never faltered." He looked at the two and tears began to stream down his face. "Forgive me; it is just so wonderful to see you two again!"

"Come," offered Lenin. "Join us for a little dinner. We will have much to discuss and to catch up on." Leading their guest into the small kitchen area, Mozger pulled out a clean tablecloth and the three men sat down at the table to dine on a simple meal of beef and potatoes. Constantin ate ravenously as he listened to his colleagues. The animated Lenin talked nonstop, updating Constantin on the progress of the Bolsheviks. "We are making slow but steady progress," assured Lenin. "Better to have a small cadre of disciplined followers than a large, unwieldy 'democratic' lot. Revolutions are not built with input from everyone. Party discipline must be strict and firm!" He confessed that he no longer worked on the revolutionary journal *Iskra*, but had begun instead to edit a new radical newsletter called *Vperyod!*, or *Forward!* He then began to describe the various activities involving the Bolsheviks. These activities included organizing strikes, paying off policemen, publishing and distributing their newsletter, and moving party members throughout Europe.

Finally, Constantin broke in. "Comrade Lenin, where do you get the financing for all of this? All of this must cost a fortune."

Lenin looked over to Mozger, and they smiled at one another. The grinning Mozger answered him. "We steal, my friend. We rob banks to raise our financing. After all, stealing from capitalists is not really stealing! The ends justify the means."

Constantin looked up with a stunned expression on his face. He saw his colleagues smiling mischievously back at him. "I don't mean to be disrespectful, but you two hardly look like bank robbers to me! We, well ... aren't we more intellectuals than ruffians? I mean, I can't picture any of our comrades as bank robbers. Has anyone been caught?"

Mozger smiled. "Of course, Comrade Lenin and I only oversee operations. Our followers, well, we're still relatively new at the game. But we've had first-class instructors who have been teaching our people how to do it. They also teach us how to make bombs, to extort people, and various other handy skills."

"Who in God's name teaches you these things?"

"Who, indeed! The masters themselves. Our teachers are the *vors*. In return for their tutelage, we give them a cut of the plunder. It has proven to be a very beneficial relationship. You must have had many dealings with *vors* at Solovetsky Island."

"Yes, I did. They are the most ruthless vermin on this planet. They are like an entirely different race of creatures, and we have the misfortune to inhabit the Earth with them. How can you stand dealing with them?"

"Comrade, when you want to cause terror, you go with the terrorists," interjected Lenin. "That's why they are so perfect for our purposes. They are feared by all, and they teach us well. They are so ruthless that no one, I mean no one, would ever stand up to them."

"I wouldn't necessarily say that," replied Constantin, with a smug look on his face. "I know someone who put them in their place."

"What?" exclaimed Lenin and Mozger almost simultaneously. "What on Earth are you talking about?" exclaimed Mozger.

"It's true. On Solovetsky Island, in the prison camp, one of my fellow prisoners, named Moryak, he not only stood up to them, but he actually dominated and intimidated them! The *vors* were genuinely afraid of him. He is fearless, I tell you! And he is a great man! Do you know who he is? He's the man who led the mutiny aboard the *Potemkin*. He is an extraordinary man. He's an intellectual, a revolutionary, and a savage animal—all rolled into one man!"

"Moryak?" asked Mozger. "The 'Sailor'? I think I may have heard of him. The rumors have it that he actually killed several *vors* at Solovetsky."

"Those aren't rumors, Comrade Mozger. I saw this with my own eyes. He kills and then he sleeps like a baby. I am not exaggerating when I tell you that he saved many of the political prisoners' lives with his courage and his power over the *vors*.

"Hmmm," Lenin thought out loud. "A man like this would be very useful to us. Is he a committed revolutionary?"

"I believe so. I would also classify him as a world-class cynic. Then again, if I had spent two years in solitary confinement, I believe that I would be a cynic also."

"Will he ever be getting out of prison?"

"He should be released in a couple of years. That's the other thing about him. He works constantly—physical work, I mean. At first, everyone thought he was crazy, but he manages to always get extra rations because he works so hard. For a man in prison, he is extremely fit." Constantin thought for a minute before he continued. "He is a frightening man in many ways. He almost seems to enjoy killing."

Lenin sat quietly with his hand on his chin, deep in thought. Finally, he spoke. "Comrade Verontov, correspond with this man and keep in contact with him."

"He is not allowed any mail, either in or out of the prison."

"Then write to another one of the prisoners and have them pass him a message. Tell him he is welcome here when he is released. Yes, a man with these talents would benefit our organization very much indeed!" He looked over at Mozger. "Imagine that. A man, an intellectual, who actually beats up and then kills *vors*. A man who makes *vors* fear *him*! I would very much like to meet such a man!"

Mozger grinned back at Lenin. "So would I, comrade. So would I."

After they dined, the three walked over to the fireplace and sat down. Constantin, in his eagerness to learn what had gone on in his absence, couldn't stop firing questions at his two colleagues. "Tell me about the party, Comrade Lenin. What are we achieving in St. Petersburg?"

"Great things indeed! Great things," said Lenin with enthusiasm. "We are small but growing. We even have six members of the Bolshevik party as elected members to this fourth Duma. Our influence grows."

"I wish I were so enthused, comrade," replied Mozger in a cynical tone. Lenin shot him an annoyed look. "In this regard, you are too trusting," Mozger continued. "I warn you, I am still somewhat concerned."

"Concerned about what?" inquired Constantin.

"Malinovsky, for one thing," said Mozger, referring to Roman Malinovsky, one of the six Bolshevik deputies to the Duma. "He drinks too damn much and has a big mouth."

"You're too hard on Comrade Malinovsky," countered Lenin. "I think you resent the fact that he's a genuine working-class man, unlike the three of us, I might add. He certainly has some rough edges, but he is a true representative of the working class, the proletariat. We need him there. He lends much credibility to our revolution that is led by the workers of Russia."

"Well, he's only part of the problem," snapped Mozger. "He's only one of several in our party in St. Petersburg that I don't trust. Many of them live beyond their means and to me that indicates that they're taking payoffs and bribes from the police. I wouldn't be surprised if many are on the Okhrana payroll as informers!"

"You are a cynic, Comrade Mozger. I can certainly vouch for the veracity of Comrade Malinovsky. Now, this conversation is over. I'm sick of having you slander Malinovsky. For your information, if anyone is caught in the act of betraying us, the penalty will be death, do you understand?" His voice rising slightly, he continued. "Loyalty to the party is everything, including from you, comrade. If you feel you cannot continue to give me your loyalty, you are free to leave. Now, having said this, I am tired of you trying to paint Comrade Malinovsky with the brush of decadence and disloyalty. This stops now!"

Several seconds of awkward silence passed as Mozger stared down at the table in front of him. He gradually lifted his eyes and stared at the other two. Slowly shaking his head, he began to talk in a soft voice. "Of course, you have my undying loyalty. I apologize. This won't happen again." The rare occasions when Lenin displayed anger toward him were difficult for him to accept. He desperately sought his leader's approval. "My life has been dedicated to the party and therefore to you. I need only remind you two of the past life that I gave up to join the party as proof of my commitment. Rest assured, I'll never question you again about Comrade Malinovsky."

Lenin stood and smiled at the other two. "Good then. Come! Let's take a walk and tell Comrade Verontov about some of the recent achievements that we have accomplished. By the way, did you know that Stolypin was killed by one of our party members, Comrade Bogrov?

"I didn't know that," replied the impressed Constantin. "We had no details of his death."

With a smile Lenin added, "See the great things our party can achieve? We had Comrade Bogrov trained as an assassin by the *vors*! Yes, we're small, but we're growing. The future belongs to us!"

Aboard the imperial yacht Standart
Gulf of Finland
June 1914

Tsar Nicholas II always looked forward to enjoying the annual family vacation aboard the imperial yacht *Standart;* they would sail to various ports of call in Finland. "No business, only family," he always dictated to his staff. However, late on the afternoon of June 28, he received a telegram that shocked him. In Sarajevo, Archduke Franz Ferdinand, the heir to the throne of Austria-Hungary, had been assassinated by a radical student who was a member of a Bosnian Serb underground group. Nicholas feared that Emperor Franz Joseph of Austria-Hungary would soon use this act as a pretext to declare war on Serbia.

Emperor Franz Joseph in fact would make demands on Serbia so untenable that they amounted to a declaration of war. When they were delivered in late July, Nicholas finally realized the seriousness of the explosive political situation. After all, Russia had always been the guardian and protector of the Serbs, and Nicholas had promised to defend Serbia's independence. This well-known policy now threatened to drag Russia into war, a war for which it was ill-prepared. On July 28, 1914, Austria-Hungary declared war on Serbia, and within a very short time, the world was at war.

Nicholas responded to the war declaration by ordering the mobilization of his armies along the Austrian border. "Certainly, Cousin Willy will understand why I must do this," he reasoned. Kaiser Wilhelm of Germany had thrown his support to Austria, believing that his timid cousin Nicholas would not respond. When Nicholas ordered a general mobilization, war became inevitable.

The outpouring of public support for Russia's entry into the war elated the Tsar. "Look, darling," he gushed to his wife. "See how the country is now unified for the first time in years! Best of all, it will be a short war!"

***

In England, Mansfield Cumming read his intelligence reports as well as the London Times. He felt a touch of self-satisfaction. His department had been expanded and they stood ready. If anything, the prospect of what was to come over the next few months and possibly years excited him even more. After all, he was a military man, a man of action.

Several blocks away, a very distraught Sir Edward Grey, England's foreign secretary, felt quite differently about the world events. He had watched the world situation deteriorate before his eyes despite his most ardent efforts. With a somber frustration and knowledge that the world would never again be the same, he uttered, "The lamps are going out all over Europe. We shall never see them lit again in our lifetime."

***

In his small apartment in Berne, Switzerland, Lenin sat at his table reading about the world events in the Geneva newspaper. He knew that the outbreak of war would be the straw that would break the camel's back. Surely, the Russian people would rise up against the Tsar for leading the country into a senseless war fueled by capitalistic greed. Instead, they surprised and disgusted him with their enthusiastic support for the Tsar and his war. Even more shocking to him was the support that the European Marxists had given to their governments for their war efforts. He tried his best to fight off depression, convinced that history was on his side.

With smug satisfaction, Lenin observed the Bolshevik strength slowly but surely growing stronger with each passing day. The various worker councils within Russia, the soviets, had become stronger and more influential. More Bolsheviks had been elected to the Duma. Yes, history and time are on our side, concluded Lenin. Even with their growing presence in the Duma, he had to concede that Mozger was correct about one critical issue that they disagreed on: Malinovsky had to go. He had become a heavy drinker, as Mozger had reported. His behavior had become more erratic, and it brought negative attention to him. He had become an embarrassment to the Bolsheviks. With personal sadness, Lenin informed Malinovsky that he would be resigning his seat and leaving St. Petersburg, or Petrograd, as it was now called. Malinovsky surprised Lenin by volunteering to join the Russian army to fight the Germans. Mozger was right all along. His behavior had been too erratic, and he could not be trusted.

Lenin continued to disagree with Mozger on one key issue regarding Malinovsky- he never doubted his party loyalty. And he totally disregarded Mozger's suspicions that he acted as an informant for the Okhrana.

***

In the Solovetsky Monastery, Stephen Morrison first learned of the outbreak of war from a fellow political prisoner. In one of their never-ending political discussions, one of the prisoners read a letter from a friend that detailed the assassination of Archduke Ferdinand and the subsequent events that had plunged the world into war. The news made most of his fellow prisoners ecstatic, but not for the reasons that Tsar Nicholas would have wanted. "Don't you see, comrades, this situation is playing into our hands!" exclaimed one of the prisoners. Morrison knew that he must be another of the Bolsheviks. Their numbers had been steadily growing at Solovetsky Island.

"Do you really think so?" asked Morrison, trying to understand their mindset.

"Yes, of course! Don't you see? At most, this will be a diversion from all of the internal domestic problems of Russia. Soon the people will tire of war, tire of the shortages and the effect on their lives. Tire of a war being fought for the glory and benefit of the aristocracy. Tire of the certain death that in the end will not change their lives or status one bit!" The look of utter delight in the man's eyes as he spoke reminded Morrison that he lived with a bunch of intelligent, idealistic, and humorless demagogues. "Comrade Moryak, think what this means!" he said.

"I think I follow you, but why don't you enlighten us all. You're certainly worked up thinking about this, "Morrison suggested.

"Of course! The result is this: when the masses tire of the war, we provide the solution, the antidote. We will pull Russia out of the war and offer the workers a Russia that is fair and democratic. A Russia that is empowered by all of the local workers' councils—the soviets! A Russia that will lead the world in a worker's revolution!" When he finished, his colleagues around the table applauded and congratulated him for his rhetoric. Many walked over, slapped him on the back, and shook his hand. Not just the Bolsheviks, but also the Social Revolutionaries and Social Democrats.

"Well said, comrade!" bellowed Morrison, as he noted the unified response to the man's political statement. *I've been listening to this revolutionary crap for years,* he thought to himself. *Perhaps this is the future reality for this world. Some world!* He smiled as he thought to himself. *In this world, I am one of their heroes and role models, a revolutionary agitator and mutineer, the Moryak! In this world, craziness, political demagoguery, and murderous violence all exist to allow me to become their respected and admired leader. What an insane world this is!* With a rueful expression, he added to his thoughts, *What a pathetic waste of my life!*

In his cot that night, he thought to himself that he had less than two years left. He had asked one of the prisoners if the United States was in this war. They told him that their president, a man named Woodrow Wilson, was determined to keep America out of the war. As he drifted off to sleep, Morrison dreamed of his past shipboard life. He could return to his prior life only in his dreams, and that was when he wasn't having his nightmares. He had given up hope. He still dreamed of killing Sidney Reilly. Perhaps that was now his purpose in life. After all, he reasoned, God would not have let him survive this far only to deny him such sweet vengeance.

***

Several months later, Sergei Witte lay on his deathbed. His beloved St. Petersburg's name had been changed by the Tsar to Petrograd to eliminate the German sound of its name. Before his health declined, he had strongly opposed Russia's entry into the war, further alienating him from the imperial court. Now it was nearly over. Cancer continued to eat away at his body, and his family could barely rouse him as they kept a deathwatch at his bedside. Intermittently, he opened his eyes and uttered some words that were largely garbled. He had several seemingly lucid moments when he finally succumbed on March 13, 1915.

Members of the press stood watch at his home when he died and began to pepper the family with questions. It had been no secret that he had fallen out of favor with the Tsar years ago, and the reporters chose to ask questions about this fact. "Did he harbor any bitterness about his treatment at the hands of the imperial family?" asked one reporter. "I mean, after all of his service to Russia, it is common knowledge that he had been largely tossed aside and ignored."

"Actually, no," replied his son. "Father always remained loyal to the Tsar, even when they disagreed. To the very end, he remained a loyal servant of the Tsar. In the past twenty-four hours, he remained largely somnolent and barely conscious. Yet, on at least three occasions, he opened his eyes and clearly exclaimed, 'Double Eagle!' In fact, the last time he said it, he had tears in his eyes. Double Eagle, the symbol of the Romanov dynasty. The last thing my father said in this world was 'Double Eagle.' Gentlemen, I think that speaks volumes about what my father was thinking when he died."

Petrograd, Russia
September 1916

Stephen Morrison stepped down from the train platform, his muscles slightly sore from the long train ride. Walking into Moskovsky Railroad Station, it occurred to him that the last time he had set foot in this city, it was called St. Petersburg, and that was eleven years ago. Now a free man for the first time in over ten years, he wanted to savor every minute of it. Walking into the men's room, he passed a mirror and stopped to look at his reflection. At age forty-six, his lined face reflected a difficult life. Gray flecks lined his hair and beard stubble. Where to go from here? That would be the next issue to address. At the moment, he didn't have a clue.

Several days before, he had left the Solovetsky Monastery that had been his prison home for over a decade. His fellow prisoners gave him enough money to purchase a train ticket to

Petrograd along with a few items of clothing. The Bolsheviks had given him one of their prize leather coats that they favored, along with a leather cap. Morrison gratefully accepted their gifts, and as he watched Solovetsky Island fade into the distance from the ferryboat, he began to plan the rest of his life. He wasn't sure what to do; he only knew that he needed to start in Petrograd. At least he had an address to start with. Constantin had forwarded him a contact's address in Petrograd and had invited him to join them in their revolutionary struggles. Morrison couldn't care less about their politics, but he needed to start somewhere.

As he walked toward the center of the city, he thought about his former life as an officer in the United States Navy and as a husband. He immediately tried to put such thoughts out of his mind. *Don't torture yourself,* he kept telling himself. *That life is over. Start thinking ahead. One day at a time.* He kept walking for no other reason than to clear his head. The sheer joy of being able to walk where he wanted as a free man continued to exhilarate him. He now had time to plan his next move. *After all,* he smiled, *what else do I have to do?*

The city looked dirtier than he remembered. Revolutionary posters containing workers' slogans seemed to be pasted on every building. Many of the notices that Morrison saw littering the streets announced an upcoming labor strike, or a planned street demonstration. The political situation mirrored exactly what his fellow prisoners had described. Many armed troops and police patrolled the streets. In the decade since he had last been there, it was as if a dark, somber veil had descended over the city, and the once vibrant capital of Russia had turned into a cauldron of discontent. After reflecting on his life, Morrison sat on a bench and thought out loud to himself, "God, how I hate this goddamn place!" He purposely spoke in English, just to savor the sound. It occurred to him that he hadn't spoken English aloud for over a decade.

He kept walking and soon he arrived on Nevsky Prospekt. Suddenly, the streets seemed vaguely familiar, and he remembered several shops and stores that he had seen in 1905. His thoughts turned immediately to his mission and his former partner Sidney Reilly. *How I would love to break his neck*, he thought to himself. After all these years, his bitterness had not abated. He readily acknowledged that it was the thought of avenging his betrayal that kept him alive. Casually walking, he strolled up the street to the Passazh Arcade and entered. To his total amazement, in a few minutes he stood in front of the import-export office that he had been in eleven years before. The signage on the door now read "Allied Machinery Company," and below it the name of the proprietor, S. Reilly. He blinked in disbelief and again read the name. Could it actually be Reilly after all of these years? Can it really be this easy? He stood in front of the door for a few minutes, debating with himself whether to enter, and decided against it. As he walked on to the end of the row of shops, he heard the door opening behind him. He turned to look, and saw Sidney Reilly emerge from the office and walk toward the opposite corner.

This must be fate, Morrison thought to himself as he followed his former partner down the streets. *This is the moment I've waited over ten years for!* There was no mistaking it. His moustache was gone, but it was the same man who had left him to be captured by the Okhrana over a decade ago. Reilly crossed the street and entered a small restaurant as Morrison followed behind at a safe distance. He walked over to the front window and saw Reilly being seated at a small table by himself, his back to the entrance. His heart pounding, Morrison entered the elegant restaurant, and the maitre d' immediately stopped him. "Can

I help you?" he inquired, eyeing the patron's leather coat and hat with obvious distaste.

"That man dining over there is expecting me. Thank you anyway," he replied as he entered the dining area. Within seconds he stood directly behind Reilly. As Reilly lifted a glass of wine to his lips, he suddenly felt someone behind him grasp his wrist. Leaning over to Reilly's left ear, Morrison whispered, "Give me one good reason why I shouldn't kill you right here and now." He then walked around the table and sat down facing the British agent.

Reilly stared back at the intruder, seeming more confused than scared. "Is there something that you want of me?" he inquired. "You know, you're really not properly attired to be dining here. I'd appreciate it if you'd leave, right now." He again raised his glass, but the intruder once more grabbed his wrist.

"Take a good look, Sidney Reilly," Morrison ordered.

Reilly glared into the eyes of this annoying stranger. Something was vaguely familiar about him, he thought. *Those eyes, I've seen them somewhere before today.* Then the realization hit him. His eyes widened in disbelief as he blurted out, "Oh, my God! It can't be! For Christ's sake, they hung you at Peter and Paul Fortress! Double Eagle—Morrison, isn't it? How can this be? I mean, I know—"

"Will you shut the hell up?" snapped Morrison, cutting him off in mid-sentence. "Never mind how I got here. I asked you a question a moment ago, and I'd like an answer. Give me a good reason why I shouldn't kill you right now! I've been dreaming of this for over ten years now. I really don't give a damn why you set me up, only that—"

"Set you up?" blurted out the startled Reilly. "What in heaven's name are you talking about? Both of us were set up by someone working for the Okhrana. I barely escaped myself. Jesus Christ, Morrison! Is that what you believed all these years? You fool; you stupid fool! I was nearly killed myself!" Morrison still held Reilly's wrist tightly. "Please let go of me and calm down." Morrison let go and sat back, his eyes filled with hatred. "That's good," Reilly said as he motioned to the waiter, who promptly came to the table. Taking a sip of his wine, he looked at his old partner and then turned to the waiter. "Ask my guest what he would like to drink, please." Morrison ordered vodka. Dumbfounded, Reilly continued. "How did you escape the hangman's knot? I know they announced in the papers that you were hanged."

"Never mind that for now."

"And where the hell have you been for all these years?"

"On Solovetsky Island. Doing hard labor. My first two years were in solitary confinement. In fact, I was released several days ago. I just arrived in St. Petersburg today."

"By the way, it's now called Petrograd. Less German sounding, you know. You do know there's a war going on, don't you?" At that point, the waiter arrived with Reilly's dinner. "Forgive me, how rude," he announced to the waiter. "Please bring my guest a menu."

Morrison continued to glare at Reilly. "Do you still work for the British?"

"Of course. I have multiple passports, multiple identities, and only two loyalties—to myself and to His Majesty, the King of England. Tell me, Double Eagle, why are you dressed like a Bolshevik? All that dark leather stuff. It makes you look quite menacing, you know."

Morrison perused the menu and ordered his first real meal in a decade. When the waiter left, he looked up at Reilly and told him, "The reason I'm dressed like a Bolshevik is because

I've been living the life of a Bolshevik. In prison, they thought I was one because I assumed the identity of a prominent prisoner when I left St. Petersburg. Do you remember the *Potemkin* mutiny? Well, I'm the sailor who led it. And then I was imprisoned at Solovetsky Island. At least that's what everyone believes. I'm called Moryak, the famous revolutionary." Over the next few minutes he recapped the details of the past ten years of his life, including his plans to kill the man with whom he was now dining.

"That's an incredible story, my friend. Now let me tell you what really happened to our mission." Reilly recounted for Morrison the specifics of their failed mission and how they had deduced that Okhrana double agents had exposed them. When Morrison's food arrived both men dined without talking until it was time for dessert. Reilly broke the silence with a question. "Tell me, what will you do now? Where will you go?"

Staring off into the distance, Morrison sighed. "I don't know. At least not yet. I've got a contact here in Petrograd, a former prisoner with whom I served. He's an active Bolshevik. He contacted me in prison and invited me to join them when I got out. Apparently, he's told the great Lenin all about me, and Lenin himself wants to meet me. Who knows, maybe it's a job. Isn't that the ultimate irony? Here I am, an American, posing as a Bolshevik, and the Bolsheviks want me to work for their top dog! Well, if it's a place to sleep and it buys me some time, I'll think about it. I just don't know. Yeah sure, I would love to go back to the United States, but I know that's impossible. Besides, I'm not the same man who left there many years ago. To survive I've had to become … well, let's say I'm not proud of what I've become. I just don't know. I'm going to have to think this through. For the first time in over a decade, I'm free." Inside, he felt like he was still imprisoned by this new life and new person that he had become.

Reilly ordered them some after dinner cordials and proposed a toast to his partner of long ago. "Why the hell would I want to toast anything that has to do with you?" snarled Morrison.

"Just you wait, my friend. You might just find that we have much to celebrate," countered Reilly. Morrison stared at him and slowly raised his glass.

When they finished, he invited Morrison to walk with him. They strolled though the city and finally ended up on the banks of the Neva River. No words were passed between them as they walked, but Reilly's mind raced with ideas. Since leaving the restaurant, he had formulated a plan, and he grew more enthused as they walked. Finally, he stopped and looked at Morrison. "I think we should talk. Come; let's go back to my office where we can talk in private. I think I can help you in your dilemma." When Morrison shot a cynical look at him, Reilly blurted out, "No, really, we need to talk. I think we can actually help one another!" Shaking his head with skepticism, Morrison followed behind as the two former partners headed back to the Nevsky Prospekt.

Entering the back room of Reilly's office, he offered a chair to his guest. Reilly immediately excused himself. "Please wait here, I have a business appointment scheduled that I'm going to cancel. We'll talk in a few minutes." Reilly left for the front office and pulled the door shut behind him as he went straight to his telephone.

When Reilly returned to the room a few minutes later, Morrison noticed that he seemed somewhat animated as he began to talk. "Morrison, I've been thinking. You probably don't recall, but I am quite a businessman, in addition to being one hell of an agent. I have a business proposition for you. Why not work for me, for the Allies? You are in a very unique position that could do us a lot of good."

"What are you saying? Why would I want to work with you again? I believe our last venture together cost me over ten years of my life."

"Come now, Double Eagle, think of it. The Allies- England, Russia, and France- we're at war with Germany. I predict that the Americans will soon be entering this war on our side. We all know that Russia is the wild card. There is so much discontent and anger in Russia over this war. It is bleeding the country dry. The Tsarist government is trying to build up public support for the war, but this effort grows more futile every day. And here's the crux of the problem.

"The revolutionary groups, especially the Bolsheviks, want Russia to pull out of the war. That would be disastrous for the Allies. It would free up Germany to fight a one-front war, and as a result they just might win this damn thing."

Morrison stared back at Reilly and asked, "What does all of this have to do with me?"

"Don't you see?" Reilly asked. "You have lived as a Bolshevik all of these years. They think you are one of their inspirational heroes. You could infiltrate them and work for us. They are a group that we worry about quite a bit. This Lenin character, if he ever got power, would pull Russia out of the war immediately. Now you have the golden opportunity to get close to him, to be part of his inner circle. I've watched them grow in number and influence, and I have contacts within their group. Hell, in some places I even pose as one of them, but no one is close to the power. There is no agent who can get near Lenin.

"You are out of your goddamn mind!" replied Morrison, standing up. As he turned toward the door, Reilly leaped to his feet and grabbed his arm. "And where the hell are you going to go, *Moryak*?" he taunted. "You have no money, and you are considered a dead man in America. Where are you going to go? What are you going to do? From what you've told me, the only thing you're good for now is killing and posing as a revolutionary hero. Don't be stupid, Morrison, you have nowhere else to go, and you know it." Morrison stopped at the door. "That's right, Moryak, use your head," pleaded Reilly. "We need an inside agent to penetrate the Bolsheviks and get close to Lenin, and you are in a unique position to do the job. Besides, you are still an officer in the United States Navy. You could be ordered to do it and under the circumstances, if you ever even remotely dreamed of going back to America, this just may be the price you'll have to pay." Hearing the last threat, Morrison turned around and faced his former partner.

"By the way, my friend, do you recall that I told you I had a business appointment that I had to cancel? Well, I lied. I went into my office and called the United States Embassy. Commander Gaine, the naval attaché, is a close working partner of mine. I told him that the agent of yesteryear, Lieutenant Stephen Morrison, is alive after all these years. That bit of news is already being sent back to America. So, yes Lieutenant, you will be subject to orders once again.

"Also," continued Reilly, "I made a second phone call. I now have a network of agents assembling outside of this building. They have their orders, too. If any harm comes to me, you're a dead man. I hate to do business this way, Double Eagle, but your talents and skills are an asset we cannot afford to lose!"

Morrison sat down heavily and sighed. It seemed too incredible to believe. "You know," he said, "I'm just so goddamn tired of this all. I'm tired of Russia; I'm tired of living a lie. I just want some semblance of a real life back. Hell, I don't know what I want."

Reilly sat down next to Morrison. He looked at his former partner, who just stared straight ahead. "Do you recall a conversation we had before we embarked on our mission back in 1905?" asked Reilly in a soft voice. "I told you that we were the same type of people and that I saw right through you. I believe I told you that given our backgrounds, we both yearned to belong, but I, at least, knew that it would never be possible. You were the kind of man that yearned for respect, acceptance, and possibly friendship. I told you then, Double Eagle, that it wasn't possible, at least not in our world. However, you did get your wish in their sick world, the world of revolutionary Russia. From what you've told me, you are respected, widely accepted, and certainly, they all want to be your friend. Why? It's because you are the famous Moryak, a ruthless and fearless killer. Congratulations. You've finally gotten what you've wanted all of your life."

Morrison stood up, his back to Reilly. His anger had crested as he realized that Reilly's comments were true. Once again, it seemed to him that he was being sent on an impossible mission, only this time he wasn't volunteering. He was back in a prison of a different type. He stared straight ahead, saying nothing for a few minutes as Reilly stood and said, "Of course, I'm not that big a bastard, Morrison. You are quite a courageous man, whom I do admire. If I can help you in any way—"

Morrison turned around and interrupted him. "Here's what I want from you. You find out what has become of my wife Helen. Find out what my actual status is back in the United States. Find out if it's even possible for me to come once they learn that I'm alive. Then we'll talk. In the meantime, I'm tired, and I don't want to talk anymore. I just want to rest and forget the whole world for a night, including you. Hell, I don't even know where I'm going to find a place to sleep."

"That won't be a problem. I have a couple of safe houses that I maintain around the city. You can stay in one of them. Let me contact London and see if I can find what you want to know. When I have all of it, we'll talk again. Meanwhile, take this," he said, pulling out his wallet and removing some cash. "Buy some decent clothes. Just relax, Morrison, and clear your head. I'll contact you as soon as I hear back from London."

Morrison took the money and pocketed it. As both men began to head out the door, Morrison turned around, grabbed Reilly by the collar, and slowly pulled his face toward him, until they were inches away from each other. "Be certain of this, Sidney Reilly," said Morrison in a soft voice. "When this is all over, I *will* kill you."

"I don't doubt it for a second," replied Reilly without hesitation.

10

Springwood
Hyde Park, New York, USA
October 1916

Assistant Secretary of the Navy Franklin D. Roosevelt had been somewhat perturbed by the tenor of his cousin's message. Although they were distant cousins, Franklin always affectionately called him "Uncle Teddy." During the phone call that he had received several days before, the former president seemed very subdued and almost secretive in his request to come up to Hyde Park for a private meeting. He specifically requested that this be a private meeting between the two of them. Because Franklin's family currently resided in Washington, that wouldn't be a problem. Still, this mysterious behaviour seemed so unlike his perpetually exuberant cousin.

Theodore Roosevelt arrived at Springwood, the Hyde Park estate, exactly on time and Franklin greeted him at the main drive in front of the mansion as the motorcar pulled away. "So nice to see you, Uncle Teddy," exclaimed the younger man as they shook hands. "Please, come on in. As you wished, none of the family is here." The elder Roosevelt's appearance alarmed Franklin. Uncle Teddy looked tired, and his complexion sallow. He had lost weight and just didn't appear to be the vigorous man that he once was. Everyone knew that he had never really seemed the same after his South American expedition that followed the 1912 campaign.

As they entered the sitting room, Franklin complimented him on a recent article he had published in National Geographic magazine. To Franklin, Theodore looked as if he had aged considerably over the past one to two years. As they sat down, one of the servants brought a tray of sandwiches and iced tea. Franklin thanked him and instructed him to close the doors behind him when he left and not to disturb them.

"So Uncle Teddy, what is this mystery meeting about?" asked Franklin enthusiastically.

"It's about this," replied the former president as he reached into his leather document bag and removed a cable that he had received three days prior from London. Handing it to his young cousin, he requested, "Please read this, Franklin, and then we can discuss it." The young man adjusted his pince-nez glasses and began to read. As he read, his cousin sat there, admiring him. *Here he is, thirty-four years old, handsome, athletic, and already an Assistant Secretary of the Navy,* thought the older man to himself. *His potential is limitless. He is also a savvy politician. It must run in the Roosevelt bloodline. Oh, to be that young again!* The elder Roosevelt admitted to himself what he sensed his young cousin could already see. He was no longer a vibrant or well man.

Franklin looked up at his cousin when he finished. He already had a bad feeling about what they were about to discuss. "Uncle Ted, what does this mean? Who is this Double Eagle who has now suddenly resurfaced? Why was this cable sent to you?"

"You can see that the cable envelope is addressed to 'Former President Theodore Roosevelt: FOR YOUR EYES ONLY,'" offered the older man. "It was sent to me by Sir Mansfield Cumming, the head of the British Secret Service. I am the only person in the United States who knows of this. Double Eagle was an American agent, a young naval officer that I authorized to go on a mission with the British back in 1905." He detailed the entire affair, from the preparations for the Portsmouth Peace Conference and the visit from Sergei Witte, through the dispatching of Stephen Morrison on his volunteer mission. Franklin listened to every detail, transfixed by the story.

"So you actually authorized a mission to kidnap a foreign head of state?" questioned Franklin.

"Franklin, Witte convinced both the British and me that the Tsar would never agree to a peace treaty. We made the choice we thought was right at the time. Considering the outcome, I've regretted the decision ever since, and I've lived with the guilt of having sent that young man to Russia. We had heard that he was caught and by all accounts he never revealed his identity nor the fact that he was an American agent on a government assignment. He never broke. We learned that he was hanged in St. Petersburg in October 1905. Now, like a ghost out of the past, I find out that he is alive and in Petrograd. The information given to Cumming was supplied by a British agent in Petrograd. In essence, they are asking my advice on how to proceed.

"Did this Morrison have any family? What were they told?"

"He was recently wed when he left on the mission. A cover story was generated that he was killed in England in some industrial shipboard type accident. He was buried with full military honors at Arlington National Cemetery. I attended the funeral, you know. His father-in-law was a close acquaintance. He was my Secretary of Commerce, the first Jew to ever serve in a cabinet position."

"Morrison is a Jew?"

"Yes, he was the adopted son of Congressman Caleb Morrison of New York. His real father was a rabbi in New York."

Franklin took a sip of iced tea and started to eat his sandwich. "Please, Uncle Teddy, have a bite to eat." As the older man began to eat his meal, Franklin became lost in thought. Finally, he said, "So the British are in essence asking you what to do with him now that he's resurfaced. Good God, how can the man come back to the United States, given his mission and the fact that he's been legally dead and buried for eleven years? What a conundrum! What are you going to tell Cumming?"

The elder man put his plate on the side table next to him and stood up. Placing his hands behind his back, he paced back and forth as he began to speak. "You can see from the cable, Franklin, the British think he'd be an ideal agent to penetrate the Bolsheviks and get close to this Lenin character, something they have been unable to do. You, of course, realize that if these revolutionaries come to power and destabilize the government, they will pull Russia out of the war and sign a separate peace treaty with the Germans. That would be absolutely disastrous!"

"You have a point. Someone who would spy on the Bolsheviks and report back on their plans would be very valuable indeed. If we can counter their moves with prior knowledge of their intentions, we just may be able to keep Russia in the war."

The former president stopped pacing and sighed. "Yes, that's what I've been thinking. You know, Franklin, the reason

I'm here and telling you all of this is because I want to turn this affair over to you. The truth is that I've been wracked with guilt over this Morrison fellow for over a decade, and now I'm in somewhat failing health. I seriously doubt that I can handle this situation anymore. You tell me, Franklin, what should be done in this case? My mind tells me to recommend one thing, but my heart tells me otherwise. I can no longer be objective about this or to be honest, think about it without guilt."

The young man folded his arms and stared ahead. "Hmmm," he began and scratched his head. "A most difficult dilemma. It seems that we have an agent in place that could really help the war effort. In addition, the man is believed to be dead already. There doesn't appear to be much of a down side to the British request that he work as an inside agent."

"Hasn't he done enough already? Isn't a decade in prison enough? I tell you, every time I think of his imprisonment, my heart gets sadder."

"I'd say let him work with the British and spy on Lenin and the other revolutionaries. As soon as we can be assured that Russia will remain in the war, we can extract him and bring him home, if it is at all feasible. I'm not sure how we'll do it. Maybe we'll give him a new identity. But we will certainly try to bring him home. We owe him that much."

Theodore Roosevelt sat back down. Quietly, he said to his cousin, "Thank you." He picked up the cable again and said, "That is what my instinct tells me is the right course of action. I suppose I can respond to Cumming—"

"No, Uncle Teddy, I'll take it from here. I'll respond and be the only American at this point who knows of the plan. Let's see," he said as he took the cable and re-read it. "It looks like Morrison has a few requests before he would begin working for the British. Hmmm, what about his wife? What has become of her?"

"There's a complication here. Let me fill you in on it."

"Right. Don't worry, sir, as we say in the navy, I've got the conn."

For the rest of the visit, they exchanged pleasantries and some good-natured kidding over the fact that Franklin was a Democrat. As they walked the grounds of Springwood, the athletic young man with a spring in his step couldn't help but notice how easily the former president became winded, even after a short walk. *He's definitely failing,* Franklin thought to himself. So sad to see a man who was once so vigorous now in the autumn of his life.

As the afternoon drew to a close, Theodore Roosevelt's car arrived to take him to New York City. They wished each other well, and Theodore told him how proud he was of him and his niece Eleanor. They shook hands firmly as they always did, and then the older man surprised Franklin by giving him a bear hug and holding him for a few seconds. "Thank you, Franklin," he whispered into his ear. The older man got into his car, and it began to drive off. As Franklin waved to him, he hoped his cousin would take it easy. He had a terrible feeling that his Uncle Teddy was worse off physically than even he admitted.

Sitting in the back seat of his motorcar, Theodore Roosevelt laid his head back and closed his eyes. *Yes,* he thought, *Franklin is a decisive, action-oriented leader. He is an adept politician. His potential is limitless.*

11

Petrograd, Russia
December 1916

Sidney Reilly knocked on the door of the nondescript apartment in the heart of Petrograd. The apartment served as a safe house for western agents, and Reilly frequently used it as a meeting place for his many paramours around town. A barechested Stephen Morrison opened the door, bathed in sweat from exercising. He invited the British agent to enter.

"You certainly look fit, Double Eagle! One would never guess that you are recently out of a prison camp."

"The exercise and the discipline are what got me through it," Morrison replied with a straight face. "Let me get a towel. Have a seat." As Reilly pulled up a chair and sat down, Morrison picked up a towel and dried himself off. "You said you got the information from America. Well, let's hear it." He pulled up the other chair from the small kitchen table and sat facing his former partner.

Mansfield Cumming had conveyed the information to him that the Americans had sent. The information would not help the situation. Helen Morrison had remarried after four years and remained happily married. She and her husband had two children. Both Cumming and Reilly agreed that this news should be kept from Morrison. Better to eliminate this awkward circumstance from affecting their agent's concentration. Instead, they concocted a different story that would be shocking, but also provide a form of closure.

Reilly cleared his throat and began in a quiet voice. "Stephen, some of the news I have is not very good. I'm sorry to be the one to bring it to you." Morrison knew when Reilly called him Stephen, the news would be ominous. "I have information about your wife, Helen," Reilly continued. "She had a long grieving period after your funeral. By the way, you were buried with honors at Arlington National Cemetery in Washington, D.C. Everyone was told that you died in a shipyard industrial accident or something like that. Anyway, your wife never remarried. She never stopped mourning you."

"Jesus," sighed Morrison, feeling pangs of sorrow within himself.

"Stephen, I've got worse news for you. After a while, she was institutionalized for severe depression. After several months she seemed herself again, but—"

"But what? *What?*"

Reilly looked Morrison in the eye and spoke. "She committed suicide in the winter of 1909. I'm so sorry to have to tell you this news. I know this will not be much of a consolation, but she is buried next to your burial site at Arlington National Cemetery. Please, Stephen, accept my condolences." He noted the stunned expression on Morrison's face as Morrison just stared directly at him. His eyes started to glaze over. His breathing increased slightly, and to Reilly he appeared to be trying to control his emotions. "It's all right, Stephen, to grieve and—"

Morrison stood up and in a loud voice spat out, "Screw you, Reilly! Screw your British Secret Service, screw this shithole country Russia, screw the Bolsheviks, screw the Tsar—screw you all!"

"I understand, but—"

"You understand nothing!" He began to pace back and forth across the room, and Reilly could see the tears streaming down his face. Meanwhile, Reilly got up and walked over to a kitchen cabinet where his liquor was stashed. Finding a bottle of vodka, he poured two glasses, walked over to Morrison, and handed him one. After several minutes of pacing back and forth, Morrison finally sat down in his chair facing Reilly. "What else did you find out?" he asked.

Reilly could sense that his former partner had calmed down a bit and absorbed the terrible blow that the initial news dealt him. *I may as well deliver some more news that will likely set him off again,* thought Reilly. "The Americans also think it would be a good idea if you worked for me, as I had suggested to you earlier. They concur that you should penetrate Lenin's inner circle and spy for us. This service would be invaluable for all of the Allies. Once your mission is adjudged complete, you will be taken out of Russia, and we will have you sent home to the United States. Of course, you can't go back as Stephen Morrison. They would create a new identity for you. It's really that simple. You would report to me and Mansfield Cumming, head of the MI6, our secret intelligence service. We will supply you with money and communications materials, as well as contacts."

"That sounds just great!" Morrison replied sarcastically.

"Stephen, I was told to remind you that you are still an officer in the United States Navy and that these directions should be construed as direct, lawful orders. These are orders from your superior officers. In fact, I have a paper copy of these orders to give to you." Reaching into his coat pocket, he pulled out several papers and handed them to Morrison. "Of course we will burn them after you've read them. Oh, by the way, congratulations! You've been promoted in your absence, twice in fact. You are now a lieutenant commander and all of your back pay has been deposited into a secure bank account in Washington, D.C."

Morrison snatched the orders from Reilly and began to read. They began, "To: Lieutenant Commander Stephen L. Morrison, USN", and corroborated what Reilly had told him. He was ordered to infiltrate Lenin's inner circle and spy for the Allied powers. After he finished reading them, he threw them back at Reilly. Reilly produced a match from his pocket and lit it. Holding the match to Morrison's orders, he watched the papers go up in flames. "So, Stephen, it appears that Double Eagle has come out of retirement. Once again, we're partners. Trust me, this time our collaboration will produce much benefit for the Allied cause." He poured them each more vodka and asked, "When can you make contact with the Bolsheviks?"

"My contact is named Constantin. He gave me an address here in St. Petersburg, excuse me, Petrograd. I can go to that address anytime." Drinking his vodka, he said, "You know, Sidney Reilly, you've got a valuable and dangerous agent on your hands. An agent who is famous for leading mutinies and for killing. One who doesn't give a damn if he lives or dies."

Reilly smiled as he reached into his billfold and produced a roll of rubles and handed them to Morrison. "Anytime you need funds, let me know. They come from a bottomless well as far as your mission is concerned." As he walked to the door, he turned and said, "I really am looking forward to working with you again, Double Eagle! Oh, by the way, did you hear the good news?"

"What news?"

"They murdered that dog Rasputin earlier this week. They just fished his body out of the Neva River. Apparently, some royal cousins of the imperial family had finally had enough of his destructive influence over the Tsar and killed him. That may just help us in our goals. Anyhow, have a good day, Double Eagle!"

As the door closed, Morrison mused over what had just transpired. *I am now an American agent again, one with a vital mission. However, this time it's different. I am no longer the mission-driven patriot I was years ago. No longer am I a cynical outsider, trying his best to further the interests of the United States and be accepted for my accomplishments. This time it's very different. This time I'm blackmailed into the mission. This time I have absolutely nothing to lose. And this time, I am much better prepared. This time, I am a cold-blooded killer.*

12

Zurich, Switzerland
January 1917

As Constantin and his colleague Moryak descended from the train platform, Constantin couldn't disguise his excitement over the situation. The man he admired the most, the man who had stood up for the political prisoners at Solovetsky Island and made them feel safe was now a free man and had joined them in Petrograd! "It's like a dream come true, comrade!" he had exclaimed when Moryak had appeared at his door the previous month. After catching up on each other's lives, Constantin had quickly contacted Lenin, who now lived in exile in Switzerland. With glee, he informed Lenin that the man he had told him about, the man who actually made *vors* fear *him,* was now a free man and wanted to join them! Lenin remembered the stories he had heard about the man they called Moryak and quickly extended an invitation to come to Switzerland. With much work to be done, Lenin had no doubts that he could use a man with Moryak's talents in the party's never-ending struggles. "There he is!" shouted Constantin as he pointed to a short man at the end of the station platform. The two walked over to him rapidly.

"Comrade!" blurted Constantin as he embraced Lenin and kissed him. "Comrade Lenin, it is my honor to introduce to you Comrade Moryak. He's the famed revolutionary that I told you about!"

"A pleasure to meet you, Comrade Moryak!" said Lenin as he shook the man's hand. "Your reputation precedes you. Thank you for joining us."

"The honor is all mine, Comrade Lenin. I've been looking forward to this very much. Ever since our dark prison days, I have been looking forward to meeting you. I have read many of your works, and they are inspiring."

"You flatter me, Moryak. Come, comrades, let's get a cab back to my apartment."

"Where's Mozger? I expected him to be here with you," inquired Constantin.

"He left two days ago for Petrograd to meet with Comrade Zinoviev. You know what an compulsive, detail-oriented fellow he is. God, he is the most suspicious man I know. He has to see everything for himself and be in total control. Hopefully, he won't be gone too long."

After a short ride, they arrived at Lenin's modest apartment in downtown Zurich. Lenin offered the extra bedroom to his guests, and they unpacked their small bags in short order. Afterward, the three of them met in the small dining room of the apartment. As they sat and exchanged pleasantries, Morrison studied the man he had been sent to spy on. Having never seen so much as a photograph of the man, he was surprised to see a small, balding individual with a moustache and goatee. *Pretty unimpressive looking,* thought Morrison. However, Lenin's gift was his mind and his oratory. Just hearing him speak, with his detailed knowledge of virtually any subject and his commanding presence, impressed everyone. *No doubt, the man is a formidable intellect,* assessed Morrison. *It's easy to see why he's the real leader of the revolutionary movement.*

For his part, Constantin's recruit greatly impressed Lenin. Moryak seemed obviously very intelligent and well versed in revolutionary thought and theory. To Lenin, he appeared to be in excellent physical condition, despite his recent release from the harsh prison camp. He had brown hair streaked with gray, as well as a gray-flecked short stubbly beard and moustache. But it was his eyes that intrigued Lenin the most. They looked like the eyes of an angry man who had lived too long and seen too much in his lifetime. Lenin had heard of Moryak's handling of the *vors,* and it both thrilled and impressed him that the man seemed to have no fear. *This would be a very handy man to have around,* Lenin thought to himself.

"Tell me, Moryak, how does one get the courage that you have to confront and actually intimidate the *vors*? Constantin has told me all about your exploits at Solovetsky Island. In fact, your exploits are an underground legend. I must tell you, I'm very impressed."

"Thank you, comrade. You flatter me too much."

"No, I'm sincere. After all, you are also the man who led the *Potemkin* mutiny. What courage it took to accomplish that! You have been an inspiration to all revolutionaries. To have the nerve to execute all of the officers! Inspiring!"

"Again, thank you, comrade."

"What are your plans for the immediate future?"

"I have no definite plans. When I take inventory of myself, I seem to have limited talents. I know how to fight, and I know how to kill people. I used to be one hell of a sailor, and I probably retained most of my skills in that regard. Otherwise, I'm not sure I have any marketable skills that I can offer anyone."

"How about as a committed revolutionary?" countered Lenin, as Constantin shook his head in agreement. "You would have much to offer to us Bolsheviks. Believe me, our time will come in the future, and we will need committed revolutionaries such as you."

"What are you saying, comrade?"

"I would like you to stay here with us for a while. I can use your help with our newsletter. There is also some physical work that we can have you do for us, if you know what I mean," he said, winking at Morrison. "Also, I don't have to tell you, there are many Allied agents who would like to see me dead. Many Tsarist agents would like to do the same thing. I could use you around me as sort of a protecting agent."

"You mean a bodyguard?"

"Well, something of that sort, but with a myriad of other responsibilities. Comrade Moryak, at least consider my offer."

"Yes, Moryak," added Constantin. "We would benefit greatly from your presence here. Please think very hard about the offer. After all, Comrade Moryak, what other prospects do you have to consider?"

"Well," replied Morrison with a sigh, "I guess I'll have to seriously consider your proposal. I suppose it will be good to get back into meaningful revolutionary activities again. Now, before we discuss anything further, is it just me who is starving to death, or are you two gentlemen also hungry?"

Lenin threw back his head and laughed. "You know, I am getting very hungry myself! Thank you for bringing it up. By the way, Moryak, once you get to know me a little better, I don't think you will bestow upon me the title of 'gentleman' anymore!"

***

Constantin could hardly contain himself as he burst through the door. "Comrades, it has started! It has begun!" Rushing to the table where Lenin and Moryak sat, he pulled up a chair, barely able to breathe. "Calm yourself, Comrade," ordered Lenin. "What are the latest reports?"

"On February 23, thousands of workers from the textile industry went on strike and shortly thereafter they were joined by thousands of revolutionary demonstrators. Within three days, the streets of Petrograd filled with over a quarter of a million demonstrators! The city was paralyzed!"

Lenin's jaw dropped. Even he had not expected this to happen so quickly. Morrison was also stunned by the information. He had only been in Zurich with Lenin for a month. As Lenin absorbed the news, Constantin continued.

"The Tsar wasn't even in Petrograd. He attempted to return, but the Petrograd garrison quickly joined the revolutionaries. They stopped his train in Pskov and arrested him. They forced him to abdicate his throne! It is over! The Romanov dynasty has ended!"

"Is there anyone in charge of the government?" asked Morrison. "Maybe I should ask, is there a government at all?"

Constantin replied with a grin. "I suppose there is. They have formed a Provisional Government, with Prince Lvov acting as the prime minister."

Lenin stood up, a smile spreading across his face. "This is it! We must return to Russia immediately. Comrades, start packing!"

"How are we going to get back there?" Morrison blurted out. "We'd have to get across Germany. I doubt that they'll just let us waltz across the country."

"My dear Moryak," smiled Lenin, "I'm already on the German payroll. I always play both ends against the middle. They pay me to keep fomenting revolution in Russia; as if I need to be paid to do that." He laughed. "Come, we're off for the German embassy!"

That afternoon, they arrived at the German embassy where the German ambassador to Switzerland soon met with them. Morrison watched with amazement how haughtily Lenin dealt with the German officials. *What an orator*, observed Morrison. *He speaks with confidence and authority, dominating every conversation.* After a while, the Germans agreed to his demands. They would arrange for a train for Lenin and his entourage. This train would be diplomatically sealed as it traveled through Germany; it would not be boarded or inspected by any German officials. Its journey would not be hindered in any way. In return, Lenin guaranteed that he would attempt to overthrow the Provisional Government, which had already announced that it would continue the war against Germany and its allies. Lenin also guaranteed that once the Bolsheviks seized power, he would sign a separate peace treaty with Germany, effectively freeing Germany from a two-front war.

As they left the German embassy for the final time, Lenin enthusiastically turned to Morrison and announced, "Now our real work is to begin. Get some rest, Moryak. We are going to be very busy."

"Yes, indeed, Comrade Lenin. I'll meet you back at the apartment. I want to pick up supplies for our trip. If this train is sealed and won't be stopping, I don't want to run out of food or ammunition." With that, they split up, and Morrison headed to a market that they often frequented. Before he got there, he stopped into a library and sat at a desk deep in the back. Making sure that no one was around, he composed a message describing the results of the negotiations earlier that day and then sealed it in a plain envelope. He addressed it to a house on the other side of Zurich that served as a combination of safe house and way station for the Allied powers. The envelope would be taken directly to the British Embassy. Arrangements had been made for similar information drops in Petrograd by Mansfield Cumming's agents. In addition, they had arranged, largely through bribe money, a series of "safe" telegraph transmitters in several of the largest cities throughout Russia. Morrison had memorized all of their locations.

The next evening, Sir Mansfield Cumming knew of the deal stuck by Lenin with the Germans to have him spirited back into Russia. The work of this new inside agent delighted him. However, the thought of Lenin returning to Russia made him very uneasy.

Later that evening, Cumming had a summary of the field report by Double Eagle transmitted to the United States directly to his American liaison for the agent. *Odd coincidence,* he thought to himself. *Theodore Roosevelt was no longer involved, but instead, another Roosevelt, his cousin Franklin, would be the new contact. These are crazy times in a crazy world,* Cumming thought to himself as he sealed the report and proceeded to pour himself another drink.

13

Finland Station
Petrograd, Russia
April 16, 1917

Vladimir Lenin had a growing sense of excitement and destiny as the train approached Finland Station just before midnight. Other than a brief six-month visit around the time of the first revolution in 1905, Lenin had been in exile for seventeen years. This return to Russia would truly be a real homecoming. Although not physically present in Russia during all of those years, his revolutionary influences had been felt throughout the land. Between his well-circulated pamphlets and the Bolshevik newspaper *Pravda*, Lenin's revolutionary credo was now widespread and gaining in influence as time marched on. "Mark this moment well, Comrade Moryak," he beamed as the train slowly ground to a standstill at the train station. "History is being created by us, the true transformers of Russia!"

Their journey had begun over a week ago. They had been escorted by German authorities to the Swiss town of Gottmadingen where they boarded the train. As per the stipulations of the agreement, the train was never boarded by authorities during the entire trip, nor did any of the train's occupants leave the train until it arrived in Petrograd. Just before boarding the train in the Swiss border town, Lenin had finished drafting his plans in Bolshevik terms for continuing the revolution in Russia, and he continued to refine them during their journey. All of Russia would soon know Lenin's plans for transformation to a Bolshevik state.

All of these thoughts raced though Morrison's mind as the train's engines shut down, and they began to descend to the platform. As they reached the end of the platform and departed the station to the public square in front, Lenin's entourage found itself greeted by an assembled crowd of soldiers, workers, and musicians, all offering wild applause. Even Lenin seemed taken aback by the enthusiastic welcome. *The man is some sort of returning folk hero,* thought Morrison, as they began to work their way through the noisy crowds.

Lenin, visibly moved, finally climbed up onto the hood of a parked car, and began speaking in a fiery rhetoric that mesmerized the adoring crowd. In his speech, he denounced any Bolshevik cooperation with the Provisional Government, as some of Russia's Bolsheviks were currently endorsing, along with many Social Democrats and Mensheviks. He also announced that the worldwide Socialist revolution had now begun. The statement that drove the crowd into a frenzy came when he ended his speech with the cry, "All the power to the soviets!" They proceeded to escort him through the streets of the Vyborg district. Morrison remained at his side, keeping him from being overwhelmed by the admiring crowd. As they walked, Lenin grumbled to Morrison, "Where the hell is Mozger? He was supposed to be at the station!"

"I thought you heard. They arrested him last week. He's in jail. Now that we're here, we'll work to get him released." As he spoke, Morrison helped Lenin into an armored car, and the crowds escorted them to the Bolshevik's headquarters, the Kschessinska Palace, prior residence of one of the Tsar's former mistresses.

The following morning when Morrison greeted Lenin, he asked him how he slept. "I didn't sleep at all, Comrade Moryak! I was too excited, too keyed up. Today we take over the revolution. No more waiting, no more compromise! We lay out our agenda, and we forcefully advance it!"

"Easy, comrade," chuckled Morrison. "You know I'm totally in agreement with you. By the way, there is bound to be some real hostility to our agenda at the Duma. We know we are altering our platform, but the Social Democrats and their allies do not. I will be on the podium with you and I'll be armed. After all, I am your bodyguard, and I will willingly take a bullet rather than have harm come to you."

Lenin looked at Moryak with delight in his eyes. Never one to demonstrate personal courage, he greatly appreciated what Moryak had just told him. "Thank you, Moryak, thank you indeed. History will bless the day when you came to us in Switzerland." He embraced his friend and bodyguard.

Morrison's prediction proved to be very accurate. He served as one of the armed escorts for Lenin when they arrived at the Tauride Palace, home of the Duma. When it was Lenin's turn to address the Duma, Morrison escorted him to the speaker's podium and then sat down in a chair off to Lenin's side. The crowd hushed as Lenin pulled out his notes and began to speak. In a few moments, he had the crowd in an uproar. No longer would the Bolsheviks endorse or tolerate a bourgeois stage of the revolution that most of the other groups had endorsed. The power must now go immediately to the proletariat. The soviets must rule, not a parliamentary body. As he spoke, occasional boos and jeers arose from the audience. Intermittently, a cry of "traitor!" burst from the audience. Undaunted, Lenin continued.

Morrison noted that Lenin was nearly shouting as he outlined the Bolshevik agenda in a policy statement that he called his "April Theses." Its main tenets emphasized no cooperation with the Provisional Government, total opposition to the war, and disestablishment of the army, police, and all state bureaucracies. At the conclusion of his speech, a sizable portion of the Duma jeered him, but Morrison observed that the majority of the Duma representatives stood up and applauded. Lenin remained at the podium, watching the turmoil in the audience with a stern look on his face. After several minutes, the tumult had nearly died down when he shouted out, "All power to the soviets!" The audience exploded into a frenzy, just as Lenin had planned. The standing ovation accorded him by the majority of the Duma representatives lasted ten minutes. They all watched as he was led of the rostrum by an armed escort, a man known to many of the delegates; the man called Moryak.

The Bolsheviks retired to their headquarters to plan future strategy. Lenin called his leadership back into the drawing room in the back of the building. As Morrison sat down, he glanced around the room. After entering the room and seating himself at the head of the table, Lenin began to introduce the others to him. "Comrade Moryak, these are Comrade Zinoviev, Comrade Stalin, Comrade Trotsky, and the only one missing is Comrade Mozger."

Morrison saw Trotsky staring at him for a few seconds when he erupted with, "My goodness, it is you! We were in Peter and Paul Fortress back in 1905. You were called Number Ten!"

Morrison smiled at him and replied, "Yes, I remember you, comrade."

"Gentlemen," continued Trotsky, "this man is a genuine hero! He saved my life and stood up to a vile scum of a prison guard who nearly killed me. Why didn't you tell me then that you were the hero of the *Potemkin* mutiny?"

"It didn't seem relevant at the time."

As they spoke, Joseph Stalin stared at Moryak and puffed on his pipe. Scratching his pockmarked cheek, he studied Morrison, judging him to be both violent and dangerous.

"Comrades, Moryak suffered for ten years in the Tsarist prisons for his bravery," exclaimed Lenin. "He will be a valuable asset to our cause. Now, let us begin to formulate our strategy. I'm sorry Mozger isn't here. We need to work to get him out of prison." They proceeded to formulate specific plans, with Lenin assigning various tasks to each of them. At the end of the meeting, Lenin asked Moryak and Trotsky to stay behind. When the others left, they shut the door and returned to the table. "Comrade Trotsky, tell Moryak what you've learned about the sailors."

"Ah, yes, I thought we'd want to let the famous Moryak know of this!" beamed Trotsky. You know, Comrade Moryak, the sailors at the Kronstadt Naval Base are committed revolutionaries. All of the ships there are controlled by revolutionary committees that elect their leaders. They relieved the officers and replaced them with elected comrades who are loyal to the party and despise the Provisional Government. They are committed Bolsheviks. They still haven't recovered from the chaos of this past February. Their energies can certainly be channeled by an inspirational leader."

"Do you mean me?" asked Morrison.

"Of course! What could be more natural than the legendary Moryak to rally and lead the revolutionary naval forces at Kronstadt? The fate of the revolution may well hinge on their actions."

"He is correct," added Lenin. "We need their unequivocal support. Comrade Moryak, I'm sending you to Kronstadt Naval Base. We've already contacted the party leader, Raskolnikov, about your arrival. Your job is to rally the sailors and prepare them for the coming workers' revolution. We will continue our agitation here in Petrograd. I also want to look into the situation with the Romanovs. You know, they will be placed under house arrest at Tsarskoe Selo. I'm not sure what the Provisional Government is planning on doing with them. Get some rest tonight, Moryak. Historic times are about to begin."

"Yes, Comrade Lenin. I'll leave as soon as it is feasible. I'll certainly keep you posted on my activities."

But he failed to inform Lenin of his activities the following day when he dined in a discreet restaurant with a man whose passport read Gregory Reilinsky, but whose real name was Sidney Reilly. All of the details of Lenin's return to Russia and his speech at the Duma were conveyed that night to London. When Morrison left the restaurant, Reilly sat back and relished his success. He couldn't believe what a stroke of luck it was to have Morrison reenter his life. He was proving to be worth his weight in gold. He had heard about the discord at Kronstadt and had already thought of a possible plan of action for Double Eagle. He planned to share his thoughts with MI6 in London.

***

The cold winds of the early May morning stung Stephen Morrison's face as the boat approached Kotlin Island in the Gulf of Finland. It brought back an eerie feeling, reminding him of his journey to Solovetsky Island so many years before. At that time, he was known as a traitorous mutineer from the *Potemkin*. Now he was approaching the docks of the Kronstadt Naval Base as Moryak, the revolutionary hero. *It truly is a crazy world,* he thought to himself.

Kronstadt Naval Base was the home of the Russian Baltic Fleet, and seeing the warships moored at the piers brought a nostalgic longing to Morrison. God, how he missed the United States Navy. So much so that just seeing the warships of another country gave him a rush.

Kotlin Island was strategically located in the gulf, twenty miles west of Petrograd. According to Reilly's report, the Gulf of Finland was frozen for nearly five months a year, and only in the past few weeks had it become navigable by boat. "Any earlier, and I would have sent you there on ice skates," Reilly had joked.

Morrison had read the briefing papers that Reilly provided and memorized the pertinent details before he burned them. Two months before, the sailors of Kronstadt had revolted and overthrown their officers. At a mass meeting in the main square of the base, they formed their own soviet and elected their own naval leaders. Over eighty officers and bureaucrats had been killed in the uprising. "Be careful, Double Eagle, these people are crazy fanatics. They are the most strident of all of the Bolsheviks," warned Reilly. When Morrison stepped onto the pier, with Reilly's words fresh in his mind, a huge man with a bushy beard raced up to greet him and hugged him tightly. As he kissed both of Morrison's cheeks, he gushed, "Welcome to Kronstadt, Comrade Moryak! This is truly an honor to have you here!"

"Please," protested Morrison modestly, "the honor is all mine."

"I'm F. F. Raskolnikov, leader of the Kronstadt Soviet. I'll be hosting you while you are with us. We have a full agenda for you. There are many here who want to see the great Moryak. You are a legend, you know."

"Well, comrade, I'll try not to disappoint too many of you."

Raskolnikov roared with laughter at that comment. Taking Morrison's arm, he guided him into the waiting car. As they got in, Raskolnikov explained, "I wanted to take you along the piers and show off our ships. I know that it has been many years since you sailed. You must miss it." The car lurched forward, and they began their tour of the waterfront. As they approached the main piers, Raskolnikov began to describe the three ships currently moored. "We have two dreadnoughts anchored here. The first is the *Sevastopal,* and the next one is the *Petropavlovsk.* You certainly must remember the horrid winters we get on the gulf. The ships have actually been frozen in place all winter, as they are every winter."

"And what is that smaller ship?" asked Morrison, pointing down the waterfront.

"Ah, that is the battle cruiser *Aurora.* She's a real beauty. Say, comrade, while you're with us, would you like to go to sea for a short while, to get your sea legs back?"

"I would like that very much," replied Morrison with total honesty.

"We can arrange that. Moryak, you must be hungry. Let us have some lunch. Afterward, I've taken the liberty of arranging a speaking engagement for you. I hope you don't mind."

"Not at all," Morrison said as the car turned away from the waterfront toward the main city of Kronstadt, a walled fortress of a city. They motored around to the main gate, facing the east and appropriately called the Petrograd Gate. In a few minutes, they parked in front of a large galley, and Raskolnikov escorted his guest inside. Several other members of the soviet joined them and their lunch included a voluminous amount of vodka. *How the hell do these people get any work done after a lunch like this?* Morrison wondered.

"You know, Moryak," said the eager-looking man on Raskolnikov's right, "most, if not all, of the sailors here were youngsters when you performed your heroic deeds. You were a bedtime story that many of them were raised on. And now you're here! This is too good to be true."

"Is it true you are going to address us all after lunch, Comrade Moryak?" asked another of the diners.

"Apparently so," chuckled Morrison. "I hope I'm not too much of a disappointment."

"Nonsense! You will be an inspiration. Tell me, is it true that the *Potemkin* revolt erupted over rotten food?"

"Yes, it is," Morrison replied, glad that he finally learned the essense of what had caused the mutiny. "It was actually maggot-infested meat. But you know, comrades," he said, looking around at all of them, "the rotten food was symbolic of a rotten system, one that didn't care for the little men, the workers, the producers. That's why we did what we did." He continued for a few more minutes in that vein, satisfied that he had enthralled them all with his exploits. He could tell by their expressions that they believed every word that he had spoken.

The soviet member at the end of the table clearly seemed to be the oldest member of the small entourage. "You know, Moryak, the years have been kind to you. I met you briefly before the mutiny, and you were quite a scrawny specimen. Our comrades in Petrograd must have been feeding you well."

"Indeed they have, comrade, indeed they have. Also, I exercise regularly. One must keep fit if he is going to be active in leading a revolution, don't you agree?" All of the heads around the table nodded in assent.

After their meal, they left the galley and saw streams of people heading into the main square of the city of Kronstadt, known as Anchor Square. As they walked through the crowds, the people recognized Raskolnikov and many realized that the stranger next to him must be the legendary Moryak. Many pointed at him and shouted revolutionary slogans as they waved to the small group heading toward the speaker's platform.

Finally, they climbed the platform, a place where revolutionary speeches had become the order of the day. Raskolnikov stood and raised his hands over his head, signaling the crowd to settle down. In minutes, the crowd of over ten thousand Kronstadt sailors had quieted down and looked up at them. At that moment, Raskolnikov began to speak.

"Comrades, fellow sailors of Kronstadt, we have a special honor here today for us, courtesy of Comrade Lenin! Our guest needs no real introduction. He is a legend and an inspiration to us all. Comrade Moryak was the leader of the first meaningful act of the revolution—the mutiny aboard the battleship *Potemkin*! He paid dearly for his courage. He spent over a decade in the criminal Romanov's prison on Solovetsky Island. Yet he has persevered, and he is here with us today, to help us along the revolutionary path! Comrades, it is my honor and privilege to present to you, Comrade Moryak!"

As Morrison stood at the speaker's lectern, the crowd erupted into a deafening roar. It took a full ten minutes before the crowd quieted enough for him to speak. As Morrison began speaking, he noted that the audience listened in rapt attention. *I'll have to feed them every revolutionary cliché I can think of,* he mused to himself as he spoke. Familiar with all of the revolutionary groups in Russia, he was able to touch upon every facet of Russian politics and proceeded to strongly condemn the Provisional Government. When he finally decided he had manufactured enough party rhetoric, he decided to close his speech with a personal, inspiring touch. "Comrades, it has been twelve years since I've sailed in the Russian Navy. That is way too long for my taste. I am first and foremost a sailor, a worker, who has committed his life to the revolution and to the Bolshevik cause. I will be sailing with you again shortly! I will be fighting with you against the oppressive government shortly! I will be working to bring Russia out of this criminal war shortly! Who is with me? I repeat, *WHO IS WITH ME??*"

The crowd roared with approval as Morrison stepped down from the lectern. The screams of approval and the applause were again deafening as their small entourage left the speaker's platform. The crowd parted as they walked through it, with many of the people reaching forward to touch Moryak and to shake his hand. It took nearly half an hour for them to reach their car. Sitting in the back seat as they drove away, Raskolnikov smiled at his special guest. "Well done, Comrade Moryak. You had them eating out of the palm of your hand. What can we do for you next?"

Morrison looked at him. "You know what I would like to do more than anything? I'd like to take you up on your offer. I want to spend a little time at sea with your men. Can you arrange it?"

"Of course we can. We'll have you back at sea in a few days, my esteemed friend."

***

Morrison stood on the stern of the *Sevastopal* as the sun began to set. They had just completed two weeks of training and maneuvers, and he watched the wake being churned by the battleship's propellers. As he stood there reminiscing about his prior days at sea, he suddenly heard a voice asking, "How does it feel to be back at sea, Comrade Moryak?"

He looked over to the young sailor who had joined him, a junior petty officer who couldn't have been more than twenty years old. The look of admiration on his face made Morrison smile. He replied, "It feels wonderful, comrade. You know, I first went to sea when I was about your age. Once the sea gets in your blood, you can't escape its allure. I dreamed of this moment for over ten years when I was a prisoner."

"Did you ever give up hope when you were in prison all those years?"

"Not really. I always believed I would get out and that I would make a difference in the world." *I certainly never thought I would become an Allied spy again,* he ruefully thought to himself.

"I want to be just like you, Comrade Moryak. I want to dedicate my life to the revolution, to a fair and just Russia! If I die for the cause, it is of no consequence for me. I pray that we can go into battle with the government soon!" Morrison smiled and nodded at the young sailor. *He is so typical of all of these sailors,* he reflected. *They are almost fanatical in their devotion to the revolution.* Virtually all conversations aboard ship during the past two weeks centered on the upcoming revolution. It had been the same even before they got underway two weeks ago. The city of Kronstadt had only one thought in its collective mind—destruction of the Provisional Government.

For the past two weeks, the crew was thrilled to have the famous Moryak walking in their spaces and taking part in the ship's exercises. Morrison was, in fact, familiar with the dreadnought class from his work in England with Admiral Fisher. He, of course, had to pretend that it was a new concept to him. While the ship itself had impressive capabilities, he was largely unimpressed with the ship's material condition and maintenance and appalled at the seamanship and abilities of the crew. The ship was dirty and most of the equipment was not well maintained. Their gunnery skills were minimal. The atmosphere aboard was more of a philosophical debating society rather than a warship. It was a stark contrast to the United States Navy. *No wonder the Japanese kicked their asses at Tsushima,* he laughed to himself.

He had been very pleased with his accommodations aboard ship. In deference to his status as a hero of the revolution, they berthed him in the admiral's quarters and had a mess steward wait on him around the clock. In return, he attempted to do some instructing, and the crew seemed amazed that Moryak still maintained many of his seamanship skills. He especially impressed them with his technique for more accurate gunfire, a skill that he promised he would teach them in the future. All in all, it had proven to be a pleasure to be back at sea, even aboard a Russian naval vessel.

After returning to Kronstadt, Morrison profusely thanked the officers and crew of the *Sevastopal* and then went to thank Raskolnikov personally. It was early June, and Morrison was supposed to return to Petrograd to report back to Lenin. He promised Raskolnikov that he would return in a couple of weeks to inspect and possibly go to sea on the other ships. He complimented the head of the soviet on the revolutionary fervor that boiled in Kronstadt by saying, "Keep the cauldron bubbling, Comrade Raskolnikov. It won't be long at all until we'll need the sailors of Kronstadt to be the tip of the spear! Believe me, it won't be long at all!"

14

Petrograd, Russia
July 1917

The early morning July sun started to pierce through the thin curtains in his office as the new prime minister, Alexander Kerensky, continued going over his paperwork. He remained very concerned over the recent demonstrations in Petrograd and the growing influence of the Bolsheviks. *We were lucky this time,* he thought to himself. *Those ruffians nearly pulled off a coup the other week. At least we drove that scoundrel Lenin into hiding, somewhere outside of Russia, I am told. We need to be better prepared.* His personal secretary opened the door, interrupting his thoughts, and announced, "They're here, Prime Minister." Kerensky stood and ordered that the new arrivals be brought into the office.

Colonel Eugene Kobylinsky, a tall and distinguished-looking member of the Russian army, entered the room. He had been assigned by the Provisional Government to oversee the confinement of the former imperial family at Tsarskoe Selo. At his side stood the former Tsar of Russia, Nicholas II, who was now simply called Citizen Romanov. Both men wore military garb, but the contrast in their sizes accentuated the diminished status of Nicholas Romanov. "Sit down, please," ordered the prime minister.

Nicholas had been concerned all morning about this meeting. What could the prime minister want with him? Why had he been summoned to Petrograd? Nicholas fidgeted uneasily in his seat, staring at the man who now controlled Russia. *He's a distinguished, professorial-looking man,* Nicholas thought when Kerensky started to speak. "Citizen Nicholas Romanov," began Kerensky, "I ordered you here today to inform you of two developments that have great impact on you and your family. I felt it best to tell you these things face-to-face."

"Thank you, Mr. Prime Minister," replied Nicholas in a low, even voice.

"First, there is a dramatic change in the status of your future residence. Your cousin, King George of England, has refused your request for asylum in Great Britain."

"What?" blurted out the former Tsar, stunned by the news. He had been certain his cousin would welcome him and his family with open arms. His family had long been planning an idyllic retirement in the English countryside. "How can this be?"

"I'm not one hundred percent certain. I believe it has to do with the labor unrest in England. I suppose he fears that by taking a former autocrat who is considered an enemy of the working class into his country, perhaps his kingdom would also be overthrown. I'm not entirely sure, but it is irrelevant. You will not be going to England, Citizen Romanov.

"This certainly complicates matters, and not only for you. My government is fighting off the extreme left-wing lunatics that are threatening us. Last week, we nearly had a coup d'état. As a result of all of this turmoil, I no longer believe it is safe for you and your family to remain in this region. You see, unlike the Bolsheviks and their ilk, we are not savages. We believe in the rule of law."

Kerensky paused to pour himself a glass of water. As he did, Nicholas began to speak. "Mr. Prime Minister, I have a request. If I am to remain in Russia, I would like to request that my family and I be allowed to retire to the Crimea, to live in the Livadia Palace on the Black Sea. I believe this would suit us well." As he spoke, he thought of the many happy times that they had there. Even when he was Tsar, he always had a yearning to retire to Livadia Palace and live the life of a country gentleman.

"Your request is denied," shot back the prime minister. "I say this not out of any sense of cruelty or vindictiveness. I say it out of a sense of practicality. We cannot provide adequate security in the Crimea. No, Citizen Romanov, we are sending you to Siberia, to Tobolsk. It is peaceful there, there is no real industry, and hence no workers or radicals. We have a government detachment there that can provide security. Lastly, Tobolsk has an appropriate residence for you and your family, given your status as a former ruler of this great country."

Nicholas sat there, taking in the news. It bitterly disappointed him that his cousin had rejected him. This news totally caught him off guard. He thought about Tobolsk, a place he knew well. The family would probably do quite well there. The situation could be much worse than the solution that Kerensky had proposed. "How long will we be in Tobolsk?" he asked.

"I don't know. If the situation here in Russia calms a bit, I would say at least six months to a year."

"When would you have us leave, Prime Minister?"

"In less than two weeks. That is all I have to tell you today. Colonel Kobylinsky, take the prisoner back to Tsarskoe Selo immediately." With that, the two visitors stood and began to walk to the door. As they did, Kerensky called out, "Citizen Romanov!"

Turning around, Nicholas replied, "Yes, Prime Minister?"

Standing, Kerensky stared directly at Nicholas and said, "Make no mistake about this, Citizen Romanov. If these radicals such as the Bolsheviks get their hands on you and your family, they will surely kill you all."

15

Petrograd, Russia
October 1917

Lenin returned to Petrograd in October just as Mozger was released from prison. "I'm able to feel it in the air, to breathe it, comrades! The revolution is imminent!" Lenin proclaimed with glee. The Bolsheviks assembled in their version of the Duma, the Smolny Institute. This former girls' school had become their refuge ever since they had been forced out of Tauride Palace after the attempted July coup. On October 10, Lenin proposed the immediate overthrow of the Provisional Government. Not all of the Bolshevik Central Committee stood in agreement with him.

"Comrade Lenin," commented Zinoviev, "we're just not sure if the masses will rise up at this time. We know that the momentum is growing, but I fear that now may not be the time. Besides, the All-Russian Soviet Congress is meeting later this month on October 25. Would it not be better to further stoke the flames of rebellion during the conference to bolster our support?"

"You've missed the point entirely!" shot back Lenin. "The government must be ours to hand over to the All-Russian Soviet Congress when it meets! Do you not see the historic importance of this? Do you not see the historical necessity?"

"No, we do not," countered Comrade Kamenev. A rancorous fight followed, but the pit bull-like Lenin prevailed. The resolution that passed, however, had been toned down, calling only for the rebellion to occur in the "immediate future." Lenin manipulated the situation to his advantage by going public and denouncing the committee members who opposed him. Suddenly, all of Petrograd knew of the Bolsheviks' intentions.

"You see, comrades," said Lenin with delight, "the idiot Kerensky continues to play directly into our hands. Now, he has decided to send the Petrograd Garrison, his praetorian guard, to the front. That leaves him totally naked."

"You missed the bigger picture, Comrade Lenin," grinned Mozger. "It is a moot point. I've just learned that the Petrograd Garrison has mutinied. They are with us now!"

"Then that's it! Russia will be ours shortly!" proclaimed Vladimir Lenin.

On October 23, the revolution began. Lenin unleashed the people and the Red Guard troops throughout the city. The situation developed largely into a bloodless coup, with many of the people eagerly joining them. All of the increasing street protests occurred while delegates for the All-Russian Soviet Congress arrived in Petrograd. Seemingly without effort, the Bolsheviks took over most of the government buildings, and in short order, much of the city fell under soviet control. The perimeter of the city around the Winter Palace where the

Provisional Government was in session was all that remained. Irritated, Lenin again insisted that the coup d'état must be completed before the All-Russian Soviet Congress could meet the following day. The delays for the final assault on the Winter Palace served to agitate him. Because of poor planning, the Bolsheviks failed to check the artillery pieces at the Peter and Paul Fortress that they needed for the final assault and bombardment of the Winter Palace. As a result, the plan became delayed for hours.

Several days earlier, the cruiser *Aurora* had gotten underway from Kronstadt. The ship would play a vital role in the October Revolution. Aboard was their legendary naval hero, the man known as Moryak. Earlier that week, he had received instructions from Lenin and Stalin and conveyed them to the naval command at Kronstadt. The ship would steam to Petrograd and enter the Neva River. It would dock at the English Embankment and prepare to fire on the Winter Palace. All of the ship's activities would be under the authority of Moryak. On his order, the ship would fire a blank shell at the Winter Palace. This would serve as the signal for the Red Guard troops to begin their final assault on the palace.

Morrison stood on the bridge of the *Aurora* and looked out over the city. Through the darkness of the hour, he could see several fires blazing at different points throughout the city. In addition, he heard occasional gunfire that crackled like fireworks. The commander of the ship, a fanatical Bolshevik named Korzatsky, stood next to him when the petty officer from the communications shack approached them. "Comrade Moryak, I have an urgent radiogram for you."

Morrison thanked him, and after reading it, he handed it over to Korzatsky. Looking up, Korzatsky said, "So, this is it, comrade!"

Morrison looked at his watch. It was just past 9:30 in the evening. "Yes, this is the moment. Captain, instruct your gunners to execute the plan. One blank round with a double powder charge aimed toward the Winter Palace." The six-inch gun crew had been manning their station for several hours and would no doubt welcome the order to execute their mission. Korzatsky summoned a runner to deliver the order, but then turned to Morrison. "Comrade Moryak, I've been thinking. I've got a suggestion to make."

"What is it?" asked Morrison, miffed at this last minute annoyance.

"Well, why not fire a live round at the Winter Palace? Would that not make a much greater point? Wouldn't that be more inspirational than just a blank round?"

"And wouldn't it make a hell of a lot more sense if you just followed your orders?" snapped Morrison. "Are you second guessing our leaders, or do you just want a greater piece of glory? Captain, when the runner arrives in a few seconds, your order to him better be to have the forward gun fire the blank round just as I have instructed, or you had better be willing to suffer the consequences of your insubordination. Have I made myself clear?"

The captain looked at Moryak and saw the savage fury in his eyes. He became genuinely frightened. "I, eh, of course, comrade. It will be a blank round, double powder primer charge. Just as you ordered. Please, accept my apology." Just then, the runner arrived, and the captain conveyed Morrison's exact instructions to him. At 9:40 P.M., a thunderous *boom* erupted from the forward gun of the *Aurora*. The purpose of the double charge was to make it an extremely loud explosion, but the intensity of the sound actually surprised Morrison.

The deafening sound of the blast from the *Aurora*'s gun caused all of the ministers in the Winter Palace to dive immediately to the floor, paralyzed with fear. In the silence that followed, many of the ministers promptly left the building, realizing that their position was hopeless. Several minutes later, the second order was given and live shells erupted from both the *Aurora* and the Peter and Paul Fortress. While the bombardment ensued, the delegates of the All-Russian Soviet Congress had begun their meeting at the Smolny Institute. Lenin was in his usual uncompromising mood. The power struggle continued between the Bolsheviks and the Mensheviks who were allied with the Social Revolutionaries.

No consensus arose among the revolutionary delegates, and many of them finally walked out. "The fools," Lenin said to Stalin and Mozger, "those glorious, ignorant fools! They've handed it to us on a silver platter. No need to compromise now."

Shortly after 2:00 A.M., the Bolshevik-loyal Red Guards entered the Winter Palace. The remaining ministers realized that the end was near. In a few minutes, a Red Guard leader, accompanied by Lenin, entered the room and placed all of the remaining ministers of the Provisional Government under arrest. It had ended. Lenin and his Bolsheviks had seized control of the government of Russia.

***

Their control over Russia was very tenuous. By the following week, Lenin realized that they needed a strategic plan if they were going to survive. At the Winter Palace, he convened a meeting of his brain trust to outline his vision. Present were Stalin, Mozger, Trotsky, and Zinoviev. After some sharing of thoughts, Lenin began to expound on his vision. "Terror," he began, "is the key. No compromise, no mercy. Already counterrevolutionary forces loyal to the central government, even to that worthless bastard Tsar Nicholas, are fomenting problems and are actively agitating against us. Our most immediate problem is in the Lower Volga and the southern approach to the capital." Turning to Stalin, he said, "Comrade Stalin, I'm sending you there to crush the resistance. You are now commissar for that region. Use any means necessary! Mercy is a word I want you to expunge from your vocabulary!"

Stalin puffed on his pipe and calmly replied, "I don't know what that word means. I never have, comrade."

"Excellent! Our second major issue is the war. We have to sue for a separate peace with Germany. This will not be easy. They will not bargain easily, for they will be negotiating from strength. Comrades Trotsky and Mozger, you will be the ones to go to Brest-Litovsk to negotiate with the Germans. You are the two most eloquent intellects of us all. You have free rein to bend over backward to accommodate the Germans. Just get us out of this war! There will be a civil war shortly, and we need to dedicate all of our resources toward it."

Turning to Zinoviev, he said, "Comrade, you will stay here with me to head up the Petrograd Soviet." Zinoviev nodded in assent.

As the meeting was drawing to a close, Trotsky asked, "What about Comrade Moryak?"

"Ah, yes, Moryak!" smiled Lenin. "I'm bringing him back from Kronstadt next week. He will be in charge of security for me, and for the party. There is a great need around here for a man of his intellect and ruthlessness."

After the meeting, Mozger took Stalin aside and asked him if they could talk in private. Choosing a dark tavern to assure privacy, they ordered vodka as Mozger began to confide his concerns to Stalin. "You know, Comrade Lenin is our leader and inspiration, but I fear at times he is blind to the dangers around him."

Sensing where the conversation appeared to be heading, Stalin replied, "You mean Trotsky?"

"Yes, I do. The man is vainglorious. He believes that his oratory skills and his organizing talents have pre-selected him to be Lenin's heir apparent. I never trust a man who has that much confidence in himself. Not only do I distrust him, but also I am starting to despise him. He is dangerous, Joseph, and I have a feeling that you and I had better prepare for the future. He and all of the other Jews in our party are a bit too ambitious for my taste!"

"You know, I've come to the same conclusions," acknowledged Stalin as he stared into his glass. "Comrade Lenin is too trusting of the Jews, especially that yid Trotsky. It is his main weakness." Smiling, he looked up at Mozger and said, "This is where we come in, my friend. We will prevent Trotsky or any of those damned Jews from assuming the mantle of leadership. Believe me, I have already given this much thought." With that, he raised his glass and said, "To the revolution and to the party! Our work now begins in earnest, comrade."

After their meeting, Mozger returned to the small apartment where he lived by himself. The sparsely furnished room with books scattered all over provided the basic necessities that suited Mozger's needs perfectly. He had never married and never had any serious relationships with women since totally dedicating himself to the party years ago. In his solitary hours, he continued doing party work. He continually read all revolutionary literature and constantly wrote revolutionary tracts for publication. He lived and breathed the revolution.

He had no regrets about his life. He had cast aside his prior life of privilege to join the Bolsheviks, and he had never looked back. He had become the living embodiment of Rakhmetev, the main character of Chernyshevsky's book, *What Is To Be Done?* He led a life of denial of pleasures and riches to devote himself totally to the revolution. It gave him much inner pride. Many of his fellow Bolsheviks and other revolutionaries claimed to be followers of Chernyshevsky, but they only gave lip service to his ideals. He, Mozger, actually lived the life of a man dedicated only to the party. It steeled him and made him stronger. Unlike Lenin, he would never turn a blind eye to the weakness and treachery of others, especially Jews like Trotsky.

He liked and admired Stalin. He considered him a dedicated party man whose ruthlessness and talent existed in equal measures. He believed that it would be Stalin, not Trotsky, who would be Lenin's successor. He would keep a close watch on Trotsky and keep him in line. His energies now would be focused into making that succession a reality. Focus- he liked that word. His life had become focused on Bolshevism. Nothing would ever interfere with that focus.

***

The message arrived the next day at Kronstadt. It was Raskolnikov who insisted on a banquet in Moryak's honor before he departed for Petrograd. The farewell reception, attended by hundreds of Kronstadt sailors who wished to show their respect and reverence for their inspiring leader, evolved into a gala celebration. It turned into a night of continuous toasting. Consequently, Morrison was drunk by the time Raskolnikov called him to the podium, where he praised Moryak for his inspiration and leadership, and invited him to say a few words. Thunderous applause erupted at that suggestion. Morrison staggered to the podium and waited until the applause and the screaming had died down. He began speaking, uttering a few inspirational clichés, peppered with an occasional joke and humorous anecdote. The crowd loved it and frequently applauded.

Finally, he knew he should close. He was drunk and began to fear he would slip up and say something inappropriate. "Comrades," he exclaimed, "I must close now. The hour is late. Allow me to tell you that I never dreamed I would be here, addressing such a fine group of sailors as yourselves." The crowd roared its approval. "When I spent all those years in the Tsar's prison camp, I never forgot my mission, my destiny! Mission and destiny, my friends! It is what drives me and must drive you all. I swear to all of you assembled here, I swear to our Bolshevik leadership—I *will* fulfill my mission and destiny, or *I WILL DIE ATTEMPTING TO DO SO!*"

The crowd erupted in a frenzy when Morrison finished with those inspirational words. "Moryak! Moryak!" the crowd began chanting. Sailors ran up, grabbed Morrison, and lifted him in the air on their shoulders. The entire crowd paraded after them for at least an hour. Before the impromptu parade had dissipated, Morrison had passed out from all the alcohol.

16

The Kremlin
Moscow, Russia
March 1918

As Lenin sat writing at his desk, he reviewed the events of the past several months. He was not proud of everything he had done, but all of his actions were for the sake of the revolution and therefore needed no other justification. In spite of the intense negotiations, the Germans still threatened to overrun Petrograd. As a precaution, Lenin ordered the city to be evacuated and moved the capital of the new government to Moscow. Lenin and the ruling Bolsheviks had been entrenched in the old Kremlin Fortress in Moscow for nearly a month. As he thought of the recently ratified Treaty of Brest-Litovsk that had finally removed Russia from the war, he knew that it was a necessary first step. Yes, the cost was high, he admitted, but it is the only way to proceed. Russia had been forced to give up all of its European lands, including Poland, Finland, and the Baltic states. The massive discontent over the terms of the treaty further accelerated Russia's descent into civil war. It was the looming civil war that occupied his thoughts that morning.

The Senate Building, also known as the Yellow Palace, had become the seat of the new government within the Kremlin, where the ruling Political Bureau, or Politburo, met. To ensure the survival of the struggling new government, that day the Politburo focused on two tasks in particular. "We need to prepare for the internal struggle," he explained to the Politburo. "Two things are critical: an effective army and internal security. I have given both items a great deal of thought.

"Because of his genius for organization, I am appointing Comrade Trotsky head of the Red Army. He will train his army and engage the organizing White Armies, which consist largely of loyalists to the monarchy and other anti-Bolshevik factions. Comrade Trotsky, you have a free hand in your methods. Terror tactics and mass executions should be your weapons of choice." Trotsky smiled broadly as Lenin spoke.

"Security and protection of the Bolshevik party is paramount for Russia. Last December, I appointed Comrade Felix Dzerzhinsky to head this critical task. I would like for you all to meet the man about whom you no doubt have already heard." All of the members around the table turned to the man known as Iron Felix, so named because of his fanatical devotion to the revolution as well as his incorruptible nature. Standing in the corner of the room, Morrison looked over at the dwarf-like Dzerzhinsky and felt nothing but disdain as he looked at the head of the Bolshevik's security service, its so-called "sword and shield," the Cheka. The dreaded Okhrana had now been replaced by an even more repressive government secret police.

Morrison had been in the room that day in December when Lenin gave Dzerzhinsky a charter for the Cheka. He recalled that Lenin stood behind the seated Dzerzhinsky and placed his hands on his shoulders. "My dear Felix," he began, "I don't need to remind you that the purpose of terror is to terrorize. That is your mandate; that is your reason for existence. We have many enemies, and we are hanging on to power by our fingernails! Murder and executions of all enemies of the party are sanctioned and encouraged. To preserve our revolution, the streets must flow red with blood. The blood of our enemies. You have been chosen because there isn't a timid bone in your body. You are the staunch proletarian Jacobin that is needed to do the job. Comrade Dzerzhinsky, you have a free hand!"

The short Dzerzhinsky stood up and, without smiling, looked directly at Lenin and spoke. With the everpresent serious look on his face, he stated, "The Red Terror is about to begin."

17

MI6 Headquarters
London, England
April 1918

Bruce Lockhart lit his cigar as soon as a break occurred in the conversation with his old friend, Sir Mansfield Cumming. The other guest whom Cumming had invited, Major Terence King, was late. The evening was young, and Lockhart was in no hurry. When he stood to stretch his legs, Cumming saw that he still appeared to be in excellent shape. Lockhart had been a popular rugby player during his school days and was still known to participate when invited. However, it was not for his rugby skills that Cumming had summoned him for this meeting.

Lockhart, a diplomat, had been the acting consul-general in Moscow before the revolution and had recently been asked by the British government to return to Russia in an effort to encourage the new Bolshevik government to remain in the war against Germany. "Mansfield, you know how I feel about these damn Bolsheviks. They are a bunch of deceitful liars that can't be trusted at all," Lockhart had protested when Cumming told him he would be going back to Russia. "That treaty with the Germans was bad enough, and now they announce they're repudiating all foreign debts. The unbelievable gall of these people." Cumming reassured him that although he was the first official British envoy to the Bolshevik government, Lockhart's real mission would be to help bring about the government's downfall.

A few minutes later, Cumming's secretary announced the arrival of Major King and then escorted him into the office. Cumming managed the introductions and proceeded to tell King that Lockhart would be leaving for Russia to assume his new duties. King was ordered to brief Lockhart on the project that he was currently directing.

King looked back and forth at the two gentlemen and began. "It's really quite simple in principle. As we all know, His Majesty's government doesn't trust the Bolsheviks at all. While we're forced to deal with the reality that they are in charge at the moment, their hold on the country is weak. There are many groups and individuals opposed to the Bolsheviks who are willing to work against them. One thing they all need and don't have much of is money.

"I have been in charge of a consortium of agents that has been involved in buying up controlling interests in Russian banks, primarily on the Siberian-Asian side of the country where the Bolsheviks have much less control and influence. We can funnel money through these banks to counterrevolutionary forces, to the White Armies, etc. We've already begun the process."

"Who else is involved in this? Are any other Allied countries participating?" asked Lockhart.

"Well, none who would admit to it, but in fact, the Americans and the French have been silent partners in the venture."

Cumming broke in. "I don't have to tell either of you that there is a strong anti-Bolshevik sentiment in the western powers. As we speak, secret plans are being formulated for the Allies to land an expeditionary force in Murmansk to assist the White Army. Their leader, Admiral Kolchak, is quite the darling of our military people."

King continued. "You need to know that there are several key agents involved in this. Recently we have turned over local operations to Sidney Reilly. He's currently in Siberia now. Do you know him?"

"No, I've never met him," replied Lockhart.

"He's quite the character. An extraordinary man, I would say!"

Cumming poured himself another drink and looked at Lockhart. "Bruce, you will be in charge of the overall situation in Russia. Reilly will actually report to you. I, we, all want you to have a free hand in stirring up the opposition to the Bolshevik government. They are a blot on civilization that must be expunged. As you now can see, you've got virtually unlimited funds to accomplish the mission, thanks in large part to the fine work of Major King.

"There is something else that the two of you should know. It had been originally assumed that the Russian Imperial family would be given asylum here in England. For a number of political reasons, King George has decided not to extend the offer of asylum to the Romanovs. They are currently prisoners of the Bolsheviks and are somewhere in Siberia. Officially, our government can make no effort to rescue them."

Sensing where the conversation was going, Lockhart asked, "How about unofficially?"

Cumming smiled and looked over at King. "Major, our meeting is over. Thank you so much for your assistance and also for the excellent work you and your men have done so far!"

King took the hint and stood up, turning to shake the hands of both Lockhart and Cumming. He left the room and pulled the door shut behind him. Cumming's expression turned serious. "To answer your question- unofficially, see if you can get the Romanovs out of Russia safely. His Majesty's government feels that the former Tsar would be an excellent unifying force, a rallying point, for anti-Bolshevik forces. We also know that the Bolsheviks will never allow the Imperial family to leave Russia alive. We want you to see if it is feasible."

Lockhart whistled quietly and said, "That's quite a task. Off the top of my head I would say that it is next to impossible to achieve that mission."

After pausing a few seconds, Cumming continued in a quiet voice. "We have an Allied agent in the Kremlin, close to Lenin. Very close. He has provided us invaluable information about the Bolsheviks. His contact is Reilly."

Lockhart's jaw dropped. Cumming's news absolutely stunned him. "You have a Russian agent in the Kremlin?"

"Believe it or not, he's not Russian. He's one of ours, and he passes as a Russian."

"How in God's name is that possible?"

"I can't say anymore. The less you know in this regard, the better. What little you do know is, of course, privileged information, never to be repeated. Understood?"

"Understood."

"Bruce, I believe this concludes this meeting. Have a safe trip back to Russia. Take care of yourself. Remember, we're counting on you."

As he walked out the front of the building onto Victoria Street, Lockhart shook his head and thought to himself- *an Allied agent passing for Russian, right under Lenin's nose! That man must have balls!*

1

Vologda, Russia
May 1918

Stephen Morrison's concern was growing. It had been over two months since he had heard from Sidney Reilly. Now that he lived in Moscow, he feared that Reilly would be harder to contact. Lenin and the rest of the Bolshevik leadership resided in the Kremlin. Morrison lived in a small apartment a few blocks away that had been confiscated from a former Tsarist official. It proved adequate for his purposes and convenient to the Kremlin where he remained at Lenin's beck and call.

His job had evolved into a general bodyguard and security agent for Lenin and other high-ranking officials. In this capacity, he met most of the leaders of the new government, and the more he dealt with them, the more disgusted he became. They seemed to him to be colorless, mindless robots, married to their revolutionary cause. There did not seem to be a glimmer of humanity in any of them. Especially repulsive to Morrison was Felix Dzerzhinsky. He seemed worse than the *vors* back on Solovetsky Island. He would have loved to deal with the head of the Cheka in a violent manner. *Perhaps that day might come,* he mused to himself.

One evening after returning from the Kremlin and as he entered his apartment, Morrison saw an envelope on the floor that had obviously been slipped under the door. There were no markings on the envelope other than two words: Double Eagle. Closing the door behind him, he entered the small sitting room and tore open the envelope. It contained a short note from a Major Homer Slaughter of the United States Army, which instructed him to get to Vologda, report to a certain address the following week, and wait there until he was contacted. It was signed with the initials HS, and it had a postscript that instructed Morrison to "burn this after reading."

Morrison scratched his head and wondered, *Who is Homer Slaughter?* He had never been contacted by the Americans before. *Why now? Could this be a trap?* Vologda was midway between Moscow and Petrograd. Since the government evacuation of Petrograd, Vologda was now where all of the western diplomats assigned to Russia resided. Perhaps something had happened to Reilly. His gut feeling told him that he should make this trip. It would not be difficult to get away; it wouldn't be unusual at all to travel to Vologda given the presence of all of the foreign diplomats.

After considering several cover stories, Morrison concocted a story about being invited to check security at the various embassies. Lenin thought it would be a good idea to bolster the image of the new government and gave his consent. Without any difficulty or suspicion, Morrison left Moscow and traveled uneventfully to Vogoda.

The address he had been provided turned out to be a dilapidated boarding house. The mysterious letter instructed him to register under the name of Moryak and to wait. He assumed that the desk clerk would notify the mysterious Slaughter the moment he arrived and his suspicion proved to be correct. Within a half-hour, he heard a knock on the door. Morrison drew his pistol and stood behind the door as he opened it slightly. His guest walked in to find the gun immediately pressed against the back of his neck. "Take it easy, Double Eagle. I'm an American."

"Turn around slowly," instructed Morrison. He proceeded to pat the man down for weapons. Finding none, he put down his revolver and asked, "Are you Slaughter?"

"That's me, Double Eagle, or should I say Commander Stephen Morrison? Mind if I sit down? We have a lot to talk about and not that much time." Morrison promptly motioned for his guest to sit down. The man looked like a soldier. Short hair, solidly built. Although he wore local peasant garb, he looked like an American to Morrison, who asked, "What's this all about? How do I know you?"

"Actually, you don't know me, Commander, but I know a bit about you. I'm Homer Slaughter, Major, U.S. Army. My specialty is military intelligence, an oxymoron if ever there was one. I'm currently the Assistant Military Attaché to Russia and working in the Ekaterinburg region of Siberia. That mean anything to you?"

"Isn't that where they just moved the Tsar and his family?"

"Correct. You see, I'm probably the only person in the United States, other than one high-ranking government official who will remain nameless, who knows of your existence. Of course, a few Brits know, since they're currently running you as an agent. Reilly, I believe it is."

"Again, why are you here, Major?" asked Morrison.

"I'm here as another resource for you, to assist you in any way I can. You need gear and equipment; I can get it for you. I've also set up a series of safe houses around both Moscow and the Ekaterinburg for you. Most importantly, I have this for you," he said as he handed a slip of paper to him. "It's a list of paid-off telegraph operators in these regions that are on our payroll and are trustworthy. You can telegraph anywhere without worrying about the transcript tapes ending up in enemy hands. Believe me, we've used all these operators, and they're reliable. Of course, after you memorize this list, you need to burn it."

Morrison began pacing around the room. Something started to gnaw at him. He had the feeling that he didn't quite have all of the information that he should. "You know, Major, I'm in Moscow, not Ekaterinburg. At the moment, I don't see how this concerns me. Do you have any messages or orders from the United States for me about this? I think I'm missing something here."

"Well, Commander, let me fill you in on some information that should help to clarify the situation. One of my main functions in Russia is to act as liaison to the Czech Legion. You are familiar with them, correct?"

"Yes, of course," he replied. The Czech Legion had been a major source of contention during the negotiations at Brest-Litovsk. This force of fifty thousand ethnic Czech and Slovaks living in Russia had volunteered to fight for the Russian government. After Russia withdrew from the war, part of the peace treaty terms allowed transit of the legion across Russia back to Europe so that they could fight for the Allies against Germany. The passports for these soldiers had been authorized by Stalin himself.

"Well, things are going to hell in a handbasket in Siberia. The Czechs are now fighting the Bolsheviks and their Red Army. Seems the Bolsheviks were trying to disarm them at the insistence of the Germans. It's turning into a mess, but a mess that may work to our advantage. As the Legion and the White Army get closer to Ekaterinburg, their presence may cause enough chaos for us to attempt a rescue. That's one of my main reasons for meeting with you today. What do you know of the internal political situation there, sir?"

"Major, I sit at Lenin's side frequently. I can tell you this, and feel free to pass this back to Washington and London. Moscow does not, I repeat, does not have a tight grip on the soviets scattered around the country. This lack of authority is especially true in the Urals, the region around Ekaterinburg. The Urals Soviet is very independent-minded and causes Lenin and the Politburo a lot of heartburn. The fact that they are holding the Romanovs worries Lenin very much. For now, he wants the Romanovs alive. Trotsky is trying to convince the Politburo to bring Nicholas to Moscow for a show trial and then publicly execute him. The people in Urals Soviet, well, they're animals who would just as soon kill the Romanovs as take care of them.

"What I'm telling you, Major, is that if the White Armies approach Ekaterinburg, the Urals Soviet might execute the Romanovs despite what Moscow wants."

Slaughter sat there thinking and scratching his chin. "Hmmm. Washington and London really want to get the Tsar out alive. We realize it may not be possible to attempt to rescue the entire family. That's part of the reason for this visit. If there's any possibility that you can influence this situation with the Tsar, any way that you can get near and try to pull off a snatch, I'll assist you however I can. This is what I've been instructed to tell you.

"Also, there is a plot underfoot that is being run by the Brits with our help. Lockhart, the British Envoy to the Bolshevik government, is in charge. He has support for this plan from the Americans and the French, and Reilly will be assisting him in this. Apparently they have been contacted by the Latvians who want to assist in a coup to overthrow the Bolsheviks."

"The Latvians? Are you sure? They are intensely loyal to the Bolsheviks and act as their 'Praetorian Guard.' Christ, they provide the security to the Kremlin! Are you sure of this, Major? I find this hard to believe."

"Absolutely! Our sources vouch for these two. You will be contacted by Reilly shortly for a meeting during which he will outline the plot for you. If the situation favorably evolves, we'd like to pull off the rescue attempt simultaneously with the coup."

Checking his pocket watch, Slaughter stood up and announced "Jesus, Commander, I've got to get going. Remember all of the contacts points that I gave you. The operator in Ekaterinburg can reach me at any time, so don't be shy."

"I'll try not to be," mused Morrison as he walked Slaughter to the door. Slaughter suddenly stopped and turned to him. "There is one more thing before I leave."

"What's that?"

"I'd like to shake your hand, Commander Morrison. I only know broad details of your past, but to accomplish all that you have, under the most unbelievable circumstances, well, it's an honor to know you, sir. You are a great American."

"Thank you, Major," replied Morrison, with all sincerity.

19

Moscow, Russia
June 1918

Bruce Lockhart could not calm down after he finished the call. The plan had been starting to gel, and he remained highly optimistic that the mission could be accomplished. His network continued to expand, and their first detailed planning session would be taking place later in the week. In the midst of this, he learned that Sidney Reilly had arrived back in Moscow. In fact, Lockhart had been waiting for the arrival of this key agent, but the manner of Reilly's arrival totally galled the proper British envoy.

Lockhart had been drinking tea and reading the latest edition of *Pravda* when he got the call. At first, the story seemed too ridiculous to believe. Arriving less than an hour before from Siberia, Sidney Reilly had traveled directly to the Kremlin. At the gates, he announced he was an emissary of the British prime minister and demanded to see Lenin personally. His personality and semi-official looking documents actually got him in the door, but they then escorted him to the office of the head of security for the Kremlin, Comrade Moryak. Moryak was not in the Kremlin at the time, so an assistant acting in his stead spoke with Reilly. He immediately suspected that the man could not possibly be a genuine emissary, and he called the British Consulate and asked to speak to the envoy, Bruce Lockhart.

Furious, Lockhart asked to speak to the mysterious visitor. He ordered Reilly to come to his office immediately. In a short while, Sidney Reilly arrived at his office, where Lockhart ordered him in and slammed the door behind them. "Just what the hell do you think you are doing? Are you insane? Christ almighty, things are at a delicate stage, and stunts like this could ruin everything!" As he shouted at him, he realized by Reilly's demeanor and enthusiasm that he had a very likable air about him. Reilly remained silent during the berating. He looked like a schoolboy who had been caught cheating and was there to receive his just desserts.

"My apologies, sir. I will freely admit that I have a flare for the dramatic. Not to worry, my *official* documents that I presented at the Kremlin had a false name, so they won't be able to track us. Lord, I have over ten passports you know."

"So I've heard!" After several more minutes, the conversation began to soften. Lockhart had established his point. He was in overall charge of intelligence operations for England in Moscow, and Reilly worked for him. Reilly readily acknowledged his authority. Lockhart then asked for an update on the banking plan that had been funding all of the counter-revolutionary activity in Russia. Reilly assured him that the banking scheme continued to go very well in that regard. It quickly became obvious that Lockhart and Reilly would work for you to return to Moscow at this time. Sidney, the plan is coming together. It's like a wave in the English Channel; it can't be stopped. I believe the heavens are all aligned for this one."

The plan had Reilly excited. A coup to overthrow the dreaded Bolsheviks! As he thought over what he had just heard, Lockhart interrupted his thoughts by asking, "How is your inside agent doing?"

"You mean Double Eagle? You know about him?"

"I didn't know he is called Double Eagle. In fact, I know almost nothing about him, just that he exists, is close to Lenin, has provided incredible inside intelligence, and that he is run by you. How the hell we ever got an Englishman inside the Kremlin is a mystery, no, a miracle, to me."

Reilly smiled and told him, "Actually, he is not an Englishman. He's an American."

"An American! An American—how the hell? Never mind, how is he doing?"

Reilly sighed and said, "I haven't had contact with him in almost two months. Now that I'm back, I plan to contact him this week. I will tell you this, Bruce, he is an incredible man. The Allies owe this man more than they could ever attempt to repay him. When this operation is over, I will debrief you on the story of Double Eagle in detail. It is almost too bizarre to believe. In fact, even though I've been involved with him since the beginning, I still don't believe it. It's rare in one's lifetime that you get to meet a man like him."

***

Several weeks earlier, the naval attaché to the old British embassy in Petrograd, Captain Hugh Cromie, had been contacted by two members of the Latvian Guards, named Shmidken and well together, a fact that greatly encouraging the envoy. A professional bond had formed, and already they spoke on a first-name basis.

Lockhart rang his secretary and arranged for lunch to be brought in for the two of them. As they ate, Lockhart updated his prize agent on the latest developments. "Our plan is coming to a head, Sidney. The day of reckoning is near. Our plan is developing in conjunction with the Americans and the French." Pausing for effect, he said "The Allies are planning a landing of expeditionary troops - British, American, and French - at Murmansk this summer. We will be staging a coup to overthrow the Bolsheviks at the same time the landings occur."

Reilly put down his fork and looked up at Lockhart. Normally an unflappable individual, the audacity of Lockhart's statement stunned him. "Are our plans advanced enough to meet that timeline? That's only two months away."

"Yes, the plans are coming along smoothly. Tell me, Sidney, do you know Boris Savinkov?"

"Yes, I know him. He's a Social Revolutionary who despises the Bolsheviks. Quite the terrorist bomber when the mood suits him."

"Well, he's thrown his lot in with us for this endeavor. Along with my counterpart from the French government here in Moscow, Consul Fernand Grenard, we've funneled millions to Savinkov's organizations, as well as the White Army. The best news of all is that we've got a commitment from several Latvian guards to help us with the coup!"

"Really?" Reilly was impressed. "My impression of them is that they are virtually unshakeable in their loyalty to the Bolsheviks."

"Tomorrow night you will see. We have scheduled a detailed meeting of the major participants. That is why I've been so eager

Bredis. They informed him of the great dissatisfaction among the guards with the Bolshevik rulers. Cromie, in turn, reported this information up the chain of command, and eventually, the two dissidents were introduced to Lockhart who saw their participation as the key to the success of any coup attempt. The Latvian Guards were the only troops in Moscow. They were known as the Bolsheviks' protectors, their Praetorian Guard. If they were willing to oppose the Bolsheviks and join the counterrevolutionaries, then a coup was definitely feasible. Without their support, a coup would be impossible. Lockhart believed that the linking of these Latvians with Savinkov's groups, as well as the Allied agents working in Moscow, would prove to be the deathblow to Lenin and his crowd.

Now, several weeks later, as the small group assembled in the safe house selected by Lockhart, he felt almost giddy with anticipation. Each of the conspirators had taken convoluted routes to the safe house in order to avoid any detection by the Cheka. After they assembled in the small room, Lockhart did the introductions. This time Shmidkin and Bredis had brought the commander of one of the Latvian regiments, Colonel Eduard Berzin, who would be in command of the rebelling guardsmen. After introducing the Latvians, Lockhart introduced the French military attaché General Lavarge, as well as himself and Reilly. General Lavarge also had a journalist from the French mission with him named Rene Marchand. Lastly, Lockhart introduced the two other men present, a French officer, Colonel Henri de Vertement, and an American agent named Xenophon Kalamatiano.

To the assembled group, Lockhart went over the details of the plan. He specified the landing dates for the Allied expeditionary forces in Murmansk with their subsequent advance on Moscow and Petrograd. "Concurrent with this," he continued, "the Latvian Guards will abandon their posts at the Kremlin, allowing counterrevolutionary forces led by Savinkov's groups to storm the Kremlin and arrest Lenin and all of his government supporters. The Latvian Guards will then provide security for any interim government. We expect fierce resistance by committed Bolshevik elements of the Cheka and from party elements in general. Hence, to aid in the conflict between the Bolsheviks and the Allied forces, we're leaving three agents to stay behind after the Allied consulate staffs are evacuated from Moscow." Lockhart designated these agents to the group: Reilly, Colonel de Vertement, and Xenophon Kalamatiano. "Their jobs will be sabotage and espionage against the Bolshevik forces in Moscow. They will be keeping the Bolshevik forces tied up until the arrival of the Allied expeditionary forces," explained Lockhart. Before finishing the initial walk-through of the plan, Lockhart informed the Latvians that Reilly would be their direct contact for all matters relating to the plan. The discussions continued for nearly two hours. Each of the participants had questions, and by the end of the meeting, everyone seemed satisfied with the general plan; only a few details needed to be resolved. As per the initial ground rules of the meeting, no note taking had been allowed.

After the meeting ended, Reilly seemed euphoric to Lockhart. "This really is your cup of tea, I see."

"Indeed it is!" exclaimed Reilly. "I really believe we can pull this off. Wouldn't I like to march that bastard Lenin down the streets of Moscow in his underwear with his hands tied behind his back!"

"Well, I doubt that little detail will be added to our operation," quipped Lockhart. "There is another matter that I want to discuss with you. I didn't want to bring this up tonight because I'm under orders to keep this matter close to the chest. It involves you and the agent Double Eagle."

"Go on," said Reilly, getting an unsettled feeling in his stomach.

"This morning I had a visitor at my office. Our guest logs list him as a private businessman in town trying to establish a relationship with the Bolshevik government. He is, in fact, an American military intelligence agent. His name is Homer Slaughter, and he's a major in the U.S. Army. His current posting is as Assistant Military Attaché to Russia. His real job is actually running all U.S. intelligence operations concerning the Bolsheviks, especially in the Perm region, including Tobolsk and Ekaterinburg."

"Ekaterinburg!" interrupted Reilly. "Isn't that where the Reds are holding the Tsar and his family?"

"Exactly right. Slaughter met with me to inform me that our government and the Americans are determined to rescue the Imperial family and take them out of Russia. They want the attempt to take place when the Allied landings and the coup are both occurring. It is the opinion of both governments that the only way this could possibly be attempted is by your inside agent, Double Eagle. They admit they don't have a clue how the rescue can be pulled off, but they also feel that given his insider status, he is the only one who could even begin to attempt the job.

"Slaughter has already met with Double Eagle recently in Vologda and provided a series of both safe houses and multiple safe telegraph operating stations to use for secure communications. He is available to assist Double Eagle in any manner that he reasonably can. He also told Double Eagle of the coup attempt and Allied landings." Pausing for a moment, he turned to Reilly and with deadly earnest told him, "Contact him in the next few days and give him the mission. Slaughter told him that he would probably be tasked with the rescue attempt. These orders are coming from the highest levels of the British and American governments."

20

Cheka Headquarters
Lubyanka Square, Moscow
June 1918

Felix Dzerzhinsky continued with the paperwork on his desk. He had not left his office for four straight days. The Cheka, housed in the nine-story office building that served as the All-Russia Insurance Company building before the war, was located on Lubyanka Square. The place had already had become a dreaded nightmare to Moscow's residents. One of the biggest fears of any Muscovite was to disappear into the notorious Lubyanka Prison located in the basement where torture and death were the only sure things that one would encounter. Already rumors circulated throughout Moscow that no one had ever left Lubyanka Prison, except in a coffin.

Dzerzhinsky's workaholic tendencies were only worsened by his enthusiasm for his job. Sending people to their deaths did not bother him in the least. If these victims of the Cheka were enemies of the state, then dismemberment and death were the only logical actions to take. Life was that simple to this dwarfish man, a child born to Polish nobility who had studied in his youth for the priesthood. His absolute ruthlessness endeared him to Lenin. Already throughout Russia, his name was feared. This notoriety pleased him very much.

This morning he waited for several of his agents to arrive shortly to debrief him on their latest mission. He had received their signal the night before and ordered them to appear before him that morning. Although he almost never smiled, he had a slight grin on his face when the three agents arrived. After his secretary opened his office door, Colonel Eduard Berzin entered first, followed by Shmidken and Bredis. The real names of the last two were actually Yan Buikis and Yan Sprogis. All three of them were, in reality, Cheka agents, sent to penetrate the counterrevolutionary forces that opposed the Bolsheviks.

Within a half-hour, Dzerzinsky knew all of the details of the proposed Allied landings and most importantly, the details of the coup being engineered by Lockhart and his cronies. He thanked his agents for their work and ordered them to continue in their roles posing as counterrevolutionaries. "Your assignment is to string along Lockhart and his agents and to report back to me all of the developments. Comrades, you are to be commended for your excellent work thus far," stated Iron Felix.

Later that day, Dzerzhinsky met with Lenin at the Kremlin. He relayed the details of the Allied plots to him, and when he was finished, Lenin asked him for his advice on the situation. "My advice, Comrade Lenin, is to do nothing. Let us continue to utilize the Latvians as our spies and learn more about the

Allied counterrevolutionary operations. Let us milk them as dry as possible. When the time is right, we can smash them mercilessly. Let us bide our time. We know approximately when all of these activities are scheduled to occur and can act at the appropriate time."

Lenin had total confidence in Dzerzhinsky's judgment. *He is right, Lenin* thought. *We hold the advantage now, and we should play our cards accordingly.* "Of course, Iron Felix, we will proceed as you have recommended. You have a free hand."

As Dzerzhinsky turned to leave the room, he looked at Lenin and said, "You know what I am really looking forward to? Catching that smug bastard Reilly! He has been a thorn in our side for years. He is very clever and knows how to disappear in plain sight. This time, we have him." Once again, a rare smile appeared on Iron Felix's face. "And you know what? I'm going to have a special place arranged for him in the basement of Lubyanka! I assure you, comrade, it is not going to be pretty!"

21

Safe House
Moscow, Russia
Mid-June, 1918

After not hearing from Reilly for two months, Morrison received instructions for a meeting to be held at one of the many safe houses that they maintained in Moscow. There Reilly revealed the plans for the coup that would be launched that summer. After briefing him on the specifics of the planned coup, Reilly gave Morrison his assignment. "This is coming straight from the top of both our governments, Double Eagle. I know you've already met with Major Slaughter, and I know he's given you a preview of the mission. Simply put, it is this. You are to proceed to Ekaterinburg and formulate a plan to rescue the former Tsar and his family. Major Slaughter will be your primary local contact for the mission as well as your logistics source. How you accomplish the mission is up to you. Obviously, until you can get on the scene and assess the situation, specific details can't be worked out. We want the rescue attempt to occur simultaneously with the coup. That will divert enough attention away from the Urals so that Moscow will not have the capacity to respond to your actions."

"You realize that the rescue attempt is going to have to take place in the next several weeks; a month or so at the outside," responded Morrison. "The White Army is making steady advances against the Reds in Siberia. The Czech Legion is also driving them back. At the rate the campaign is progressing, Ekaterinburg could fall to the Whites within four to six weeks."

"We realize that. That is why time is of the essence. Can you manage to get to Ekaterinburg without arousing undue suspicion? Is this even a possibility, or will you simply have to vanish from Moscow?"

"Vanishing is probably not an option, not when you're a famous hero like 'Moryak'!" said Morrison ruefully. "I do believe there is a way though. Moscow still doesn't have total control over the many soviets in Russia. Probably the most independent-minded ones are in Siberia, especially the Urals. They are a real pain in the ass to Lenin and company. Unfortunately, the Urals Soviet is the one that has custody of the Imperial family. They are constantly threatening to execute them, partially to show their independence from Moscow. Lenin is deathly afraid they may actually do it. He talks constantly of his frustrations with them."

"What are you suggesting, Double Eagle?"

"I can try and convince Lenin to send me to assert Moscow's dominance over the Urals Soviet. At the very least, that would give me control over the Imperial family. What I would do at that point I'm not certain, but it's a starting point."

Reilly nodded his head in agreement. "Well, we certainly don't have much else. It is a starting point. I concur. Let's begin in the manner you described. I'll contact Slaughter and let him know what we're thinking."

***

The next day at the Kremlin, Morrison observed Lenin moping around in a depressed mood. After chairing a meeting concerning the Red Terror and internal security, he announced that he had just been briefed on the setbacks of the Red Army. He seemed to be talking to himself as he mentioned his repeated frustration and anger over the Urals Soviet. "How can I get control over those bastards?" he blurted as if talking aloud to himself.

Morrison knew he had his chance to act. "Comrade Lenin, I have a suggestion to make."

"What is it, Moryak? Please tell me something to brighten my day."

"Of course, allow me to continue. It is in regard to the Urals Soviet. I think I can improve the situation."

"Go on, Moryak," Lenin invited. Among those around the table sat Stalin, who leaned forward on his elbows to listen closely to Moryak.

"It's a simple question of power politics. The Urals Soviet needs to be shown who is in charge of Russia. They need to be taught a lesson in power. I propose to do it for you."

"Just what do you propose?" asked Stalin. All of the others at the table also leaned forward on their elbows.

"Send me to Ekaterinburg to meet with the leaders. I will tell them I am on a mission authorized by Comrade Lenin with the total endorsement of the Politburo. My mission is to assert Moscow's dominance over their Soviet and to liquidate all who oppose it. One of my first acts to accomplish this would be to take over control of the former Tsar and his family until you decide what you want to do with them. Those blowhards are always threatening to kill the Romanovs, and I believe it is just to spite you, to thumb their noses at us in Moscow. They need to be taught a lesson, Comrade Lenin. I believe you know that I am just the man to do it."

Lenin and Stalin stared at each other for a moment, briefly astonished by Moryak's audacity. Then, they both erupted in laughter. The sheer simplicity of the plan, coupled with the fact that they had nothing to lose, made it even more amusing. Soon everyone at the table sat back, convulsing with laughter. The plan even impressed Stalin. *This Moryak has the stuff that legends are made of,* he thought. He had heard how Moryak had handled the *vors* while in prison. *This is the same man who also ordered all of the officers aboard the Potemkin to be liquidated. Yes, if there is any man who could establish Moscow's dominance over the Urals Soviet, it would be Comrade Moryak.*

Stalin looked at Lenin and asked, "What do you think?"

Lenin smiled and said, "Thank you, Moryak, for brightening my day. I will have the official paperwork drafted for you immediately and also notify Comrade Goloshchekin that you will be arriving. Plan on leaving early tomorrow morning."

The meeting being concluded, they all stood when Lenin announced, "My next meeting should at least be humorous. Do you have any idea who has returned and has requested a meeting with me? None other than Comrade Roman Malinovsky!"

"Malinovsky!" blurted out Stalin. "He's still alive? I heard that the bastard had joined the Russian army after we kicked his ass out of the Duma."

"That is correct. In fact, he spent most of the war in a German prison camp. And now he returns, eager to work for the party. I knew he was a drunkard, but I never believed he was a traitor. Well, Comrade Dzerzhinsky has had the all of the Okhrana's files sent to Moscow from Petrograd, and his Cheka agents have been going through them with a fine-tooth comb. He showed me the irrefutable truths that the files contain." After pausing a second, an angry look swept across his face. "Mozger was right; I should have listened to him. The files show that Malinovsky was an Okhrana agent all along. And I trusted that bastard! He doesn't know I have this knowledge of his past. I think I'll have Comrade Mozger handle this matter for us in Petrograd. That would be poetic justice!" He had his secretary send Malinovsky in.

"Comrade Lenin, it is a pleasure, no, an honor, to see you again. Thank you so much for agreeing to see me."

"Welcome back, comrade. Do you remember Comrade Stalin?" Malinovsky enthusiastically shook Stalin's hand. "And this is the famous Moryak!" Malinovsky pumped Morrison's hand and exclaimed, "It's truly an honor, Moryak." Then it hit Malinovsky like a thunderbolt: *I've met this man before!* he thought to himself.

After the introductions, Stalin and Moryak left the room, and both Lenin and his guest sat down. They had a short conversation, and Lenin expressed his forgiveness for Malinovsky's past drunkenness. At no time did Lenin allude to the fact that he now knew that Malinovsky had been an agent of the Okhrana. Malinovsky expressed his delight when Lenin informed him that he would be working for the Bolsheviks again. He proposed that Malinovsky return to Petrograd where he would work directly for Comrade Mozger. Malinovsky could barely control his gratitude as he thanked Lenin profusely.

That evening, Lenin cabled Mozger, informing him that Malinovsky would be arriving that week. He also revealed what he had learned from the Okhrana files. He ended the message by saying, "You were right. Dispose of the problem immediately." Lenin didn't like to be made a fool, and he wanted the matter handled outside of Moscow, where no one but Mozger would know that he had been duped all along.

For his part, Malinovsky was thrilled to be accepted back in the party. On the train to Petrograd, he was filled with hope that maybe now he could pull his life back together. He had been so foolish in the past, but now it appeared that he would be getting his second chance. Still, he couldn't get the thoughts of Moryak out of his mind. Sure, he had heard of the man; everyone had. But he was certain that he had never previously met the man. The word was that Moryak was in the Tsar's prison until 1916. Malinovsky had been in a German prisoner of war camp since 1915. He couldn't possibly have met the man. Yet, he was certain that they had met. Somewhere in the past, they had met.

Malinovsky slept soundly, lulled to sleep by the rhythm of the train, when suddenly he sat bolt upright, drenched in sweat. He now remembered where he had met the man called Moryak! It was back in St. Petersburg in 1905. Of course, how could he not remember those eyes! He was a British agent then, working with Sidney Reilly. He was called Double Eagle back then. Malinovsky himself was known as Olovyanniy, the Tinman, at that time. But how could it possibly be? That operation had been aborted, and the agent called Double Eagle was caught. He knew for a fact that they hanged him shortly after his trial. But most baffling of all, how could a man who was a British intelligence agent over a dozen years ago now be a legendary hero of the Russian Revolution, a man whom they say led the *Potemkin* mutiny? How could this possibly be true?

Malinovsky pulled out his handkerchief and dabbed the sweat off his forehead. *It is not possible,* he thought to himself. Yet he was certain. It was the man's eyes. He had met the man called Moryak years before, when Moryak was acting as a British secret agent. He had no doubt in his mind that Moryak, whom he just met, was that same man.

22

*Urals Soviet Headquarters
Ekaterinburg, Russia
Late June 1918*

The long train ride to the Urals exhausted Morrison, but shortly after arrival in Ekaterinburg, he caught his second wind. How ironic, he mused to himself, that he had been sent on a mission by both the Bolsheviks and the Allied forces to Ekaterinburg. Now he sat in the headquarters of the Urals Soviet, waiting for their leader, Filipp Goloshchekin to arrive. Goloshchekin had already been notified earlier that Lenin had dispatched Moryak to Ekaterinburg on an urgent mission and requested that they meet as soon as he arrived.

At the Ekaterinburg train station he had been met by two thuggish-looking henchmen who brought him to the soviet's headquarters, located in the old municipal building. There they instructed him to wait in Goloshchekin's office until he arrived. Morrison had been waiting for about a half-hour when the door suddenly flew open and Goloshchekin walked in. "Hello, comrade," he grunted as he proceeded to sit at his desk and look directly at Morrison. The man's theatrics and attempt at dominance did not impress Morrison. He also knew that the two thugs who picked him up at the train station would be posted outside the door, acting as bodyguards. Goloshchekin, a small man, appeared to be about Morrison's age. "So, you're the famous Moryak. Tell me, comrade, what is the urgent business for which Moscow has dispatched you here? As you can see, I'm a busy man."

Morrison stared back at him and began in a soft, almost monotone voice. "Moscow is not happy with your soviet. You are too independent and cause grief to the Politburo when they have enough on their plate. I've been sent here to inform you that these days have come to an end. From now on, you will dance to Moscow's tune. Don't get me wrong, comrade, you will still run your internal affairs without interference from us, but in the big-picture issues, you will follow the party line. That's the first order of business.

"Next, I have been ordered by the Central Committee and the Politburo to assume control of the Romanovs. We have had enough of your saber rattling and threats of execution. I will be overseeing the situation until Moscow decides what it wants done." Morrison handed over to Goloshchekin the official documents from Moscow confirming his authority. He could see Goloshchekin becoming angrier by the second. He read the papers and, at first, didn't say a word. Then he called his bodyguards into the room. The two men entered and stood on either side of Morrison. "Comrades, escort Moryak back to the train station. Give him all the respect due to a revolutionary hero, but make sure he is on the next train to Moscow.

I'm sorry, Moryak, we cannot comply." He looked down to the paperwork on his desk, signaling that this relatively unimportant meeting had ended.

This response didn't surprise Morrison; in fact, he had anticipated it. He slowly stood up between the two bodyguards and then suddenly grabbed each of their closest arms and pulled them together with all of his might. The surprised bodyguards' heads smashed into each other, the impact knocking them both unconscious. As the two men collapsed, Morrison pulled his gun out of his belt and leaped across the desk at Goloshchekin, who had been caught completely off guard by Moryak's actions. The impact of the collision knocked him over backward, with Morrison landing on top of him. As he attempted to speak, Morrison pinned his left forearm across the surprised man's throat, and with his right hand, he held his gun with the barrel inserted into his opponent's mouth. Goloshchekin's eyes bugged wide open in terror.

Morrison waited about half a minute before he said anything. He wanted the moment to register with Goloshchekin, for him to remember it always. Finally, he said, "Listen, you piece of shit. What I brought to you is not a request. It is an order. An order that *will* be obeyed, understood?" When Goloshchekin didn't respond, Morrison cocked the hammer back on his pistol and repeated, "Understood, comrade?" Goloshchekin nodded slightly in assent.

"Good. We seemed to have reached an understanding. I want you to bear something in mind, comrade. I am in charge of security at the Kremlin. I personally train all of my men, every one of them. They are merciless killers as I am. If I were not to report back to Moscow, Comrade Lenin has authorized a small army of my men to return here, and their orders would be to go to your soviet, find your men, and tear their fucking hearts out and eat them for dinner. Am I making myself clear?" Again, the terrified Goloshchekin nodded his head slightly. "Excellent. I do believe that we've come to an understanding, my friend." He pulled the gun from his victim's mouth and put it back into his belt. Morrison stood and reached down to help Goloshchekin up to his feet.

The two bodyguards remained on the floor, still out cold. "Don't worry about these two. They obviously didn't hear a thing or witness our friendly little chat. So you see, this was just between us. No one will ever know how we chatted or what we chatted about. Your authority here is undiminished. It's just that now you report to and will be respectful of Moscow. Now, isn't this simple?"

Sitting back in his chair, still trying to catch his breath, Goloshchekin finally responded, "Yes, Moryak, now I understand. Your reputation doesn't do you justice. You are one crazy son of a bitch. I've heard all of the stories. I suppose that now I am the latest addition to the collection."

"It will be our little secret. Don't worry about that."

Rubbing his jaw, Goloshchekin asked, "How can I help you, Comrade Moryak? Where do we start?"

"Let's start with Citizen Romanov and his entourage. Where are they?"

"They are living in the Ipatiev House. It's a nice mansion that was owned by an engineer. We appropriated the house from him because it's large, defensible, and easily guarded. We have constructed a wooden fence around it for added security."

"Who is in charge of the security detail at the Ipatiev House?"

"We have recently had a change. Comrade Yakov Yurovsky is now in charge. I had to replace the prior leader, Comrade Avdeyev and his people, because they were a bunch of drunks who would harass the prisoners daily and steal their possessions. The guards are much more disciplined and competent now under Yurovsky."

"Very good. Notify Yurovsky immediately that I will be meeting with him tomorrow and will be assuming command of the prisoners. He will be my second-in-command. Also, comrade, I'll let you take the credit for this one. Tell them that you decided on this change if it will enhance your prestige locally."

***

The following morning Morrison, escorted by Goloshchekin, arrived at the Ipatiev House to meet Yakov Yurovsky. There, he informed Yurovsky that Moryak had now assumed control over of the detachment guarding the Romanovs. "It is for the best, comrade, and it will also bring us more in concert with Moscow, something that is becoming more and more important." Yurovsky, although obviously not pleased, acceded to Moryak's authority. Goloshchekin then departed and left the two as he returned to headquarters. Morrison first requested a tour of the outside of the house.

It was just as it had been described to him, a stately white house, surrounded by a newly constructed fence. The house stood two stories tall and had several ground level rooms on the left side that appeared to be for storage. Yurovsky indicated that the family and the rest of the entourage lived on the second floor. Morrison noted that all of the windows had been painted over with white paint, rendering them opaque. After the tour, Yurovsky invited Morrison in, and they sat down in the front-right room on the first floor that Yurovsky reserved for his own use. "What would you want to see next, Comrade Moryak?" offered Yurovsky.

"Let me ask you, how many prisoners are in this building?" inquired Morrison.

"There are eleven."

"Eleven? There are seven members of the Romanov family, correct? Who the hell are the others here?"

"You are correct Moryak. There are seven family members. The former Tsar and Tsarina, their four daughters, Olga, Tatiana, Maria, and Anastasia, and the Tsarevitch Alexei. Four other courtiers have remained with them and are in this building."

"Who are they?"

"There's their physician, Dr. Botkin. The Tsarina has a lady-in-waiting named Demidova. There's also the royal cook, named Kharitonov, and lastly Citizen Romanov's personal servant, an idiot named Trupp."

Great, thought Morrison. He hadn't counted on any others besides the family. Any potential plans were already becoming further complicated. "How has Nicholas Romanov behaved while in captivity? Have there been any problems with him or with any of them?"

Yurovsky scratched his head for a moment and replied, "By and large, there haven't been any real problems. Every now and then, the former Tsar seems to forget that he is a prisoner of the new state and gets a bit arrogant toward us. This was apparently a much greater problem earlier on. There haven't been any problems recently."

"Good! What are the living arrangements for the Romanovs?"

"The former Tsar and Tsarina, along with the Tsarevitch, live in the corner room facing the front of the house. The four daughters live in the adjacent room along the west side of the building."

After writing all of the information down, Morrison looked up and said to Yurovsky, "Bring the former Tsar in here. I want to meet with him privately. I've got a personal message to give to him from Comrade Lenin. I also want to make it clear who is in charge of this building and that I better not see or hear any 'royal airs' from him."

"Yes, Moryak," replied Yurovsky as he rose and left the room to fetch Nicholas. After a few minutes, the door opened, and Yurovsky stuck his head in the doorway and announced, "I have Citizen Romanov here."

"Send him in and close the door," ordered Morrison. Nicholas Romanov, the former Tsar Nicholas II, entered the room, and Morrison pointed to the chair next to him, indicating that he should sit down. Nicholas sat down and looked at the new head of the prison guards with a blank stare. Morrison noted that he looked considerably older than he would have thought. *Hell, he thought, it's been over thirty years since I last saw him.* Nicholas' hair, now flecked with gray, seemed to accentuate the lines on his face. *How old is he?* Morrison tried to remember, and he guessed Nicholas was about fifty years old. Dressed neatly in a gray military tunic, he sat there nervously with his hands folded. The small man appeared quite pathetic to Morrison. He remembered what an arrogant snob he was those many years ago in Japan when they had met.

Nicholas eyed this new guard. The menacing man appeared to be about his age. He had a full head of brown hair flecked with gray and several days' growth of beard. Like many of those revolutionaries, he wore a leather coat. Nicholas began to feel uncomfortable when he noted the dangerous look in the guard's eyes. The guard stood up, walked over to the door, and locked it. He sat down again next to Nicholas and stared at him for a few seconds. He then began to talk in a quiet voice.

"Nicholas Romanov, we don't have much time, and I need you to listen to me very carefully." Morrison leaned over, placing his face near Nicholas. "I am an Allied agent, sent here to rescue you and turn you over to the western forces that will soon be entering Russia. I will be attempting this in the next several days, so I need your total cooperation. The other guards believe that I am a Bolshevik, and that I have been sent by Lenin himself to oversee your imprisonment. I'll explain the entire situation over the next several days. The important thing is that—"

"No!" exclaimed Nicholas, jumping to his feet. "I don't believe you! You are trying to trick me! You want me to attempt to escape to give you an excuse to kill me and my family! Well, I won't do it! If you want to murder me—"

"Keep your voice down! Get back in your seat. You have to trust me and listen to me!"

"No. How can I trust you after you tell me such a crazy story?" Nicholas became more agitated as he continued. "You are just going to have to kill me if you want, that's all. Please leave me and stop this torture. Please!"

Morrison stood up and shoved Nicholas against the wall. Holding his left forearm against his throat, he pinned the former Tsar against the wall, and blurted out, "Shut your mouth! Just shut up!" As he did this, put his right hand on the former Tsar's chin, turned Nicholas's head to the left, and then ran his hand along Nicholas' forehead. Running his finger along the scar on the side of his forehead, Morrison asked, "Do you remember that day in Japan when you got this wound?" Nicholas just looked back at him with terrified eyes. "Answer me!" demanded Morrison. "Do you remember that day? Do you remember having a handkerchief pressed against this wound? A handkerchief that had crossed gray anchors embroidered in the corner with letters USNA above them? Those letters stood for United States Naval Academy. Do you remember that, Nicholas Romanov?" Morrison speaking with an angered viciousness in his voice, now had his face just inches from the former Tsar. "Answer me, Goddamn you!"

Nicholas stared at his assailant, his eyes reflecting obvious terror. He didn't know what to say. The man had the eyes of a killer and now asked him about an incident that occurred nearly thirty years ago. What could that possibly have to do with anything? Morrison could see the fear and confusion in his eyes, but soon the look of terror seemed to slowly change into a look of astonishment. Nicholas' eyes got wide with disbelief, and Morrison could see that now he slowly remembered that day so long ago in Japan and how he had been rescued. He backed his forearm off of the former Tsar's throat so he could breathe easier. The man started slowly shaking his head side to side, and then he finally spoke in a soft, stunned voice. "My God, how can this be? You're the American! One of those who saved my life! I don't understand. How can this be? What is happening here?"

"Nicholas Romanov," interrupted Morrison, "I'll have to explain all of this to you later. We just don't have the time now. You have to trust me. I saved your life thirty years ago, and I am sure as hell going to try and do it again. Now please, let me ask the questions." The stunned Tsar nodded in assent, still trying to comprehend what he just heard. "I just learned that there are four more people in addition to your family that are prisoners here. Is that correct?" Again, Nicholas nodded. "Are all members of the family fit for travel, travel that may be somewhat rigorous?"

Nicholas looked down for a few seconds before answering. "There is a problem with my son Alexei, the Tsarevitch. He's a hemophiliac and—"

"What the hell is that?"

"He's a bleeder. It's a genetic condition. When he gets even a minor trauma, he bleeds uncontrollably. He has had a recent bleed into his left knee. The pain is subsiding, so the bleeding has apparently stopped. But for right now, his knee is locked and he can barely walk."

Morrison sighed with disgust. "Well, that's just great!" he blurted out as he smashed his right fist into the palm of his left hand. He stood up and paced around the room a bit. "All right, all right," he said, looking at Nicholas, "I'm sorry for the outburst. Is there anything else I need to know?"

"No, that's it."

"Have you had any contact with the outside world? Has any aid been brought to you here in Ekaterinburg? Is there anyone we can rely on in the city for help if we need to?"

Nicholas thought a minute and said, "Yes. For a while, people from the local monastery were very kind and sneaked eggs and milk to us. Occasionally there were messages of encouragement for us. One day after they dropped off some food, I gave a message to one of the sisters to send to the Allied forces, but it was discovered by one of the guards before she left the grounds. I'm told she was beaten and since then we have had no outside contact. I don't believe there is anyone else out there who is willing to help you."

"All right, now listen carefully," instructed Morrison. "This conversation we just had, do not, and I repeat, do not discuss this with anyone else, not even the Tsarina. It must be a total secret, understand? I can't stress this enough. I think the attempt is going to occur within the week, so I need you to be ready at a moment's notice. When I give the word, or if anyone else gives you sudden orders to prepare to travel, we must go immediately. You have to rouse your family and get them moving immediately. There can be no delay. Do you understand what I'm telling you so far?"

"Yes, I do. I assure you that I will not discuss this at all. You have my word on this."

"I might as well tell you this. I don't have an exact plan. I'll be formulating it over the next day or so. I plan on returning here to speak with you then. By the way, the former head of the guards, Comrade Yurovsky, he's now my assistant. He thinks I'm interrogating you at the moment." Suddenly, Morrison lashed out at Nicholas with a backhand slam across his face that sent him sprawling over backward and cut the corner of his lower lip. He then walked over to Nicholas and offered his hand to help him up. All the flustered Nicholas could think to say was, "What the devil?"

"Sorry. They think I'm interrogating you, so I have to make this somewhat believable. Your bruises and cuts will help our cover." *This is just a small payback for what you did to my family,* thought Morrison. As Nicholas held a handkerchief to his cut lip, Morrison told him, "I have a feeling we're going to have to act sooner than later, much sooner."

"Why do you say that?"

"Do you hear that distant rumble? It's not thunder. As you can see, the skies are clear. No, that's artillery fire. The battlefront is approaching. The White Army will be here soon." He then put his hand on Nicholas' shoulder and smiled. "Courage, Nicholas Romanov. Remember, not a word to anyone. I'll be back with a plan." Opening the door, he called out "Guard! Escort the prisoner back to his room!" As Nicholas exited the room past Yurovsky, the Bolshevik could see the bruises and cuts on the former Tsar's face. The sight of the bruises made him smile. He liked Moryak's style already. As Morrison exited the room, Yurovsky asked him, "How did it go?"

"It went well, comrade. He got arrogant with me only once. I doubt it will ever happen again." Yurovsky chuckled at that. "Comrade Yurovsky, have the guards assembled in the back. I want to meet them."

In the backyard of the Ipatiev House, Yurovsky assembled the fifteen men who comprised the guard detail. Morrison could see that they were plainly ruffians. Some appeared to have been drinking. Yurovsky proceeded to introduce the detail to their new commander, the Bolshevik hero Moryak. A general murmur of approval arose from the group. Morrison gave them a general talk, outlining what he expected of them and of the importance of central control of all soviets by Moscow. He spoke forcefully and confidently. Finally, when he finished, he asked if anyone had a question. One of the guards named Pavel spoke out. "I have one, Comrade Moryak."

"What is it?"

"Will we still get the honor of killing the Romanovs, and when?" All of the others nodded their heads. Morrison could clearly see that this question had been on all of their minds. He had to reassure them.

"Comrades, you will all certainly have that honor! It is simply a question of when we get the authorization from Moscow. Once we do, we will proceed. But I tell you this. I am in total command of this guard detachment here at Ipatiev House. Do you all understand that clearly? When we execute the Romanovs, it will be under my command, and we will proceed exactly as I direct you to. Is that understood?"

"Yes, sir!" they answered enthusiastically in unison. As they did, another faint distant boom was heard.

"Another thing comrades. Do you hear that which sounds like thunder in the distance?"

"That's not thunder, Comrade Moryak!" shouted one. "That's gunfire!"

"That's exactly right. The White Army approaches. We will have to carry out our mission very soon." Turning to Yurovsky, he ordered, "Dismiss the men and then let us review the latest battle reports from the front."

23

Safe House
Ekaterinburg, Russia
July 15, 1918

Stephen Morrison gently knocked in the prescribed pattern on the nondescript door of the small cabin located on Ekaterinburg's outer border. A few seconds later, the door cracked open slightly and Morrison could hear the voice of Homer Slaughter saying, "C'mon in, Commander." After closing the door behind then and locking it, Slaughter invited his guest to sit down at the small table in the middle of the room.

As he sat, Morrison said, "I'm glad you got the message I had sent. You're right, your team of paid-off telegraph people is very reliable."

"Indeed they are!" replied the major. "Can I offer you some booze, some real stuff instead of the shit vodka we get here all the time? I brought a bottle of Jack Daniels with me. I thought it might have been a while since you've had some."

"I'd love some, thank you." The major poured and they toasted. "To the mission," they said in unison. As the liquor went down his throat, Morrison couldn't remember when he had had such a delicious drink. "Ahh, it's been too long!" he said as Slaughter refilled his glass.

Putting down the bottle, Slaughter noticed the smile on Morrison's face. "You seem pretty damn happy tonight, Commander."

"Oh, it's nothing really. I was just sitting here, thinking how wonderful it is to hear English spoken and to speak it myself. You know, for so long in the prison camp, I worried I would forget how. I forced myself nightly to think in English and, hell, I even talked to myself when I was in solitary confinement to stay proficient."

The major grinned and again thought to himself how much he admired this man. They then got down to business. "I assume you read my message," stated Morrison. "You realize the other four prisoners—you know, the doctor and the others—well, they have to be considered expendable."

"I agree. Especially under the circumstances."

"I spoke with Yurovsky after I met with the guards. They already have a plan for the executions. They are planning on taking them all into one of the cellar rooms and killing them there. I inspected the room with him. It's not very big. As I mentioned in my telegram, I seriously doubt that I can get the family out. There are just too many guards involved. If I try to cut back the number of executioners, it will immediately arouse suspicion that something is wrong. Major, I'm afraid we may not be able to pull this mission off. It will be impossible to get the family out of there by myself. You did let your superiors know this, right?"

"Yes, I did," replied Slaughter. He said nothing for a few seconds and his face remained impassive. "Hmm, this is not good. The Allied command is really looking for a person to rally all the forces; they had their plans pinned on the Tsar getting out. Tell me, Commander, do you think it's possible to get even one person out?"

Morrison thought for a second before replying. "As I mentioned in my message, probably the easiest one for me to work with would be the son. I think that possibly I could control the situation enough to attempt to rescue him. I think that a best-case scenario would be if I can get one of them out, he'd be the most logical candidate. Unfortunately, I don't see how it can be the Tsar. There's no way he can get out of that room alive, even with me in control of the situation as much as possible. Did you communicate my concerns up to the chain of command? What did they think?"

Slaughter lit a cigarette and slowly exhaled the smoke. He offered one to Morrison, but he declined. "I did hear from General Graves, who in turn was in touch with the Brits as well as our American in charge. When they heard the exact situation at Ipatiev House, they were quite discouraged, I will admit. They concurred with you in that they didn't see how a rescue would be possible given the current situation. It's funny, but your proposal to rescue one of them was entertained, I understand. In fact, there was discussion of this as a backup plan. Naturally, the first choice would be Tsar Nicholas, but under the circumstances, this option certainly didn't appear feasible. They actually do think that there would be a lot of value if the heir, Tsarevitch Alexei can be rescued. You know, the chance to use the heir to the Romanov throne as a rallying point for all of the counterrevolutionary forces can be a very powerful tool. They've authorized you to proceed with that plan if, in your judgment, it is the best course of action."

"Did you let them know about the hemophilia?"

"Yes, they now know. Again they've authorized you to proceed if feasible."

"Major, the intelligence that Yurovsky gave me indicated that the White Army and the Czech Legion are no more than three days from Ekaterinburg. You realize that means the mission has to be undertaken no later than tomorrow night."

"Tomorrow night!" blurted out Slaughter, causing him to have a minor coughing spasm as he exhaled another cloud of cigarette smoke. "Christ, that's cutting it mighty close! Are you ready to go, Commander?"

"It looks like we have no choice. Just before I left to come here, I was given a telegram that Lenin himself sent me. As the latest reports indicate, Ekaterinburg is going to fall to the Whites in days. Lenin has now ordered the execution of the Romanovs, under my direction, in no later than forty-eight hours. We have to make our move tomorrow night." Looking down at the table at the items that Slaughter had placed there, he said, "I see you brought the things I requested."

"Yeah, I got 'em. You said you carry a Nagant M1895, right? I don't like that gun. The pull on the trigger on those pieces of crap is like trying to lift weights. I know, I know, you gotta play the part, but you should try this sometime." Reaching into his belt, he pulled out a new Colt 1911 .45 caliber semi-automatic. "This is what we now issue in the U. S. armed forces."

Morrison picked up the new pistol and looked at it admiringly. "Semi-automatic?" he asked, handing it back to Slaughter. "I wish I could use something like this." Pulling out his Nagant M1895, he asked, "Are those the cartridges I requested?"

"Yes. 7.62 caliber blanks. I got you ten of them."

"Very good," said Morrison as he picked up a small box and removed a small vial from it "What is this?"

"The command thinks you may well need that. It's a sedative. The doctor who supplied it said that drinking half the vial will cause one to be quite sedated. Drinking the whole thing will probably knock someone out. They were thinking about the boy. He'll probably need it."

Morrison held the vial of yellow liquid up to the light. "I don't think that I'll be able to give it to him."

"Commander, you said you were going to meet with the Tsar one more time. Give it to him so he can give it to the boy. He's the only one who can logically do it." As Morrison pondered the suggestion, Slaughter continued. "You said that the original plan was to drive the bodies in a truck to an abandoned mine northwest of Ekaterinburg, off of Koptiaki Road. I've obtained a safe house on the road heading northeast of the city, about eight miles up the road. You'll recognize it easily enough because there will be a red lantern burning in the window as you approach. If you're able to rescue the boy, that's where you transfer him to me. Even if it's not possible to bring the boy out, you meet me there. From that point on, you're going with me, even if it's only the two of us. Do you understand what I'm getting at?"

"I'm not sure exactly."

"You better maintain your English language proficiency. You're going home, Commander! This comes straight from the top. This is your last covert mission for the government. Yep, Double Eagle is being retired after this mission. I've been told to inform you of that tonight. Also, I'm to tell you that the government is grateful for your services. In a couple of weeks, you are going to be back in the United States. Christ Almighty, how long has it been, sir?"

"Nearly thirteen years. You know, Major, there are complications, such as my original mission."

"I've been told to inform you not to worry about things like that. These issues are being addressed as we talk. Not to worry, you are definitely going home. And I, for one, definitely feel that this calls for one more drink." He filled both of their glasses and then raised his. "To Double Eagle's last mission!" They both downed their drinks and he asked, "You know, Commander, I know a lot about your original mission and some of the other details, but I have to ask you, where did you learn to speak Russian like a native? I mean, you pass so easily."

"Actually, I was born in Russia, in Perm. I didn't move to the United States until I was eleven years old."

"Tell me, why the hell do they think you are this Moryak character?"

Morrison smiled and said, "That's a long story. Why don't I save that for sometime after tomorrow night? Then we'll have all the time in the world to talk."

"It's a deal!" The men continued to talk for another hour and one more time went over the details of the mission. As Morrison prepared to depart, Slaughter stood and shook his hand. "Good luck, Commander. I hope you'll be able to pull this off. Remember, I'll be in the cabin with the red lantern burning in the window. Once you and, hopefully, the Tsarevitch get there, we're heading home!"

Morrison smiled at him and simply said, "I'll be there."

***

Two days earlier, Mansfield Cumming prepared a message for Sidney Reilly after reviewing the report from Major Slaughter. He felt quite disappointed when he learned that rescuing the Romanovs would not be possible. That was it, then. There would be no more use for the agent called Double Eagle, especially after the coup engineered by Lockhart and Reilly. It was a shame, he noted, that this Major Slaughter seemed to be so admiring of Double Eagle. It would be best if the good major never knew of the instructions that he was about to send Reilly. Certainly, the American in charge will never be told of my decision.

With little remorse, Cumming instructed Reilly to have Double Eagle rendezvous with Slaughter as planned, immediately after the Romanov murders. Slaughter would then arrange to have the man brought to Reilly's agents, and he would not be informed of what was to follow. Reilly was to ensure that the agent called Double Eagle never made it out of Russia alive. His existence was too big a liability for the British and American governments to deal with. *After all,* reasoned Cumming, *the man has been officially dead since 1905, and he's now, once again, outlived his usefulness.*

24

Smolny Institute
Petrograd, Russia
Morning, July 15, 1918

Mozger sat at his desk, trying to get through the mountain of paperwork that had piled up over the past week. As head of the Petrograd Soviet, he remained a constantly busy man who would often sleep in his office rather than go home to his tiny apartment. The other members of the soviet respected and feared him. He lived the life of the consummate Bolshevik, the new party man. Zinoviev himself actually resented Mozger, for he felt he should have been given the honor of heading the Petrograd Soviet. Trotsky agreed with Zinoviev, but it appeared that Mozger had allied with Stalin and those two continued, in Zinoviev's opinion, to maneuver to get closer to Lenin. Mozger couldn't care less what Zinoviev thought. All he cared about was the party.

His thoughts that morning were interrupted by his secretary, who announced, "Your guest, Comrade Malinovsky has arrived." Mozger instructed her to escort the man into his office.

"Comrade Mozger! What an honor and delight to see you again after all of these years." As he spoke these words, he approached Mozger and vigorously shook his hand. Mozger smiled at him and invited him to sit down. Malinovsky reveled in the thought of how good it felt to be back in the party's good graces. "Comrade Lenin no doubt wired you that I would be arriving?"

"Indeed he did, comrade, indeed he did."

"Excellent. He told me that you would have important work for me here in Petrograd, working in the soviet. I can't tell you how excited the prospect of that makes me."

Mozger got up and walked around his desk to him. Sitting on the edge of his desk right in front of Malinovsky, he smiled and then suddenly lashed out with a vicious kick to his guest's groin. Malinovsky collapsed to floor, crying out in pain. "Comrade," he gasped, "what are you doing?" A wave of nausea swept over him.

Mozger leaned over him, grabbed him by the hair with his left hand and slapped him across the face with his right. "What am I doing? What am I doing, you ask? I'm beginning to administer justice to a traitorous pig! To a cunning, devious enemy of the party! To a man I suspected all along was an Okhrana agent!"

"No, comrade, you're wrong. Please, that is a lie. Comrade Lenin himself sent me here to you!"

"Comrade Lenin was duped by you for years. I had warned him about you, but he wouldn't listen." He kicked Malinovsky in the ribs and then continued. "You miserable piece of shit. Don't you know that we've read the entire contents of the Okhrana's files. Your treachery is outlined there as clear as day. So don't lie to me and tell me you are as innocent as driven snow. I know you are a traitorous bastard and so does Lenin. The party has been on to you for quite some time. You stupid imbecile, don't you realize that Lenin sent you to me so I can kill you?"

Mozger sat down in a chair and watched Malinovsky slowly get up and finally sit in the chair facing him.

Malinovsky tried to catch his breath as tears streamed down his face. In a low voice he said, "You know comrade, I've spent nearly three years in a German prisoner of war camp. Isn't that enough atonement for my sins? I wish nothing else for the rest of my life except to serve the party. Can't you forgive me for my past transgressions? Please, I beg of you!"

Mozger remained impassive and simply replied, "No."

"What are you going to do to me?"

"The penalty for treason is death. I'm going to have you taken out back and shot when we're done with our business here."

Malinovsky's head dropped into his hands, and he cried openly. His shoulders shook rhythmically as he wailed loudly. Mozger allowed him to cry for nearly two minutes before saying, "It's time."

"Wait!" insisted Malinovsky, looking up at Mozger. "I have information, very important information that the party needs to know. That Comrade Lenin himself needs to know! Let us make an arrangement of sorts. I give you the information, and you let me live. I'll leave Russia, I swear, and you'll never see me or hear from me again. Please, Comrade Mozger, I beg of you!"

Mozger sighed with disgust. "You miserable, pathetic wretch. What information could you possibly have that I could give a damn about?"

"Please comrade, trust me. You'll want to know what I have to offer."

Mozger stood up and slapped him hard across the face. "Tell me this priceless information right now, and I'll decide if it's worth letting you live. Do you understand me?"

Sobbing again, Malinovsky began in almost a whisper. "The man they call Moryak, he's not who they think he is. He is an agent of the British who was sent here years ago."

"What?" shouted Mozger. "You are one crazy bastard, do you know that? Moryak is a national hero! Is that your priceless information? I should put a bullet in your head right now!" He pulled his Nagant M1895, the favorite sidearm of the Bolsheviks, from his belt and held the barrel against Malinovsky's forehead.

"Please, Comrade Mozger, hear me out," he implored. "I was working for the Bolsheviks back in 1905, and it is true I was also an informer to the Okhrana. I freely admit that now. Anyway, I was contacted by this British agent named Reilly. He was fluent in Russian and could easily pass for a Russian himself. He paid me to assist him on some mission that the British had designed to kidnap the Tsar and spirit him out of Russia. He had with him another undercover agent, but the mission never was attempted and the other agent was arrested. I thought they hanged him. That other agent is the same man that is now known as Moryak. I'm certain it's the same man."

"How hell can a man who was hanged be alive today? Do you realize how incredibly stupid your story sounds? An authentic Russian hero is actually a British agent who was executed years ago! If that's your precious information that you were counting on to keep you alive, you are sadly mistaken, my friend."

"I tell you, Comrade Mozger, I can see it in his eyes. Those serious, angry eyes. I don't know how it can be, but I tell you it is the same man! Have you ever seen Moryak's eyes?"

"Interestingly, even though we've communicated often, we've never actually met. Our schedules have never permitted it."

"Please, comrade, I beg of you! I've given you this valuable information—"

"You've given me nothing but a fantastic, ridiculous story!" He walked over to his door and called out to his secretary. "Have Goretsky sent in!" Within a minute, the man he sent for arrived and Mozger instructed him. "Comrade Goretsky, take this man in the back," he said, pointing at the crying Malinovsky, "and shoot him, now!"

***

For the rest of the morning, Mozger couldn't concentrate. Something continued to eat away at him. Something that Malinovsky had told him. His story he had told about Moryak was preposterous. It amazed Mozger that he actually thought that it might save him. Still, something continued to bother him, and Comrade Mozger just couldn't let go of the thoughts in his head. It all centered on that year he had mentioned, 1905. So many changes had occurred that year. It was the year that he had made the commitment to devote himself totally to the Bolsheviks, the year he forsook his prior life. Many other important events also occurred that year. He couldn't let go of these nagging thoughts and felt he had to find out things for himself. As he left the office, he informed his secretary that he would be going to the Peter and Paul Fortress.

The Peter and Paul Fortress once again continued to do a bustling business only now the prisoners were enemies of the new Bolshevik government. Mozger knew this because he had been personally responsible for sending many of the current prisoners there. One particular prisoner had Mozger's interest that morning, and he prayed that the man was still alive. He would possibly have the answers that he sought. Upon arrival, he told the guards that he had to see the People's Jailer immediately. Without any hesitation, the guards escorted Comrade Mozger to the office of the People's Jailer, who in spite of his lofty title, was basically the warden of the old prison. In fact, he utilized the same office that all of the past wardens had used for over a century.

"Comrade Mozger, to what do we owe this honor?" greeted the People's Jailer ebulliently. You should have called first, I would have arranged—"

"Thank you, Comrade Jailer," Mozger interrupted, "but I don't have the time. I need to know. The warden of this prison under the Tsar, how long was he the warden? It was quite some while, as I recall."

"Yes, it was about twenty years, I believe."

"Is he still alive, here?"

"Yes, of course, comrade. We don't necessarily kill everyone, you know," he replied, somewhat amused with that witticism.

"Good! Take me to him immediately."

"Of course, comrade. Whatever you wish. They say that he is quite depressed now. I suppose going from jailer to jailbird can do that to someone." The People's Jailer erupted into laughter as the two of them left his office.

The People's Jailer led Mozger down a dank, dark corridor. Finally, they stopped at a cell, and the People's Jailer unlocked the door and opened it. "Come back for me in fifteen minutes," instructed Mozger. He then walked into the cell and saw the solitary occupant lying on his side on the cot. Mozger walked up to him and shook him, saying, "I am Comrade Mozger, head of the Petrograd Soviet. You were the Tsar's warden here all of those years, correct?"

Lee Mandel

The man in the cot didn't answer so Mozger kicked him in the small of his back and the man blurted out, "Yes! Yes, I was."

"Turn around and face me now!" ordered Mozger. The man complied and sat up now with a forlorn expression on his face. He appeared to be in his sixties and also appeared to be in ill health. Every few seconds he would have a mild coughing spasm. "Tell me, in 1905 you had a prisoner here from the *Potemkin* mutiny, do you remember?"

"That was so long ago, what does that matter?"

Mozger grabbed the prisoner by the throat and said, "It matters to me! Now, do you remember him?" Unable to speak, the former warden just nodded. "Good," said Mozger, releasing the man's throat. "Tell me, whatever happened to him?"

The warden looked apprehensively at his tormentor and replied, "Well, he served in a labor camp for a decade and is now the famous Moryak, right? Everyone seems to know that."

Mozger removed a switchblade knife from his pocket and opened the blade. He placed the point right under the man's chin until the blade drew blood. "Listen to me and listen well. Nothing else is going to happen to you for what you may have done in the past. I'm not interested in punishing you further for whatever you might have done back then, but I do need to know if the man you sent to that prison camp was the man who led the *Potemkin* mutiny. If you don't answer me honestly, I will shove this blade upward and skewer your brains. I hope I'm making myself clear."

The terrified warden could barely breathe as the tip of the knife blade stung his skin. Finally, he whispered, "No, he's not the same man. The man who I sent to the prison camp was some sort of undercover agent from England, I think. He was convicted of trying to kill the Tsar, or some other nonsense like that."

"Whatever happened to the mutineer?"

"Please, put down the knife, and I'll tell you what I can recall!" Mozger slowly dropped the blade, and the warden breathed a sigh of relief. He swallowed and then cleared his throat before continuing. "The mutineer, I had him hung in the British agent's place. I sent the British agent to the labor camp in the place of the mutineer."

"Why would you do such a thing?" asked Mozger, getting a very uneasy feeling in the pit of his stomach.

"I don't remember exactly. I think he had killed a guard whom I wanted killed, and I thought I would reward him and spare his life—if you call being sent to a Tsarist labor camp sparing one's life."

"What was the British agent's name? This is important."

The warden didn't answer at first. Finally he said "I'll be honest you; I can't remember. Only that it was an Anglo-sounding name. I'm sorry."

"So you know who this one they call Moryak actually is then?"

With his head down, he softly replied "Yes, I suppose I do, but the secret is safe, given the fact that—" Mozger suddenly grabbed the man's hair and then jerked his head up. With one fluid motion of his right hand, he took his knife and slashed the warden's throat. As blood spurted from his carotid arteries, the warden collapsed with a look of shock in his eyes. He fell forward against Mozger, who pushed him off of himself and onto the floor. A large pool of blood soon formed around the dead prisoner's head. Mozger cleaned the blade off on the warden's prison blouse and walked out of the cell just as the People's Jailer had arrived for him. "Take me back to your office immediately," he ordered.

Back at the office, Mozger sat down and asked, "You have kept the archives of all of the prison's intake photographs, correct?"

"Yes, we have them all."

"Good, bring me the archive books from June through December of 1905." Within a half-hour, ledgers from those seven months were on the desk in front of him. Mozger ordered the People's Jailer out of the office and began to open the ledger dated June 1905. Organized with six entries to a page, each entry had a name, along with front and side-view face photographs. The far right-hand column of each entry listed "crimes charged with." He tried to remember the real name of the *Potemkin* mutineer. After a few minutes, it came back to him—Matushenko! Something like Anatoly Matushenko, he recalled. After a few minutes, he found him. The man had been sent to Peter and Paul Fortress at the end of that June.

The photographs of Anatoly Mantushenko did not look familiar to him. That didn't surprise him, for he had never actually met Moryak face to face. It would be the other prisoner that would give him the answers to his questions. The other man who had been arrested that fall. Mozger decided to start with September. He scanned every entry, not certain of the name he was looking for. He focused in on the crime that each man had been charged with. He scanned every entry for September, but found nothing that interested him.

He next opened the ledger from October. It amused him greatly when he found an entry in the middle of the month for "Leon Trotsky" along with his photographs. *Your day is coming, soon, Comrade Trotsky,* he thought to himself. Shortly after that, he stopped at an entry when he noticed that the crime that the prisoner had been charged with was listed as "foreign conspiracy to assassinate the Tsar." This had to be it! He looked over at the name, an Anglo-Saxon name: Brian Anderson. He then gazed at the front and side view photographs, and his heart nearly stopped. His worst fears had been realized.

There was no doubt in his mind that the pictures were of his good friend from so many years ago, a United States naval officer named Stephen Morrison! He had no doubt! He had been the one sent to the labor camp at Solovetsky Island and then assumed the life of the one called Moryak. As soon as Malinovsky told him his tale, he had developed the uneasy feeling that this might possibly be the case. It was the year, 1905, that triggered his paranoid suspicions. His good friend Stephen Morrison had just died in October of that year in an industrial shipyard accident, he had learned. The one non-Russian person that he truly admired in the world was gone, and he took the loss very badly. The whole story of his death seemed so improbable to him at the time, and he never quite believed it. He had been convinced there was some sort of cover-up involved. True, he was a paranoid at heart, but he just couldn't accept the fact that his admired friend had died in such an undistinguished manner. He was actually depressed for months afterward. It was only his work for the Bolshevik party that kept him focused. Hearing Malinovsky's tale threw a switch in his mind. This British agent had been arrested in St. Petersburg at the very moment he later learned that his good friend had perished! That was quite a coincidence, a little too much for such a skeptic such as himself. Things didn't happen this neatly in reality. He didn't believe in coincidence. He had to know for certain. Now he did know, and he felt sick to his stomach.

He looked back at the photographs and put his fingers on them. "Stephen," he said in a soft voice, "I believed in you so much. I had such hopes for you." His mind drifted back to the times that he and Stephen had traveled across Russia so many years before. Those were such good times. It tore at his heart to think of them again after so many years. It was a lifetime ago.

He was not the same man he was then. He had attempted to erase from his memory banks all thoughts of his prior life. He then tore the two photographs out of the ledger and closed it. He stacked the seven ledgers in monthly order on the desk and proceeded to walk out of the office. As he approached the entrance to the prison, the People's Jailer saw him and ran after him. "Comrade Mozger," he asked breathlessly, "did you find what you were looking for?"

Without turning to look back at him, he answered "No, I didn't. But thank you anyway, comrade. I'm sorry I wasted your time."

Mozger went directly back to his office at the Smolny Institute, his mind going over and over the meaning of what he had just discovered. As he walked past his secretary, he instructed her that no calls be forwarded in to him and that no visitors be admitted. "What about your scheduled appointments this afternoon?" she asked.

"Cancel them all," he barked at her as he entered his office and closed the door behind him. He locked the door, went to his desk, and sat down. Reaching into his pocket, he took out the two pictures of Stephen Morrison and placed them on the desk in front of him. As he did, he noticed that his hands trembled. His heart pounded rapidly as he thought of the ramifications of what he had just learned. What alternatives did he have? He was a Bolshevik, the one they called the "ultimate party man" behind his back. He would have to inform Lenin and the rest of the Politburo. The man they knew as Moryak was a spy, a traitor who must be liquidated, for the good of the country. It galled him to think of how many times he criticized Lenin for being too gullible and trusting, yet here he was with the knowledge that a former close friend was an enemy spy! The thought of this dilemma continued to nauseate him.

He thought of his friend from years back as he gazed at the photographs and of the correspondence that they had over the many years. He had so much hope for his friend. He had been convinced that Morrison would be a man who could change the world. Back then, when he was called Yuri Kodarov, he dreamt that a just workers' society would evolve in Russia and that America would be a strong ally in their cause. And it would be Stephen Morrison, no doubt a future admiral in the United States Navy, who would be the link between the two great countries. Oh, how he had admired his friend!

He began to rationalize to himself. *Of course, I never met Moryak face to face. How could I possibly know? It was Lenin and that stooge Trotsky who were so enamored with him all along. They really had been responsible, not me.* He proved to be the vigilant one who discovered the treachery of Moryak. *I am*, he reassured himself, the *ultimate party man*, the one who dedicated himself to the party and had no life at all outside of the party. *I should not be the one who should bear any blame in this sordid affair.* That conclusion seemed crystal clear.

He laid his head in his hands and actually began to weep. Such ambivalent emotions tugged at his soul. For years, he had never experienced feelings of conflict about anything in life. Now, he broke down and cried uncontrollably for several minutes. When he finished, he stopped and abruptly sat straight up. *What am I doing? How dare I show emotions, or worse, let emotions factor into my life. I have no emotions! I had excised them from my life when I swore my life and loyalty to the Bolsheviks. Bolsheviks, true Bolsheviks, have no emotions. They are for the weak. I am the ultimate party man. I am Rakhmetev, the embodiment of the revolutionary man.* He suddenly knew what he had to do.

Reaching into his desk drawer, he withdrew some stationary and envelopes. At first, he crafted a short telegraph message to

Lenin. He now realized that Moryak, who had assumed control of the Romanov family in Ekaterinburg, had likely maneuvered himself into that job, probably to attempt a rescue and try to deliver the Romanovs to the White Army. He composed a short telegram that got right to the point:

MORYAK A DOUBLE AGENT WORKING FOR ALLIES STOP MUST BE NEUTRALIZED IMMEDIATLEY STOP EVIDENCE UNDENIABLE STOP PROOF WILL ARRIVE ON NEXT TRAIN FROM PETROGRAD STOP MOZGER

He folded the message and then placed it into an envelope. Next, he began writing a letter to Lenin, explaining the accusations of Malinovsky concerning Moryak. He decided that he would not go into his past association with Stephen Morrison; it was irrelevant to the issue. He explained his suspicions after Malinovsky's confession and also detailed his visit to the Peter and Paul Fortress. He described the details of the failed 1905 British mission that he had gleaned from the prison records. He reassured Lenin that the Tsar's warden, the only other person who knew the real identity of Moryak, had already been killed. Like he himself, his letter showed no emotion. He simply signed it "Mozger" and then folded it neatly, placing it into another envelope. Before sealing it, he inserted the two photographs of Stephen Morrison. He then called out to his secretary to send for Goretsky.

Goretksy promptly arrived, somewhat out of breath from running up the stairs. "How did your prior assignment go?" asked Mozger.

"Perfectly, Comrade Mozger. The prisoner cried like a girl all the way to the end. It was a pleasure to finally shut him up with a bullet!"

"Good, very good. I have another task for you, Comrade Goretsky. This is a vital assignment, you understand." He handed the man the two envelopes. "Take this one to the telegraph office and have it sent immediately. Take the transcription tape from the clerk and burn it immediately. Do you understand me?"

"Yes, comrade."

"Good. This other envelope needs to be hand-delivered to Lenin himself at the Kremlin. Only to Lenin. Now, there is a train leaving for Moscow this evening. You will be on this train and make sure that this message gets to Lenin. Are my instructions clear?"

"Yes, comrade!" Goretsky replied enthusiastically.

"Good then! Be gone now and close the door on the way out."

After the door closed, Mozger arose, walked over to it, and locked it again. He slowly walked back to his desk and seated himself. Taking time to arrange everything neatly on his desk, he reached into his belt and removed his pistol. Placing it on the desk, he looked at it admiringly. He loved the Nagant M1895. It spoke power and authority. In his career, he had used it not infrequently to send enemies of the party to justice. *How appropriate,* he thought. He picked the weapon up with both hands and pointed it toward himself. Inserting the barrel into his mouth, he placed both of his thumbs on the trigger. Using his right index finger, he cocked back the hammer. With slow, deliberate pressure, he pressed his thumbs against the trigger. He wanted to savor the moment. He wanted no pity, only absolution for his momentary weakness of several minutes ago. His last thought before the bullet shattered his brain was of Stephen Morrison.

25

*Ipatiev House
Ekaterinburg, Russia
Morning, July 16, 1918*

Stephen Morrison assembled all of the guards in the small guesthouse on the grounds of the Ipatiev House. He had instructed Yurovsky to make sure that they reported sober, as he had critically important news for them. They filed into the sitting room of the house and as instructed, they all appeared sober. Morrison instructed them to all sit down as he stood in the front of the room.

"Comrades, you don't have to be a weatherman to know that the thunder of gunfire that we're hearing is getting closer. Our intelligence is telling us that the White Army is converging on Ekaterinburg. It is anticipated that they will arrive the day after tomorrow." A murmur of excitement swept over the men as he continued on. "I have been instructed that we must evacuate these premises tomorrow and retreat eastward to link up with Bolshevik forces near Tobolsk. The biggest concern that the party masters in the Kremlin have is that the Romanovs must not, I repeat, *must not,* fall into the hands of the enemy. Accordingly, the entire entourage must be eliminated before we evacuate." The men began to cheer at that point. *Sadistic bastards,* Morrison thought to himself with disgust.

Yurovsky shouted to the men to quiet down, and they promptly complied. "Sorry, Comrade Moryak," he said, motioning for him to continue. Morrison thanked him and continued.

"The plan is already designed, and there must be no deviations from it, do you understand? No deviations! Including Comrade Yurovsky and myself, I will need nine other shooters. I'll need two of you to stand guard at the doors. In addition, I need a driver who will drive with me to the site where we will dispose of the bodies."

"Where will we execute them, comrade?" asked one.

"We will bring them down to the middle room of the basement where the executions will take place."

"When will we do this?"

"Sometime tonight, probably after midnight. Comrade Yurovsky will awaken them and inform them that they will be moved to a safer location. We'll tell them that we will be having them wait in the basement room for cars to arrive." Immediately, the room began buzzing with comments from the guards, each claiming that he would be the one to execute the Tsar and laughing at his individual boast. After about thirty seconds of the banter, Morrison ordered them to be silent.

"Shut up!" he shouted. "Now listen up! This is the plan, and there will be no deviations at all, is that understood?" When there was nothing but silence in response, he shouted, "*Is that understood, you maggots?*" The sudden outburst both startled and scared them, and they all meekly replied affirmatively. "Good then, now keep your mouths shut and pay attention. I will be the one to execute both the Tsar and the Tsarevitch. Is that clear? I will be the sole executioner of these two. If any of you fire at them, I will kill you on the spot. If any of you doubt that, then you haven't been listening to all of the exploits of the legendary Moryak. Believe me, I will have no qualms whatsoever about firing a bullet into any of your disgusting faces. Is that understood?" Again, the assembled men nodded their heads. Yurovsky was smiling. He had to admit, Moryak certainly knew how to communicate a point.

"Good! I can see we're all going to work together just fine on this assignment. Next, it is Comrade Yurovksy, and only Comrade Yurovsky, who will execute the Tsarina. That instruction, I trust, is crystal clear. Now for the good news. There are nine other people left in the Romanov entourage. You each can pick who you want to kill. I don't give a damn whom you choose. Just work it out amongst yourselves and inform Comrade Yurovsky within the hour." Immediately the room buzzed with excitement as the men bantered over whom they wanted to execute. Morrison and Yurovsky smiled at each other as they headed for the door. Before departing, Morrison turned back toward the men who had quieted down.

"There is one more thing," he began. "None of you are to speak at all with any of the prisoners today. Not a word. If even a glimmer of the plan gets out, if any of the prisoners suspect what is going to happen to them tonight as a result of interacting with any of you, I will shoot every one of you myself! Make no mistake, I will kill every one of you and don't doubt me. I haven't killed anyone this week, and it's really starting to bother me." He and Yurovsky walked out the door.

"You certainly have a way with words, comrade," quipped Yurovsky.

"Yes, I do, don't I? You know, Moscow wanted me to grill the former Tsar one more time. Something about overseas accounts and money that he may have stashed all over the world. Have him brought to my room in about a half-hour."

"Certainly, comrade, with pleasure!"

***

Morrison sat on the edge of the sofa when the knock on the door occurred. Ordering him to enter, he stood as Nicholas Romanov entered the room. Morrison thanked the guard who had escorted him and dismissed him, locking the door behind him. He motioned for the former Tsar to be seated and pulled his chair up next to him.

"Listen carefully, Citizen Romanov. It is on for tonight. The White Army will be in Ekaterinburg within two days, and Moscow has ordered that we evacuate. We have been given instructions to execute all of you before we leave. I have met with my Allied contacts, and they have given me instructions. Let me start by saying that I'm sorry but we won't be able to get most of you out."

"What do you mean?" asked the startled Nicholas. "I thought, well, you said—"

"I know what I said. The situation here is untenable. I am the only agent on scene. If I wasn't here, all of you would be murdered tonight. As it turns out, I can probably get only one of you out alive, and that's being a bit optimistic. There are over twenty guards here, and one slightly suspicious move will result in my liquidation. Then all of you will die for sure. The Allied command has instructed me to attempt to get the Tsarevitch, your son Alexei, out. It is felt that there is a great value in spiriting the heir to the throne out of Bolshevik hands. It would be a great rallying point. I believe we can certainly attempt it."

Nicholas just stared at Morrison. He sat there expressionless, taking in what he had just been told, that he would die tonight. He began to tremble and his eyes glassed over, but he soon composed himself. "There isn't any other way? You're sure of it?"

"I'm afraid so. You realize what I'm saying to you, don't you?"

"Yes, yes, of course I do." After pondering a moment, Nicholas looked at Morrison and said, "It looks like you won't be able to work your magic like you did back in Japan some thirty years ago, will you?"

"No, I won't be able to, Nicholas Romanov."

Sitting upright in a most aristocratic manner, Nicholas asked, "So tell me, what is the plan? What is going to happen?"

Morrison stood up and began pacing the room as he spoke. "Sometime after midnight you will all be awakened and told to get dressed, that you are being moved to a safer location so that the White Army won't capture you and that the local Reds won't kill you. They will have you all assemble in one of the basement rooms and wait."

"And then?"

"An execution squad, led by me, will enter the room and the killing will begin."

"How is it possible to save even Alexei? Remember, I told you he can barely walk."

Returning to his seat, Morrison leaned forward toward the former Tsar and began explaining in a low voice. "I have assigned different executioners to different people. I am the only one with the authority to shoot both you and your son, no one else.

I promise you that your death will be clean and instantaneous. You will not suffer. When I shoot Alexei, it will be with a blank cartridge." Nicholas appeared to be confused, so Morrison continued on. "Once I shoot Alexei, it will be the signal for the rest of the guards to begin firing. It will be over quickly."

"I still don't understand. I mean, Alexei—"

"He will be virtually unconscious," interrupted Morrison. Pulling the vial of medicine from his pocket, he held it up and said, "About midnight, have him drink this. It's a sedative provided by my contact agent, and it will sedate him to the point of unconsciousness. He won't be aware of anything after that. You'll have to carry him down to the basement, and you must hold him in your lap close to you. Do you understand that? You must hold his head close to your chest. That is critical for the plan to work.

"When it is all over, I will personally carry him out. The rest of the guards will assume he's dead. When we transport all of your remains, I will be delivering Alexei to an Allied agent who will be waiting en route. I know this sounds cold as hell, but it is the best I can come up with under the circumstances and given the very short fuse."

With a forlorn look on his face, Nicholas asked, "Do you really think you can save my son? It sounds very tenuous."

"All I can say is that if I don't succeed, I will die trying. I will follow my orders to the letter, and my orders are to get your son out of the hands of the Bolsheviks." For the next few minutes, they said nothing. Morrison wanted to make sure that Nicholas had absorbed all of the information. It pleased him that the man seemed relatively calm, considering he had just heard his own death sentence.

Morrison considered the improbability of the entire situation. *Here I am, the son of a rabbi, forced out of Russia to the*

United States of America, who once participated in the rescue of the Tsar of Russia's life, and now thirty years later, after serving ten years in a Tsarist prison camp, I will once again attempt to rescue a member of the Romanov family. He was pondering the irony when Nicholas began to speak.

"You know, my wife and daughters, they brought a lot of their jewelry with them on our exile. They have sewn most of the diamonds and gems into their stays and corsets to keep them hidden. Do you think that this may protect them?"

It seemed like an absurd thought, considering the caliber of the assassins. Out of compassion, he offered, "That probably may help somewhat."

"Tell me sir, it there anything else we need to discuss?" asked Nicholas.

"I believe we have covered it all." Morrison handed the vial of sedative medicine to Nicholas and told him to be careful with it. "Remember, he must take it about midnight." As he stood up, he turned to Nicholas and said, "I implore you to keep what I've told you a secret, even from your wife. No one must know, as it will result in all of your immediate executions. If any of this plan leaks out, you will all die. Of course, I will be killed along with you. You have to act as calm and as normal as possible. Nothing must be leaked. I know that I'm almost asking the impossible, but you must try. If not, your son will die."

Nicholas looked up. Morrison noticed his eyes had glazed over again. "It's time for you to leave," Morrison informed him, walking to the door. As he did, Nicholas asked, "May I say something?"

"Of course."

Nicholas stood up and faced him. "I don't even know your name. I only know that you are an American and that you saved my life years ago. I want to thank you again for that. Thank you for what you are about to attempt to do. You are a brave and honorable man." He then made the sign of the cross and said, "May Jesus Christ protect you and Alexei tonight, and may He watch over you and protect you for the rest of your life."

26

The Kremlin
Moscow, Russia
11:00 P.M., July 16, 1918

No greater example of the inefficiencies of the centralized government functions of the Bolshevik regime could be found than the railroads. Goretsky had left Petrograd on the 7:00 P.M. train to Moscow. He and many others hadn't yet recovered from the stunning news of the death of Comrade Mozger. Goretsky remained especially affected, for he believed that he might well have been the last man to see Mozger alive. It was Zinoviev who had discovered his body slumped over his desk. Goretsky was deathly afraid that he would somehow be implicated in the comrade's death. He reasoned that the best way to conduct himself would be to carry out the assignment that Mozger had given to him. It had to be of the greatest importance.

МОЯУАК

Unfortunately, the transit took several hours more than usual. In addition to problems with track repairs, the scheduled delivery of coal to the Petrograd Station had been delayed. The train had to stop for a few hours at one of the intermediate stops and wait for more fuel to be delivered. He didn't arrive at the Kremlin until nearly 10:00 P.M. the following evening. After presenting his identification, he received permission to wait outside of Lenin's office in the Yellow Palace. Lenin was in a prolonged meeting with Stalin and had left instructions not to be interrupted under any circumstances. It wasn't until after 11:00 P.M. that Lenin finally emerged from his office. "What do you want at this hour?" he demanded.

"Comrade Lenin, I bring you a critical letter from Comrade Mozger. I have been instructed to hand-deliver it to you."

"What?" barked Lenin. "Mozger is dead! What are you talking about? I should have you killed!"

"Comrade, I didn't know that Comrade Mozger was dead until after I left Petrograd," fibbed Goretsky. Lenin absolutely terrified him, seeming to imply that somehow he had been involved with Mozger's death. "You were supposed to have received a telegraph from him explaining the purpose of my visit. Did you not get this?"

"I don't know, let me check. I've been extremely busy all day." Turning back into his office he saw a pile a letters and messages that he had not had the opportunity to address. Looking back at Goretsky, he asked, "What is it you have for me?" Goretsky handed the letter from Mozger to him. Lenin thanked him and ordered him to leave. Walking back into his office, he sat behind his desk as Stalin puffed silently on his pipe. Rapidly sorting through the stack on his desk, Lenin finally found the telegram from Mozger and ripped open the envelope. He read the short telegram and gasped. With a stunned expression, he looked up at Stalin and handed it to him. As Stalin read the telegram, Lenin next read Mozger's letter. He held the two photographs in his hand and stared at them, shaking his head from side to side. He then handed the letter and the photographs to Stalin.

After Stalin read the letter, he looked at Lenin and said, "You know what needs to be done. Comrade, you'd better act quickly. Moryak may well be up to something tonight."

"You are exactly right," Lenin replied. He sat at his desk and began writing out a telegram. He addressed it to Filipp Goloshcheckin and kept it short and direct. It read:

COMRADE MORYAK GUILTY OF TREASON STOP ARREST IMMEDIATELY STOP PREFER HIM ALIVE AND SENT BACK TO MOSCOW TO STAND TRIAL STOP MAY BE PLANNING RESCUE OF ROMANOVS STOP DO NOT LET HIM ESCAPE STOP LENIN

Lenin called for an aide and instructed him to send the telegram to Ekaterinburg immediately. He turned to Stalin, who calmly continued to puff on his pipe. He seemed to almost be talking to himself as he said over and over, "How can this be? How can this be?" Stalin noted that beads of sweat had developed on Lenin's forehead. *Your days are numbered, comrade,* he thought to himself. *You are weak. Bolsheviks never sweat! Don't you know that?*

27

Ipatiev House
Ekaterinburg, Russia
2:00 A.M., July 17, 1918

Stephen Morrison sat motionless, absorbed in thought while Yakov Yurovsky sat nearby, blowing smoke rings as he exhaled his cigarette smoke. Morrison looked at the small clock on the desk in the second floor room of the Ipatiev House. He and Yurovsky had gone over the plan several times after the two of them returned to the room over an hour before. They both felt confident that their men understood their assignments and would follow their instructions to the letter. Finally, Morrison spoke. "It's time," he said softly.

Yurovsky stood up and said, "We'll meet you outside the cellar door in about forty-five minutes."

"Just keep the men in line and quiet. We'll get this thing over with." As Yurovsky left the room, he smiled and said, "Don't worry, Comrade Moryak, all will go as planned."

Lee Mandel

Once Yurovsky had left, Morrison pulled the Nagant M1895 pistol out from his belt. From his coat pocket, he removed the cartridges that Slaughter had provided to him. He carefully laid out two live rounds and five blanks. As he loaded the seven bullets into the chambers, he was careful to align them so that the first round he would fire would be a live 7.62 round, followed by five blank rounds. The last of his seven rounds would be a live round, just in case he needed it. Satisfied that his weapon was prepared, he sat back and stared at the clock. Just over forty minutes to go. With any luck, he would be with Homer Slaughter later that morning and begin his journey back to the United States.

Yurovsky opened the door to the Tsar's bedroom. The light from the hallway cut into the darkness. Nicholas Romanov lay there awake, only pretending to be asleep. "What is it? What do you want?" he asked.

"Citizen Romanov, you and your family must get up and get dressed. You will be in danger if you remain here. We will be transporting you to safety. You must hurry!"

"Where will we be going?" asked the Tsarina.

"You will be told when you are all assembled downstairs. Now hurry!" Noting that the Tsarevitch wasn't even stirring, he angrily said, "Awaken your son and get him moving!" He stomped out of the room to begin awakening the rest of the family and entourage. One by one, each person was awakened and ordered to quickly get dressed. After about a half-hour, all eleven prisoners had assembled in the hallway. Nicholas stood holding his son in his arms. The boy appeared to be in a deep sleep. "Everyone, follow me!" ordered Yurovsky. Walking slowly, he led them down the stairway on the east side of the house to the basement room. They cut through the lower floor until they entered the small basement room in the center of the west side of the house. "Wait in here," he ordered.

The barren room contained no furniture and they stood near the back wall, facing the door that led to the side yard. Staring around at the green and white striped wallpaper, the Tsarina began to complain before Yurovsky left the room. "What, no chairs?" she said angrily. "We need to sit! My baby is not well."

Yurovsky left the room and walked to the team that had assembled outside. "Where's Moryak?" he asked. No one seemed to know. "Well, get two chairs for them in there. One for Nicholas and the other for his damn wife so she will shut up." After a few minutes, one of the men returned with two wooden chairs. He carried them into the room where the prisoners had assembled.

He remembered the diagram that Moryak had drawn for them, indicating where he wanted the Tsar and his wife to be. He placed the chairs in the front row of the prisoners, directly in the center. Pointing at Nicholas and Alexandria, he indicated, "These chairs are for you. Sit down." Nicholas sat in the chair on the right, cradling his son in his lap. Next to him sat Alexandria. She wondered, *How can he sleep so soundly through this?* Then the waiting began. They had been told that trucks would be coming for them to take them to Tobolsk. Alexandria looked over at Nicholas and saw that his forehead was wet with perspiration.

Nicholas hoped he appeared calm enough. He tried not to look at his wife, fearing that his expression might betray him and reveal the disaster that very soon would engulf them. It would end here, in the basement of a stranger's house, as a prisoner of Bolshevik rabble. It was nearly impossible for him to comprehend that his life would end this way. Yet, to add to the incredulity, this man had appeared, the same man who had rescued him thirty years ago. Who he was, and why he was attempting to rescue Alexei was also beyond comprehension.

Nicholas could only pray to God for a merciful death and that He would look over Alexei and spare his life. Oh, how the thought of his son ate at his soul! The boy was born to be emperor of all Russia and instead was now a cripple as a result of an inherited disease. Now he held his beloved son as if he was still a baby and gently kissed his forehead. As he did, he felt a tear tickle down his cheek. *Courage*, he thought to himself. *It will all be over soon. Soon we all will sleep, and the nightmare will be over.* He began to rock ever so slightly. As he did, he felt his beloved wife rub his arm. The minutes seemed to go on forever as they waited.

The rest of the entourage stood behind them and Nicholas could sense a growing restlessness developing amongst them. *Why are we not leaving? Why had they awakened us for this in the middle of the night?* No one spoke. The room remained deathly quiet.

After what seemed to be an eternity, the door to the outside opened and eleven of the guards entered the room and spread out along the entrance wall in two rows. The guards had been led into the room by the new commander, the cruel-looking one they called Moryak. Next to him stood the old commander Yurovsky, who had a piece of paper in his hand. As soon as each of the men got into their assigned position, one of the guards closed the door and locked it. Nicholas held his son close to him against his chest. At that point, Yurovsky started reading from his paper.

"Nicholas Romanov, you and your family have been charged with crimes against the Russian people and for attempting to communicate with outside forces for the sole purpose of attempting escape. Accordingly, it is the decision of the people of the Ekaterinburg Soviet that you and your family are to be executed immediately!"

Since they had entered the room, Nicholas' eyes had been locked with Morrison's in an almost understanding way. When

Yurovsky finished speaking, Nicholas turned to Yurovsky and blurted out, "What? *What?*"

Yurovsky repeated the death sentence, and when he did, Morrison walked to within two feet of Nicholas and pulled his revolver out, pointed it at the center of his forehead and fired. The impact of the bullet entering his skull and shattering it threw Nicholas over backward, still clutching his son close to him as all of the women began to scream. Morrison took another step forward, aimed his pistol at the Tsarevevitch, and fired twice in rapid succession before stepping back and turning to the other executioners. This was their signal. He stepped back and they all began to open fire at their respective targets.

The fusillade lasted about thirty seconds. The room immediately filled with smoke from the gunpowder, and the screams continued. Morrison could feel ricocheting bullets whizzing by as the assassins continued their firing. After what seemed like an eternity, the screams stopped and it appeared that the task had been completed.

"Cease fire!" ordered Morrison. The firing continued, and he bellowed out, "*Cease fire, now!*" The other assassins looked over at him through the misty smoke, awaiting further instructions. They then heard moaning coming from the young daughters, and the men looked up as Moryak for guidance. "You can finish them off," he said, wondering if the bullets had ricocheted off of the diamond-encrusted corsets that the former Tsar had mentioned. The men clubbed the girls' heads with the butts of their rifles and, for good measure, fired a bullet into each of their heads.

As they began to approach the girls, Morrison had placed his pistol in his belt and walked over to Nicholas, who lay face up. The smoke made it difficult to see and stung his eyes. "Open the damn door and vent this room!" he yelled as the guards murdered the girls. Nicholas lay motionless, his eyes wide open. The starburst entry wound of the bullet in his forehead had splattered blood over his face, and he still had Alexei over him, clutched to his chest by his lifeless arms. Morrison leaned over and lifted the motionless boy up over his shoulders. "Okay now," he ordered, "everyone grab a body and let's get them loaded into the truck." As each of the executioners began to lift a body, he complimented them. "Well done men, well done."

He could see the look of satisfaction in their faces. Not only had they gotten to kill the Romanovs, but the famous Moryak had complimented them on their work. As he walked from the room with Alexei on his shoulder, he noted that the boy still remained unconscious from the sedative, but he could detect shallow breathing. Exiting the basement room into the warm summer air, he noted that the full moon illuminated the sky brightly, despite the late hour.

The open-bed truck, driven by one of the guards named Lytenko pulled up to the side of the Ipatiev House. Morrison nodded over to the line of men that had formed, each carrying a bloody body on their shoulder and they began to walk up to the rear end of the truck. One by one, they tossed the dead bodies of the Romanov entourage onto the truck bed. The space had been lined with bed sheets that rapidly turned red from the blood exiting the many gunshot wounds. In the bright moonlight, it could all be seen very easily. One of the guards stood in the truck bed, helping to arrange the bodies, when Moryak walked up with the last body, that of the Tsarevitch Alexei. "I'll take care of this one, comrade," he said as he gently placed the boy's seemingly lifeless body in the very back of the truck bed. The other guard then jumped out and they closed the tailgate of the truck. As he walked around to the front of the truck, he saw that Yurovsky had mustered the execution squad over by the door to the basement. He motioned for him to come over to the truck.

"Comrade Yurovsky, please convey my compliments to the men for a job well done." Looking up at the bright moon, he announced, "The hour grows late. Dismiss the men. Lytenko and I will deliver the bodies as planned." He stepped up into the passenger seat of the truck cabin as Lytenko started the engine. "Well done to you, Comrade Yurovsky! I'll see you in the morning."

"Thank you, Comrade Moryak!" Yurovsky slammed the truck door shut, and the truck began to pull away. *That Moryak, he thought to himself. What an efficient, cold-hearted bastard. His reputation is well-deserved!* As he watched the truck drive down to the main street, he noticed that Lytenko had turned in the wrong direction. *Oh well, Lytenko always has been an imbecile. Moryak would straighten him out.* He then yawned, stretched, and headed around to the front of the building. He needed some sleep. It did not please him to see one of the Bolsheviks from the soviet running down the street toward him yelling, "Comrade Yurovsky! Comrade Yurovsky!"

Yurovsky stopped and waited as the man approached. *Now what the hell can he want at this hour?* Finally, the man was at his side, out of breath from running. "Well," demanded Yurovsky, "What is it that you want at this hour? Couldn't it have waited until later?"

Still gasping for breath, the man finally said, "No, comrade, it can't wait!" Reaching into his pocket, he produced a folded telegraph message and handed it to Yurovsky. "It's urgent that you read this. It's from Moscow, from Lenin himself! Comrade Goloshcheckin ordered me to deliver it to you personally!"

The puzzled Yurovosky opened the message and rapidly read its contents. His breath seemed to be taken away by what he read. "It can't be!" he exclaimed out loud. "This is unbelievable!" Looking at the messenger, he ordered, "Come with me, quickly!" The two men ran into the Ipatiev House, and Yurovsky began to shout, "Everyone down! Everyone get down here, now!" The startled guards, who had been drinking in the kitchen, rapidly assembled before Yurovsky, who appeared livid and quite agitated. "You!" he ordered, pointing to the nearest man. "Go out back and get the car, now! Bring it around to the front." He pointed to two others and demanded, "Get your rifles and meet me in front at the car immediately. Move, *now!*" he screamed. That bastard Moryak! So that's why the car turned the wrong way! I should have known that something was up!

***

As they headed up the uneven dirt road, Morrison estimated that they should be at the safe house in about fifteen minutes. The plan seemed to be working, almost better than he had dared to hope. He actually now started to believe that before too long, he would be back in the United States. Neither of them spoke as the truck prodded along, the two headlights piercing the moonlit darkness in front of them. Finally Litenko spoke. "How did it feel, Comrade Moryak?"

"How did what feel?"

"How did it feel to kill the criminal Nicholas Romanov? You must feel quite honored to have done so!"

Morrison pictured the final look in Nicholas' eyes as he pulled the trigger. "How did it feel? It felt about the same way it will feel to me when I kill you." Litenko's head rapidly turned toward him with a look of terror on his face. "Just kidding, comrade, just kidding. Keep your eyes on the road." He heard the younger man exhale a sigh of relief as he concentrated on the road. *Too bad I'm not kidding,* Morrison thought. *I will be killing you in several minutes. Hopefully you'll be the last man I will ever have to kill.* The somber truth depressed him at that point. He had survived all these years because he had, in fact, become a killer. A cold-hearted killer who killed and then slept like a baby.

"You know, comrade," said Litenko, "you shouldn't kid like that, because—" A sudden explosion shattered the rear windshield and a bullet entered the back of Litenko's head, smashing it against the windshield. The sudden, violent action momentarily stunned Morrison as the skull and brain fragments splattered all over him, the seat, and the windshield. Litenko had been thrown against the steering wheel, dead on impact. Morrison turned around and he could see two headlights behind them, several hundred yards back. He saw a muzzle flash come from the pursuing vehicle as another bullet whizzed by his head and shattered the front windshield. The truck began to swerve to the left and Morrison tried to grab the steering wheel to control it. Litenko's lifeless body, pinned against the wheel, made steering impossible. *Shit! How did they know? How did they find out?* About a half-mile ahead, illuminated by the bright moonlight, he could see a small cabin up ahead. He could just make out a small red glow in the front window. *God, we are close! So close!* The truck swerved over to the left, careened into a small creek, and quickly lodged in the muddy water, with the front of the truck angled down into the creek bed.

We've got to get out of here, he thought. *We're so close.* Looking back, he could see the headlights in the distance still approaching as the gunshots continued, with bullets raising small sprays of water from the creek. Morrison jumped out of the truck and ran around to the back. Unlatching the ramp, he quickly saw Alexei lying there. The child groaned and began to stir. They only had one chance. Morrison looked over to the cabin. He could see no trees or shrubs. They had to try and make it to the cabin through the open field ahead. He lifted the semiconscious boy up and threw him over his shoulder. Climbing out of the creek, he began to run toward the cabin through the thigh-high grass.

The boy weighed about one-hundred-twenty pounds and running with him on his shoulder proved to be difficult. As he ran in the open field, Morrison could hear the other car getting closer and gunshots continued to whiz around them. Alexei now groaned louder as Morrison tried to run as fast as he could. He could see the cabin getting closer. They had to make it. Every step seemed an effort with the boy on his shoulder. *Keep going,* he told himself. *You'll be home soon! You're going back to America!* Suddenly, he felt as if a club had been smashed against the back of his right leg as he heard the last rifle shot. He collapsed in agony. The tall grass momentarily provided cover for them as their pursuers continued to approach.

In the cabin, Homer Slaughter heard what sounded like distant gunshots and ran outside of the cabin. Holding his high-powered binoculars to his eyes, he could make out the headlights of the two cars. The second car appeared to be getting closer to the first, which appeared to be stuck in the creek. *Christ Almighty,* he thought. *How did this happen? I am definitely not prepared for this!* He had no backup at the cabin, just him, and his only weapon was his Colt 1911 semi-automatic pistol. He got a sick feeling in his stomach as he scanned the field in front of the car for any sign of Morrison. The bright moonlight made it easy to spot the figure of what appeared to be Morrison

МОЯҐАК

with the boy on his shoulder, running from the creek toward the cabin. After one rifle burst, they collapsed in the tall grass. "Come on, Commander!" he said out loud, "Get up! Get up!"

Morrison knew he had been hit. *Got to keep going*, he said to himself. He attempted to get up, but he knew instinctively that his thighbone had been shattered by the bullet. He couldn't stand. He reached down to his right thigh and felt a pulpy mass of splinted bone, torn muscles, and flesh. Blood gushed from his gaping thigh wound. He unbuckled his belt, removed it, and wrapped it around his thigh proximal to the gunshot wound in an effort to control the bleeding. He would not make it; of this much he was certain. But the boy—Alexei! He lay on the ground next to him, moaning. Morrison reached over, grabbed his arm, and began shaking him. Finally, he slapped him across the face, and the boy's eyes flew open. "Alexei, listen to me. Wake up!" Another bullet hit the ground right next to them, further startling the boy. "Listen to me! Get up! You need to make it to that cabin!" he implored, pointing to the red light in the distance. Slowly, the confused Tsarevitch struggled to get to his feet. Morrison could see that the boy couldn't straighten his left knee. As he prodded the young boy, Morrison could feel himself becoming light-headed "Over there!" he pointed. "Go now!"

The boy started to stumble in the direction of the cabin. "Run, Alexei, *run!*" screamed Morrison. His face now drenched in sweat, he fell backward onto the grass. He looked straight up to the perfectly clear, starlit sky. His breathing had become rapid and shallow. His mind drifted back to a time when he was nine years old, back in Russia, and he and his father had sat in the back of their little shack of a house, pointing up at stars. "The stars are the lights that point the way to God's kingdom," his father had told him that night. He also reflected on those nights in Perm when he and his friend Yuri Kodarov sat and talked in the night, looking at the beautiful starlit Russian nights. Now, here he lay, once again staring at the Russian skies. *Born in Russia, only to die in Russia,* he thought. *My mission is now over.* He only prayed that the boy would make it to the cabin.

Then all went dark.

28

*Lubyanka Prison
Moscow, Russia
September 1, 1918*

As the car approached Lubyanka Square, Joseph Stalin reflected on the events of the past several days and smiled, feeling quite pleased. Circumstances had completely changed, and now his star had begun its ascent. He felt events couldn't possibly be going any better. It all began two days before, when Lenin gave a speech in Moscow to a group of factory workers. After he finished and the crowd swarmed around him, several loud *pops* were heard and screaming began. A Social Revolutionary, a woman, had shot Vladimir Lenin three times.

Lenin refused to be taken to a hospital and instead insisted that he be taken to the Kremlin. After visiting him, Stalin learned that the doctors felt that he would survive. It would be a while before he convalesced adequately, so Stalin began to make his moves. He already had a plan. While he would promote the cult of Lenin, he himself would be maneuvering for more power and neutralizing his rivals. Yes, the star of Stalin was beginning to ascend! One of his first actions had been to order the immediate arrest of all of the members of the Lockhart conspiracy. *Little did those fools realize that we had infiltrated them from the start!* Almost simultaneously, all of the plotters were arrested, with one exception: Sidney Reilly.

Reilly had been tipped off and had escaped before the Cheka arrived to arrest him. His escape infuriated Stalin. He wanted that "boastful British bastard" badly and he remained determined to capture him. He knew exactly who would betray Reilly to him; that was the purpose of his visit to Lubyanka Prison that morning.

Moryak had been captured by Yurovsky and his men the night that the Romanovs were murdered. They found him unconscious in the grass field, his leg shattered by a bullet. He had lost much blood and was taken to a nearby hospital. He had remained in a coma for over two weeks. No attempt had been made to treat his shattered right leg, only to control the bleeding. When he was finally deemed well enough to travel, Lenin had ordered that he be returned to Moscow. The Tsarevitch Alexei was found about halfway in between Moryak and an abandoned cabin that he appeared to be attempting to reach. Yurovsky's riflemen had aimed well. A bullet had entered his back and pierced his heart, killing him instantly.

Initially, Morrison had been brought to the hospital in Moscow where the ruling Bolsheviks received their medical care. It was Lenin's intention to have him recover his health enough for him to stand trial in a public forum. It would send a strong message to the people. If the Bolsheviks could uncover treason in a national hero like Moryak and then publically try him, humiliate him, and execute him, this action would only enhance the adamant and ruthless image of the new rulers. Lenin's near-assassination changed the picture.

It was Stalin who ordered that Moryak be brought to Lubyanka that day and be interrogated for information. There were three things that Stalin needed to know. He had to find out where Reilly was and capture him. He needed to know what other Allied agents remained in Moscow and may have been involved with the Lockhart conspiracy. Stalin had to learn one other thing: who the man known as Moryak really was and whether he working for the British or the Americans.

Felix Dzerzhinsky waited for Stalin at the entrance to the Cheka headquarters. After their greetings to one another, Stalin asked, "How is the interrogation going? Have we learned what we need to know yet?"

Dzerzhinsky took him by the arm and said, "Come, Comrade Stalin, let's go downstairs to the basement and find out what has been learned. I haven't been down there since Moryak was brought in last night." Both men entered the stairwell and descended into the notorious torture chambers of the Lubyanka Prison. "He's in the last interrogation room," indicated Dzerzhinsky, pointing to room number six. He opened the door for Stalin and the two men entered.

Even Stalin, a sadistic thug by nature, gasped at what he saw when he entered. In the center of the room, Moryak sat tied to a wooden chair, naked except for bloody bandages around his right thigh. His jaw appeared to be broken, and his face was swollen black and blue. Both of his eyes had swelled shut, leaving only narrow slits. His nose had obviously been broken. Multiple cuts, gashes, and lacerations all over his face gave testimony to the beating he had received over the past several hours. Fresh cigarette burns covered his chest and arms, filling the room with the odor of burning flesh. His head slumped forward and he seemed barely awake.

On one side of Moryak stood the interrogator, an owlish man named Trepolov. On the other side stood a very muscular, bare-chested man who had been administering the torture. He wore leather working gloves and had a fresh cigarette dangling from his lips. Stalin could see many scattered cigarette butts on the floor around Moryak's feet. Dzerzhinsky looked at Trepolov and barked, "Well, Comrade Trepolov, what have we learned?"

"This one doesn't talk much," he said, pointing his thumb at Moryak. "In fact, he doesn't talk at all, no matter what we do to him. And you can see, my friend here has been beating the living shit out of him and torturing him continually." He nodded over to the torturer who removed the cigarette from his lips and held it against Morrison's chest, producing a fresh burn. Morrison seemed to wince slightly.

"He hasn't said anything?" Stalin asked incredulously.

"Well, at first he would hum and sing something in English. I am fluent in English, Comrade Stalin. Now he's fading and is barely arousable."

"What was he singing?" asked Dzerzhinsky.

"He doesn't make a whole lot of sense. Something about him being a yankee dandy, whatever that is!"

"Hmm," thought Stalin, "a yankee. Could he be an American?"

"Who can say, comrade?" Trepolov laughed. "One thing we did learn is that he is Jew, most likely."

"What? How do you know that if he hasn't spoken?"

"Look what's hanging between his legs. He's been circumcised!"

"I'll be damned," replied Stalin. Walking up to Moryak, he leaned over and looked at his face closely. "We're wasting time here, Moryak. There is information that I want from you right now. Where is that bastard Reilly? Who else is involved with you here in Moscow? Who are you really, Moryak, and who are you working for, the British or the Americans?" He put his hand on Morrison's shoulder and shook it gently. Morrison lifted his head slightly and said nothing. After about a minute, Stalin stood and motioned over to the bare-chested muscular man and nodded toward Moryak as he stepped back.

The torturer stood directly in front of Morrison and delivered a crushing blow to the right side of his head. Everything suddenly went white to Morrison. He now could see only a bright white field. He could make out the form of someone emerging from that field, walking toward him. As the figure approached him, it seemed to be saying something. The figure got closer and he could see that this stranger wore a frock coat and wide-brimmed hat.

Suddenly, his father, Rabbi Zvi Kambotchnik, stood directly in front of him with his arms folded. He had that disgusted look on his face, a look that Morrison hadn't seen in over thirty-five years. Finally, the rabbi spoke. "Lev, you will always be the biggest disappointment of my life!" The rabbi seemed to slowly vaporize into a mist as Morrison attempted to speak to him, but no words formed in his mouth. Finally, the rabbi disappeared. His senses seemed to be returning.

The torturer then smashed his iron-like fist directly into Morrison's face again stunning him, and all went white again. Morrison could see someone walking up to him in the brightness. He appeared to be a well-dressed man of means. As he came closer, Morrison recognized him; it was his father-in-law, Oscar Leavitt. Leavitt stopped in front of him and smiled. In his right hand, he held a champagne flute. He raised it into the air as if to toast his son-in-law. "After all, Stephen," he said with a beaming smile, "you are a man of honor. And if we have honor, we can live and die with dignity!" He downed the champagne, smiled at Morrison, and threw the glass off into the distance. Morrison tried to smile, but his face, now a mass of broken bone and torn flesh would not permit the smile to form. Like Morrison's father before him, Oscar Leavitt began to fade into a vaporized mist and then disappeared altogether.

The torturer then smashed his right fist into the left side of Morrison's head with such a vicious impact that it knocked him and the chair completely over on his side. As Trepolov and his aide placed the chair back upright, once again a strange whiteness enveloped Morrison. Again, a figure seemed to be approaching from the distance. As he came closer, Morrison could see that the man was wearing a tuxedo. Finally, he recognized Sidney Reilly, who stopped in front of him and leaned forward until he was directly in Morrison's face. "Well, congratulations, Double Eagle," he sneered. "I once told you that we were both striving for something in this life. Well, you've finally earned it, everything that you've been hoping for all along. Respect, friendship, and admiration." Reilly stood up for a moment and as if to gather his thoughts. "Oh, you stupid fool!" he continued, again placing his face inches from Morrison's face. "Did you really think that serving your country honorably as a naval officer would earn you these things? No matter what you did, to them you would always be that rabbi's boy, that Jew from Russia! You've now come full circle and you're back in stinking Russia where you came from. No, Double Eagle, you got your acceptance and earned what you craved by becoming a killing machine. You've become a brutal, emotionless killer in a sick and chaotic world. Congratulations once again." Reilly stood up and smiled. Morrison could feel the fury and the anger well up inside of him as the image of Sidney Reilly vaporized.

Stalin came up and pushed the torturer out of the way. Moryak's silence both frustrated and angered him. Leaning over him, his began to speak. "Listen to me, Moryak, the end is near. You can't endure much more of this. You are dying. If you can still hear me, you know that what I am saying is true. We can end this pointless nonsense. All you have to do is to tell me what I want to know. It's that simple! Once you do, I swear we will take you to the hospital for medical treatment. After all, we will need to get you back into a good state of health so you can stand trial. So let's be reasonable and end this senseless violence. Make your choice, Moryak, make your choice. Now, tell me. Where is Reilly? Who else is involved with you? Who are you working for, the British or the Americans?" After nearly a minute when Morrison failed to respond, Stalin grabbed his shoulder and roughly shook it. "Goddamn you!" he shouted. "Tell me what I want to know!"

Morrison's head lifted slightly. They all noticed his swollen, lacerated lips trembling, as he appeared to at last be attempting to speak. "That's good, Moryak, that's excellent!" said Stalin. Leaning to place his face only inches from Morrison's, in a soft voice Stalin again ordered him, "Tell me what I want to know." As he ordered this, the other three in the room gathered around Stalin, also inches from Morrison's face.

Morrison's lips continued to tremble as if trying to form words. He could no longer see, and all seemed to be fading around him. The whiteness now began to return. It was over. His mission was about to end. He was dying, and he knew it.

He suddenly spoke three words in flawless English: "Go fuck yourself!"

Stalin stood up with a puzzled look on his face. He did not speak English and had no idea what Moryak had just said. He looked over at Trepolov, who seemed embarrassed, and ordered him to translate for him. With reluctance, Trepolov complied with Stalin's demand.

Stalin's complexion reddened with anger. He shot a look of fury at the other three in the room. Dzerzhinksy could not remember when he had last seen Comrade Stalin so livid. Stalin turned around, walked rapidly to the door, and opened it. As the others watched him, he pulled the door shut behind him, but suddenly he stopped and stuck his head back into the room. He then spoke two words: "Kill him!"

EPILOGUE

Arlington National Cemetery
November 11, 1950

Jerry Thurmond, ace reporter for the *Washington Herald*, fidgeted in his seat as President Harry S. Truman continued delivering his Veteran's Day speech. This annual ceremony at the Memorial Amphitheater had taken on a special significance, considering the ongoing combat actions in Korea. For the first time, armies now fought under the flag of the United Nations. Truman had referred to the conflict as a "police action" in which United States armed forces played the crucial role in combating communist aggression. Thurmond continued to jot notes as the president spoke.

Thurmond was known around Washington, D.C. as a man who had a 'nose for news'. His special talent was coverage of presidential events, and he always seemed to have an insider's perspective of White House events. His success had less to do with a nose for news than it did with the fact that his college roommate, Peter Geiseiker, worked in the White House appointment scheduling office. Whenever an interesting event found its way onto the president's schedule, Geiseiker was sure to alert his ex-college roomie and current drinking buddy Jerry Thurmond. The price for the hot tips was that Thurmond had to buy the drinks.

Earlier in the week, Geiseiker had called Thurmond, who was just leaving the newsroom, with another one of his famous "I didn't tell you this, but—" tips. They met that night at Lloyd's, their favorite watering hole in Georgetown. Sitting at a small table, Geiseiker handed over a scrap of paper to his friend. Thurmond read it, looked up, and asked, "What the hell does this mean, pardner?"

"I'm not sure. All I know is that this guy, a naval officer named Lieutenant Commander Logan had an appointment with the president last month. It was an add-on job, and I had to cancel some other pretty important appointments to accommodate this guy. The orders came right from the Chief of Staff."

"What was the meeting about?"

"Seems like some papers turned up at the White House. The Chief of Staff did mention that they belonged to President Roosevelt, and this Logan guy wanted to personally brief the president about them."

"Wait a minute," protested Thurmond. "Truman is living over at Blair House. The White House is undergoing a major renovation. How the hell can papers just turn up like that?"

"Apparently they were in a strong box that was hidden in an alcove behind some of the cabinetry in Roosevelt's old study. Next thing I know is that I'm ordered to add this appointment on to President Truman's schedule, to take place right after the press conference at Arlington National Cemetery on Veteran's Day. As you can see, there will only be two other people there with him." Thurmond looked again at the paper and read: *Stone replacement graveside ceremony following speech and press conference: SECNAV and LCDR Logan in attendance.*

"SECNAV? Secretary of the Navy Francis P. Matthews? Wow! Hey Pete, who the hell is the other guy?"

"I checked him out through my sources at the White House. This guy, Logan, is Naval Intelligence's liaison officer to the CIA. That's all I was able to find out."

"The president, the secretary of the navy, and a CIA spook," said Thurmond as he lifted his glass. "What do you think this meeting is all about, my friend?"

"Jerry, I have no idea. There is the word out that this conference is absolutely not a meeting for public consumption. The president is adamant about it. No press, no publicity. He wants this ceremony, whatever the hell it is, to be private, and he doesn't want it interrupted or degraded for any reason. And so, my esteemed ex-roomie, I implore you not to get too close when you observe the goings-on and to be discrete. The job and the ass you save just may be mine, old friend."

"Buy me another round, and my discretion is guaranteed!"

Thurmond shivered slightly as he wrote in his notepad. Although quite cold, the sky remained cloudless, and the air had an autumn crispness signaling that winter's arrival would be just around the corner. He had to remove his gloves to write his notes. After listening to Truman speak for about twenty minutes, he could tell that the president's speech would be ending shortly.

Turning to the last page of his speech, Truman continued "... and so, on this most important of days, a day when we honor the men who have worn the uniform of the United States armed forces, we acknowledge that our young men are once again in harm's way. This, less than five years' time after the most horrific war the world has ever known. We can never repay our debt to the men in uniform, but to them I offer this: to all who have worn the uniform of the United States armed forces, past and present—we salute you! To all who have worn the uniform of the United States armed forces, past and present—we thank you! Finally, to all who have worn the uniform of the United States armed forces—God bless you! And God bless the United States of America!" As the president finished, thunderous applause erupted from the audience in the form of a standing ovation. Truman beamed as he waved to the crowd. After a few minutes, the other members of the press headed toward the conference room of the Memorial Amphitheater for Truman's press conference. *My cue to exit,* thought Thurmond.

The day before, he had visited the offices at the entrance to the Visitor's Center at the cemetery. Never averse to slipping twenty-dollar bills to people who could supply him with information, he soon found a willing recipient for his money. He learned that the private ceremony was being held fairly close to the chest by the White House staff. All that his informant was able to tell him was that the private ceremony would be held in an older part of Section 60. He didn't know whose headstone it was or why it needed to be replaced. He only knew that Section 60 would be closed to the public right after the president's press conference began. With that tip, Thurmond decided to walk toward the road that bordered the northern edge of Section 60 when the president ended his speech.

As he approached the northwest corner of Section 60, he saw a small flatbed truck moving onto the road and turning toward him. He waved for the truck to stop and walked toward the driver as he reached into his pocket. The driver rolled down the window and asked, "What's the problem, Mac?"

"Nothing, nothing's the problem. Say friend," asked Thurmond as he reached to shake the driver's hand with a twenty-dollar bill in his palm, "did you just come from that gravesite where they're switching the headstone?"

Looking at the money in his hand, the driver smiled and responded, "Yep, we sure did. Got the old headstone in the back."

"Tell me, what's so special about this headstone that it needs to be switched? Mind if I take a look at it?"

"Look, Mac, that I can't do. Besides, the stone is face down and already wrapped up. It's the same name on both stones. Looks like they got his rank wrong or something." Motioning back over his shoulder with his thumb, he continued. "Hell, you can see the back of the new stone from here, toward the back of the section. All the other headstones in the section are slightly faded with age. The new one is a little brighter. Can't miss it."

"Thanks for the tip," offered Thurmond, as he handed the man another twenty-dollar bill.

"Thank you, Mac. You see all the people headed toward us? Those are Secret Service guys. The section's about to be cordoned off, so enjoy the view of the ceremony because this is about as close as you're gonna get."

***

Thurmond wandered around the graves in the section just north of Section 60, along with other tourists and visitors. He knew that the press conference was scheduled to last about a half-hour. He had also anticipated that he wouldn't be able to get close to the ceremony, so he had come prepared. Around his neck hung a pair of high-powered binoculars. Right on schedule, he noticed a small entourage of Secret Service approaching with President Truman and his guests. Turning south toward the far end of Section 60, the Secret Service agents took their positions in various pre-designated places. Finally, the president and his two guests reached their destination, a gravesite that had what appeared to be a new headstone, judging by its brighter appearance as compared to the surrounding headstones.

Through his binoculars, Thurmond could see the bright white back of the new headstone. The president faced the front of the headstone, and in so doing, he also faced Thurmond. On his right, he recognized the Secretary of the Navy, Francis P. Matthews. On his left stood a naval officer, wearing service dress blues and a bridge coat. *Must be that guy Logan,* thought Thurmond to himself. The president appeared to be speaking as the other two men stood in a parade-rest posture. The president continued to talk for about four more minutes.

Suddenly, all three of them snapped to attention as Secretary Matthews handed a folder to Truman. Truman opened it and began reading, while Thurmond tried unsuccessfully to lip-read. When Truman finished reading, the lieutenant commander reached into his pocket and handed the president a small box. Opening it, the president removed what looked like a ribbon and placed it around the top shoulders of the headstone. With amazement, Thurmond watched as the three men stood at rigid attention and then saluted the headstone. They held their salute for nearly a minute. As Thurmond scanned their faces, he noted that tears had formed in President Harry Truman's eyes. Tears also streamed down the face of the lieutenant commander.

***

MORYAK

Thurmond waited for the presidential entourage to leave and then slowly approached Section 60. He remained intensely curious to find out who had been honored by the ceremony that he had just witnessed. Pretty damn impressive, he thought, to get the president of the United States to a private ceremony. He must have been some important warrior from years past!

Thurmond's heart raced a bit as he approached the gravesite from the north. The new white stone did stand out from the other more aged stones. Time and the elements would soon take care of that. Finally, he reached the row where the ceremony had been and headed right, toward the new headstone. After a few seconds, he arrived and stood in front of the gravesite where the president had stood only twenty minutes ago.

The plain headstone arose from the ground in front of him, identical to the others that surrounded it in Section 60. Below a Star of David was inscribed:

Stephen
Lee
Morrison
LCDR
U.S. Navy
Allied Expeditionary Force, Russia
JUN 15, 1870
SEPT 1, 1918

A blue and white ribbon nestled around the shoulders of the headstone. Suspended from the ribbon hung a Navy Cross, the nation's second highest award for combat valor.

"Christ Almighty," blurted out Thurmond, "a Navy Cross!" He walked over and held the medal in his hand. As a veteran of the U.S. Army, he knew what one had to do to earn that award, and it impressed him greatly. He stepped back a few feet and stood facing the grave that only a short time before President Truman and Secretary Matthews had faced. He stood at attention for a few seconds and then delivered a crisp salute.

Turning to walk away, he shook his head and thought to himself, *Lieutenant Commander Stephen Lee Morrison ...*

Never heard of him.

Printed in Great Britain
by Amazon.co.uk, Ltd.,
Marston Gate.